The
Cookbook
of
Common
Prayer

Francesca Haig grew up in Tasmania and is an author and academic, whose poetry and YA/crossover fantasy have been widely published. She lives in London with her husband and son.

The Cookbook of Common Prayer

FRANCESCA HAIG

ALLEN&UNWIN

Published in hardback in Great Britain in 2021 by Allen & Unwin, an imprint of Atlantic Books Ltd.

This paperback edition first published by Allen & Unwin in 2022

10 9 8 7 6 5 4 3 2 1

A CIP catalogue record for this book is available from the British Library.

Paperback ISBN: 978 1 91163 092 0
E-book ISBN: 978 1 76087 480 3

Printed in Great Britain

Allen & Unwin
An imprint of Atlantic Books Ltd
Ormond House
26–27 Boswell Street
London
WC1N 3JZ

www.allenandunwin.com/uk

For James Upcher, 1979–2017.

Always brilliant,

always beloved.

Prologue

Dark water rising.

It comes up faster than you'd believe, but it doesn't wait for your belief, or need it – the water is its own permission. It's black, and cold enough to make your lungs clench. If you scream, or shout, you don't hear it over the indifferent water. It swallows your words, swallows the world.

The water tells only one story, and it's the story of water.

Teddy

It's Papabee who taught me to understand stories. My grandpa read me so many stories that I learned how they can come outside of their pages, until a story is something you can move around in, like a house, or a forest, all dark up above and sideways and down below too.

When I was small (even smaller than I am now), Papabee used to read me *The Lorax*, and the bit at the start went into my head and never came out.

If you want to hear the story of the Lorax, the book says, you have to go and ask the Onceler. The Onceler's a sort of monster-person that you never even see properly – just a glimpse of green hands, or a peek of eyes through a window. From way up high in his creepy tower, he sends down a bucket on a rope, and the only way to hear the story is to put in exactly the right things: fifteen cents, one nail, and a snail shell. Not just any snail shell, either – it has to be from an ancient snail, a grandfather four times over.

Papabee used to read me *The Lorax* over and over – it was one of our very best books. So since all the bad things started happening, and our house started to fill up with stories that nobody will tell, I've known exactly what to do. The stories are building up, like the dust in Dougie and Sylvie's bedrooms. Mum and Dad are stuck, and Sylvie's stuck, and Dougie's stuck too, in his own way. Our whole family's stuck tight, and nothing can be fixed until they find a way to make their stories word-shaped.

And everyone's so busy being stuck that nobody notices me at all any more. I'm only small, after all – eleven years old and mainly knees and elbows, and always in the way, like SausageDog.

I know it's not easy to make people tell the truth. I'm still learning about how there are different kinds of truths: the right ones and the wrong ones. When our cat died, my teacher said, 'I'm sure she's gone to a better place.' I said, 'I think he's in the freezer at the vet's.' That's the wrong kind of truth, apparently, because Mrs Conway made me pick up rubbish in the playground at recess, for being rude.

But I know how to fix my family, and how to shake the stories loose. Because of *The Lorax*, and Papabee, I understand something about stories that the others don't: if you want someone to tell you their story, you have to find the price, and pay it.

Gabe

When we named him Douglas, we didn't know that it meant *dark water*. Those were the days before endless online forums about baby names, and we chose Douglas without much deliberation, because it had been my grandfather's name, and he'd died only a year before Gill got pregnant. I'd been close to my grandfather in a way I never was to my father. And Gill and I both liked how the name sounded: *Douglas*. The solidness of it; those reliable, hard sounds. When he was born, our first child, bunched up and wrinkled as a tissue that's been through the wash, the name seemed to suit him.

It was only nineteen years later, after Dougie had died, that I found out what his name meant. I was staying up late every night, scouring the web for more details than the official accounts had given me. There'd been a flurry of coverage in the first few days – long articles in the local press, and short ones in the big national papers. After the first week, the reporting died down, and my nightly search threw up the same articles, which I could recite like scripture.

That night, nearly two weeks after he'd died, I typed in my usual search (*Douglas Jordan Dead Cave Floodwater*) and one of the hits, several pages deep into the search results, was a listing on a baby names website. *Douglas (boy). Means: Dark water.*

Ever since then I've blamed myself and Gill, accidental prophets. I blame us for choosing a name that turned out to be a promise.

PART ONE

Omelette for the day the police come to your house to tell you that your son is dead

Take six eggs (large; ideally free range).
Crack them, one by one, carefully separating
the yolks and whites into two large bowls.

Throw them away.

Gill

This is how it happens:

There's a knock on the front door. It's Sunday, mid-morning. Teddy's gone to soccer practice with Papabee and I'm back in bed with the papers, SausageDog asleep across my legs. Gabe, still in his dressing gown, is in the bathroom.

I get up, the dog protesting. I see them as soon as I reach the corridor. One man, one woman, their blue and white uniforms unmistakable even through the dappled glass panels of the door. I'm surprised it's the police – in the past, whenever Sylvie's gone downhill, the hospital has always called us. That's how I know it must be really bad.

For a second I want to hide. If I never let them in – if I freeze, or drop very slowly to the ground so they can't see my silhouette, and crawl back into the bedroom and never answer the door – then they'll never be able to tell me the news.

They knock again, and call out, 'Mr and Mrs Jordan?'

I can't move. I'm frozen in a crouch, staring at the pattern on the hallway rug and trying to ignore the hammering on the door. From the bathroom I hear Gabe, voice thick with toothpaste. 'Gill? Can't you get that?'

I'm still stuck there, half-crouched on the rug, when he comes out from the bathroom, holding his toothbrush. He sees me, sees the police at the door.

'Shit,' he says, and goes straight to the door, and opens it.

Will I ever be able to forgive him for opening that door? If he'd just left them outside, and stayed here with me, the police would never be able to come inside and say the words, *Your daughter has died.*

But it isn't our daughter. It's our son.

When Dougie first went away for his gap year, I didn't really grasp that he'd moved out until the pasta fell on me. The corner shop used to do a special pasta deal: five packets for five dollars. When Dougie was in high school, I'd pick up a pasta deal at least once a week. From the instant he hit puberty, he was always eating. He ate WeetBix in a pasta bowl because it was bigger than a cereal bowl; ten WeetBix at breakfast, and sometimes the same after school. Our fridge was crammed with cartons of milk, and still we couldn't keep up. His friends were always coming over after school, and they'd cook pasta before heading off to hockey or basketball practice. Jars of cheap tomato pasta sauce; mounds of grated cheese. I was forever buying cheese – huge bricks of cheddar. Gabe and I used to laugh about it. 'Jesus,' he said, when we were out of cheese and milk again. 'It'd literally be cheaper to buy a cow.'

Then Dougie left for his year away. After he'd been in England for five weeks, I still hadn't consciously changed my regular shopping routine. One afternoon I opened the pantry and twenty-five packets of pasta came tumbling down on me from the top shelf. I sat on the cold tiles of the kitchen floor and cried. I wasn't hurt – not even bruised. But it was the first time I really understood that Dougie had left home.

Now there are two strangers in my house telling me that he's dead, and I think: *I need a moment like the falling pasta to make it real.* He's already been away for more than four months. We've become used to not having him here, and it will take something as tangible as twelve and a half kilos of pasta falling on my head to prove to me that this is different. Then I could hold the fact of his death, as solid as all those crinkling packets of spaghetti and penne that I had to pick up from the floor. Instead, all I have are these police officers in their neatly ironed uniforms, and their words that I can't make sense of: *accident; caving; flash flood; coroner.*

They use phrases that I've heard on TV shows – *Perhaps you should sit down; We're terribly sorry to have to tell you; Every effort was made* – but the officers seem sincere. The man even has tears in his eyes while he explains what happened. He's very young, probably only early twenties, with a few spots still lingering on his forehead. He sits opposite us, leaning forward as he talks, his shirt coming untucked at the back. I remember Dougie's school uniform shirt, always untucked. I find myself comforting the policeman, saying, 'It's OK, don't cry. Don't cry.'

The dog, excited to have visitors, is trying to lick the policewoman's ankle. His tail's wagging, not just from side to side but round and round like the crank on my coffee grinder.

'Do you have someone who can be with you?' the policewoman asks, trying to push SausageDog away without being rude.

'Sue,' I say, at the same time as Gabe says, 'We'll be fine.' I want Sue here – my best friend. I want somebody to translate the police officers' words into something that I can understand. There's a ringing in my ears. Several times I ask Gabe, 'Can you hear that?' and he keeps shaking his head.

I give the policeman my phone and he calls Sue. I hear his voice from the corridor. 'If you can come straight away, I think that would help.'

'We have to be there,' Gabe says. 'In London. I'll book flights.' He wipes the back of his hand across his eyes. 'We'll ask Sue if she'll keep an eye on Teddy and Papabee. And Sylvie, too.'

'Oh God,' I say. 'Sylvie. This'll kill her.'

Gabe

The policeman gives us the number of the Buckinghamshire police. I get put through to a woman and I put the phone on speaker so Gill can hear too. The lady is nice – terribly, convincingly nice, as if what happened to Dougie is an unprecedented shock, even though it's presumably her job to deal with death on a regular basis.

'I'm afraid I can confirm that they found Douglas's body last night.'

'It can't be him,' Gill says immediately. Her eyes are jammed tight shut, her fists too. 'It can't be,' she repeats. 'It must be somebody else.'

'There's been a preliminary identification, and—'

Gill interrupts her. 'Who?'

'We're confident that it's Douglas, Mrs Jordan.'

'That's not what I meant,' says Gill. 'Who identified him?'

There's a shuffling of paper. 'A Rosa Campbell,' the woman says.

'Dougie's mentioned her,' I say. 'She's his girlfriend. She teaches there, at the school where he works.' Should I say *worked*? Through which hole in language has my son slipped from the present to the past tense?

'She could be wrong,' Gill says. 'How can she be sure it's him?'

'They know him.' I look down at my hands. 'Rosa's his girlfriend, for God's sake. If they're sure, they're sure.' *And it's not as though the caves under the Home Counties are crammed with the bodies of young men*, I want to add, but it seems too flippant, too harsh.

'You can view Douglas's body at the hospital,' the woman says.

'The hospital?' I echoed, stupidly. I was expecting it to be a morgue, or a funeral home or something. Why is he at the hospital? He's dead. He's already been dead for – I counted hurriedly in my head – at least twenty hours. There's nothing they can do for him at a hospital.

'The deceased are kept at the hospital,' she explained. 'Until they can be released to the care of a funeral home.'

She gives me the number for the hospital, and the address of her own office. Gill's crying more noisily now, so I end the call quickly, with apologies that the woman politely brushes away.

I'm angry at Gill for forcing me to be the sensible one. For taking all the hysteria for herself, and for leaving me to handle things: talking to the police; booking the flights. Meanwhile, Gill sobs, and rocks herself forwards and backwards, and the policeman says something about making us sweet tea, for the shock.

I walk to Gill and lean close to her, my forehead against hers.

'How are we going to tell Sylvie?' I ask.

Gill

'How are we going to tell Sylvie?' he asks.

I have no answer for him, so it's a relief when Sue arrives, a shriek of brakes outside. She lets herself in the back door, all noise and tears. 'Fuck,' she says. 'I can't believe it. I can't fucking believe it's real. Is it real? You poor loves. My loves. How can it be real? Fucking fuck.'

She grips my hand and I grip back and I'm glad that she's punctured the orderly calm of this scene, and the rehearsed condolences of the police officers. She clutches me to her, then Gabe, and then me again. My lungs are an accordion being squeezed. An atonal gasp bursts from me.

'I'll pick up Teddy and Papabee,' she says.

I nod. I haven't even been able to think properly about them yet. Teddy, and my dad.

Once, years and years ago, we left Teddy behind at the hockey club's end-of-season barbecue at the reservoir. My sister, her partner, and their kids were staying, so there were four adults and six children. It was chaotic – Dougie had eaten too many chocolate bars and thrown up, and we were rushing to get home, herding the kids into two cars, everyone assuming Teddy was in the other car. We got halfway down Waterworks Road before I realised. When we rushed back we found Teddy, unaware we'd even left, playing with his friends among the trees by the water's edge. For weeks afterwards I'd wake at night picturing him in the reservoir, the water closing over his little face.

Standing at the counter, I crack the eggs, one after another. I separate the yolks and whites, cradling each yolk in my palm while the white slips through my fingers to the bowl below.

'I don't think I can eat,' Gabe says. 'Can you?'

'No,' I say, and I keep cracking the eggs. When they're all done, the yolks make a slurping noise as I tip them into the bin. The police officers must have gone; I didn't even notice Gabe showing them out.

Footsteps outside the back door – Sue's brought Teddy and Papabee back. She hasn't told them anything yet, and my dad's as oblivious as ever, but Teddy already knows something's up.

'Sue wouldn't say what's happened,' he says, looking from Gabe to me and back again. His transparent plastic soccer mouthguard is still in his hand, like the teeth of a ghost.

We tell Teddy and Papabee together, because they do everything together and it doesn't seem fair to separate them for this. Papabee doesn't say anything at first, while Teddy cries, and collapses into Gabe's embrace. Then Papabee says, 'Why don't you telephone Dougie? I'm sure if we just ring him, he'll be able to sort all of this out.' He picks up the remote control from the coffee table and holds it out to me. 'Gillian – just telephone him.'

'We can't, Papabee,' Gabe says, and eases the remote from my dad's hands. 'He's dead.'

Then Teddy cries so much that he wets himself, which he hasn't done for more than five years, and I'm grateful to have something to do, rushing to put on a load of washing and run him a bath. I sit on the edge of the tub, stroke his hair and tell him that we love him, which is true, and that it will be all right, which is not.

'Teddy. Teddy-bear. Teddy,' I say, kissing the top of his head.

He was never meant to be called Teddy. We named him Edward, Papabee's name. Except we never called him that

– people called him Teddy from the very start. At first, we always corrected them, said 'No, it's Edward.' Then, when we started calling him Teddy too, we promised ourselves it would be just for a few years. *Teddy's OK while he's little,* we agreed; *It's cute for a baby – but not for a big boy, let alone a man.*

But we didn't ever get around to making the change. On his first day of school his teacher called him Edward, and Teddy didn't answer because he didn't even know that was his name.

I sit on the edge of Teddy's bath. He's lying on his back, staring at the ceiling. 'Mum? Was it dark?'

'What do you mean?'

'In the cave,' he says. He fiddles with his flannel, draping it over his bony knees. 'Would it have been dark?'

'I don't know.' I try to make my voice gentle. Teddy looks very small there, in the water.

'I think it must have been dark,' he says, 'if it was a cave underground.'

I bend my head to his and stay there for a long time.

When I go back out to the kitchen, Sue's making us sweet tea. Gabe's taken Papabee into the living room, patiently explaining again and again what's happened. Papabee says, 'How extraordinarily sad,' and 'Quite, quite dreadful,' over and over, but then he stoops to pat SausageDog, straightens again, and asks Gabe, 'Will Sylvie and Dougie be joining us for dinner this evening?'

'I know you won't feel like it,' Sue says to me, 'but you should eat something.' She opens the fridge. 'Any eggs?'

I shake my head. 'We're all out,' I say. I can't explain why they're all in the bin.

'When are you going to tell Sylvie?' Sue asks.

Teddy

I can hear Mum and Sue in the kitchen now, talking about Sylvie.

'I don't know how to tell her,' Mum says. 'Jesus Christ. This'll be the end of her.'

'Don't say that,' Sue says. 'Sit down. Drink some tea. We'll get through this.'

'How?' Mum says. 'How, though?'

I lean my head back and let the water fill my ears, so I don't have to hear Mum talking like that. I used to think Mum and Dad had all the answers. You think that, when you're little. I'm still little – I can still stretch out in the bath and get my whole body underwater and my knees don't even make an island – but lately I'm not so sure about Mum and Dad and answers.

When Mum and Dad were trying to tell me and Papabee about what had happened to Dougie, I couldn't stop looking at the big pile of eggshells on the counter. I was trying to understand what Mum and Dad were saying, but I was also thinking about the eggshells, and why there were so many of them. And when an egg cracks, is it broken or is it coming true?

Papabee kept saying, 'Quite, quite dreadful,' but he said it like 'Quate' because he used to live in England, so his voice is posh even though he's not posh at all. And I remembered how Dougie used to do a really good Papabee voice, when Papabee wasn't around: *Quate, quate extraordinary*, Dougie would say, and do his big Dougie laugh. So I was hearing Papabee's voice and Dougie's at the same time and Mum and Dad's too – until I couldn't hear anything properly at all.

After a while, my ears got less muddled and noises started to creep back in. I could hear two seagulls outside doing their croaky seagull yells. *The seagulls must know about Dougie,* I thought. *They get it.* What the gulls were saying made more sense than all of Mum and Dad's words. The seagulls were telling the whole truth about Dougie being dead. They were yelling, *carrrrrr carrrrrr carrrr*, and it sounded exactly right.

Then I did so much crying that I let go of everything, even my wee, all hot down my legs, way hotter than you'd think, and Mum was trying to clean me up and a bee had come in the window and Mum was saying to Dad, 'For God's sake can you deal with that?' and it didn't seem right that this moment should have become about wee and getting the washing on and chasing the bee out the window instead of Dougie being dead, which was The Big Thing.

While Mum was helping me out of my wet trousers and wrapping me in a towel, I listened to the gulls, and I thought, *How do they know? How can they know this exact feeling?* If I were a gull I'd fly away. Miles away. I'd fly straight up up up until our house is just a square of roof like on Google Maps and all the people are tiny LEGO-people, then tiny ant-people, then nothing at all. Right up as high as I could go and all I'd take with me would be my own gull-voice that sounds like *gone gone gone.*

I'd rather be Bird-Teddy, even if it meant eating worms. Warm mouth, worm mouth. I'd rather be any Teddy than this one. If I was Bird-Teddy, all my thoughts would be bird-thoughts and all my questions would have bird-answers, and none of my questions would be about caves.

I swish the bathwater with my fingers, then hold out my hand and watch the drips falling off the end of my fingers. How does the water always know how to point down? How does it find the way? How did it find Dougie, and what did he do? Dougie always seemed so big to me, but he's never seemed bigger than now. My big brother drank the river, all the clouds and their rain. The whole wet sky and everything underneath. He drank all of it.

I lean my head back and close my eyes. I'm trying to figure out how Dougie being dead is going to work, and what language I can miss him in because I don't know the words for this in English. Through the door I can hear that Mum and Dad and Sue are back to talking about Sylvie and how they're going to tell her. Part of me wants to yell at them: *Dougie's dead! Why are you talking about Sylvie?* I want Dougie's death to belong all to him. But I know that it can't – no chance – because everything that we do ends up being about Sylvie. It's been like that for three whole years. Like a computer game that's stuck on a loop, and everything always ends up back at the same bit: Sylvie. Sylvie.

The water's dripping off my hands, little *plink plink* sounds, and I make up a little rhyme in my head, in time with the drips. A rhyme like in *The Lorax* or one of my other old picture books. *Mum and Dad have two sons and a daughter. My sister in the Boneyard, my brother in the water.*

There's a word for Sylvie's sickness, but I know a secret: it's not really a disease at all. It's a place.

It's a place because we all live in it now, and there's no outside of it. I call it the Boneyard. It smells of hospital (which smells like a toilet that's just been cleaned), and it tastes of nothing, and if it had a colour it would be grey-blue, the exact colour of her skin and the hospital floor. That's the Boneyard. We live there, since she got sick. I suppose Dougie lives there forever, now. He's stuck in the Boneyard for good.

I have a sister. I have a brother. A sister in the Boneyard, a brother in the water. In the black water in the blackest cave.

I have a sister made of books and bones. I have a brother made of dead.

I'd like to give Dougie back his own death, like a present. It'd be the worst present ever – even worse than socks, which is what Papabee always gives me for birthdays and Christmas. But if I can't stop Dougie being dead, then at least I can try to give his death back to him.

That broken game again, stuck on a loop, round and round – because to give Dougie his death back, I have to fix Sylvie. Three years ago, something happened to my sister. Something broke in her. Just like that: *snap*. I never knew until then that a person can break, like a zip or a rubber band. I never knew a whole family could get broken too. I never knew a disease could be a place, and a whole family could live in it.

If I want to know what happened to Dougie, in the deep down blackness of that cave, I need to know what happened to Sylvie. I need to find out her story.

Sylvie

PART TWO

PART TWO

Gill

It doesn't start out as such a big lie.

'We can't tell Sylvie yet,' I say.

'What are you talking about?' Gabe asks. He's finally got off the phone from the airline, and the phone's still in his hand. Sue's gone, and Teddy's in his pyjamas, playing cards with Papabee at the dining table.

'What are you talking about?' Gabe says again. 'We don't have a choice.'

'It'll kill her.'

He's silent, so I go on.

'I'm not being melodramatic. The shock could literally kill her. You heard what they said about her heart.' The nurse told us just last week, when she checked Sylvie's obs, that if somebody came to A&E with a heart-rate like that, they'd be sent straight to intensive care.

When people say that the heart is a muscle, it's not just some inspirational meme about love, circulated on Facebook by your annoying aunt. It's a fact: the heart, that vigilant muscle, wastes away along with the rest of the body. If your body is starved for long enough, the heart loses mass. The walls get thinner, and weaker. The heart can't pump enough blood, or stay steady. There's only so long that the body can sustain that sort of strain. Ever since the day Sylvie stopped eating, her heart is a timer, counting down. The nasogastric tube keeps her alive by carrying food directly down her nose into her stomach, but whenever I look at it hanging from her nostril, I can't help but see a fuse.

'We can't lie to her,' Gabe says. I envy his faith in what's right. He's a good man. I knew it thirty years ago, when we were walking home from our second date and he bent to pick up a snail from the wet pavement and move it to the grass so it wouldn't be crushed.

But I'm not a good person like he is. I'm a mother.

'I want to do the right thing too,' I say. 'Of course I do. But not at any cost. It'll kill her. You saw what happened, after Katie P died.'

Katie P was in the same ward as Sylvie. After Katie killed herself, Sylvie's silence grew more and more implacable. The row of perfectly straight cuts on the inside of her left arm moved higher and higher. For her brief stays at home, we'd learned to hide all the knives and medicines in a locked box under our bed. But she used whatever she could lay her hands on. A chisel from the shed; a loose screw from the desk in Dougie's room. Each time the doctors said she had to be readmitted, I felt guilty at my own relief. At least in hospital they could keep her safe.

Gabe shakes his head. 'It's not the same as when Katie died. Sylvie needs to know. He's her brother, not just some girl she used to see around the ward.'

'Exactly,' I hiss. 'If she was that bad after Katie died, imagine how badly she'll cope with hearing about Dougie. She got sick right after your dad died, for God's sake. She doesn't exactly have a great track-record of dealing with loss.'

'We can't lie to her about this.'

'We won't be lying. We just won't tell her yet.'

So my first lie is to Gabe, not to Sylvie. Because I already know that it will be more than just omission.

'She'll hear about it. Christ, Gill, this is Hobart. There aren't any secrets here.'

'How could she hear? There aren't any laptops or phones allowed on the ward. No internet. She's in isolation. Nobody can visit her without our permission – and we'll tell our friends why they can't say anything just yet.'

Paediatrics 3 is a completely controlled environment. Locked doors, and windows that don't open. No mobiles, no internet access.

'It's not just the dodgy stuff online – all those pro-ana websites,' the nurse had explained to me, when Sylvie was first admitted, and they made me take away her phone. 'There are privacy implications for other patients, too, now that every phone has a camera. And stuff gets nicked all the time, so we discourage people from having valuables on the ward – that includes phones. And then there's the cords.'

'The cords?' I asked.

'Charging cords,' she said. 'You know, for phones and laptops.'

I still didn't get it.

She raised her eyebrows and lowered her voice. 'They're a hanging risk.'

'Of course,' I said. But even as I said it, I was thinking, *How did this become an 'Of course' moment? How have we arrived in a place where it's considered obvious that our daughter will try to kill herself with anything she can form into a noose?*

I grab Gabe's hand. 'It'll only be a few days. We'll tell her later. Just a few days. Maybe a week, while we get over to England and sort this out.'

Gabe doesn't need to say it out loud. He just looks at me, and lets my words marinade in their own stupidity: *Sort this out.* As if it's a muddled hotel booking, or a broken toe, and not my son in a morgue somewhere on the other side of the world.

'Just a week,' I repeat. 'Just until she's a bit more stable.' Sylvie's obs have been bad since last weekend. Heart-rate jumpy, blood pressure low. Before weigh-in on Tuesday a nurse caught her loading up with water, straight from the bathroom tap, and now she isn't even allowed to go to the toilet unaccompanied.

'Don't make it more complicated than it already is,' says Gabe.

'Is there a simple way to do this?' I snap. 'I'm not an expert in dealing with my son's death.'

'Our son's death,' he says quietly.

Gabe's right, of course. My grief leaves no room for his. There is only room for me and Dougie, just as there was when he was born, his face outraged, wrinkled and purple as the cross-section of a red cabbage. For weeks, a baby's eyes can't even focus enough to make out anything beyond the orbit of their mother's face. It was just me and Dougie, so hungry that he almost took my left nipple off with the urgency of his suckling.

I'd never imagined that the fierce intimacy of those newborn days could be recreated, but now I learn that I was wrong. This is the same: the same reeling sleeplessness; the same raw-skinned, ripped-open love. It allows for nobody and nothing else – not even Gabe. I don't claim that it's right, or fair. But it's a fact. Nobody warns you, before you give birth, about the savagery of that love – a love that starts when you're still bleeding and does not stop.

I know that I have not lost a son. I've lost a thousand sons: the baby, milk-drunk and heavy-headed. The toddler, with his absolute determination to swallow stones. The six-year-old, with his growing fluency in his own body. The fourteen-year-old, mortified when I hugged him in public. The seventeen-year-old, who let Teddy beat him in arm-wrestles. The nineteen-year-old whom we put on the plane in January, hiding his nervousness behind bravado. The man he would have become, and the father he might have been, and all the hundreds of futures I'd imagined for him. I'll never be able to count the many

Dougies that were lost in that cave. It's too much – too much for me, and certainly too much for Sylvie.

'We can't tell her,' I say again.

'Gill,' Gabe says. 'Love. You're not thinking straight. You know we have to.'

'I will not bury two of my children.' My words are a freshly sharpened blade.

This time he doesn't correct me, doesn't say *Our children.*

Teddy's quiet at bedtime. I figure it's best if we keep to our normal routine as much as possible, so I brush his hair, and Gabe reads him two chapters of *The Horse and His Boy* and kisses him goodnight.

I know how to do this, I think, as we go through the evening's rituals with Teddy. I know how to ease the knots from his curly hair. I know to put a clean glass of water on the bookshelf next to his bed, and to leave the door open just enough for SausageDog to get in and out in the night. I know how to be his mother.

But I don't know how to be a mother to a dead child. What can I do for Dougie now? What does he need from me?

And how can I be a mother to Sylvie, who wants nothing from me except to be allowed to die?

'Is it real?' Teddy asks us, before I turn out the light. 'Is he really dead?'

'Yes, sweetheart,' Gabe says. 'I'm afraid so.'

For hours, Teddy's question and Gabe's answer rattle around in my head, the words coming loose. *Is it real? Really? I'm afraid so. I'm so afraid.*

Gabe

All through that night we barely sleep, and when I do slip into the oblivion of dreams, waking is a new torture.

'Where has he gone?' I say into the dark, not expecting an answer. 'Where has he gone?'

I feel the shaking of Gill crying, her back pressed tight against mine.

In the morning, we drive to the hospital, leaving Teddy with Papabee.

Gill turns to me, before we get out of the car. 'How do I look?'

'You look beautiful.'

'You know what I mean. Do I look like I've been crying?'

'A bit,' I say. 'We both do. But it won't be the first time she's seen us like this.' We've done plenty of crying in the parked car outside the hospital over the last three years.

It's only going to be for a little while, I say to myself, as we walk up the hospital stairs. A white lie; a stopgap, until Sylvie's stronger. Until Gill and I can say Dougie's name without our breath faltering. We've spoken to Louise, Sylvie's doctor – she's agreed that we can't break the news to Sylvie until we're back from London to support her. Louise has given the order to the nurses – nobody to say a word.

Sylvie has lied to us every day, for years. *Yes, I drank my Sustagen. No, the doctors said I could exercise as long as it's only an hour a day. Yes, I put butter on my toast like the dietitian said*. I don't hold it against her – it's part of her illness, we know that. But it still makes it easier to justify this lie.

Anorexics are wonderful liars. They're accomplished magicians. Watch for the meals slipped to the dog, or into a hand, or a sleeve, and palmed off into the bin. The little parcels of food concealed everywhere.

And the greatest lie of all, the climactic disappearing trick: the body itself, vanishing.

How did Dougie learn this trick, to disappear so completely?

Gill

We try to hug Sylvie, but she's adept at leaning away from our embraces, and turning her face from our kisses. Today, I barely notice. I'm concentrating on not sobbing. I start the words that I practised in my head, all through last night.

'Sweetie, we have some bad news.' It isn't all lies you see – it's a version of the truth. 'There's been an accident, on a caving trip that Dougie was doing. A flash flood, and he was hurt. Nothing serious, thank God, but he broke his leg. It's been a nasty scare. He'll be in hospital for another few days, and he'll be stuck on crutches for at least six weeks. Probably more.'

She looks very young, her mouth opening and staying open.

'Jesus,' she says. 'Is he OK?'

'He's fine,' I say, a little too quickly. 'The leg's painful, and it was a frightening experience, but he's going to be fine. But we really ought to go – just to help him get back on his feet. He won't be able to work for at least a month. And when we told him we were coming, and we'd be there for my birthday, he went online and got us tickets to the Chelsea Flower Show.'

Gabe shoots me a look at this unexpected piece of improvisation. I think, *Sylvie's not the only accomplished liar in this family. Just watch me*.

'I've always wanted to go,' I say.

'I can't think of anything worse than being dragged around the Chelsea Flower Show,' Gabe says, and rolls his eyes. 'The things I do for your mother.'

I know he isn't talking about the flower show, and I squeeze his hand.

'But Dougie's OK?' Sylve asks. It's the first time in a long time that she's asked for anything from us. She and Dougie have always been so close. How can I refuse her?

'Of course.' I lean closer and say conspiratorially, 'But I think he's missing us, though he'd never admit it. He tries to act so grown up, but this whole thing's given him a shock. And it's a bad break, the leg. There might be more operations needed, depending on how it heals. So we're flying out tonight.'

'OK,' she says, nodding. Even through her pyjama top I can see her ribs poking out, a birdcage made of bones. I try not to think about her bones, or Dougie's.

Gabe sees me pause and picks up where I left off. 'Papabee will help out with Teddy,' he says. 'And Sue and Dan are going to keep an eye on both of them, and you too.'

But already Sylvie's withdrawing from us again, and she just shrugs. The nasogastric tube comes out of her right nostril, is taped in place across her cheek, and tucked behind her ear. It's connected to the feeding pump that hangs from the drip-stand by the bed. The pump makes its rhythmic, gassy hum. *Shhhhh. Shhhhh.*

On the drive back home, I rest my hand on Gabe's leg. He's wearing old corduroy trousers, the ridges soft under my fingers. He puts his hand on top of mine and squeezes tight. The lie we've told feels more irrevocable than a promise. More than a marriage vow.

Sylvie

Mum and Dad leave me with my silence, and it rises around me like water.

(Doing this to myself isn't the hard bit. The hard bit is doing this to them.)

Did it hurt, when Dougie broke his leg, and how much? Was he afraid? I know about fear (don't ever make the mistake of thinking I am not afraid). I know all the shapes of it. If Dougie were here, and if I could find my way back to talking, I'd like to ask him about the shape of his fear, when the water flooded the cave.

I can't imagine Dougie laid up with a broken leg. He's always doing something. Always the basketball bouncing on the driveway; the cricket ball thrown against the side of the house. Visiting me in the hospital, he could never sit still. He'd rock backwards and forwards on his chair; sometimes he'd borrow a wheelchair and balance on the back wheels at the same time as talking to me. I hardly ever spoke back, but since he went away, I miss those visits. I used to watch him from my hospital bed, and think: *How does he do that? How does he occupy his body without thinking about it?*

He's always been like that. I used to be like that too.

Nothing changes. Everything changes. All those summers at the old house at the Neck, always the same and always different. The tin dinghy tied under the jetty was there one year and gone the next. Still the same bit of loose carpet tripped us on the stairs; the same shelf in the fridge was broken. One year the sea was full of jellyfish, suspended in the water like kites, trailing their tentacles, and only Dougie dared to swim. For an entire summer it didn't rain, the huge tin water tanks nearly empty, so that if a cricket ball hit them they rang like a gong. Papabee got sunburnt on his bald spot, and when we tried to rinse the sand from our feet, the outside tap was too hot to touch. The creek near the blowhole disappeared, then returned with the autumn rains. Teddy got too big for me to carry. Still the cockatoos gave the same cry from the pine tree behind the house. Papabee offered to make the lunch and on the beach we unwrapped nine very neat marmalade and lettuce rolls. Sue and Dan's daughter Ella was away that year, on a school exchange to Spain. Dad's dad, Papa J, came down from Sydney for the whole summer. Ella came back again. With a rolled-up newspaper I squashed a mosquito high up on the bathroom wall. The mark stayed there all summer – a black smear, with a tiny splat of my own blood.

Gill

It's dark when Sue arrives to watch the sleeping Teddy, and we take a cab to the airport. Gabe loads the suitcase into the boot. I can't remember anything that I packed, though we must have done it. We must have stood in our room and chosen things, and put them in the case. How is it possible that we did this? *Gabe will have taken care of it*, I think, though I know it's unfair to expect him to be any more lucid than I am.

I close my eyes and let myself imagine that, instead of the airport, we're going to Eaglehawk Neck – to Sue's family's beach house, where we've been going since before our kids were born. Instead of this taxi, I imagine we're in our rusty white station wagon, Papabee and the kids in the back. Dougie and Sylvie are elbowing each other for more space, and SausageDog's drooling on Teddy's lap. There at the Neck, that thin stretch of land linking the Tasman Peninsula to the rest of Tasmania, the old house will be waiting for us, the broken fly-wire on the windows curling at the corners. Sue and Dan, with Nathan and Ella, will be there already, and we'll park in the shade of the macrocarpa trees, and everything will be just as it always was. Spiders will scoot between cracks in the walls; the stack of boogie-boards will be leaning against the shed. Dougie and Nathan will cheat at cards, and Sylvie and Ella will sunbathe on the water tanks, and Teddy will fall asleep on the couch, trying to stay up as late as the big kids. My children will go barefoot on the beach, and the air will smell of sun cream and distant bushfires. Nothing will have changed.

I force my eyes open. We're going to the airport, not the Neck. The taxi sweeps past Cornelian Bay and along the riverfront, the city ahead of us, spread out along the river's western shore, and the mountain looming above it. Then we turn onto the bridge, and I lean my forehead against the glass window, watching the other lanes of traffic and the river beyond.

The Tasman Bridge fell once, in the mid-seventies. A ship crashed into the pylons and brought half the bridge down, killing twelve people. I wasn't even living here then, but if anyone in Hobart ever tells you they haven't thought about that crash as they drive across the bridge, they're lying. We've all done it – imagined that forty-five metres of falling. Asked ourselves: What if the kids were in the car? What would I do? Would my last words be *Brace*, or *Get out*, or *I love you*? How would I spend my last breaths, my last moments? We've all done it – prodded ourselves in the tender places of our hearts, trying on somebody else's heartbreak. Edging as close as you dare to somebody else's disaster. Until you wake one day in your own disaster, a perfect fit.

The letter ambushes me while we're waiting at the boarding gate, and I'm rifling through my handbag for an aspirin. There are various bits of paper in there – my boarding pass, half-finished recipe notes, old receipts. Then I see Dougie's handwriting. The letter is addressed to *Sylvie Jordan*. I remember taking it from the letterbox a few days ago and putting it in my handbag to take to Sylvie in hospital – but after the news I completely forgot.

Sitting in the plastic chair beside Gabe, I hold the envelope like it's a bomb, or a gift. Dougie's writing across the front; his saliva on the seal on the back.

Since he went to England, he'd written to Sylvie every couple of weeks. Real letters, because she isn't allowed any internet. For all my moans of 'Would it kill you two to include Teddy?', I've always been quietly proud of how close Dougie and Sylvie were. Before she got sick, I used to love seeing them walking on the beach at the Neck, those two sets of footprints close together, and Teddy trailing behind. I liked hearing the big kids talking in Dougie's room, after dinner. I even liked the way their voices stopped when Gabe or I walked past the door.

If they hadn't been so close, her descent into silence wouldn't have hit him so hard. If they hadn't been so close, I'd be able to contemplate telling Sylvie the truth.

He always sent the letters to the house, because she'd changed wards a few times, and we'd learned that the hospital mail room was unreliable at best. So the letters came to the house, and we'd take them into hospital for her.

'Gabe,' I say, nudging him. 'Gabe.'

He knows it straight away for what it is. When he takes the letter from me he holds it as though he should be wearing gloves, like a curator at a museum with some priceless artefact. He swallows, then clamps his eyes shut.

'Jesus,' he says. 'Jesus.' He presses the envelope to his forehead, leaning forward and rocking slightly.

'This must be the last one, right?' I ask. 'If it came just the other day?' Gabe straightens, and we check the postmark. It was posted a little over a week ago. Dougie wrote to Sylvie regularly, but not weekly. There will be no more.

Gabe's still holding the envelope, but he makes no move to open it. 'Keep it safe,' he says. 'We'll have to give it to her when we're back.'

Teddy

In the morning, Mum and Dad have gone, but I don't even have any room to be sad about it because all my sadness is full up with Dougie.

Even though it's Monday, Sue says I don't have to go to school today. I tell her that Papabee can drop me at the hospital instead.

'Are you sure you want to go?' Sue asks.

I nod. Definitely. It's definitely better than sitting at home watching Sue try not to cry, or watching her try to tell Papabee again and again what's happened. Going to see Sylvie is the opposite of that, because there isn't allowed to be any telling about Dougie.

'It's not that we want to lie to her,' Dad said before they left last night. 'But she's just not well enough to deal with it. We need to think carefully about how to tell her, and when.'

I get it. I know what he and Mum are thinking about, because when Sylvie first got sick I Googled anorexia and it says *twenty per cent mortality*, which is one in five. And it seems like Sylvie might be the one in five, because her words stopped, ages ago, and her skin's all grey and kind of scaly, like the feet of the pigeons that hang around the rubbish bins in Franklin Square. On her left wrist there are scars I'm not meant to notice, all purple and shiny. If she dies, as well as Dougie, then the Boneyard will never finish for us. We'll all be there forever.

I never used to think I could do anything to change Sylvie, because if three years and a whole enormous hospital and all the doctors and dietitians and grown-ups haven't fixed her, then obviously I couldn't. She's been in hospital for more than a quarter of my life, after all.

I used to think, too, that if anyone could fix Sylvie, it'd be Dougie. Because they were the big kids, the two of them, always together, always talking. So I thought maybe Dougie could teach her how to eat again, the same way he'd taught me how to swim and ride my bike. I always thought that he could do anything – that's what big brothers do, especially Very Big Brothers like Dougie, always so far ahead of me. I used to hear him and Sylvie while I was falling asleep, when they were talking next door in Dougie's room. I knew all the sounds of their laughing, and even their arguing – Sylve's yelling (*Jesus Christ, Dougie – you're so immature*), and Dougie's yelling (*Why the hell are you such a pain?*).

But when Sylvie stopped eating, the talking stopped, and even Dougie couldn't fix her. After he went away, I started thinking that it might have to be me that fixes her after all.

'If you're sure you want to go see Sylvie,' Sue says, 'd'you want me to come with you?'

'No,' I say, then (quickly), 'thanks.' I've got a job to do, and I can't do it if anyone else is there.

'Remember what your parents said, about not telling her just yet. Not a word, OK? I know it's hard, but she just can't handle the news while they're away.'

'I know.' I don't think she'll handle it when they're back, either, but I don't say that out loud.

I take my school backpack with me to the hospital and I hang on tight to both shoulder straps as I walk through the hospital corridors. I hear my footsteps – *clonk clonk* on the hard shiny floor – and that rhyme comes back, in time with my steps: *Sister in the Boneyard, brother in the water.*

I press the buzzer to be let in through the big locked doors of Paediatrics 3. The doors slide open, and as I pass the nurses' station a nurse squeezes my shoulder in a way that makes me know for sure that she's heard about Dougie.

'How're you doing, sweetie?' she asks, and I just say 'Fine, thanks,' and keep walking, because if I tell her the truth I'll start crying and then I won't be able to lie to Sylvie. Maybe it's good practice, lying to the nurse: it's like a warm-up for the big lie I have to do in Sylvie's room.

The rooms on each side of the corridor have glass doors, and all the way along I count the girls – I count them every time, because of the one-in-five. Six girls today. Dougie used to call them *the rexiles*, all the anorexic girls in Sylvie's ward. But today I squish Dougie-thoughts out of my head, because if I cry in front of Sylvie I'll ruin everything.

She's in the last room, sitting in her bed. She looks just like all the others: like her head's way too big for her body. I pull the curtains around her bed so the nurses can't see us through the glass.

She doesn't say hi, just asks, 'Any news about Dougie?'

'Nope,' I say, and it's not a lie, because there really isn't any news. Once somebody's dead, that's the end of news for good.

Yesterday I heard Sue say to Mum that it's a bad idea, not telling Sylvie about Dougie. But looking at Sylve now, I get why we have to do it: Dougie's death is just so big, and Sylvie's made herself so small. It's obvious – there's no way it could fit inside her. She's always been the one with secrets, but now it's us. Sylvie's made of nothing but bones, and Dougie's death would snap her bones right open.

But I'm only small too. What will it do to me?

'Mum and Dad are in the air right now,' I say, to fill up the silence. She doesn't answer. Normally it would annoy me that she's not even interested, but this time I'm glad she's not going to ask lots of questions.

I take one last peek at the gap between the curtains. There's nobody nearby, so I pull the brown envelope out of my schoolbag and pass it to Sylvie. She scrunches her nose as she rips open the flap to look inside.

'Jesus, Teddy.' She shuts the envelope, looking quickly to the gap between the curtains. 'What are you doing? Have you been dealing drugs or something?'

'It's my Papa J money,' I say.

Papa J is the reason Papabee is called Papabee. Papabee had to be Papa B, for Barwell, because there was also Dad's dad, Papa J, for Jordan. But Papa J lived on the mainland and hardly ever came down to Tasmania, except for the last summer before he died. Then he had a brain haemorrhage and died on his loo. That was three years ago, and now all that I have of Papa J is the framed photo in the kitchen, of him and Dad on the beach, and five thousand dollars, which he left each of us grandkids. Mum and Dad set up a bank account for me, because I didn't have one yet. The money's mine, and I have a bank card with a PIN and everything, but when I asked them if I could use it to buy some Technic Lego, they did a big speech about university and charity and compound interest.

So I didn't tell Mum and Dad when I began taking out my money. I started nearly two weeks ago – before Dougie had even died. Every day on the way to school I went to the ATM next to the bus stop, and got out six hundred dollars. That's the most you can take out in one day, unless you go actually inside the bank and ask for your money – and I was too scared to do that, in case they said no, or called Mum or Dad. So it took me eleven days – nine school days, plus the weekend when I couldn't get to the ATM without anyone noticing. I kept the money in an envelope, and by the fifth day it was already getting full, stuffed with notes. By yesterday, when Dougie died, I already had all the money ready – but my plan feels even more urgent now.

A nurse walks past the door, peeks through the curtains

and smiles. Sylvie ignores her, and keeps her hand on top of the envelope.

'What are you doing, bringing this here?' she hisses, when the nurse has gone. 'You can't just walk around with five thousand dollars in your schoolbag. What if you got mugged? What if you lost it?'

'Well, I didn't. Anyway, it's not for me.' I wait for a second. 'It's yours.'

'My Papa J money's in the bank, same place yours should be.'

I shake my head. 'I'm giving mine to you.'

'What for?' She sounds tired instead of curious. But she keeps looking at the money. Even if this isn't the right price for Sylvie's story, it's still doing something. Because she's talking – way more than usual. For such a long time she's been a snail in a shell made of silence. But now she's talking. It's the huge chunk of money on the bed between us that's done it. You can't ignore it. You can't argue with it. It looks so solid – such a big, fat chunk of notes. She can't just pretend it isn't there.

I push the envelope a bit closer to her.

'It's the whole lot – five thousand,' I say. 'You can count it, if you like. It's for you – if you'll tell me why you stopped eating.'

'Jesus,' she says again.

She picks up the envelope very carefully, folding the top over twice, holding it between the very tips of her finger and thumb like it's something dirty – like it's one of SausageDog's poo bags. She reaches for my schoolbag, drops the envelope inside, and zips the bag shut.

'I don't want his money. Take this to the bank tomorrow morning. Don't tell Sue – get Papabee to take you. You might need your passport, or bank card or something, for ID. Put it all back in, right away, and don't ever do anything this stupid again.'

'I want you to have it. You don't even have to start eating again right away. Just tell me why you stopped.'

'You idiot,' she says. She leans forward and hugs me. It should be nice – it's been ages since she's hugged me. But the bones of her arms are poking my sides, and I'm scared of the tube up her nose touching me. Worst of all, she has this gross smell all over her. It's called *ketosis*, Dad told me – the fat in her body burning. I hope she doesn't notice me holding my breath.

She's the one who ends the hug, pushing me away.

'So you're not going to take the money?' I ask.

'That's not how it works.'

'So how does it work, then?'

'Go home, Teddy.' She sounds tired again.

I got it wrong today – the price for Sylvie's story isn't money. But now Dougie's dead, and Mum and Dad have gone away, it's up to me to find out what the price is. In the doorway I turn back and look at Sylvie's face again. Skull too big, skin too small. It doesn't even look like a face any more. *Sister in the Boneyard. Brother in the water.* I don't have long.

You put a tooth under your pillow for the tooth fairy and hang the stocking on the fireplace for Santa, and I know none of those things are real but the price still matters. So what's the price for Sylvie, and to make Dougie's death fit into the world? What's her price because I will pay it, no matter how many teeth or anything else. I will pay it.

Sylvie

Cordelia. Nothing, my lord.
Lear. Nothing?
Cordelia. Nothing.
Lear. Nothing will come of nothing. Speak again.

'Tell me why you stopped eating,' Teddy says.

Speak again. Speak again, they say. Mum, Dad, Dougie, and now Teddy. *For God's sake, Sylvie, when are you going to start speaking again?*

Everyone is always so hungry for my story, my secrets. It's a relief that Mum and Dad are away. When they come to see me, they don't stop talking. Mum especially, pointedly, each word aimed at my silence.

If I spoke, I would say: *Stop trying to fill my silence. Stop trying to fix it.*

Listen.

We're not girls any more, here in Paediatrics 3. We've made ourselves into martyrs, saints, tiny bone-gods. Visitors come to us with offerings. I sit cross-legged on my hospital bed and, month after month, they come: Mum with her tears, and her plastic containers of home-cooked food, which I don't open. Dad, with his own quiet sadness, unmistakable as his beard. Papabee, with his bafflement. Dougie's letters from England, always so determinedly cheerful. And Teddy, little Teddy, coming here today with his ridiculous envelope of cash.

I can only offer them Cordelia's *nothing.*

I can only give them someone else's words. My own are
all broken.

PART THREE

PART THREE

Gabe

I can't work out, at first, why everyone's being so nice to us. At Check-in, the lady looks at our boarding passes, consults her computer, and immediately starts speaking to us in a hushed voice.

'We've upgraded you to Premium Economy,' she says confidentially, 'and I've seated you in a row with no other passengers, so that you'll have some privacy.' She gives us new boarding passes, with *COMP* printed in the corner. I'd seen the same thing when I'd printed ours at home and had wondered what it meant. *Complimentary?* (Hardly – I paid thousands for those tickets yesterday when I called Qantas, barely coherent and with no time to shop around, telling the man over and over, *My son has died and we need to be in London now.*)

I ask the woman behind the check-in desk, and she explains that *COMP* is a code: *Compassionate.* It turns out that if an airline knows you're flying because of a death, or some other horrible circumstance, they put this code on your boarding pass, so the staff will take special care of you.

Then she asks me whether we have frequent flyer numbers.

'No,' I say. 'I mean, we do, but I don't know where they are, and—' I peter out.

'Don't worry about it. You'll have twelve months to claim the points,' she says, as though that will be a tremendous relief for me. As though there'll come a time when we'll care again about frequent flyer miles.

All the way through the journey, we're treated with the same solicitousness. At Security, the man looks at the boarding pass and waves us through to the fast-track lane. At boarding, one of the flight attendants takes us aside before the main boarding call and leads us through the empty gate, all the way to our seats. She gives us her name, which I promptly forget, and she squeezes Gill's hand and tells us to call her if we need anything at all.

On the plane, food comes and goes, on neat little trays – I even manage to eat something, with a vague thought that I'll need the energy. I don't know for what – I don't know what a death like this involves; what will be required of me. But there will be things to do, things to organise, I tell myself, forcing myself to chew and swallow. And Gill will need me. She's not eating; she's sitting there, her bag clutched on her lap, and her whole body weirdly rigid. At one point she starts a movie, but she doesn't even put her headphones on. Just sits there, staring at the screen while the actors gesture sincerely at one another.

She's hardly spoken, but after we change planes at Dubai, she turns to me suddenly and bangs at her chest, as if trying to knock loose something lodged in her windpipe.

'It hurts here,' she says. 'Do you feel that? Right here?' She strikes her sternum again, hitting hard enough that she leaves small red marks on her skin.

'I know,' I say. 'But we'll be OK. We'll get through this.'

I have no idea whether that's true. The pain she's talking about, I feel it too – a compression, my whole chest encased in concrete. I'm sure I've seen articles about people literally dying from heartache. Something about blood pressure, or a change to the ventricles. Maybe that's happening to us now. A heart attack at 35,000 feet would seem no more strange or terrible than anything else that's happened since the police came to the door more than forty-eight hours ago. Ever since then, the world is a jerky old movie, grainy and monochrome, the sound out of sync. I grip the armrest tighter and watch the flight attendant patrol the aisle, dispensing coffee as if it, or anything else, matters.

Gill

I used to roll my eyes at people who sprang up as soon as the plane landed. I'd stay in my seat, smug, watching them scurrying for their bags and standing, hunched over, in the aisle, even though it never got them off the plane any faster. Now, at Heathrow, it's me ignoring the seatbelt sign and wrenching open the overhead locker while we're still taxiing to the gate. I turn my phone back on, and while it's loading I play in my head all the scenarios I've imagined on the flight. The missed calls from the consulate, and from Sue. Thirty voicemails. *A terrible mistake. It was another boy.* I can almost see the messages: *The body wasn't Dougie after all. It's a miracle – he's been found. An air pocket. A hidden tunnel. Another exit from the cave.* And a voicemail from Dougie himself. *Mum. Dad. It's me – I'm fine. I'm so sorry to have got you so worried. Gonna have some great stories to tell!*

That's what I was imagining, all through that endless flight – even while I tried to distract myself by watching a movie. There was a pain in my chest. I could feel every membrane of my heart, and the whole thing being slowly and deliberately pulled apart, like a ball of mozzarella being shredded for a salad. From time to time I let my hand grope in my bag for Dougie's letter to Sylvie. I pressed it between my thumb and forefinger and rubbed it. I ran my fingers along the envelope, front and back, as though I could read the letter inside like braille.

I'm queueing in the plane aisle when my phone finally boots up. I scroll past an automated message from my mobile provider. *Welcome to the UK*. There's text from a UK number. *This is Elena, from the Australian High Commission, just confirming that I'll be available tomorrow to speak to you and explain the consular assistance we can offer. Please call this number when you've arrived and we can arrange a time at your convenience.*

A text from Sue. *All OK here, darling. Sylvie and Papabee both fine (mad, but no madder than when you left them). Teddy fine too. Sending all the love. Call any time – bugger the time zones.*

Eleven texts from other friends, which I only hurriedly scan – they're all variations on *sorry for your loss,* interspersed with questions about the funeral date. Why is everyone in such a rush to commit my son to the dirt? I shut my phone back off.

I hate them all: the phone company; the helpful woman from the High Commission; my friends; even Sue. I hate the man ahead of me as we file off the plane, for walking so slowly, and I hate the two blonde children in front of him, for being alive, when one of mine is dead and another is doing her best to be.

Gabe

From Heathrow we take a taxi to the flat that Sue booked for us before we left home. 'I found somewhere close to Dougie's school,' she'd told me. I wasn't sure if we should base ourselves there, or closer to the caves, or the morgue, or the coroner's office. But I just thanked Sue and took the piece of paper on which she'd scrawled the address. In the back of the taxi I squeeze it so tight that the ink on *Edgware* has smeared. Beside me, Gill barely speaks. The stiffness in her body has given way to a gentle shaking. She's like a gong that's been struck, shaking until she almost shimmers.

'I can't make it stop,' she says, and I'm not sure whether she's talking about the shaking, or Dougie's death. It doesn't make any difference.

We've been in the cab for half an hour when I realise we have no English money, and I have to ask the driver to stop at an ATM, all while Gill sits there shaking, her head pressed against the window. I don't mind, now, that she isn't coping, because it forces me to cope. It gives me something to do with my hands: loading the bags into the boot; counting the money; checking that our passports are zipped into her handbag.

We drive past a restaurant, Ottolenghi, and I recognise the name from Gill's cookbook shelf. I'm about to point it out – a kind of habit, my old life momentarily forgetting that it's over. I lower my hand and close my mouth before the words are out. We aren't tourists, here for restaurants and walking tours and gawking at monuments and palaces.

'She going to be all right?' the driver asks, gesturing to Gill as he helps me hoist the suitcases from the boot. She's crying silently, people detouring around her on the pavement and pretending not to stare.

'It's not been a good day,' I say, and pay him far too much because I'm not sure how much to tip in England, and I don't have any change.

'You take care now,' he says, with a pat on the arm, and a look that might be sympathy, or might just be a response to that wad of notes, fresh from the ATM.

The suitcases are heavy – it takes me two trips to get them up the stairs. So heavy that I don't see how the clothes I threw in can account for it. I imagine the cases loaded with the lie that we told to Sylvie. We've brought it with us, that great unwieldy lie. I'm hauling it up the stairs, the suitcase handle cutting into my hand. It's here with us, in the small rented apartment on the first floor.

Gill stands in the middle of the living room as though she's forgotten how to sit down.

'My baby boy,' she says, and it sounds strange, because that's what she often calls Teddy. I've forgotten, until she says it now, that she used to call Dougie that, all those years ago.

'I want to see him,' I say. 'I want to know how it happened.'

She doesn't seem to hear me.

I run a glass of water, and put it down, undrunk.

'I guess we should try to sleep,' I tell her.

'I can't.'

The flat has the immaculate dullness of all rented flats. The kitchen is basic, and there's no food in the cupboards except olive oil and a box of sugar cubes. I pace the kitchen, from the sink to the empty fridge and back again.

'I'll make something for dinner,' says Gill.

'We don't need to cook,' I tell her. 'We can go out. I'm not even hungry.'

But Gill says she wants to cook, and I can see that she can't keep her hands still, so I find my way to the nearest supermarket. The woman at the till asks, 'How are you?' and I don't know how to begin to answer. I don't say anything, of course – I just mutter the obligatory 'Fine, thanks.' I need the airline compassionate code for everyday life. A small tattoo on my forehead – *COMP* – so that people would understand. They'd look at me and right away they'd know I'm the father of a dead son.

I come back to the flat with a bag full of veggies and a supermarket baguette that's already turning stale. Even while we're too dazed to make words, Gill fills the sterile kitchen with cooking smells. I'm grateful for the noise of the onions browning on the stovetop, to fill the silence. But neither of us can eat.

'We should call that woman, at the High Commission,' I say, staring at my food.

'I'll wash up,' says Gill, picking up the untouched plates.

'Do you want me to put it on speaker, so you can listen?' I call after her, but she doesn't hear me over the clatter of dishes in the sink.

Gill

Over the sound of the kitchen tap running, I can hear him on the phone in the next room, still talking to the High Commission.

My bag is on the kitchen counter. As I wash up, I keep looking at it. Twice I put down the sponge and move towards the bag; once I even go as far as drying my hands. But each time I stop myself, sinking my hands back into the water. It's too hot, my skin turning a broiled red.

Before today, I would never have dreamed of opening one of Dougie's letters. I never even peeked – it wouldn't have occurred to me. It would have been like eavesdropping on my own children – like creeping barefoot up the corridor and pressing my ear to Dougie's bedroom door when he and Sylvie were having one of their endless chats.

But this is different. Of course I'm going to give Sylvie the letter – I'll do it as soon as we're back. But she won't know its significance. That it might be the last thing he ever wrote. Gabe doesn't seem to understand it either – that somehow the cave has changed it from a letter into a testimony.

Gabe's still talking in the living room. *Why did it take so long to recover the body?* he asks, and I lean over the sink, trying not to throw up. I put the last glass in the draining rack, dry my hands on a tea-towel, and pull the letter from my bag. I slide a fingernail under the flap and give a tentative tug. Nothing. I remember that, in the spy novels I read as a child, people were always steaming letters open, so I boil the kettle, but all that I manage to achieve is a soggy envelope, and a scorched right wrist.

In the end I ease a sharp knife under the crease and peel it open that way, a little at a time. I stand with my back to the kitchen door, in case Gabe comes in, but he's still on the phone, still asking for details.

The letter's typed, not handwritten, which shouldn't have surprised me – Dougie and his generation use laptops for everything, even for taking notes in class.

Dear Sylve,

Missing you lots and hope all OK there (relatively speaking – you know what I mean).

Went to Bath last weekend and met up with Lucas Kane, who was at school with me (red hair, remember?) – he's doing a gap year at a school there. I used to think he was a tosser at school, and I was only catching up with him because I don't know anyone else in Bath. But actually we ended up having a really good time. Bath's v posh, and Jane Austen everywhere – you and Mum would have loved it, but I never finished Emma for English in grade 10 even though I wrote an essay on it – thank you, Wikipedia! (DON'T EVER TELL MUM. SERIOUSLY. OR SUE.) And actually I think Lucas is OK. Really interested in Aus politics so we had a good chat about that, a nice change after the students at my school here who don't care at all or (worse) think Tasmania is Tanzania (!! – so much for the expensive education they're getting...). Anyway, it was good to see Lucas. You'd say maybe it was me who was the tosser at school...probably you're right.

I can still hear Gabe's voice – something about viewing the body, and the morgue. I want to run out of the kitchen, interrupt him, wave the opened letter at him. Drag him away from that Dougie – the one of coroners and bodies and morgues – and offer him this Dougie instead. Our Dougie.

But what if Gabe doesn't understand? What if he tells me I'm wrong? By reading the letter, am I keeping faith with Dougie, or betraying him?

So I stay where I am, my back to the kitchen door. I run my thumb over and over the typed words, and read on.

Things with Rosa are v good, though it's a bit weird working together (have to call her 'Miss Campbell' in front of the kids! etc.). But I'm actually missing home more than I expected. I miss the Neck – miss being in the sea. And I swear you can actually TASTE the pollution in the air in London. Tas is one of those places you can't wait to leave, and then afterwards you start to appreciate it from a distance.

And I worry about you, and Mum and Dad too and T and P (not Sausage, cheeky little bastard, who will probably outlive us all, like the cockroaches). I know you have your own stuff going on, but try not to freeze out the parentals. Yes, they drive us up the wall sometimes, but I also know they worry about you and miss you like crazy.

Lots of love
Dougie xx

The parentals. I'd forgotten that he used to call us that. How much else have I forgotten already?

PS: Off next week for an excursion – Outward Bound sort of thing, for some of the younger kids. Caving,

*archery, rock-climbing (all crucial life skills for
contemporary urban rich kids!). Will be good to have a
break from usual school routine (and school meals!) –
and Rosa's coming too, though a coach-load of 12-year-
olds means it's not exactly a romantic getaway...*

My hands are shaking so much that I'm worried I'll tear the
paper, still soggy from the steam.

Next door, Gabe's thanking the woman on the phone and
saying goodbye. I tuck the damp letter between the pages of
a book, and shove it back into my bag.

Mediterranean vegetable soup for the day you land in England to collect your son's body

During the meal, you will want something to do with your mouth, which won't be fit for speaking. Chop the celery only roughly, so that you'll be picking the long threads from your teeth for hours. For the same reason, it's important not to de-stone the olives. Leave the stones in, and when you are eating, take your time loosening each one with your tongue. Use your fingers to fish them from your mouth like dislodged teeth.

Teddy

'You don't have to go to school today if you don't want to,' Sue says. She's trying to get out a piece of toast that's stuck in the toaster. She burns her finger and yells 'Fuck!', then drops the burnt toast onto my plate.

I remember once, when Mum told off Dougie for swearing, and he said, 'You never tell Sue off when she swears, and she swears all the time.'

'Have you ever tried telling Sue off?' Mum said, and we'd all laughed, because nobody, not even Dougie, the bravest of everyone, was brave enough to tell Sue off.

Sue skids the butter across the table towards me. 'Seriously,' she says. 'Don't go if you don't feel up to it. I'll be around all day anyway.' Normally she flies up to Melbourne almost every week for work meetings, but she tells me she's cancelled them for this week. 'I'll be here until your folks get back. Just to keep an eye on you and Sylvie, and Papabee.'

'I keep an eye on Papabee myself,' I say.

'I don't doubt it.' She gives me a kiss on my head. 'So: school, or not?'

'Mum said it's probably best to try to keep going like normal.'

'OK.' She nods. 'Fair enough. This isn't really normal, though, is it?'

My turn to nod. 'But I think I want to go anyway.'

I don't tell her that it's the day we're presenting our science projects. I want to be there to show the rocket that Alasdair-Down-The-Road and I made. We spent ages building it, and Mrs Hooper said we can even take it out to the oval

60

and see how high it will go. Does it make me a bad person, that I still want to do it, even now that Dougie's dead? I don't understand how two such different things can fit in my head at the same time. *Rocket. Dougie. Rocket. Dougie.*

Sue rests her hand on the back of my neck. 'Do you want to talk about it? About Dougie?'

'No.' I wouldn't mind talking about it, but I don't know how. Dougie being dead is still just a thing in my head. It hasn't made it as far as my mouth yet.

'OK,' she says. 'Don't worry – I won't make you talk. But if you want to, or if you have any questions, I'm around.'

I look down at the dog, instead of her. I bend forward and squish my head down so my face is in SausageDog's fur, and I close my eyes and I wish I could be Dog-Teddy and burrow under fences, squeeze under tree-roots, find all the hidden places. I'd be a real dog, even the gross bits: bum-sniffing, wet-nosed. I'd roll on my back and show my belly, which is how a dog says *Yes* with its whole body. Pissing proudly on every tree: *Yes! Yes! Yes!* Chase my nose into every hole. Smell-chasing, cat-chasing, wave-chasing in the shallow water at the Neck. I wouldn't have to lie to Sylvie because dogs can't tell lies – their tails always tell the truth. And if I was Dog-Teddy I wouldn't be afraid of bones.

Sue drives me into school, instead of making me catch the bus, which makes today feel even less like normal. We drive past the shops and the newspaper display outside the newsagent says *Hobart Boy Killed in Cave Tragedy* and for a second I think the cave's called Cave Tragedy and I think *Why did they even take them into a cave called Tragedy?* and it almost seems funny and then I remember that there's nothing funny about it. Sue says, 'Thank Christ your mum's not here to see the *Mercury* having a field-day with this,' and drives faster.

At school, Mrs Conway and the other teachers are extra nice to me, and even my friends must've heard the news because Alasdair-Down-The-Road says, 'Are you OK?' and gives me a pat on the arm that's kind of a cuddle and kind of a shove. He doesn't say anything else about it, but at recess he gives me his whole muesli bar. I think he wants to say something about Dougie, but he doesn't know how, and I don't mind, because it's the same for me.

All day Elsie Parr and Chibek Deng keep staring at me. I'm not sure how I'm supposed to be acting. Am I doing this wrong? Elsie's the only person who actually says anything about Dougie. She comes up to me in the art room and says, 'How exactly did it happen?' and Alasdair tells her to shut up, but afterwards he looks at me like he's waiting for something, and I realise that he wants me to tell him too.

'He drowned,' I say quietly, so Alasdair can hear and Elsie can't. 'In a cave.'

'But he could swim, couldn't he?' Alasdair asks.

I've been thinking that too. Dougie was a really good swimmer – better than Mum and Dad. At the Neck, he could swim out so far that we could hardly see him, and Mum got nervous about sharks and would shout to him from the beach. When I was smaller, Dougie could even swim with me holding onto his back. It doesn't make sense that somebody like him could drown.

'I think it's different underground,' I say. 'I think maybe it was too dark.' I haven't worked out yet exactly how the dark makes a difference, but it seems important.

I don't want to talk about it any more, because that would mean thinking about Dougie drowning. So I don't say anything else to Alasdair, and just pretend to concentrate really hard on my painting.

After school, Papabee picks me up, just like normal, and we go back to his tiny little flat, just like normal. While I hang up my blazer on the hook on the back of the door, he's already getting out the dominoes.

'I thought we might have a biscuit while we play,' he says. 'What do you think?'

I say yes – I always say yes, even though I've learned to check the biscuits for mould, and to sniff the milk before he makes me a hot chocolate. Papabee doesn't really cook any more – not properly. That's why Mum and Dad bought him a microwave for his flat, last year. A few months later he said, 'That television that you very kindly gave me doesn't seem to be working,' and Dad went around to see what Papabee was talking about, and there was the microwave, set up on top of the chest of drawers in Papabee's bedroom.

I wonder if I should tell Papabee again about Dougie, but it seems mean, and anyway I don't want to, so that Papabee's flat can be one place where Dougie isn't dead, and Sylvie isn't sick, and I don't have to imagine being Bird-Teddy or Dog-Teddy or any other kind of Teddy at all. Instead we play dominoes, and I show him movies on my phone of penguins falling over, and he says, 'How extraordinary.' I show him another penguin movie, and he laughs again. I'm not good at very many things, but I'm better than pretty much anyone at making Papabee laugh.

Papabee makes hot chocolate, and when he puts the milk away in the cupboard next to the cups I take it out again and put it in the fridge, without saying anything. I show him another YouTube movie, of dogs knocking over toddlers, and just at the bit when the big white dog pushes the toddler into a puddle, I remember that Dougie is dead. Properly, totally, dead. Papabee's still looking at the movie. He points at the boy onscreen and says, 'I hope that poor little chap suffered no lasting ill-effects. Is he a friend of yours?' But my tongue has got too big in my mouth. It feels like the ox tongues on display in the window at the butcher on Argyle St – bigger than you'd believe, great big heavy chunks of muscle so thick and grey that when we go down that street

I make Mum and Dad cross the road with me to walk on the other side.

A bit of me wants to yell, *Dougie's dead, remember! Don't you know?* And another bit of me wants to take Papabee's not-knowing and crawl under it with him, the way I used to crawl right under the covers in Mum and Dad's bed when I had a nightmare. I want to pull Papabee's not-knowing right over my head and stay in there with him and never come out.

When it's time to go down the road for dinner, I remind Papabee to lock the door, and make sure he puts his key in the top pocket of his jacket. I counted once: one hundred and seventy steps, from Papabee's front door to our back door. Inside our house, when Papabee bends down to let SausageDog lick his ear, his hat falls off, like it always does, and I pick it up and hang it for him on the hook by the door, like I always do. I love the sameness of these things, now that Dougie's dead and it feels like normal has gone away for good.

Sue's in the kitchen, and she says, 'You're looking particularly handsome today, Papabee,' and kisses him on both cheeks.

Papabee smiles, such a big one that his moustache goes up at the ends like a cartoon smile. 'You must forgive me, my dear, if I don't remember your name,' he says to her, 'though I do, of course, recall you most fondly.'

'I would forgive you anything, Papabee,' Sue says. She's always like that with Papabee – she flirts with him even though she's married to Dan, and even though Papabee's super old. Sue's old too, but only Mum-and-Dad old, not proper old-person old.

He asks about Mum and Dad, and Sue says, 'They're away for a few days, remember?' and he says, 'Of course, of course,' and she doesn't remind him why, and I'm glad. Sue makes it all the way through dinner with me and Papabee without crying, but afterwards, while Papabee's drinking his coffee in the lounge room and I'm helping Sue to load the dishwasher, I catch her doing it again, just like Mrs Conway did – the kind of trying not to cry that's so obvious that you might as well just actually cry.

'It's OK if you want to cry,' I tell her. 'I'm not going to cry right now. But if you want to, I don't mind.'

'Thanks, Teddy,' she says. She puts down the plate she's holding and stands there, letting the crying happen for a minute or two. Then she blows her nose – a really good, loud, snotty blow, and says, 'Do you know what? I might be finished with crying for now. But if I need to have another one later on, I'll go for it.' She gives me a little salute, with just one finger.

On the third morning, Sue makes us pancakes. Most of them she burns, and when she's scraped them off the pan they're all scrunched up. But she eats the squished ones herself, and gives me the good ones.

'I don't normally get pancakes for breakfast,' I say, with my mouth full.

'I thought you might like a treat.'

'Because Dougie died?'

For a moment she doesn't say anything. 'I suppose so.'

I really like pancakes – even Sue's burnt ones. But it doesn't seem like a good deal to me. I try to work out what kind of deal would be fair, for a dead brother. A new PlayStation. Being able to fly. No homework ever again. I can't think of anything that would be big enough to make it a good deal.

I still eat all the pancakes though. They're not very good – burnt on the outside, and squishy on the inside – but I eat them anyway, and pass the blackest bits to Sausage under the table.

'Hospital after school, or Papabee's?' Sue asks. 'I can give you a lift to the hospital, if you want.'

'I'll go and see Sylvie, I guess,' I say. I won't be able to figure out what her price is if I stay away from her. But when I think about going in there, and trying not to let anything slip about Dougie, my tongue feels like ox tongue again: too thick, too wet, too heavy.

But I know I have to do it. If I can work out Sylvie's price in time, she might not be the *one* from the *one-in-five*. Because I'm starting to think it's all joined up: what happened to Dougie, and what's happening to Sylvie. *Sister in the hospital, brother in the water* – it's part of the same thing, and it's got something to do with stories, and something to do with bones. I remember the last summer before Sylvie went into hospital, when I sat on the beach and stared at her sharp shoulder blade. The triangle of bone looked just like a signpost. I think that when Dougie went into that cave he was following the signpost on Sylvie's back. He followed the bone sign all the way down.

Gabe

We have a morning appointment with a woman from the coroner's office. We need to catch a train to Beaconsfield – she explained on the phone that even though Dougie was living at the school in London, the accident was in Buckinghamshire, so the local coroner has jurisdiction. I almost fall asleep on the train, drunk with jet lag or grief, and Gill has to nudge me awake when the train slows at the station.

When we're shown into the coroner's assistant's office, she introduces herself as Heather, but although I say, 'I'm Gabe, and this is Gill,' as I shake her hand, she insists on calling us Mr and Mrs Jordan throughout.

'You've come a long way,' she says.

'Of course we came,' I say, abruptly. My capacity for small talk has been left somewhere between Hobart and Heathrow.

'Of course,' she echoes, and I feel bad for my rudeness.

'Please,' I say, softening my voice. 'Can you explain what happened?'

'We don't yet have the whole picture, I'm afraid. What we can confirm, so far, is that the flood happened suddenly, when the caving expedition was well under way. I've got you the contact details of a police officer who should be able to give you more details.' Heather glances at her computer. Her office feels like just that: an office. There are filing cabinets, a battered desk with piles of forms. It could be an office at a car hire firm, or an insurance company. I'm grateful for the administrative surroundings. If this conversation were happening somewhere cosy – on a couch in somebody's living room – I'd fall apart. This is better. The printer on top of the filing cabinet, its red light blinking; the sound of people talking in the next office. It doesn't feel like a place in which it's appropriate to cry, and so I don't.

'I understand that someone from the Australian High Commission has been in touch with you,' she goes on. 'They told you about the inquest?'

'No. I mean, yes, I spoke to a woman. But I don't remember anything about an inquest. Maybe she did mention it, but there was a lot to take in.'

'Of course,' she says again. 'In cases like this, where the death doesn't take place in the hospital, and where the cause isn't entirely straightforward, there has to be an inquest. But the important thing for you to understand is that you don't have to wait until the inquest to move forward with the funeral, or burial.'

I haven't got as far as that in my head: the process, the reality of Dougie's body, and what we'll do with it.

'The inquest has been opened,' Heather continues.

'Without us?' I jump in. 'Why? Shouldn't we have been told? We should have been there.'

She raises her palms. 'There isn't a *there*,' she says patiently. 'It's not something that happens in a courtroom, or anything like that. It's just a technicality, so that we can start the process, record the death and the identification of the body. The inquest's already been adjourned, while we investigate. It'll be months, minimum, before the inquest itself. But I do need to inform you that there'll have to be a post-mortem examination.'

'There's no need,' says Gill, straight away. 'Surely there's no need? They know what killed him. They fished him out of the cave. There were other people there, when the flood happened, right? This isn't an episode of a detective show. We know what killed him.'

I put my hand on her arm. 'It might not be as simple as that.'

'Your husband's right, Mrs Jordan. I know that the idea of a post-mortem can be confronting. But the inquest is about establishing the precise cause of Douglas's death. We don't know for certain whether equipment failure might have been a contributing factor. Whether the guides followed correct protocol, or whether search and rescue procedures were properly followed. Whether Douglas's death was even drowning, strictly speaking. As I'm sure you can imagine, there are other injuries.' I hadn't imagined – though now I can do nothing else. 'The post-mortem will hopefully be able to give us more information about the exact sequence of events and which of these injuries might have resulted in his death.'

'I don't want to know any of that,' Gill says, turning away.

I do. I want to know it all, I realise. I want to know exactly what happened to my son.

Heather's still talking – something about how future tragedies might be averted, if they can learn a lesson from Dougie's death.

'He's our son,' says Gill. Her voice is very calm, very dignified. 'Not a cautionary tale. What if we say no to the post-mortem? Do we have the right to do that?'

'In ordinary circumstances – if Douglas had died after an illness, say – then yes, you would. But in a situation like this, when the post-mortem has been ordered by the coroner, then no, I'm afraid there's no choice.'

Gill's holding my hand so tightly that I can feel her pulse, or my own, at the point where her fingers crush against mine.

Heather continues. 'But, as I said, we'll be able to release the body as soon as the post-mortem is finished, so that you can move on with your own arrangements.'

Gill lets go of my hand. 'So you're going to cut up our son, and we have no say in it?'

'I can reassure you that the whole procedure is done with great care and respect. You'll be able to view Douglas's body afterwards, and it's probable that you won't even notice a difference.' She refers to her notes. 'Also, you have the power to make decisions about any tissue removed during the process.'

Gill looks as though she might be sick. I turn back to Heather.

'Tissue?' I ask.

'It may be necessary for them to take small amounts of tissue, for further analysis. If this happens, then after any testing is finished, you can choose whether you would like these to be returned to you, or cremated, or donated to science.'

'Donated to science,' I say. 'I think so, right?' I look to Gill, but she's looking down at her hands, her fists clenched tight as if clutching an invisible rope.

'You don't need to decide immediately,' Heather says. 'You can decide closer to the post-mortem itself, which should be in a matter of days. You'll get the preliminary results almost immediately, though toxicology results might take a bit longer.'

'What do you mean?'

'I'm afraid processing these things takes time—'

'No, that wasn't what I meant. I don't mind about it taking time. But why do they need toxicology? It was a caving accident, early in the morning. He was hardly going to be drunk.'

'We always need to get the full picture, Mr Jordan. And remember, it's about understanding what happened, rather than allocating blame. Any alcohol or drugs that might have impacted his reactions—'

Is that what this is all about? Are they looking for a way to blame Dougie for what happened to him? If it turns out he smoked some weed the night before, will they claim that this is his fault?

A few times during Dougie's final year of school, Gill and I smelled the unmistakable waft of marijuana from his bedroom, when he had friends over.

'It smells like bolognese,' Gill had said. 'Really good bolognese.' She took a slow, deep inhalation. 'Should we say something? Stop them?'

I liked those parts of parenting. The not-knowing, when Gill and I were together in not having a clue. It made me feel young again – sitting there with her, giggling through our whispers, while the weed smell grew stronger.

'He's not injecting crack into his eyeballs,' I said. 'He's just having a joint. We did the same thing when we were young.'

'Not that young. He's seventeen. And they've got exams.'

'It might relax them,' I say. 'We should be grateful it's just weed.'

Maybe we were too easy on him. We were so thankful to have a kid doing normal kid things, instead of starving themselves to death in a hospital. Between the smell of burning fat on Sylvie's breath, and the smell of Dougie's weed drifting through the dark air, we would choose the weed every time.

Here, in the coroner's office, I blink several times, and try to focus on Heather, who's still talking about the post-mortem.

I interrupt. 'Can I be there?'

She raises her eyebrows. 'At the post-mortem itself?'

'Yes.'

'You have the right to request that a representative be there, on your behalf. A doctor of your own choosing, though I believe it would have to be at your own expense.'

'He doesn't need a doctor,' I say. 'He's dead.'

Gill flinches, shifting away from me. I don't know if she's embarrassed by my rudeness to Heather, or whether it's the starkness of those two syllables: *He's dead*.

'He needs his father,' I continue, 'not a doctor. Why can't I be there?'

'A post-mortem is still a medical procedure. No onlookers are allowed, except for doctors.' She pauses. 'This is for your benefit, Mr Jordan. It would be distressing, for you to witness this.'

'Heaven forbid that I should be distressed.'

'Naturally you're distressed.' She nods, and keeps nodding, like one of those nodding cat ornaments that you see on the counters of Chinese restaurants. 'Of course you are. But why make it worse for yourself?'

I almost laugh at the concept of my distress as something that could be worsened, any more than it could be improved. It's absolute – when your child dies, there are no sliding scales of distress.

'My being there can't hurt him. He's dead. What harm can come to him now?'

'Gabe,' cautions Gill.

'I mean, if he wasn't dead already, we wouldn't be here. So tell me why I can't be at the post-mortem?'

'It's not permitted,' Heather says, shuffling papers.

I have no energy left to argue. And I feel sorry for Heather – she's only young, probably no more than thirty, and her job can't be easy. At the edge of her top lip, some of her lipstick has smeared. It makes her look like a child dressed as a grown-up.

'As I said,' she continues, 'the body will be released immediately after the procedure. If you want to repatriate Douglas, for burial, then he will have to be embalmed.'

'And what's the other option?' I hope there is another option. *Embalmed* sounds only one step removed from taxidermy. My grandfather used to have a stuffed fox in a glass case in his dining room. I remember all those childhood afternoons at his house, trying to avoid the gaze of that fox, which looked too alive to be dead, and too dead to be alive.

'Cremation,' Heather says. 'That can be organised through a funeral parlour. We're not permitted to recommend any firm in particular, but the Australian High Commission can give you a list of reputable local companies. Once you've chosen one, they can collect the body and advise on the logistics – cremation or repatriation, whichever you choose.'

I look at Gill. 'Love?' I ask. 'What do you think?'

When I was young I used to want to be buried. In recent decades, cremation's started to make more sense. Maybe it has something do with being older – the body becomes fallible, and you become less attached to the idea of it. But is it different for Dougie? He's nineteen years old, his body still perfect. Invincible, except for being dead. It seems like a waste, somehow, cremating him. But I don't want to embalm him and haul him all the way back to Tasmania.

'I can't,' Gill says. 'I don't know. You decide.'

'This is important. We should decide together.'

'You don't need to decide right now,' says Heather. 'Take your time.'

'No,' Gill and I say at once.

'We should decide today,' I go on. 'I don't want him waiting in a morgue any longer than he has to.'

'Yes,' Gill nods. 'I don't know. Cremated? Do you think that's what he would have wanted?'

Then I catch myself laughing, and Gill gives a kind of snort, and for a moment we're both laughing, because the question is so absurd. Dougie wouldn't have wanted any of this. He was nineteen, and alive, aggressively alive, always too hungry and too noisy and still growing. Not once have we spoken with him about his plans for death.

Our laughter stops as soon as it starts. The room is so quiet that I can hear the buzz of the fluorescent lamps in the ceiling, and a printer going in the next office.

'I think it's best,' I say. 'Cremation. Then – later – we can take his ashes home. Choose where to scatter them.'

'Or keep them,' Heather offers helpfully. 'Many people do.'

What might seem normal for the death of a parent or grandparent seems incongruous for Dougie. Do many people keep their teenage sons on the mantelpiece? Is that really a thing?

This whole situation feels so bizarre that I half-believe that it might be an elaborate prank. None of this can possibly be real. I look around the room, expecting some American TV host with suspiciously white teeth to burst out from behind the door and shout a catchphrase, followed by Dougie, grinning.

'You don't need to make any decisions right now,' Heather says again. 'Take the paperwork, look it over when you've had a chance to rest.'

We thank her, take the papers that she gives us, and leave. Halfway down the corridor, I stop.

'Where are you going?' Gill asks, but I'm already on my way back.

Heather is startled when I come barging back into the room without knocking. 'What about his organs? Can they be donated?' I ask.

Gill has caught up with me. Behind me, in the doorway, I hear her intake of breath.

Heather gives a grave smile. 'It's very generous of you to be thinking of that. But I'm afraid that's not an option. The circumstances of your son's death—' There's a long silence. 'The delay in finding the body, and the immersion in the water, meant that the doctors wouldn't have been able to harvest any usable organs.'

I wince at the word 'harvest' – it's so utilitarian. So agricultural.

Heather's come out from behind her desk now and is walking towards the door, so we have to move with her. 'And even if they'd been able to, I'm afraid the inquest and the post-mortem rule out organ donation.'

'Gabe,' Gill says, her hand pulling gently at mine. 'Love. We should go.'

We call the number that Heather gave us, and a policeman called Richard introduces himself as a Family Liaison Officer, and offers to come to the flat.

'How did this happen?' I ask him, when the three of us are sitting in the living room.

'There was an accident on the field trip,' he says. He speaks very clearly, a little slowly. He's probably used to dealing with people like us – people who are seeing everything as though from a distance. Hearing things as though underwater.

'We won't be able to confirm the exact sequence of events until the coroner's findings,' he says. 'But this is what we do know. There were eight children in the group, all aged twelve or thirteen. Two staff members, including your son.'

'Who was the other one?'

'Rosa Campbell.'

I nod. Rosa. Dougie's girlfriend. He'd mentioned her a few times – a bit cagey, but enough to make it clear that they were seeing each other. They'd travelled to Prague together at Easter.

'And two expedition guides, from a company called Intrepid South-West. One guide in charge, and an assistant. They drove to the caves – a cave network called the Smith–Jackson System. The group entered the caves shortly after ten am, after a safety briefing in the car park. By about ten forty-five, there was a sudden rise in water levels.'

'How was that allowed to happen? How could they be taken underground if it was raining?'

'It wasn't raining at the time,' he says. 'Though it seems there were brief but heavy rains overnight, raising water levels in the reservoir upstream. One of the theories is that the reservoir walls were breached, and that it took a long time for the water to soak through to the cave system.'

'One of the theories?' I ask. 'How many theories are there?'

'Again, we don't yet know every possibility. There's a chance that the water was rising earlier, but that somehow the guides failed to realise it. There's a chance that an internal wall in the cave system gave way, releasing a surge of water. And there are probably other options that we're not even aware of yet.'

So many options. But the result is always the same: Dougie, dead.

'So the water's rising,' I say.

'Yes. Rapidly, by this stage. The group had all reached Cavern 2, which took some time – it's down a narrow, fairly steep tunnel. One of the guides then led Douglas, Miss Campbell, and two of the kids down to another cavern – Cavern 3. This was a big descent, on ropes. And by this point it became clear that there was a problem. The guide said that the water there was already deep – above knee height, and rising. He escorted the children back to the central cave.'

'Leaving Rosa and Dougie?'

'But he came back for them. At some personal risk, by all accounts. The water was cutting off the cavern entirely by this point. The guide went down again, swam back to the cavern, and was able to rescue Miss Campbell.'

'But not Dougie,' I say. It's a statement, not a question.

'No. Conditions were deteriorating rapidly. The guide claims that he was barely able to get the young woman out safely, and was concerned that it would be futile to go back again, and that if he himself was lost, the other guide mightn't be able to safely lead the remaining children out of the caves.'

'What was his name?'

'Who?' Richard asks.

'The head guide. The one who left Dougie in the cave. What was he called?'

He checks his notes. 'There was an assistant guide, Terence Wan. But the guy in charge was Phillip Murphy. Goes by Phil. He owns the guiding company, too.'

I don't want to write the name down, not now while the policeman is staring at me, but I repeat it in my head, committing it to memory.

'Mr Jordan, I've got to advise you not to attempt to make any contact with Mr Murphy. Our own enquiries are under way, and I can assure you that they're going to be extremely thorough.'

'But you're saying that he was responsible?'

'It's the coroner's job to find out exactly what happened. All I've said is that Murphy was leading the group. If you try to contact him, you'll only muddy the waters.' An awkward pause, for his awkward metaphor. 'It could even jeopardise the investigation.'

'I'm not looking for any trouble,' I say. What am I looking for?

'The main group was able to exit the cave system shortly after eleven,' the policeman says. 'They raised the alarm immediately. Local police attended, and volunteers from the local potholing club came too. The guides were also helping, once they'd been checked over by paramedics. But because of the water levels, the rescue teams weren't cleared to re-enter the cave system until after seven that night. Douglas's body was located after midnight, in a cavern slightly downstream from where he had last been seen.' He checks his notes again. 'Cavern 4. It took several hours to safely remove the body.'

The body. When did that happen – when did he cease to be Dougie and become *the body*? I feel a wave of relief that we haven't told Sylvie. This would destroy her utterly.

'Do you have any questions?' he asks.

And I shake my head, my mouth flooded with questions that I cannot ask:

What was the last thing my son saw before he died?

Can you tell me why my daughter won't eat?

Can you tell me if Dougie was afraid?

Gill

PC Holden says, right at the start, 'Please, call me Richard,' and I think, *Richard Holden, Christ, school can't have been easy for little Dick Holden*. Then I think *Shit, concentrate, concentrate*. My mind keeps darting off in different directions. I try to focus on what the policeman is saying, but my mind skitters from his words like cumin seeds in hot oil, fizzing and skidding.

There was a field trip, Richard said – we knew about that already. An outdoor adventure day for some of the school's boarders, who were bussed off to different activities: rock-climbing; horse-riding; orienteering.

'On Friday morning, one group was taken potholing,' Richard says.

The police at home already told us this. They'd used the Australian term: *caving*. Not *potholing* – that sounds too innocent, too safe. Nothing deeper than a pothole on a country road. *Potholing* evokes kids in yellow gumboots, splashing in puddles. The word contains nothing about underground canyons, or narrow passageways. I think of Teddy's question: *Was it dark?*

It isn't just that *potholing* sounds deceptive – it sounds silly. Trivial. It has none of the seriousness or gravity of a proper pursuit like rock-climbing.

Because I haven't answered, PC Holden seems to think I haven't understood. He tries again. 'Spelunking? That's what they call it in America. I don't know about Australia. But you know what I mean: exploring caves, underground, sometimes with underground rivers too.'

Spelunking. That's even worse than *potholing*. The jaunty, unbearable onomatopoeia of that word. *Spelunk* – the sound of a rock tossed in a puddle. Not the sound of a body winched up from the blackness.

I can't bear those names. They seem grossly inappropriate. He keeps talking, but each time he mentions potholing I wince, hearing in my head that embarrassingly sprightly sound. *Spelunk. Spelunk.* Gabe keeps interrupting him, asking all kinds of questions, but I can't seem to make myself follow the conversation, or join it. What can I say? *I don't have any idea about the technical aspects of the expedition, or the flood, or the attempted rescue. But I have some complaints about the vocabulary.*

So I stay quiet, and drink my sweet tea, even though I can't taste anything. People keep offering us sweet tea. Those first police officers at home; Sue; the flight attendant. Now this policeman, who made tea for us in our own flat, dropping sugar cubes in one after another (*Spelunk. Spelunk*). 'Sweet tea – good for shock,' he said. How does everybody seem to know this except for me? Where did they learn it?

'Phillip Murphy,' the policeman – poor Dick Holden – is saying to Gabe. 'Goes by Phil.'

I don't know who he's talking about. I don't want to know. I'm thinking about Dougie – everything else is just a distraction.

I loved cooking for Dougie because he was hungry in the way that only teenage boys can be. He was hungry with his whole body. *Is there more of this?* he was always asking. He'd eye up anything left on my plate. 'Are you going to finish that?' he'd ask, already reaching out. I worried about him, always so ravenous. 'You must have worms,' I used to say. 'You sure you don't have an itchy bum?'

'Of course not,' he'd protest. 'Jesus, Mum, you're so embarrassing.'

Sometimes, if we had visitors for a meal, Gabe or I would have to issue a whispered command of 'F.H.B.' to the kids. It stands for *Family Hold Back*: no seconds, and no firsts until the guests had served themselves. It was mainly Dougie that we'd have to tell, because otherwise there was no stopping him, or the guileless hunger of his growing body. In the corridor, out of hearing of the guests, I'd have to grab Dougie's arm. 'F.H.B. on the pudding, Dougie. I mean it. It came out smaller than I thought.'

'You're starving me,' he'd groan.

I thought about that later, when Sylvie stopped eating. Dougie must have remembered it too, because he made a joke about it.

'She's taking F.H.B. a bit literally, isn't she?' he said. But I was too tired to laugh. I'd just come back from the hospital, where Sylvie had ignored me to lie with her face to the wall.

Teddy overheard Dougie's question. 'Does she think there isn't enough food?' Teddy asked. He was barely nine then, when Sylvie was first hospitalised. 'Is that it? You should show her the top of the cupboard, where all the tins are, and the big packets of pasta.'

'That's not it,' I said. 'Dougie was just making a joke. It's got nothing to do with not having enough food.'

'Plenty of food at my place too, Gillian,' said Papabee, looking up from the newspaper. 'Only have to ask.'

'No, Papabee, that's fine,' I said, trying to keep my voice calm. 'Thanks, but it's all fine.'

I'd been so glad when Sylvie suddenly showed an interest in cooking. After she turned fourteen, she was suddenly in the kitchen all the time, watching at first and then joining in. And I was secretly smug about it. While some other girls her age were trying out their fake IDs at Knopwood's pub,

Sylvie was in the kitchen with me, learning how to pierce a drizzle cake with a skewer so the sugar syrup penetrates all the way down to the bottom.

'Maybe she'll be a chef too,' I said to Sue. We were watching Sylvie making an apple cake; layering thin slices of apple in the base, pressing them flat with her fingertips.

'She'll be better than you soon,' Sue said. 'I'm gonna ditch you as a client and take on Sylvie instead.'

During the hospital years, I ran through those moments again and again: Sylvie in the kitchen, by the window, lifting the beaters from the cake mix; holding them high to check the consistency of those viscous ribbons of batter; using a wooden spoon to shift the last scraps from the beaters to the bowl.

I should have known then. Anyone else would have licked the spoon.

Papabee was the first to realise what Sylvie was up to. 'Do you think Sylvie ought to be quite so thin?' he said to me, one day after dinner, when the kids had left the table.

'She's just growing,' Gabe said, stacking the plates.

'And you know what she's like,' I added, reaching over Papabee's shoulder for his glass. 'We can't keep her out of the kitchen. She eats all the time.'

Papabee didn't argue with us, because he never argues with us. But what I should have understood was that cooking all the time isn't the same as eating all the time.

Sylvie made cakes for birthday parties, special occasions, and for no reason at all. Dougie loved it – he was sixteen, and always hungry. He'd grab a slice of something every time he passed through the kitchen. Or he'd sit on the counter while she cooked, Sylvie slapping his hand away when he tried to swipe the choc chips or scraps of shortcrust pastry.

Then we could no longer ignore the way her collarbones had grown sharp as a wire coat hanger under her skin.

She kept getting thinner, and I got fatter. In those months before her admission, she was baking so much, and was so insistent. Every afternoon, something new from the kitchen: rugelach biscuits, rolled tight like little fists; Baklava, layer after layer of pastry, heavy with sugar syrup and encrusted with pistachios. 'Go on,' Sylvie would say, 'I made it for you.' My clothes grew tight across my hips, and when I took off my trousers the waistband left a mark, a ring bisecting my waist. I had wandered into one of those fairy tales or myths, where the witch-mother consumes the child.

Sylvie never ate the things she made. 'Go on,' she'd say, when Gabe patted his full stomach, or when I waved away the offer of another slice of carrot cake. 'I made it for you.' She and Dougie had always been close, but there was something new in the way she watched him eat now. His hunger, and her hunger. When she offered us the cakes she'd made, she wasn't offering – she was goading. 'Go on,' she'd say, again and again. 'Mum will have seconds, won't you, Mum.'

She loved cooking for us. And she did love us – that wasn't counterfeit. She loved us, and she despised us. She loved us, because she despised us. Such a precise combination of love and disdain, generosity and disgust – she balanced it carefully, like the cinnamon and powdered ginger in the gingerbread men that she pressed out on the flour-dusted countertop. Each time she baked, and we ate, it was proof of our weakness, and her strength. She was reshaping our bodies, and her own. Pressing down with the cookie cutters, sharp and exact.

In the end, we had to refuse. My clothes didn't fit any more, and she was sharpening, all angles and edges. I didn't want to exile her from the kitchen, but we couldn't let it continue. When she bent to open the oven door, I couldn't take my eyes off her spine, that dorsal ridge of bone.

'We have to be strict about it,' Gabe said to me and Dougie.

'It's getting ridiculous.'

'No more cakes?' Dougie asked, with a theatrical moan. 'Are you serious?'

'No more cakes,' I said. 'Not unless she eats them too.'

So we sat her down, still in her apron. The apron strings that used to tie at the back now passed all the way around, tied at the front in a triumphant bow.

'We mean it,' I told her. 'We won't eat what you cook unless you eat it too.'

And that was the end of it. She didn't cook another thing.

The policeman's still answering Gabe's questions. Something about how Dougie's body was removed from the caves – the difficulty of manoeuvring it through the narrow tunnels. I think of Dougie's mouth full of water. Sylvie's mouth, always empty. Sylvie's hands, clenched around her silence. Dougie in the kitchen, when Sylvie cooked, his hands, snatching at scraps of pastry. His hands, reaching for air.

I want to slip back to the bedroom, to where Dougie's opened letter still sits inside my book. I want to take the book to the toilet, lock the door, and read the letter again and again. *I'm actually missing home more than I expected. I miss the Neck – miss being in the sea.* I want Dougie's voice in my head, not the policeman's.

'The caves aren't re-opened to the public yet,' the policeman says. 'And before they are, our own investigators will be searching them thoroughly.'

Don't, I want to say. *Block up every entrance. Set explosives and bring the whole thing down.*

Teddy

The newspapers at Papabee's flat give me the idea. He forgets to chuck things out, so the newspapers always pile up next to the loo, and Mum and Dad have been in London for four days, so they haven't been able to come up to his flat to clear out the rubbish. I'm sitting on the loo at Papabee's, looking at the newspapers, and reading some of the headlines:

Deadly Superbug Thriving in Australia

Leaked Brexit Email Claims David Cameron has 'Starved' NHS

So many stories squished in those folded-up pages. If Sylvie isn't going to tell me her story herself, then maybe I can find it in there.

'Can you please help me with a history project, for school?' I ask Papabee, when I come out. 'I have to look at some old newspapers.'

He drives me to the library. When he parks in Bathurst St, it takes him twelve goes of back-and-forward to get into the right spot. Counting Papabee's tries at parking is a game Dougie used to play. The record is nineteen. That time, Dougie and Sylvie and I were all in the back seat, counting in whispers, and we laughed so much that Dad turned around and said if we were rude to Papabee he'd make us walk home.

Could some of Dougie's laughing still be here, stuck in the back of Papabee's car, wedged down the side of the seats and in the footrests, along with bits of biscuit, and pieces of SausageDog's hair? I like the idea that Dougie might have left something behind.

Even after twelve goes, the back of the car still pokes out a bit into the road.

'A somewhat rakish angle,' Papabee says, looking over his shoulder. 'But it will have to do.'

In the library, I ask the man at the counter if we can see the old newspapers.

'How old?' he says.

'From 2012,' I say. It was 2013 when Sylvie first went into hospital, but I figure I'd better look a bit further back than that, just in case.

'Looks like you and I have very different definitions of *old*,' the man says, then smiles at Papabee as if they're sharing a joke.

Papabee smiles back politely. 'Indeed,' he says.

'Indeed' is like a disguise for Papabee – he says it all the time. It's good manners, and it makes it sound like he agrees, without showing that he doesn't understand. I've even tried it myself, a few times. Once Dad was helping me with my French homework, and he said, 'You haven't made the verb agree with the subject.'

'Indeed,' I said – but it didn't work, because Dad just looked at me funny, and Dougie laughed and said, 'Why are you talking like someone from the olden days?'

The man behind the counter points us down to the basement, where another librarian asks us, 'Local or interstate papers?'

'Both, please,' I say. I'm not quite sure of the difference, but it's safer to look at both. I want to do this job properly.

She shows us how to log in to see the old newspapers online – the *Mercury* and *The Age* and *The Australian* and *The Guardian Weekly*. All the ones that I can remember seeing around our house, because they're the ones Sylvie would've seen. I scroll and scroll, stopping whenever I see a headline that looks interesting.

Some of them are about things I sort of remember, even though I was only eight or nine back then:

Man kills family at health spa

Health plea for asylum centre

Terrorists break hearts of Tassie victim's family

Others I can't understand at all, even now:

Medicare gap widens: Doctors raise fees but rebate frozen in Budget

Victory for besieged MP Commission clears Thomson of electoral breaches

We spend almost two hours there. Papabee doesn't get bored. It's one of the things I like most about him. He never hurries me along, like other people always seem to. A few times he asks me to remind him what we're there for, and I tell him again that it's a history project, and he has a few goes of scrolling up and down the screen, and says, 'What an ingenious contraption.' We stay there until it's nearly six, and the librarian is stacking things on her desk, extra noisy, and staring at us, and finally she starts turning off the lights in the far side of the basement, so we have to leave. I realise that, for the whole time, I haven't thought about Dougie being dead.

'Did we find what we were looking for?' Papabee asks, when we're walking up the stairs.

'I'm not sure,' I say.

I've written down a few of the headlines that seemed most important – the ones that are so scary or sad they might've got stuck in Sylvie's brain, playing over and over like a song you can't get out of your head. The ones that might have scared her enough to make her stop eating.

Children will be exposed to the worst effects of climate change, says UNICEF

Doctors involved in terror torture

After the bloodshed, Cairo begins grim search for relatives

I can see how those kinds of stories could've made Sylvie afraid, or upset. But the rest of us were around back then too, and saw the same headlines, and we didn't stop eating.

While Papabee's driving backwards and forwards and backwards again, trying to squeeze out of his parking spot, I re-read the headlines in my notebook. I know I have to choose really carefully. I got it wrong when I tried to give Sylvie my Papa J money. If I'm going to find the price that will make Sylvie's secrets come rushing out, it has to be exactly the right thing.

Even before we get back home, I already know that the newspapers aren't what I need. The history in all those headlines is too big. It isn't going to answer my questions about Sylvie. It's the wrong kind of history – politicians and countries and tornadoes; big news stories. The kind of history I need is smaller, and closer to home.

When we come in, Sue yells out from the dining room. 'TeddyandPapabee? That you?'

Before Papabee moved here from England, I was just Teddy. Or, a lot of the time, *HurryUpTeddy* or *NotRightNowTeddy* or (from Sylve or Dougie) *ShutUpTeddy*. When Papabee came, the big kids were almost teenagers, big and busy with homework and sports practice and sleepovers, and without much room in their lives for an old man, or a little boy. But I was five when Papabee came, and it turned out he had exactly the right amount of room in his life for me, and I had exactly enough room in my life for Papabee. He arrived, and we turned into TeddyandPapabee.

Sue's dishing up dinner – it's one of the casseroles that people keep dropping off since Dougie died, and since the *Mercury* had *Hobart Boy Killed in Cave Tragedy* on the front page. Sue's started calling them 'Death Casseroles'. There've been a lot of them. If you could measure how bad something is in casseroles, Dougie's death is Nine Casseroles worth of bad.

'Jesus, Teddy,' Sue said the day before, bringing in another two casseroles from the front verandah. 'You're going to need a bigger freezer. We're all set for the apocalypse now.'

I thought: *Maybe this is the apocalypse. Maybe it's not like in the movies, with aliens or bombs or asteroids, and all the capital cities blowing up, one after another. The White House – Boom. The Sydney Opera House – Boom. Maybe this is how it really happens, instead: a little apocalypse, one person at a time. Sylvie – Boom. Dougie – Boom.*

So we eat the lasagne that Sharon-Over-The-Road made for us, and nobody talks about Dougie, or Sylvie, or where Mum and Dad are. After dinner I don't have any homework, so we watch *Pride and Prejudice*, the old one that Sylvie loved, before she got sick. When the episode's over and we turn the lights back on, Papabee says, 'Ah. It appears that the dog has eaten my trousers.' He stands up and we can see he's right – the whole time that the dog was nuzzling and snuffling at his feet, Sausage was actually eating right around the bottom bit of both Papabee's trouser legs, very neatly. Sue and I start laughing, and Papabee's laughing as well, and saying, 'Goodness me,' and now that his trousers are cut off short I can see that his socks don't match, one grey and one black, and that makes it even funnier, and we're all laughing, and I think about Dougie, who used to make us all laugh, and Sylvie, who lost her laugh like Papabee losing his car keys. And I wonder how these three things can be true at the same time: that Dougie's dead, and Sylvie's in hospital, and the dog ate Papabee's trousers. What kind of day is it, that can hold three things like that at once?

Mum and Dad ring when I'm in my pyjamas.

'We miss you,' Mum says. 'Are you being good for Sue?'

I tell them about Papabee's trousers, and Mum says, 'Oh God, it probably says something about how grubby his suit is. We'll get him a new one when we're back.' And I can tell the real funniness of it isn't making it all the way to London, where it isn't night-time, and they can't see Papabee's trousers or his odd socks.

'What time is it there?' I ask.

'Morning,' Dad says. 'Ten o'clock.'

'Which day?'

'Tuesday, same as there,' he says.

It's Tuesday night here, which means Dougie has been dead for longer here than there. And even though I know that's not actually how time zones work, I wish Mum and Dad had been able to keep flying, round and round the world chasing the time difference backwards all the way to the moment Dougie died, back far enough to stop him. And then back even further, right back to before Sylvie got sick, to stop her too.

I first noticed Sylvie getting skinny at the Neck.

I mean, I'd noticed already that she was getting skinny. But I didn't know whether or not it was normal. I didn't know what happened to girls' bodies when they were teenagers. Just before that same summer, Sue's Ella had come back from her exchange in Spain suddenly taller, and thinner, and with boobs that she never had before. So I thought maybe getting skinny was part of turning into a woman, like boobs and periods.

But at the Neck, when I saw Sylvie in her bathers, I realised she wasn't normal-skinny. She was a kind of skinny that made me want to stare and look away at the same time. She'd changed colour, too. The rest of us got browner and browner that summer, but even though Sylvie lay on the beach like the rest of us, she stayed a kind of grey-blue. When she helped me to zip up my wetsuit, her hands on the back of my neck were freezing cold.

I hoped the Neck might fix her, because of the magic that's there. Every year, I start to feel the magic as soon as we get close. The drive takes an hour, but we usually stop at Forcett to buy a box of cherries from the truck at the side of the road. We eat the cherries, redder than any red thing, while we drive, and Dougie and I spit the pips out the window. One day there'll be cherry trees growing all the way along the highway, both sides.

Across the skinny bit of land at Dunalley, the bush gets thicker, and I know that we're coming into the magic. When we open the car doors and I hear the waves going *shhhh shhhh*, I know for sure that the sea never stops telling itself secrets. I can feel the magic even when nothing's happening, which is the most happening thing of all, because at the Neck I can notice that the sky's happening, right up there, and the big trees behind the house are happening too, and the seagulls, and my body, all of it, busy with happening.

The magic at the Neck isn't magic like the man with the fake moustache pulling a rabbit out of a hat at Alasdair-Down-The-Road's birthday party. It's not good magic or bad magic – the magic at the Neck is crabshell gumtree bushfire magic, and it belongs to itself and you can't even argue with it. It's magic like the big eagle that flies above the beach, going round and round, writing O O O on the sky.

When we were younger, we used to go searching for Tasmanian Tigers in the bush above the beach, getting ourselves so excited that we could almost believe we could see their striped fur through the trees. Back at home I don't believe in Tasmanian Tigers – I know they've been extinct since the olden days. But at the Neck, I can believe in anything. I can almost smell the Tigers hiding there in the bush – a doggy smell, like SausageDog but more wild. Sharp smell, like the smell of being afraid or being excited, or both.

Right through that summer on the beach, while the others were talking and eating and chucking the tennis ball around, I watched Sylvie carefully. I made myself into a detective, or a spy. I watched her bones get bonier and her skin get more and more grey. And I figured out that the magic at the Neck must have gone wrong. All that time I was watching her and wishing for her to be fixed, Sylvie was staring at the sea and putting her own wishes into it. And the Neck made Sylvie's wish come true, instead of mine. Because she wanted to disappear, and she did.

After she was in hospital, we couldn't go to the Neck as much, and when we did there were only three big kids left: Dougie, Nathan, and Ella. Ella was by herself in the girls' room now. In the boys' room, Dougie and Nathan had the top bunks, and they'd talk in whispers, and keep their big-boy secrets up there, too high for me. And in the day, most of the time they were off with Ella, doing their big-kid things, and I was with Papabee, or by myself. I didn't mind. I'm lower down than all the others, so I see things that they don't see. In the corners of the house I found the dead bodies of slaters, curled up into little dry balls. Under the shallow water I saw the holes in the sand, and learned where the crabs were waiting. When the tide went out, the crabs came out like they were looking for the water. I watched how they moved – *fast, slow, fast* – across the sand. I've always liked crabs because they're full of crab – full up right to their shells, busy with being nothing but crab. Dougie was like that: he was always exactly Dougie. Even after Sylvie disappeared, Dougie was still the same. Out of everyone at the Neck, Dougie was always the loudest, the funniest, the fastest. Best at swimming, best at snapping tea-towels in the kitchen, and best at rowing the dinghy. Strongest of the big kids, even though Nathan was actually older. When Dougie was there he was the most there of anyone – he was the exact opposite of disappearing.

If I was a crab, I could understand how Dougie disappeared. I'd be Crab-Teddy, moving sideways and seeing the world sideways out of googly eyes. I'd wait in my hole and when the tide came in the water would be my sky. I'd keep my soft body inside the shell like a secret. Does a crab even know about the secret of its own body?

I lie in my bed and think about secrets and bodies and the different ways a person can disappear. Next to my feet, SausageDog's dreaming about chasing rabbits, his little legs dig dig digging. Maybe somewhere a rabbit is dreaming about being chased. Down the corridor, Dougie's room and Sylvie's room are empty.

I'm the littlest – I'm used to being left behind. But not like this. How can I catch up with Sylvie and Dougie now?

Sylvie

I used to be a girl, instead of a body or a patient or a ghost.

I used to live in my body without thinking about it. Imagine that. It didn't used to be a weapon, or a secret, or a bomb ready to detonate. It didn't used to be an anchor, heavy with yearning for the bottom of the sea. It didn't used to be any kind of metaphor at all. It was just my body: a thing I lived in. I was as careless of it as any child is. I scraped my knees on the gravel of the driveway of the Neck, racing against Dougie; I carried Teddy to the water when the sand was too hot for his little feet. I bit my nails (I still do this).

Listen: I don't know how to stop looking for answers in the knife drawer. I don't know how to let my body be. I don't know how to trust my body to be itself.

It never gets dark in the ward – not properly. All those Exit signs and backlit machine monitors, and the strip lights in the corridor. It's never quiet, either – drips and feeding pumps and the cleaner's trolley trundling along the lino floor.

In the not-really-dark, I dream I'm at the Neck again. I'm standing at the front door, the fly-wire sagging at the right-hand corner. Somewhere, a black cockatoo is screaming; further away, I can hear the sea.

Dougie and Teddy are already inside. They stand there, holding the door, waiting. SausageDog is there too, ears raised, waiting for me.

Are you coming in? Dougie and Teddy ask. *Aren't you coming in?*

Watermelon and feta salad for when you're in London but can't stop thinking of Tasmania

Wash the mint first, so it has time to drain before you add it (you don't want water diluting the sweetness of the watermelon juice).

Cut away the watermelon rind. If the black seeds in the melon bother you, flick them out with the tip of a knife. Chop the melon into satisfyingly solid cubes, about an inch wide, and the feta into slightly smaller chunks.

Tear the mint (patting it dry with a clean tea-towel if it's still damp) and add it to the melon and feta. It's important to rip, rather than to chop – it releases more flavour, but it also keeps your hands busy for longer.

With a fork, whisk together the juice of a couple of limes, a quarter cup of olive oil, a lot of ground black pepper, and a miserly pinch of salt. Pour over the salad, tossing through only very gently, preferably with your hands.

Gill

I write down the recipe on the back of one of the forms that the coroner woman gave us. Then I fold it in half, and in half again.

These new recipes are mad – I know that. I'm not writing them for a cookbook, or for the magazines or newspaper supplements that usually publish me. I'm writing them because I can't seem to help it.

I shove the tightly folded paper between the pages of my unread novel, where Dougie's letter is still hidden. I don't want Gabe to see the letter again until I've found some glue to re-seal it. And I can't do that yet, because it would mean no more sneaking off to re-read it on the toilet, or under the covers at night by the light of my phone, while Gabe sleeps. So for now I keep the letter hidden, along with my recipe notes.

I place the huge glass bowl of salad in the middle of the table. It's so bright – the green mint and the pink melon, their colours so unabashed. I've made too much – enough for a whole family.

Earlier, Gabe rang the coroner again, so I went to the shops for the melon. The last of the spring blossom was mounting in the gutters, and the late-afternoon sun was bright on the shopfronts and vans of Edgware Road. The horizon was blurred with smog, and I thought of Dougie's letter – *And I swear you can actually TASTE the pollution in the air in London.* I carried the melon home in my arms, heavy as a baby.

Gabe and I stare at the salad in its glass bowl. I think of Teddy at home, and Sylvie in her hospital bed, and Dougie, cold in the basement of a hospital. In Hobart it will be dark now, the thick darkness of the descending autumn. The dolerite of the mountain will be lichened with frost.

Here, in London, the windows in the flat are locked shut, the room too stuffy. Outside, a man shouts something, and a woman laughs. The afternoon light refuses to be ugly. Watermelon juice cool in my mouth, and my heart out of season.

Gabe

I phone the hospital to make an appointment to visit Dougie.

'Ordinarily, the appointments are for half an hour,' the man on the phone says. 'But you can make another appointment for the following day.'

'Just half an hour? Can't it be for longer? It's our son. We've come all the way from Australia.'

He pauses. 'It's to protect the deceased.'

Nobody says *dead*, I've noticed. It's always *deceased*.

'We have to maintain them at a suitable temperature,' he continues.

It hasn't occurred to me to think about temperature. Somewhere, probably beneath the hospital, there'll be a morgue, with refrigerated drawers. When I put the phone down I steady myself against the kitchen counter.

Gill doesn't want to go with me. She shakes her head convulsively. 'I can't do it.'

'Are you sure?' I ask. 'I mean – you might not have a chance later. Don't you think you might regret not seeing him?'

'I can't,' she says, still shaking her head as if shaking something off. 'If I see him like that, it'll be in my head forever. I won't be able to unsee it.' She grabs my wrist with both of her hands. 'Are you sure? You definitely want to see him?'

'I want to.' What I should have said: *I need to*.

Before I go, I ask her, 'Are you going to be OK?'

'OK?' she says, and the word hangs in the unfamiliar air. 'Am I going to be OK?'

In her voice, my words sound exactly as absurd as they deserve to.

It takes two trains and a bus to reach the hospital, which is outside London, and I'm so tired that a car nearly reverses into me as I cross the car park, and I find myself apologising to the driver. Inside, after I've found the right wing, a chaplain is called to the reception desk to meet me. She introduces herself but I immediately forget her name. I was expecting something like a priest, but she's determinedly non-denominational in her clothes and her words. I've never been at all religious, but I wouldn't have objected to a dog collar, or even an offer of prayers. I would take anything I could get.

'How does he look?' I ask, once she's ushered me along a corridor and into a small waiting room.

'Douglas looks fine,' she says. 'He looks as though he's sleeping. But you should prepare yourself for the fact that Douglas has some bruising on his face.' She's diligent about using his name. It feels a bit too conspicuous – like somebody who's gone to a networking seminar and been instructed that using people's names creates rapport.

'Some of the bruising might be from injuries Douglas sustained; some of it's likely due to the body's natural process after death, when the blood begins to pool.'

I swallow, and nod. 'Are his eyes open?'

'No, they're not.'

That's that, then: I won't see Dougie's eyes again. I keep stumbling against these new losses, each of them tiny and vast.

'The other thing that you need to know,' the chaplain says, 'is that, if you choose to touch Douglas, he will feel very cold. You need to be prepared for that, because it's not a natural feeling, and it can come as a shock.'

I'm not sure what could constitute a shock, after all that's happened. I feel incapable of being shocked.

'But I can still do it?' I ask. 'I can touch him?'

'Of course.'

'OK,' I say. That's something, at least.

'Douglas is currently covered by a sheet. Do you have any particular clothes that you'd like him to wear? For when the body is released, after the post-mortem?'

'Not yet. I have to go to the school – where he was living – and get some of his clothes.'

'That's not a problem. You can bring them in any time, and we can dress him for you. Or you can dress him yourself, if you like, but family tends to find the process difficult. His body won't move in the way that you expect.'

'No, that's OK. You do it, please.' It's been years since Dougie let us see him naked – I don't want to intrude on him now.

On the far side of the waiting room is a small window, with curtains drawn across it, and a door.

'Is he—' I gesture towards the window.

She nods. 'If you don't feel ready to go in, you can view Douglas through the window first. We can pull back the curtain.'

'No. I'd rather just go in.' I don't want those pleated beige curtains being pulled back. I don't want to view my dead son like something in a Punch and Judy show.

She stands. 'Are you ready?'

When Dougie was a baby, I used to be paranoid that his breathing had stopped. He was our firstborn, and I worried all the time. I'd go into his room three or four times at night, to check on him. If he was lying still, I'd creep closer, risking the creaking floorboards, until I could hear his breathing.

I've never forgotten the relief, each time I could finally make out the rise and fall of his chest.

Looking at Dougie's body, lying on the trolley in the centre of the small room, I understand how wrong I was. There's no mistaking a dead body for a sleeping one. This is a totally different kind of inertness. Absolute stillness. His body, neatly arranged, has become a place outside of time.

It takes me three steps to reach him. I reach for his hand. I'm glad that the chaplain warned me about how he would feel. His hand isn't only cold, but also hard. Nothing yields in my grip. His nails are broken, and there are scratches on his hands, but the wounds look bloodless and oddly clean.

There's a bruise across one side of his face, a deep red-purple blotchiness – but I can't read his body for clues of what happened. Nothing of what I see makes any sense. His body is written in a different language now.

I bend down to kiss him on the forehead, and leave my lips pressed against his cool skin for a long time. He doesn't smell like himself. He smells of nothing.

The chaplain has followed me and is hovering by the door.

'He doesn't look bad – not as bad as I expected,' I say.

'Most of the head wounds are at the back,' she says. I'm thankful for the straightforward words, and the no-nonsense tone of her voice.

He looks so clean – soaked and scrubbed. He's very pale, except for where the bruising has left his face reddened in precisely delineated patches. Even his hair looks lighter, as though it's been bleached. It's fluffy – none of the gel that he used to add. Somehow that's the hardest thing – not the wounds, but this baby-chick fluffiness of his hair. He always hated it, that fluffiness. From the age of about twelve he put stuff in it to make it spikier. We used to tease him about it – about how long it took him, standing in front of the bathroom mirror rearranging the strands. And if I hugged him, or if Teddy was roughhousing with him, Dougie would shield his hair with his hand, or yell, 'Not the hair!'

'He always put stuff in it,' I say, touching Dougie's hair now. 'Some kind of gel. I don't suppose I could fix his hair for him?'

It feels like a very frivolous request – such a trivial thing, compared to the fact of Dougie's cold body. I'm learning to do these small things, because they're all that I can do.

'That's no problem at all,' she says. 'We have a selection of hair products.' She goes away for a few minutes and returns with a lidless shoebox containing a collection of jars and sprays. She chooses a blue jar, passes it to me. 'This kind of thing?'

The words on the jar are gibberish to me: *Volumising, Texturising, Wet-look.*

'Is this the kind of thing that young men use?' I ask, blinking blindly.

She nods.

'Do you think you could do it?' I say. 'Please? I've never done it for him. I don't know how.'

She scoops a small amount of the gel into her hand, rubbing it between her palms to soften it. Then she bends forward and runs her fingers through his hair, gently teasing it upwards.

I take deep breaths. The gel smells a bit like the stuff he used to use. The chaplain works patiently at it, the two of us leaning together over this silent baptism.

Back in the flat, Gill hasn't moved from the armchair by the window. The dark has come, but she hasn't turned on the lights.

'He looked—' I search for words. None of the ones that people usually use to refer to dead people seem to fit. He hadn't looked calm, or peaceful. Neither of those emotions, nor any others, had anything to do with him any more. What could I say to her about the scratches on his hands, or the bruises? The awful stillness of his face.

I want to say, *Do you remember, before the kids were born, when we swam in Lake Rowallan?* The hydroelectric company made the lake by flooding the valley. The drowned trees remain, ghost trunks that pierce the water's surface, as though the lake is always dreaming of trees.

I want to tell her: *Dougie's face now is no more a face than those white spars of wood are trees.*

Instead I say, 'He looked OK. Not badly roughed up, honestly.'

'I can't hear about it,' she says, still looking out the window. Her hands are on her stomach, and I remember the day she went into labour with Dougie; how she'd pressed her hands to her stomach as the contractions first started, saying, *Shit, I think it's really happening. It's really happening.* Her laugh, giddy with pain and excitement, her hands pressed just where they're pressed now.

When we Skype Teddy, he's eating breakfast, Sue moving in and out of the shot behind him, dropping things in the kitchen.

'Have you been to the Tower of London?' he asks. 'Did you see the Beefeaters, and the ravens?'

'It's not that sort of trip,' Gill says.

'What about Dougie? Did you see him?'

As if Dougie's body is one of the sights: *Be sure not to miss the National Gallery, your son's dead body, or the Tower of London.*

'I saw him,' I say. 'Mum didn't feel up to it.'

He doesn't ask anything else for now, and I'm relieved.

'Are you OK, sweetie?' Gill asks him.

Teddy shrugs. 'I don't know. Sue and I are crying quite a lot. Sometimes we take turns. Sometimes we do it together.'

'That sounds fair enough,' I say. 'We're crying a lot here, too. How's your sister?'

Another shrug. 'Same as usual. We haven't been doing any crying when we go to see her. We haven't said anything about Dougie.'

'Good boy,' says Gill.

When Sylvie began to disappear, the vet was one of the first clues. Three and a half years ago, SausageDog suddenly started getting fat, despite being fed the same amount as always.

'Jesus Christ,' Sue said when she came around. 'From a bird's eye view, that animal is basically circular.'

Then, one Saturday, I'd made a stew for lunch, and thrown in a few handfuls of alphabet pasta. It's the kind of basic meal that I usually make – when you're married to a chef, you get lazy. But Teddy had always loved the pasta letters, and Papabee enjoyed them too, playing a kind of scrabble with Teddy on a side-plate. Dougie was sixteen then, so of course he spelled out rude words on his plate – *BALLS SHIT BUM* – nudging Sylvie to show her, and Gill and I pretended not to see because it was nice to have Sylvie giggling, Sausage sitting on her lap. Nice to see Sylvie and Dougie laughing together. They used to be like that all the time: the big kids – those two conspirators. But lately those moments seemed to be getting rarer; Sylvie had been so teenagery – thirteen, and full of eye-rolls. My dad, Papa J, had come down from Sydney for the summer just gone – a nice change, as he'd never bothered to spend much time with his grandkids until after his second wife died. But Sylvie had been sulky for most of his visit, and I'd felt embarrassed by her behaviour, because for once my dad was actually making an effort.

'Maybe we had it coming,' I'd said to Gill, when Sylvie had stormed off to her room after I tried to tell her she shouldn't be so monosyllabic with Papa J. 'Dougie's given us such an easy ride.'

It was true – Dougie had cruised through his teenage years relatively unscathed, except for acne. He was too busy with his friends and his sports to tie himself into knots of teenage angst.

'I know,' Gill said. 'It's only fair that one of them should have a chance to be a shit. God knows, I was a nightmare at that age.'

So it was good, that day, a few weeks after my dad had left, to see Sylvie laughing with Dougie, and cuddling the dog. Good to see her forgetting, briefly, that she thought her family was deeply uncool and boring.

Half an hour later SausageDog ate some grass and threw up on the kitchen floor. There, among the barely chewed grass, was a perfect array of alphabet stew, a jumble of letters that spelled out nothing, and said everything.

I can't stop feeling that I'm in the wrong place, or the wrong time. That Dougie's death is some kind of mistake. Because it's Sylvie who wants to die, not him.

When Sylvie first stopped eating, I didn't know that it could kill her. Like most people, I thought eating disorders were a kind of rite of passage, a worrying phase that teenage girls tended to pass through, these days. Skipping a few meals, losing weight, wanting to be like models in magazines. So when we found that she'd been slipping all her food to the dog, I wasn't too panicked. Even her weird period of frenzied baking didn't worry me unduly. But after the first few doctors' appointments, and then the first hospital admission, it became all too clear that Sylvie didn't want to lose a few kilos. She wanted to disappear. The doctors talked to us about osteoporosis; infertility; liver enzymes; muscle wastage; heart damage.

'People die from this,' I said to her. 'Is that your end goal? You don't eat, you die. That's not me being dramatic, that's a basic fact.'

She said nothing.

When her friend Katie P killed herself, I hoped it might wake Sylvie up to the reality of what she was doing. But she and the other girls in the ward were more single-minded than ever. I should have guessed it. Anorexics aren't friends to one another, or even allies. They're competitors. That's why they keep them in isolation in Paediatrics 3 – they can't mingle at all. But even then, in the corridors and through the curtains and glass doors, they're always watching each other. On Tuesdays and Fridays, weighing days, the ward is thick with suspicion, as they eye each other off while they shuffle through the ward to the weighing room, wheeling their drip-stands.

For those girls, every new low weight is a new precedent, a new goal. And Katie P, cremated and reduced to ash, became the ultimate goal weight. She was the gold standard anorexic: the one who achieved perfection.

In those first months, I used to tell Sylvie all the time, *You could really die from this. It could kill you.* I never say it any more. After the first suicide attempt, and the second and third, I learned that she didn't hear it as a threat, but as an offer.

'We can't leave Sylvie and Teddy any longer,' I say when we've hung up. 'Or Papabee.'

'I know.'

'One of us needs to go back. Tomorrow, probably.'

'I know.'

I call the airline.

What we really meant, though we didn't need to say it to one another: Gill's going back. There are things to be done here that Gill can't do: dealing with Dougie's body; organising the cremation; monitoring the inquest. And things to be done at home that I can't do: maintaining a semblance of ordinariness for Teddy, Sylvie, and Papabee.

So she'll go, and I'll stay. My job, as a research physicist, can be done remotely, at least for now – my boss has been accommodating, and I can work on my datasets from England.

The next morning we go together on the tube to the airport. The Piccadilly Line to Heathrow takes more than an hour, but I don't mind. We sit there holding hands, which we don't do often these days, and she leans into my shoulder.

At the entrance to Security, I say, 'Give Teddy a huge hug from me.' No point telling her to hug Sylvie – Sylvie hasn't let us hug her properly for years.

Gill kisses me, the kind of slow kiss on the forehead that she gives to Teddy when he's had a nightmare. One of us is crying, and I don't know which one.

'When are we going to tell Sylvie?' I ask.

'We'll see how she's doing once I'm back.' She hitches her bag higher on her shoulder. 'We'll see what the doctors say.'

'We can't put it off forever.'

'We'll talk about it once I'm home,' she says.

Gill

I don't have the magic *COMP* code on my boarding pass this time. Gabe comes out to Heathrow with me, and before I check in he asks me, 'Do you want me to speak to them at the desk? I want to make sure that they'll take care of you.'

But I don't want to be taken care of, least of all by these glossy flight attendants, their big grins painted on with red lipstick, their hair weirdly unmoving, lacquered into shape. I don't want to be subjected to the scrutiny of their pity.

Onboard, I have a window seat, and I lean against the side wall and pretend that I'm flying for any other reason. A holiday. A book tour. A research trip. Anything but this.

'Heading home?' the man next to me asks.

'Yes,' I say, and I smile, and it feels almost real. I can't wait to see Teddy. I'm even looking forward to seeing Sylvie. I want to imagine that everything can go back to normal, even if normal means sitting by Sylvie's hospital bed so that she can ignore me.

The man smiles back and puts on his headphones, in the way that signals that the conversation is over. When Gabe and I flew out together, the whole row to ourselves, we'd had nowhere to hide from our grief. This time, next to a stranger, I can pretend. I sit back and put my own headphones on, and try to watch a documentary about Antarctica. I don't read Dougie's letter again, but I take out the book that contains it and I hold it to my stomach like I'm keeping pressure on a wound. When I cry, I keep my eyes closed and wipe my face surreptitiously with my cuff. For some reason it seems terribly, terribly important that this stranger next to me not think that anything is wrong. I don't want to have to explain to him, or to see the look on his face that shows he's reclassifying me as *that* woman – the one with the tragic story; the one he'll tell his wife about when he lands; the one who'll make him hug his kids tighter and think, *Thank God it's her and not me.*

It's mid-morning on Monday when I land in Hobart. I ought to be exhausted, but I'm tingling with brittle energy. I can't stop moving my hands, fidgeting my feet. Teddy's at school, and Papabee will be at his flat. Sylvie will be sitting cross-legged in her hospital bed, reading. I called her before I left London to tell her I'd be back today; I wonder if she's remembered.

Sue picks me up from the airport. My suitcase topples over when she runs to me, and I let it lie there in the gutter while we hug. We drive across the bridge, the late morning sun throwing its light against the mountain. The mountain that watches over Hobart has a real name – Mount Wellington, or (earlier) kunanyi – but everyone in Hobart calls it *the mountain*. People from the mainland find that quaint – the same way they laugh at the fact that Tasmanians call it *the mainland*. It doesn't matter – *the mountain* remains *the mountain*, the city's hulking witness, and we all live in its shadow. On the side of the mountain facing down towards Hobart are the striated cliffs, the Organ Pipes, vertical columns of dolerite.

When Dougie started high school and was learning about metaphor, I used the Organ Pipes as an example: 'That's a metaphor,' I told him. 'They're not really the pipes of an organ, like you'd see in a church – they just look like them.'

'Yeah,' he said, 'but after a while, doesn't the metaphor become the thing? Like, if somebody says *organ pipes* to me, I don't think of an actual church organ. I think of the mountain.'

What did it do to my children, growing up on this island at the bottom of the world, in this city trapped between mountain and water, in a place where metaphors become solid?

Sue helps me lug my suitcase up the steps to the house, where the dog greets me as if I'd been gone years, and not a week. There's a pile of mail on the kitchen table – not the usual collection of bills and circulars, but handwritten letters and cards. Word spreads quickly in a place like Hobart. I have a moment of gratitude that Sylvie's in the hospital, quarantined from the gossip of the real world. Then I feel sick – what kind of thing is that to be grateful for?

I open some of the letters. They're all variations on the same thing: *We're so sorry for your loss. Let us know if there's anything we can do.*

Sue never asks me what she can do to help – she just does it.

'There's cheese and milk in the fridge,' she says, 'and half of Hobart has dropped off casseroles – they're in the freezer. I didn't change the sheets on the bed, because it was only me, so bugger that. But I've ironed Teddy's school shirts, and I've done a few loads of washing. There's one load that hasn't finished yet – you'll have to hang it out when it's done.'

'OK.' I'm glad to have something normal to do. Something to fill the hours.

'I won't be turning my phone off at night,' she goes on. 'Call me any time, OK?'

'Thank you,' I say. 'Jesus. What would I do without you?'

'Don't be too thankful,' she says. 'I ate all the good chocolates, and I dropped your iron and now it's making a weird rattling noise. But that's the least of your problems right now.'

We both laugh, then hear ourselves and stop.

'I've got to get to a meeting,' she says. 'Then Ella's violin thing, after school. You sure you'll be OK here by yourself?'

I nod. 'I'll pop up to check on Dad before I go into the hospital. And Teddy'll be home in a few hours.' I'm longing to drive to the school and pick him up early, and squeeze his little body to mine, but he doesn't need more disruption in his life right now, or his mother weeping hysterically in front of everyone in the school car park.

When Sue goes, I can't get used to the quiet. In the London flat the traffic sounds never stopped, and there was always a siren in the distance. Here there are only the sounds of birds, and the washing machine chugging. Three hours until Teddy gets home from school. I should go into the hospital soon, but I'm lurking in the kitchen, looking for excuses to delay. I ring my dad, but he's out – he usually goes for a walk in the afternoons. I try his mobile, but he doesn't answer. He hardly ever does. His phone is an ancient Nokia that used to belong to Gabe. The kids call it 'The Brick', but it works, and it's simple enough that we were able to teach Papabee how to use it, though he still avoids it whenever he can. It only has three numbers saved in it: mine, Gabe's, and Teddy's.

I check my voicemail: five messages from friends, all with the same refrain – *I'm so sorry. Let me know if you need anything*. There's also a six-minute voicemail from Papabee, who does this every few weeks – calls one of us by accident from his mobile and leaves a long voicemail that's just silence, or the sound of him humming as he moves around his flat. Usually I delete these straight away, but today I listen all the way through. It's oddly comforting.

Leaning on the counter, I open more of the letters. One of them's from my sister Amy, in Perth, and she's enclosed a self-help book that she found useful when our mum died – a manual about grieving, with a soft-focus picture of lilies on the cover. Amy's always gone in for that sort of thing. Over the last few years she's given me several self-help books about anorexia. Gabe and I bought some books of advice ourselves, back when Sylvie first got sick. Reassuringly fat books full of sensible advice, by sensible people with impressive medical qualifications. I'd devoured them, even underlined some sections, and read them out loud to Gabe. None of it made any difference to Sylvie – and, anyway, there are no books about doing both at once: about losing my son at the same time as trying to hang on to my daughter.

I tuck the book underneath the other cards. I shower, hang out the washing and empty the dishwasher. Then I stand in the kitchen with a tea-towel hanging limply from my hand, and stare at the door frame where we've always marked the children's heights. Inch by inch, those little horizontal marks creep up the painted timber and through the years. Then, three years ago, Sylvie stopped growing and went into hospital: *Sylvie Jan 2013* is the last record of her.

Dougie kept growing. Now I stand facing the door frame, pressing my forehead against the wood, against *Dougie Jan 2016*, measured just before he left for England. I remember it perfectly. Dougie standing there, his back to the wood. Teddy saying, 'He's cheating! He's on tippy-toes!' until Dougie lowered his heels. Gabe rested a cookbook on Dougie's head and marked the line with the pencil.

We still have that cookbook (*Women's Weekly Children's Birthday Cake Book*). We probably still have the same pencil, in the mug with the broken handle next to the phone. How can we still have those things, and not have Dougie?

I'd like to cook something, but Sue was right – the freezer's full of meals dropped off by friends and neighbours. I peel back some of the foil lids, and squint through the frosted Pyrex dishes. Baked puddings; macaroni cheese; lasagne. It's all comfort food – the kind of things that are supposed to make us feel better, along with the cards and letters. I'm touched by their effort, their kindness. But I don't want comfort. There isn't any comfort. Instead, I dice three chillies for a meal that we don't need. Standing there at the chopping board, I look down at my red-stained hands and wipe them, very deliberately, in my eyes. I rub them across my gums, and jam my fingers up my nostrils, to feel the soft tissue there burning. I start to sweat, and that's the only thing that feels true: my body shrieking *Alarm. Alarm.* I let the oil in the pan get hot, and I toss in the cumin seeds and listen to their spiteful hiss as they spin themselves from gold to brown. When the oil spits at me, I don't snatch my hand away. I step closer to the pan, and I have to stop myself from spitting back.

When the unnecessary curry is cooling on the counter, I unpack. From the pages of the still-unread novel, I fish out my scrawled recipe notes, and Dougie's letter. I read it one last time, although by now I know it by heart. *I never finished* Emma *for English in grade 10 even though I wrote an essay on it – thank you, Wikipedia! (DON'T EVER TELL MUM. SERIOUSLY. OR SUE.)* Then I find an old glue-stick in Teddy's desk drawer, and carefully re-seal the envelope flap, pressing down hard. I put it in my handbag to take to Sylvie at the hospital.

Teddy

Mum's there when Papabee brings me home from school. She cuddles me so tight that my face is squished against the buttons of her shirt, and I don't even care.

'When's Dad coming home?' I ask.

'Soon,' she says. 'There are some things he needs to sort out, that's all. Stuff to do with Dougie, and the inquest.'

'Inquest' has 'quest' in it, which sounds like something from *Lord of the Rings*. I picture Dad on a mission, to save Dougie somehow, a bit like my own mission with Sylvie. I like the idea that Dad and I are both busy with important quests.

'Christ,' Mum says. 'It's only been a week, but I swear you've grown.'

I've always wanted to get taller, and catch up with the big kids. I was always behind them – too young, too slow, too little. Then I turned ten last year, and I started growing fast, and getting thinner, like my body didn't know any way to go except up. 'He's having a growth spurt,' Mum said to Dad, and I didn't hear her properly and thought she said, 'growth squirt', and that stuck and became one of those things we say, like *napple*, from when Sylve was little and used to say she wanted 'a napple' instead of 'an apple'.

But now I don't want any more growth squirts. Because Sylvie doesn't eat napples now, or anything else, and she's stopped growing, and Dougie can't ever grow any more either, which means one day I'll overtake them, and that doesn't seem right, because what happens if the big kids aren't bigger any more? What happens if people's names don't even fit them?

In the car on the way to the hospital I practise all my answers in my head, in case Sylvie asks questions. Practising all my lies, so that I won't mess it all up. But when we get to her ward she just says 'Hi,' without even looking up properly, and it's Mum who does nearly all the talking. Sylvie asks, 'How's Dougie? How's his leg?' and Mum starts talking at Sylvie, on and on. She talks to Sylvie like she's hitting tennis balls over the net to someone who just won't hit them back, and the balls just bounce and drop and lie there around Sylvie's feet. Mum does so much talking that I think she'll give it away for sure, but Sylve just ignores her, the same as usual, and I remember that Sylvie's too busy looking at herself to look at anybody else. I never understand how her body can take up so much space – in her head, and all of ours too – when it's so little.

'So he's OK?' Sylvie asks. 'It's going to be OK, after the operation?'

The rhyme's going through my head again, in time with the swoosh swoosh of the feeding pump: *Sister in the Boneyard, brother in the water.* I'm almost worried that I'll say it out loud. But Mum's off again, talking talking talking.

'They're still not sure if he'll need another operation. But for now, he's relying pretty heavily on Dad. Dougie can't even manage in the shower by himself – hard to say which one of them's finding that more embarrassing.'

Mum's really good at this – all the lying. She lies like it's her superpower.

What's the difference between a secret and a lie? Is a lie just a secret that's gone wrong? Mum's talking about operations, hospitals, plans, and the lie's getting bigger and bigger.

Papabee sits quietly doing his little smile and sometimes his humming. Sometimes he shakes his head, like he's seeing Sylvie for the first time, and says, 'My dear, it strikes me that you don't look well. Do you feel unwell?'

'I'm fine, Papabee,' she says.

Mum used to jump in and say, 'She's very sick, Dad. We've talked about this.' But she doesn't any more – she just lets it go.

Later, when we're walking back to the car, Papabee says, 'Does it occur to you that Sylvie's looking rather too thin?'

'We know, Papabee,' says Mum, the vein in her jaw poking out. It does that more and more ever since she got back from London.

'I expect it's the hospital food,' Papabee says. 'Ghastly stuff.'

That night, when Papabee's gone home, I get my notebook and start a list:

Napple.
Growth Squirt.
Don't be shellfish. (That's what I used to say when I was too little to talk properly, and the big kids wouldn't share their toys with me.)
Papabeen-and-Gone (That's what Dad calls it when Papabee wanders into a room and wanders out again, chatting to himself.)

On top of the page I write *TOP SECRET*, and I tuck it in my drawer where my Papa J money's still hidden. I want to make sure I have a list of all our family's private words. Dougie's dead. Sylvie's trying really hard to die, and she hardly talks anyway. Dad's on the other side of the world. Papabee doesn't always understand, and Mum's too busy talking at Sylvie to listen to me.

What happens to a family's whole private language, if nobody's left who speaks it? Where do the words go, then, and what do they mean? What if I'm the only one left, shouting *Napple Napple Growth squirt,* and nobody understands?

I know it isn't really Sylvie's fault, but when I think of Dougie, who isn't even allowed to have his own death because of her, I want to yell at her, *Don't be shellfish*.

'I need you to help me look through some photos,' I say to Papabee. Usually we go to his flat after school, but today I ask if we can come straight to the house. Mum's out – hospital, probably – and I take him into the study, and show him the boxes and albums that we need to go through. He doesn't ask why, or ask what we're looking for. He just says, 'Photographs! How delightful,' and helps me lift down the boxes that I can't reach.

A couple of years ago, Mum and Dad finally got a digital camera ('Wow,' Dougie said. 'Finally joining the twentieth century, now that we're well into the twenty-first'). But I don't bother getting the laptop out and going through those photos. The one I'm looking for is way older.

There are proper photo albums from when Dougie and Sylvie were little. There's Dougie as a fat baby, looking surprised. Sylvie as a baby on Dougie's lap, with Dad helping Dougie to hold her. Mum breastfeeding Sylvie (I quickly turn to the next page, because it's embarrassing to see Mum's boob, and double-embarrassing because Papabee's right there next to me).

A silverfish runs out from between the pages of the album and goes under the bookshelf. I can see the tiny holes in the page, where silverfish have chewed through. I'd like to be Silverfish-Teddy, down the cracks, in all the smallest places. I wouldn't be seen (I'm good at that). Nothing could be hidden from me. I'd wriggle into gaps between pages, little paper places, and I'd eat up the paper and become the stories.

I keep looking. We get older as the photos get newer. There's Dougie and Sylvie about my age, on the beach at the Neck with Nathan and Ella. Sylvie's buried in the sand, except for her neck, and Ella's making her a mermaid tail covered in shells. There's Dad when he still had lots of hair, standing next to the dinghy. Sylvie with her mouth open, and Papa J laughing at whatever she's saying.

It's almost dinnertime when I find the photo I'm looking for. It's not of a special occasion – just a picture of Sylve at the table in the back yard. She's doing that big smile, the one that shows her gums as much as her teeth. She's smiling like she actually means it, her chin pushing up and forwards. She looks like she used to look, before she went into the Boneyard. It's the last photo I can find of her smiling. There are a few photos of her where she looks older, but in all of them she's thinner and thinner, and angrier and angrier. And then she disappears from the photos altogether.

I show Papabee the photo of Sylvie smiling. He holds it a long way away from his face. 'And which of my lovely children – or grandchildren – is this?'

I don't say anything, because it feels like saying *Sylvie* wouldn't be true, and I don't want to do any more lying than I already have to.

118

Sylvie

I stare at the window. Not through it, because it's light in the ward and dark outside, and even if I wheel my drip-stand over to the window and press my face to the glass to peer out, there's nothing to see but the black windows of the office building opposite, and the pigeons squabbling over a bin, four floors down. So I stare at the reflections on the glass itself. The ward's ceiling tiles, mirrored so that they go on forever. The curtains around my bed, which make it look as though I'm on a stage.

'*Off next week for an excursion,*' Dougie's latest letter said. I try not to think of the crunch of his leg breaking. Or the water getting higher, eating up the air. I try not to think of what could have happened if he hadn't got out in time. About those moments when things change – when the water is at the mouth of the cave, and the world holds its breath and makes a choice: *this way*, or *that way*.

In last night's dream we were all back at the Neck. It was the summer that Papa J was down from Sydney. The year that an echidna snuffled its way out of the marram grass and sat near us on the beach for an hour. I found an empty abalone shell lying on the rocks, like a bowl full of sky. It was the year that Nathan hauled up an octopus on his fishing line, and Ella was so disgusted she jumped out of the dinghy and swam back to shore. The year Teddy started learning French and put Post-it notes on everything in the house, little yellow labels fluttering to the floor in the heat: *La porte. Le four à micro-ondes. L'armoire.*

In my dream we're all at the beach, and Papa J says he wants to walk to the promontory. *Are you coming?* he asks me. Then time stops: the waves are held just like that, propped up by an offshore wind that no longer blows. Ella's frozen where she kneels in the sand, helping Papabee and Teddy make a moat for their sandcastle. The moat never fills or empties. That gull in the sky stays suspended at the exact point where two clouds touch. Dougie, Dad and Nathan are held in place in the middle of their game of cricket, Dougie's arm reaching to the sky as he bowls. His raised foot never lands; the ball is never released.

Gabe

With Gill gone, I get a short-term rental on a smaller furnished flat. It's dark, and there's a patch of mould creeping from the corner of the bathroom, but it's cheaper than the first flat, and it's on the top floor, three storeys above the High Street in Barnet. I find myself doing that, these days: seeking higher ground.

The estate agent, a young man in a shiny grey suit, asks me why I don't have a UK credit history. I tell him I'm from Australia, and explain why I'm in London. He stops, and stammers something about having been to Australia once, *beautiful country, beautiful. Beautiful beaches*, and then he stops himself again, as if even the mention of water might set me off, unmoor my grief and let it flood his fancy office with its reproduction Eames chairs and its row of gleaming Macs. I think he rents me the flat just to get rid of me and the contamination of my grief.

On my first evening in the new flat, I eat nothing but a packet of salt-and-vinegar chips for dinner. I picture how much Gill would hate this, and how much Teddy would adore it, and I miss them with a suddenness that almost knocks the breath from me. I miss Sylvie, too, though that's nothing new – I've been missing her for years. I should be with them, now – I wish it for my own sake, selfishly, as much as for theirs. But Dougie's alone in the morgue, and the date for the post-mortem still isn't even confirmed. I can't leave him here alone.

All through the night the shower drips noisily, and I get up four times to check it. I spread the bathmat inside the shower to muffle the sound, but the hushed, rhythmic dripping still sends my heart skittering. The next day I take the bus into town at dawn and walk for hours. Crossing the Millennium Bridge, I find myself sweating, my breath loud in my head and my eyes clenched against the sight of the black river on each side.

I used to love swimming. All those days on the beach at the Neck; all those hours of playing with the kids in the sea, throwing them in the air and letting the water catch them. I can't imagine it now. I cannot forgive the water.

The second day after Gill left, I ring Northdale House, the boarding school where Dougie was living and working. They've obviously been expecting me to call, because I'm only halfway through explaining who I am when the secretary says, 'Oh, oh, Mr Jordan, of course – let me put you straight through to Mr Overton.'

A deep voice comes on the line.

'Mr Jordan – this is Jacob Overton. I want you to know that the thoughts of the whole school have been with you.' He keeps going, unhesitating – it's like he has access to a script. 'As parents ourselves, my wife and I have had you in our thoughts. And I can assure you that, in his short time here, Douglas made an immeasurable contribution to the school community.'

I wonder how I can get a copy of his script – how I can find out what I ought to be saying in this situation. Then I think of Sue's reaction, at home, when the police called her and she'd arrived at our house, her car parked nearly sideways across the street. 'Fuck,' she'd said. 'How can it be real? Fucking fuck.' And I prefer Sue's outburst to Overton's polite spiel, which is still going.

'And at an appropriate time, when you and your wife feel ready, we'd like to discuss how we might create some sort of lasting memorial on the school campus. We had several ideas – we thought perhaps a memorial bench on the South Lawn? Or there's a new scull being purchased for the boys' eight, and we thought it could be named after Douglas. Only with your permission, of course.'

'A skull?' I ask.

'A rowing boat. It's traditional for them to be named after esteemed members of the school community. And Douglas was involved in coaching the first eight this season—'

'Can I come to the school?' I interrupt him. I can't listen any more to this talk of boats, or to that accent, posher than Papabee's. Posher than the Queen. 'I'd like to see Dougie's things.'

'Of course,' Overton says. 'You'll be welcome here whenever it suits you to come.'

So the next day a taxi takes me through the high black gates, down the long driveway with trees on each side, playing fields to the left. Probably an *avenue*, not a driveway, I correct myself. Driveways are for normal houses – not this huge Victorian pile in its landscaped grounds. We're still in North London, but it feels like the countryside. The taxi traces the gravel loop to deposit me at the front door. Overton and his wife are already coming out to greet me.

'Mr Jordan,' he says. 'Jacob Overton – please, call me Jacob. And this is my wife, Miranda. I only wish we were meeting in different circumstances.'

I shake his hand, then hers. She wraps her other hand over mine.

'Douglas was such a lovely young man,' she says. 'I can't tell you how sad we are. Such a tremendous loss.'

'A tragedy,' Jacob says. 'We're all heartbroken.'

I notice that they say everything except 'sorry.' Sue's husband Dan's a lawyer, and he's warned me about that.

'They'll have lawyered-up,' he said, when he rang last night. 'They've probably been advised not to admit

123

liability. They'll be shitting themselves that you might sue. It already looks bad for them, publicity-wise – Dougie dead, students injured. They'll be dealing with lots of mummies and daddies scrambling to withdraw little Isabella and Sebastian.'

But as Miranda guides me through to Jacob's office, she has real tears in her eyes. I wave away her offer of tea or coffee.

'How are the others?' I ask Jacob. 'The other children, from the cave? And the teacher. Are they doing OK now?'

'They're recovering very well,' he says. 'Superficial injuries only, thank God.' A tiny shake of the head from Miranda to him, perhaps to remind him that I might not be feeling like thanking anyone, least of all God. 'Grazes,' Jacob continues hurriedly. 'A sprained wrist, two cases of hypothermia. And they're all very distressed, naturally. The injured students were all discharged from hospital within a few hours. But we're providing counselling, not just for the children on the excursion, but for any student who feels affected.'

He's slipped back into glossy-school-prospectus mode.

'I'm glad,' I say. 'Glad they're all doing OK, I mean.'

There's more small talk – more platitudes about Dougie, whom they keep calling Douglas.

'We saw relatively little of Douglas in the day-to-day running of the school,' Jacob says. 'Though we were left with no doubt of his popularity with staff and students alike. That's why we thought that you might like to meet some of his colleagues – particularly those who live on campus. They were closest to him, and I know many of them would like to give you their condolences in person, if you feel up to it. Your wife, too, if she cares to visit.'

'She's had to go back to Australia,' I say. 'Our other children—' I trail off.

'Of course.'

He leads me through to the staffroom where ten or fifteen teachers are waiting, on chairs and couches dragged into a rough circle. Several have work with them, papers hastily slipped under their chairs when we enter.

Jacob introduces me, and suggests that the assembled staff might like to tell me some of their memories of Dougie. Some of the teachers are emotional – several cry while they tell me their stories. One young PE teacher had worked with Dougie to coach the rowing team. 'He was rubbish at the early mornings,' he says. 'The alarm clock didn't cut it. I used to chuck gravel at his window from the driveway.' Jacob looks nervous at the mention of Dougie's flaws, but I encourage the teacher with a smile. 'Then he'd rush down with his tracksuit on top of his pyjamas,' he says.

One by one they speak. It's like a group therapy session, but I'm not sure who it's for. Jacob's still here, standing by the door, and nodding sympathetically as each teacher talks. He's watching me – they all are. I feel that I'm expected to offer them something in exchange for these tidbits of memories and anecdotes. Gratitude, or absolution.

The anecdotes keep mentioning Rosa. 'He and Rosa would come to the pub with us, sometimes, after Prep,' one teacher says, glancing at the pale young woman perched on the arm of the couch on the far side of the circle from me. Another woman mentions something about 'after he and Rosa came back from Prague at Easter'. But Rosa herself doesn't speak. Her left arm is in a sling, and there's a graze on her cheek. She keeps swinging one leg. A bell rings in the corridor outside, followed by a flurry of footsteps and children's voices, which subsides after a few minutes.

When the reminiscences have dried up, Jacob dismisses the staff, and they shake my hand one by one as they leave. It feels like the receiving line at a wedding, or a funeral.

When it's Rosa's turn, I hang on to her hand.

'I'd love to speak to you properly,' I say. 'I know we haven't met, but my wife and I heard a lot about you. We knew you were his girlfriend.'

Jacob interjects, lowering his voice and glancing at the other teachers. 'The school has certain policies, on relationships between staff. It's a delicate situation.'

'Not any more,' says Rosa, and I catch myself giving a snort of laughter, then slap my hand over my mouth.

'Rosa's been through a very difficult time, obviously,' Jacob continues. 'But the senior management team wasn't aware of any relationship, if that's what it was, before the accident.'

'That's what it was,' says Rosa. Her Irish accent is conspicuous among all these plummy teachers.

'Well, as I said,' Jacob goes on, 'Rosa has been through a very hard time, and the school is supporting her as well as we can.'

Rosa says nothing.

'I'd really like to see Dougie's room,' I tell her.

'Certainly,' Jacob says, as though I'd been addressing him.

'I'll show you,' Rosa says. 'If you like.'

Jacob looks from her, to me, and then to his wife, who's hanging back in the doorway.

'Rosa,' Miranda says. 'You don't think you ought to be resting?'

'I've been resting all week,' says Rosa.

'I'd be grateful if you'd show me his room,' I say to her. 'I'd like to talk to you, if that's OK. I know you were close to Dougie.' *Close* – a neutral term, for Jacob's benefit. 'And I need to pick up some of his clothes, for him to be dressed in.'

A pause. Jacob looks from me to Rosa, and back to me.

'OK then,' he nods. 'Thank you, Rosa. I'd appreciate you showing Mr Jordan to Douglas's room, and helping him find anything he needs.' He turns back to me. 'Spend as long there as you'd like. If you need anything else, I'll be in my office.'

Rosa and I don't talk on the way. I follow her higher and higher through the corridors of the huge Victorian mansion. It's rundown in the way that only posh places can get away with – flaking paint on old radiators, worn carpet, scuffed walls. We pass doors open to dormitories, the beds all neatly made. A clash of different doona covers: football teams; superheroes; cartoon animals.

On the upper floors the corridors are narrower and the ceilings lower. The doors here are closed, with staff name-plates. Then there's another flight of stairs, so narrow that Rosa has to turn sideways to avoid bumping her injured arm.

'The gap students always get the worst room,' she says.

At the top of the stairs is a single door. She opens it for me and steps out of the way.

It smells of him. Not even in a nice way, but that familiar smell of dirty sneakers and deodorant. Maybe every teen boy's bedroom smells the same way – but his is the only one I know, and I have to stop myself from kneeling right here and burying my face in the carpet, taking great undignified gulps.

'We haven't changed anything,' Rosa says. 'The cleaners come round on Wednesdays to vacuum, but that's it.'

For a minute neither of us speaks. I don't know what to say to Rosa. When I said we'd heard a lot about her, I was lying. Dougie mentioned her a few times, but in a deliberately casual way. *There's a girl here, from Ireland. Rosa. She's an assistant teacher, basically my age. She'll be travelling over summer too, so we might meet up.* Gill had raised her eyebrows when I'd read her that bit of the email, holding the iPad on my lap in bed, and she'd nudged me whenever Rosa's name had come up during Skype calls. But he'd been reticent – of course he had.

He was a nineteen-year-old boy.

Rosa starts to cry. 'I'm sorry,' she says, sniffing.

What's she sorry for? That she's crying? That he's dead? Or is it for something that she's done?

'I'm sorry too,' I say. There's a t-shirt draped over the back of the chair. I want to pick it up and smell it, but not with her standing there.

'How's the arm?' I ask.

She wrinkles her nose. 'It's not serious – just annoying. It only hurts when I bump it. But when I do that it hurts like mad.' She stops suddenly. 'Sorry – it's nothing, really. I mean, compared to—'

'It's OK.'

'You said you needed to choose some clothes?'

I nod, grateful to her for changing the subject. 'Something for him to wear, for the cremation.'

She swallows. 'Cremation? I wasn't sure what you were going to do.'

'We thought that was the best option.' It sounds ridiculous. *Best option*, like choosing a new dishwasher from a website. Not choosing what to do with your son's body.

She turns to the wardrobe. 'So what kind of thing do you want him to wear? Something smart, or just normal?'

'I don't think he'd want to dress up. Not a tie, or anything like that. That would seem weird, don't you think?'

She looks surprised to be asked. 'Maybe. He has a tie – we have to wear formal clothes for some stuff here. Prizegiving, and chapel. But I think you're right. It's not really him, you know?'

'I know.'

She opens the cupboard. His clothes on the shelves aren't folded so much as tossed. That detail gets me right in my chest, and I have to put a hand against the wall and concentrate on my breathing.

'He liked this one,' she says, holding up a grey-blue t-shirt. I notice that she uses the past tense. 'He wore this a lot.'

'I remember that one.'

I pick some boxer shorts, too – the grey Bonds ones he always wore – and some black socks.

'And he had some grey jeans that he liked,' she says. 'I think they might be in my room.'

'OK.'

'Were they the ones with holes in them?' I say. 'It's just that Gill – his mum – always hated it when he wore things with holes.' It wasn't that she minded him looking scruffy. It was the idiocy of paying for jeans that were already ripped. *You're bound to go through the knees in a month anyway*, she used to say to him. *I'm not paying an extra fifty dollars just for jeans that start off like that.*

Rosa smiles. 'Nope. No holes. I promise.'

She's young – maybe twenty-one or twenty-two – and very pale, her hair more white than blonde, and a face full of freckles. I picture her there in the cave, the water rising, her face showing up white in the darkness. Her face above the water, his face beneath it.

I blink the picture away.

'Would you mind if I take those jeans then, please?'

'I'll get them.'

Alone in his room, I walk back to the desk. On the wall above it, photos are Blu-Tacked to the wall. An old one from the Neck, showing our family and Sue's, together on the beach. Rosa, smiling on a bridge in Prague. Dougie with his school friends at a party, their faces flushed with beer or sunburn or both. Teddy and Papabee in the garden. Even a photo of Sylvie that he must have taken last year, on one of her brief home visits. She's on the verandah, scowling at the camera, one hand already raised to stop him.

His desk is as messy as his desk at home used to be. There are scrunched receipts, a snapped rubber band, envelopes and bits of paper with half-decipherable lists:

Dubrovnik hostel?
Stamps
Rowing sheds 11–12:30 Thurs
Toothpaste Phone charger Deodorant

I'll have to sort this all out at some stage; work out what to throw out, and what to ship home. The stuff on the desk is the kind of detritus that you'd ordinarily toss without thinking, but now I can't imagine getting rid of any of it, not even the broken rubber band. Perhaps this is what happens when somebody dies: everything they've touched becomes a relic.

I pick up the t-shirt from the back of the chair, and hold it to my face, gulping deep breaths. It's been worn, and it smells of Dougie in a way that Dougie's body in the hospital did not. Sweat and salt and his skin and the warmth of his breath.

I'm still there, sitting on the bed with my face pressed against the t-shirt, when Rosa comes back.

'I've done that too,' she admits. It feels an oddly intimate thing to say.

'I can't imagine ever wanting to wash this stuff again.'

She sits next to me on the bed. 'Here,' she says, passing me Dougie's grey jeans, neatly folded. 'I don't like to think of him lying there in nothing but a sheet.'

'You went to see him?'

'Of course,' she says. 'Twice.' She's watching me. 'Is that OK?'

'Of course,' I echo her. 'I just – it hadn't occurred to me, that's all.' I pause. 'It's different for everyone, I guess. Gill didn't want to go.'

'I wanted to see him. I'm glad I did.'

'Me too,' I say.

I think about asking her how she found it, that strange room with its curtained window, and the terrible stillness of Dougie's body. But it's enough just to know that she's seen it as well.

'You were with him in the cave, at the end, weren't you?'

She nods, but doesn't say anything.

'I'd like to know,' I say. 'Anything at all that you can tell me, about what happened.'

'Really?' she asks.

'Really.'

She shrugs. 'I don't remember all that much about it. It all happened so fast. The doctors said it's normal not to remember much. And the bits that I do remember don't seem important.'

'They'll be important to me. Anything at all.'

She turns to me. 'Just before it happened, I remember we were joking about peeing in our caving suits. It was so cold, you see. He said something about how at least we didn't have to worry about sharks smelling the pee – not like Australia.'

I'm smiling and crying at once. It's something Gill and I used to say to the kids when we were at the Neck: *Don't wee in your wetsuits, it attracts sharks*. I can't remember, now, if it's even true, or just something we told the kids to stop them from being revolting.

'And then?'

She shakes her head. 'I don't remember. I'm sorry. I don't remember anything after then.'

It's the sincerity in her apology that makes me doubt her. She's sorry for something, but I'm not sure it's amnesia. But I can't push her on it – not here, and not now, when all I want to do is turn my face to the bed and breathe in the smell of my son.

'So what will you do next?' I ask.

'I don't know.' She gestures downstairs, in the direction of the staffroom. 'They've given me time off, but officially staff members aren't meant to date, so they can't say why they're giving me special treatment. Lots of muttering about *We know you and Douglas were close*, or about my arm, and then awkward silence. So I'm kind of drifting around.' She hesitates.

'I think they'd probably quite like to fire me, for breaking the rule. Or at least they'd like not to renew my contract in September. But they feel bad, now Dougie's dead. And they're worried that I'm going to sue them, because of this.' She jerks her left arm, in its sling and plaster cast. 'And they don't really want me around the students, with the sling, because they're trying to play down the whole thing. So they don't want me working yet, but I still live here. So I'm sort of here, but not here.'

'Is there somewhere else you could go, even just for a while? Your parents?'

'No,' she says immediately, and then she speaks too quickly. 'I mean, they came down from Ireland straight away, when they heard the news. They were worried, obviously. But I didn't need them to stick around. I was only in hospital for a few hours.' Another silence. 'We don't talk much, normally.'

'This isn't really a normal time.'

'We don't talk much, ever, is what I should have said.'

I think about trying to contact her parents. What would I say? I hardly know this girl.

'I thought about going to stay with them for a bit,' she says. 'But they live on the west coast of Ireland, and they're both working, so I'd be stuck in the arse end of nowhere, with nothing to do. And my sister's in Mexico – she married a Mexican guy. She offered to come out, but her baby's only six months old – I said not to bother.

And I want to be here. Closer to—' She pauses, waves her arm around the room. 'I don't know. It felt weird to go. And people here have mainly been nice, even if most of them don't really know what to say.'

I nod, thinking of the attempts of our own friends and relatives, in the emails and voicemails that had been arriving ever since Dougie died. The cards and letters at home, too, that Gill's told me about. All those sound bites, skirting around the edge of what happened: *Sorry for your loss. We heard the sad news. So sorry to hear about your son.* Nobody saying the words *Dougie is dead.*

Before Rosa shows me downstairs, I take a blank piece of paper from Dougie's desk and scribble my phone number, and the address of the new flat. 'I know you probably don't want to talk about it. But when you're ready – if you're ready—'

'I told you,' she says. 'I don't remember.'

She leaves me at the door to Jacob's office. It's late – the secretary's gone, but Jacob's still there, waiting for me. He calls me a taxi, and sees me to the door.

'Let us know, whenever you decide how you'd like to deal with packing up Douglas's things. We'll help, of course, in any way that we can. And there's no rush.' He shakes my hand again. 'If there's anything that we can do, please let us know. Anything at all.'

What can I say? *Go to that hospital and take the lift down to the basement. Find my son, get him to stop being dead, then bring him back to me.*

'Thank you,' I say. I seem to be spending the whole day thanking him. I'm not sure exactly for what. After all, this is the school that organised the caving trip that killed my son. But I'm not angry with them. I feel very distant, that's all. As if Jacob and all those teachers, in this huge mansion, with their fancy voices, are creatures from a BBC Sunday night drama. Not Rosa – she seems different, and real, at least, with her freckles and her accent and her bluntness. But the rest of them – what can they possibly have to do with Dougie, or with me?

Dessert for a house with no teenagers

This is too simple to be a recipe. It's really just a way of passing half an hour. Because lately time has turned slow and viscous – molasses-thick. And the bananas are going brown, tiny flies starting to circle above the fruit bowl like miniature vultures. When you had a teenage boy in the house, bananas never got the chance to go brown. You couldn't keep enough bananas in the house. The fridge was always open; a loaf of bread would last half a day; you were always running out of Vegemite, milk, cheese.

Things are different now.

Heat the oven to 200°. Take four bananas, ideally slightly overripe (but not black or soggy – they need to hold their shape).

Don't peel them. Make a slit, longways, in the side of each banana, being sure not to go all the way through to the skin on the other side. Into the slit, press several pieces of dark chocolate or, for full nostalgic effect, some slices of whichever chocolate bar your children used to prefer, however revolting (for me: Milky Way). Resist the temptation to overstuff – it will only ooze out when it cooks. You should be able to close the slit once again, before wrapping the whole thing firmly in silver foil.

Bake on the top shelf of the oven for no more than twenty-five minutes, or until the foil darkens and the banana, when gently squeezed, has the texture of tightly packed wet sand. If you had teenage children at home, they'd make jokes about squeezing bananas. But you don't have teenage children at home.

Now (and this is the important part): eat this alone. Use a spoon if you want (I don't). If you concentrate hard on what you remember, and on what you want to forget, you can probably get through at least two whole bananas before you sit back, hands on your stomach, looking around at the leftover food and the empty table. This is very good practice. You need to get used to this.

Gill

I eat the bananas in the late morning, alone in the house while Teddy's at school. Then I make a shepherd's pie for tonight, putting some in a small container to take to the hospital tomorrow. Every day, I take Sylvie some of whatever I've cooked the night before. It's become habit now, whenever I cook a meal: a Tupperware for Papabee to take home for the next day's lunch; a smaller container for Sylvie. I only give her a tiny amount – barely five or six spoons' worth. I take the container in, and she ignores it, and the next day I take away the unopened container and replace it with a new one.

'Isn't it just a waste of food?' Dougie asked me once. 'You know what you and Dad used to say, if we wouldn't eat something: *There are starving children in Africa.*'

His imitation of me was always good.

'Sylvie's starving too,' I told him.

Even Sylvie's doctors are unconvinced by my daily deliveries. 'I'm not sure it's productive,' her main doctor, Louise, told me. 'It's a lot of pressure. If we see progress, it's going to be small – keeping down her Sustagen. Drinking half a glass of skim milk. She's not going to wake up one day and wolf down a serve of risotto.'

So far, Sylvie doesn't even open the containers, let alone eat the food. But I don't expect her to. I tried to explain to Louise that it's not about what Sylvie does. It's about what I do: I don't give up on her. I want to show her that she's still part of this family. Each of those battered plastic containers is an act of faith.

Gabe calls at noon – it must be the wee hours there. He tells me that there still isn't a date for the post-mortem.

'Something to do with a shortage of pathologists, apparently,' he says. 'I'm chasing the coroner's office about it.'

Why? I want to say. *Why do you want it to happen?* Instead I change the subject and get off the phone as fast as I can, my hands shaking.

I go into Sylvie's room. At the hospital she only has one small bedside table to store her things, so on her desk at home are the piles of things we've brought home for her over the last few years: books; letters; schoolwork.

I rifle through her papers for Dougie's letters. I find fourteen – there might be a few more at the hospital, but I don't dare ask Sylvie for them. I hold the pile of envelopes close to my face. I want to know if they smell of him – of that awful deodorant that used to make him and all his friends smell the same. But these smell of nothing but dust.

Before, I would never have contemplated reading her letters. There were a lot of things I would never have done, before the police came to the door that morning with the news about Dougie and split our lives into *before* and *after*.

I sit on the floor, spreading the envelopes out on the carpet. I don't even sort them into order before I start pulling out pages and turning them over hungrily.

Rosa and I had a BIG night on Sun in town – only just caught last train back to the school. Thought I was literally going to die the next morning when I had to help with rowing training at 6 am. You haven't truly suffered until you've been trying not to spew in a rowing boat while it's still dark outside. Reminds me of last year when Nathan overdid it at his 18th and spewed into his own sleeve in the back

of the car when Sue was driving us home. Ask Ella –
she'll tell you how gross it was.

He writes as if it was an ongoing conversation – except it
wasn't, because Sylvie never wrote back. We asked her, lots
of times, if she wanted to – we told her we'd bring in stamps,
and post the letters for her. She just used to shrug. 'That's
OK, thanks.' It makes Dougie's letters seem more poignant,
that he kept on sending them in the face of her silence. I
think of my own daily tubs of food for her and I miss him
with a new sharpness.

> *Starting to get serious about planning travels*
> *over summer. Thank God for the Papa J money –*
> *otherwise I'd be having a scenic tour of European*
> *bridges to sleep under! Even as it is, time (and*
> *money) are tight – two months travelling seems a lot*
> *longer until you start to plan it. Lots of Aussies come*
> *over here and say they're going to 'do Europe' in,*
> *like, a 10-day bus tour (only thing worse than that:*
> *Richie Yang from school who I caught up with in*
> *London last week. He's spent about three months in*
> *Scotland, and is putting on a THICK Scottish accent,*
> *I shit you not).*

I rip one of the pages as I yank it from its envelope. I can
hear Dougie's voice as though he's talking in the next room.

> *The food at the school is genuinely foul – Mum*
> *would have a heart attack if she saw what they're*
> *capable of doing to a Sunday roast. Mainly gristle,*
> *and so dry that every now and again you just have*
> *to give up and take out a chewed-up wad of meat*
> *and put it back on your plate. Classy! And they're*
> *OBSESSED with potatoes. Dinner (except they call it*

High Tea) for the students yesterday: mashed potato,
with potato wedges, and potato gems. Thank God
for gravy, and garlic salt. Looking forward to getting
scurvy.

Lots of love

D xx

PS: Remember at the Neck that time when Papabee
mistook a raw potato for an apple and just took a
huge bite?

PPS: (Sorry if all that food stuff is weird for you to
hear about – but honestly this place is enough to
turn anyone anorexic.)

PPPS: (Too soon for anorexia jokes? I'll try again
next year, when you're out of hospital and all of this
is behind you.)

Hours must've passed, and I've read all the letters at least
three times. I try to clear my head by taking the dog for
a walk before Teddy gets home from school, but Dougie's
voice follows me all the way to Cornelian Bay, and through
the scrubby bush that surrounds the foreshore path. When
I come home, his voice follows me down the side path and
in the back door.

Seen much of Ella or Nath? Nath's rubbish at
emails. Would be brilliant if you were out by this
summer, when I'm back, so we'd all be together
at the Neck, like the old days (still on the kids'
table, no doubt – even though Nath is like 6 foot
2 by now!).

His letters are full of moments like that – his optimism as reliable as his appetite.

> *Have you thought about doing something like this, some kind of gap year, when you're better? (Not England. Seriously. Winter here is grim as fuck. Spain, maybe?)*

> *Is Papabee still driving? (If you can call it that?) When you're out of hospital you can get your licence. I'll give you some lessons when I'm back.*

I wonder if he really believed that she would get better, or whether he was just performing hope for her. Was he lying to her, just as we are? Or was this his act of faith? Is there a difference?

Teddy

Dad Skypes me on Saturday morning, but Mum's already at the hospital with Sylvie.

'How's she doing?' he asks.

'Sylvie or Mum?'

'Both, I guess.'

I think about it. 'Mum's OK. She's cooking a lot.'

'Lucky you,' says Dad.

I don't know how to tell him that some of the stuff Mum's been cooking is a bit weird. Yesterday when I came home from school there were seven bananas wrapped in foil on the counter, cooked and then gone cold again.

'And Sylvie's the same as normal,' I say. I can't even remember what *normal* used to be, before she went to live in the Boneyard.

'She doesn't really like talking, when I ring her,' Dad says. 'You know what she's like.'

'Is she mad at you and Mum?'

'She's always mad at us.' He's smiling, trying to make it into a joke.

'Is she mad at you for keeping her alive?'

He stops his joking face, and he does that thing I like, where he takes my questions seriously.

'Yes,' he says. 'I think she is.'

I'm not supposed to know that Sylvie's tried to kill herself. I'm not supposed to know a lot of things. That's the thing about being the littlest: you notice more than people realise. I notice the scars on her arm, and the sharp knives and the medicines being locked snap click shut in the box every time she's allowed to come home from hospital. I worked it out for myself.

And it makes sense, because not eating is just killing yourself slowly. So it's not a big shock that Sylvie's tried a quicker way.

'How do we know it's definitely better to be alive?' I ask Dad. Because I've been trying hard to save Sylvie, but she's always been the smart one – even smarter than Dougie. So if she wants to be dead, I have to check whether she's right.

I like that Dad doesn't rush to say, 'Of course it is.' Instead, he thinks properly about what I've asked.

'I think it's hard to be alive, sometimes,' he says. 'There are a lot of difficult things, and a lot of sadness. So much, since Dougie died.' He rubs his face, and his hands pull his skin down and for a second he looks a million years old. 'And I think it's extra hard for Sylvie, these last few years, because her brain's not working properly, because of her sickness. But even after everything that's happened, I still think being alive is better. There're so many good things – amazing things.'

'Like SausageDog?' I say. 'And the Neck. And McDonald's.'

'I'm not sure that I'd count McDonald's. But yes, those other ones. And more things, too. People, most of all.'

'Papabee. And you and Mum.'

'Definitely. And all of our friends. But most of all, for me and your mum, at least, it's the three of you: you and Dougie and Sylvie. I've never wanted to be dead, because that would mean not being with you guys.'

You're not with me now, I think, but I don't say it, because even though it's true, I think it might be one of those kinds of true that you're not meant to say out loud.

I think about all the things I can't say, and all the things Sylvie doesn't say. Sylvie, with the bones on her back poking out like spikes – like the echidna that we sometimes see at the Neck. I'd like to be Echidna-Teddy, even though Dad always says they're covered in fleas. I'd make my own sky out of spikes and use it to keep the world away. Everything inside the spikes would be me, or mine, even the fleas. I'd dig tunnels and a little burrow just big enough to turn around, and that would be the world, exactly shaped like me. I would be all claws and paws, waddling at my own exact pace because Echidna-Teddy couldn't be hurried. The world would wait for me.

I get Papabee to drop me at the hospital later that morning. Usually on weekends Mum takes me in the afternoon, but she's in the study with the laptop click click clicking and she doesn't even ask why I want to go in early, by myself.

'Remind Papabee where he's heading,' she yells out. 'And make sure you get him to do the loop and drop you on Argyle Street.' It's easier for Papabee to find his way home if he's already pointing the right way.

I say hi to the nurses on the way in. I've got the photo in an envelope tucked under my jumper, because I don't want anyone asking me what it is.

'Why are you in here so early?' asks Sylvie. 'Shouldn't you be in school?'

'It's a weekend.' I forget, sometimes, how cut off she is from the real world. I look at the thick windows, locked shut. They don't even get real air in here. When Mum brings Sylvie's pyjamas home to wash, they smell like hospital.

'Where's Mum?'

'She's coming in later, so I can go home with her.'

'Guess you'd better settle in, then,' she says.

I sit on the side of the bed, and slide the envelope out of my jumper.

One of her eyebrows goes up. 'You a magician now?'

'It's for you.' I hold it out to her.

'What's this?' she says. 'Not another bribe?'

'Not exactly. It's different.'

She just leaves the envelope on the bed. She's not even looking at it, so I pick it up again and open it myself.

'There.' I hold up the photo so she can see it. 'It's you.' That doesn't feel right, so I try again: 'It was you.'

She takes the photo for a second, looks at it, and puts it down nearly straight away. She does it casually, like she's not interested in the photo at all, but I notice that she makes sure to turn it over so that it's face-down.

I turn it back over so that her face is smiling at the hospital ceiling.

'D'you have to do that?'

'Yes,' I tell her. That feels like quite a brave thing to say: *Yes. I have to do this. I do.* So I go on, feeling even braver. 'You were different then.'

'Fat, for one thing.'

That's stupid, because you can hardly even see her body in the photo, and the bits that you can see (her face, her neck, the top of her arms) aren't fat at all. But she's talking, at least, so I keep going.

'You were really happy.'

'Nobody's happy all the time.'

'Sure,' I say. 'But you weren't grumpy all the time, I mean.'

She doesn't argue with me.

'You were fun.' I'd almost forgotten about that, until I saw this photo. She used to let herself be silly. Jumping through the sprinkler with me on hot days in summer, in our undies, screaming from the cold water. Telling me made-up stories about a dragon called Teddy, who did farts so bad that they set fire to the curtains in the castle.

'I'm not here to entertain you. That's not my job.'

'I know,' I say. That's Papabee's job. 'But you were different then.'

'Of course I was. Then I grew up.'

She makes it sound like this is the way it always works: like spending three years in hospital is a totally normal part of growing up. Like everybody does it.

But she hasn't grown up – that's the thing. She hasn't done any of the things that you do when you grow up. She hasn't got taller, or gone through higher grades in school, or done any new things at all. Even the pyjamas she's wearing, the pink ones with the sausage dogs on them, are the same ones she had years ago.

'That's got nothing to do with me,' she says, jerking her chin towards the photo, and I think maybe I've got it wrong, like last time with the Papa J money. That I shouldn't have come today.

I pick up the photo again. 'How old were you?' I ask, as I slide it back into the envelope.

'Thirteen and a half.' It's the way she says it – quickly, automatically – that makes me see that the photo hasn't been a waste of time after all. She says it so fast, like she knows exactly when she started to change.

'Listen to me, Teddy.' She's sitting up a bit, staring right into my eyes, and her voice is really sharp. 'Whatever you're doing – bringing me things, sniffing around – whatever it is, you need to stop it.'

It feels like we're playing that game we used to play sometimes, me and Dougie and Sylve, when one of us would hide something and then guide the others: *warmer, warmer, cooler, warmer, hotter*. But it isn't like that game, really, because this time she doesn't want me to find it. *Hotter, hotter, hot*. She knows it's too hot. It burned her right up. What will it do to me, when I find it?

Sylvie

Teddy's here again, poking around at the edges of my secrets. He picks at my silence the way I pick at the scabs and scars on my left wrist. He can't leave it alone.

I think of King Lear, and Cordelia's silence. She couldn't heave her heart into her mouth. Shakespeare knew about hunger. He understood that my mouth must be empty for this. That *nothing* is a promise that I make to myself, as well as to the world.

Teddy's come here twice, now, with his strange little offerings. I think of Lear: *And my poor fool is hanged.*

What if the circle of silence that I've drawn around myself turns out to be a noose?

Outside, it's getting cooler, and the trees are forgetting their leaves. Down on the street, people are wearing coats. From my window I can just see the hospital's main entrance, where the smokers cluster. The wind snatches the smoke from their cigarettes and smears it across the sky.

Down at the Neck, the sea will be grey. If Sue and Dan go on the weekend, they'll light the fire, and the slaters will scuttle out of the firewood and hide under the carpet. The pine trees behind the house will scratch their needles against the windows, and walkers on the beach will have to squint their eyes against the sand that the wind throws in their faces. Waves will break against the headland at the end of the beach, and spatter it with salt spray. The high tide will leave dark clumps of kelp on the beach, each one heavy as a drowned body.

PART FOUR

Gill

'How's Dougie?' Sylvie asks.

Since I got back from London, she asks about him every day. It makes a change from her usual reluctance to speak at all. I know that if I tell her the truth, she will slip back under the surface of her silence.

'Oh, you know,' I say. 'Grumpy, actually – I think it's hard for somebody like him, being laid up like that. He's usually so active. I think he's taking it out on your dad a bit.'

The details come easily. I can picture it: Dougie negotiating corners in his wheelchair, scraping impatiently against the edge of door frames. Driving Gabe mad by endlessly bouncing a tennis ball against the foot of the hospital bed.

Keeping the secret from her seems no more outrageous to me than the outlandish fact of her hospitalisation itself. If I can get used to that, I can get used to anything. If this can be real – my daughter interring herself in a hospital bed for three years – then anything can be real. I'm as stubborn as Sylvie, after all – she gets that from me. And the lie isn't forever. Only until she's stable; until she's reached the goal weight that the doctors have set for her; until she's been discharged.

'Another week and he should be out of the chair and on crutches,' I say to her. 'And hopefully out of the hospital. He's counting the days – but Gabe's worried that he'll overdo it, push himself too fast. You know what Dougie's like.'

What I mean: *I know what he's like.* My son. I know him well enough that it's as if I'm watching the story happen, rather than creating it. I know, with perfect certainty, how it would be.

'They still haven't ruled out another operation, if the leg doesn't recover the full range of motion.'

Sylvie shifts on her bed. The nurses have removed her feeding tube temporarily, to insert a clean one, but I can still see the telltale sign: a small hairless square on one cheekbone where the tube is usually taped in place.

'But he's OK? I mean, his leg's going to be OK, right?'

'Of course,' I say. Because for three years she has wanted nothing from me, and now she wants reassurance, and I can give it.

Should I feel guilty? Remember that she's been lying to me for years. How long has it been, really, since Sylvie and I have been able to tell each other the truth?

Before I leave, I shift the books on her bedside table to make room for the tiny serve of gnocchi I cooked last night, and I pick up yesterday's untouched container, as light as the body of a baby bird.

On the way out, Sylvie's doctor, Louise, catches me and asks me to come into her office. It's down the corridor from Paediatrics 3, and so small that when I sit, I have to turn my knees sideways so they don't bump her desk.

She's reluctantly agreed to keep hiding the news from Sylvie until Gabe's return, but even though Louise is at least a decade younger than me, I feel as though I've been called into the headmistress's office.

'You know I care about you and Gabe. Teddy too. I understand why you're doing this, for now. But first and foremost, I have obligations to my patient.'

'*Do no harm*,' I say. 'Isn't that what doctors have to promise? You know the news will harm her.'

'It's a bit more complicated than that,' she says, sitting back. 'But yes: there are serious risks in telling her. But there are risks either way. We'll have to work together to plan the safest way to tell her, when she's stable. When Gabe's back.'

'Of course. When he's back. Of course.'

That night, when Gabe calls me, he asks, 'Are we doing the right thing?'

I appreciated the generosity of that *we*. We both know that it's my idea, and that he's mainly going along with it because I've insisted.

'I don't care about what's right,' I say. 'I only care about keeping her alive.'

When Sylvie quit food like a bad habit, and gave us no answers, we went looking for our own. She was in hospital, turning her head away from our questions, and staring at the pigeons doing laps of the sky. So, instead, I interrogated her doctors. Books about anorexia piled up on my bedside table. We dragged the whole family to therapy sessions, where Sylvie continued to say nothing, while Gabe and I blathered, saying too much and still coming up with nothing.

I blamed everything. Magazines; TV; school; the internet; the six months of ballet lessons that Sylvie took when she was eight; the fashion industry; the advertising industry; the patriarchy generally.

I even blamed the dirt beneath us, and the rocks, and the unforgiving sea. This island, where we had raised our kids. The thing about Tasmania is that it never forgets. The ground is thick with memories and bones. This island, drifting on the edge of a nation founded on that extraordinary lie: *Terra Nullius*. No Man's Land. What could grow on such a soil?

The longer Sylvie was silent, the more I hurled myself at answers, like a moth battering at a closed window. I allowed myself to blame everything, except for Sylvie herself. This is what Gabe and I learned to tell ourselves:

You can't blame an anorexic for being sick, any more than you could blame somebody with pneumonia. That's what the doctors, the dietitians, the counsellors and the self-help books tell us. That's how we always explain it to Teddy. *Her brain's just not working properly, sweetheart. It's a disease. It's not her fault.*

We say it and say it and say it and we might even believe it.

More than anything else, of course I blamed myself. All teenage girls turn on their mothers. I did it myself, when I was that age – for at least four years, I rolled my eyes at every single thing my mother said, and smoked cigarettes out of my bedroom window, just to annoy her. So when Sylvie stopped eating, it felt like a very particular attack on me. When she refused food, it couldn't help but feel pointed.

When she was first admitted to hospital, I asked her, 'What did I do wrong? What did your dad and I do wrong?'

'For fuck's sake, Mum,' she said. 'It's not always about you and Dad. This isn't about you.'

'Language,' I said, automatically. But I didn't care about her swearing – I cared about her dying. Her words – *This isn't about you* – were a relief and a blow, at once. Whatever had claimed her, we didn't even figure in it. It wasn't about me – it was about her, and about food.

But I'm a chef, a food-writer – how can I separate myself from food? How does a mother separate herself from her daughter?

For the first week or two after I got back from London, people kept bringing meals around, and we ran out of vases for the flowers. An expensive bouquet of lilies was stuffed into the laundry jug; a dozen roses crammed into an empty peanut butter jar; the whole house reeking of flowers on the point of going bad. But by the time the last casseroles have been eaten, and the last of the flowers have dropped their petals and been dumped in the compost bin, I've realised that when somebody dies, nothing else stops. I still have to file my articles; Teddy's school uniforms still pile up in the laundry basket; and Papabee crashes his car. I'm in the passenger seat, on the way back from helping him with his weekly shop, when he rounds a corner at about five miles an hour and steers with stately magnificence straight into the back of a parked car.

'Ah,' he says.

While I write a note with my contact details, to tuck under the other car's windscreen wiper, Papabee keeps saying, 'Far the simplest thing is for me to write them a cheque for a hundred dollars.' It's the same thing he says every time he gets a bill, whether it's forty dollars for the newspaper subscription, or twelve-hundred dollars to the plumber for a new boiler.

'You sure he's still safe to drive?' Sue asks, when she rings me that evening.

'Of course he's safe.' I'm surprised at the impatience in my voice. 'He barely dented the car. His driving's fine – it's only navigating that's a problem. Or losing the car.'

This happens a couple of times a month. He'll forget where he's parked the car, or he'll drive down to the shops, then leave the car there, and walk home. Back at his flat, he sees the car missing from the parking space and calls the police to report it stolen. These days the local police switchboard has a note on file, telling officers to call me before they file a report on his stolen car.

'Him and Teddy together most afternoons,' says Sue. 'Talk about the blind leading the blind.'

'They're fine,' I say. 'And what am I supposed to do? I can't manage the school run, work and hospital every day without Papabee's help.'

I don't say, out loud, the other reason I'm so grateful to have him around as much as possible now – because at night, when he's gone home, and Teddy and I are alone, Teddy's questions start. He lies on his side in bed with the dog tucked behind his knees, and asks me in his small voice:

'Do dead people get cold?'

'Does it hurt to drown?'

'Does a dead person know that they're dead?'

I don't have the answers to those questions, because they're the questions I would ask too, if I dared. Instead I say, 'You'll have to talk to your father about that, sweetheart.'

I must've said that a lot, because today I say it again and Teddy asks, 'How come Dad's the expert in Dead Stuff?'

I don't have an answer for that either. If I did, it would be something to do with Gabe being braver than me. Something to do with me being here, with Teddy and Sylvie, where there's no room, and no time, to face those questions.

That's why I cling to those times when Papabee's here. For those few hours of dinner and coffee and watching the news, Papabee says exactly the same things that he's said for the last six years. Lee Lin Chin comes on, to read the SBS news, and Papabee says, 'She's a very fine-looking lady, for a Chinawoman,' and Teddy and I shout, in unison, 'Papabee! You can't say things like that!' and I can almost pretend that things are normal. I can almost pretend that death is just another time zone that Dougie has travelled to.

I've started ignoring my phone, unless it's family, the hospital, or Sue. The messages and cards continue to come, and I can't avoid everyone entirely – not in Hobart. I bump into people at the Hill Street Grocer, or at the gates of Teddy's school. At first, it was condolences, and questions about the funeral, which I brushed aside, grateful for once for the inquest and the post-mortem, which at least give me a genuine reason to avoid committing to any plans. But as the weeks pass, I've noticed that people are too embarrassed to mention Dougie at all. Or, worse, they talk about him, but when they do, I can't recognise him.

A long letter arrives from Gabe's brother, in Sydney. He writes about Dougie's charity work. It's true enough – last year Dougie raised more than six hundred dollars for Amnesty in his school's annual fundraiser. He and some of his mates ran a sponsored 10k race. But when the Amnesty people gave a talk at his school, he said to us, 'For people worried about attacks on freedom of speech, they sure do go on a lot.' We'd laughed, outraged, and Gabe cuffed him on the back of the head with a rolled-up magazine. Dougie didn't even need to train for the race – he ran it easily, for fun, with the latent fitness of an eighteen-year-old boy. And he hadn't actually done much of the fundraising part – that had mainly been me and Gabe, cornering our friends and asking our neighbours; grabbing the sponsorship sheet off the fridge every time anyone came over.

Mrs Manheim, the head of Dougie's school, writes too – a really kind letter, mentioning Dougie's talent for sports, his leadership skills, his popularity with the other students. But all that I can think while I'm reading it is that Dougie and his friends used to refer to her as Mrs ManHands.

I don't remember the person these letters describe: this rule-abiding, wholesome, polite young man. Where's the Dougie who would sleep until two pm on weekends, if Gabe and I didn't drag him out of bed? The boy who played computer games all night, and lied about scraping my car along the garage wall?

Missing too, are his patience with Papabee, and the summer he taught Teddy to swim, and all those letters he posted to Sylvie.

What if Dougie was an ordinary boy – cruel, and funny, and lazy, and curious, and kind, and always leaving skidmarks in the toilet? Am I still allowed to mourn him then? Nobody but Sue wants to talk about the Dougie that I remember – the boy who seemed, from the ages of twelve to fourteen, to be masturbating more or less full time.

Sue rings on Sunday afternoon and says, 'The kids are out. I need a drink – how fast can you get here?' Teddy's at Papabee's so I grab a lemon from the tree by the clothesline, like I always do, and by the time I drive over the bridge and park in Sue's driveway she's already got the gin poured. We've been doing this for so many years that I only have to think of her to catch myself patting my side pocket, expecting to feel the bulge of a lemon.

Sitting on her porch now, with a gin and tonic cool in my hand, I ask her if she remembers Dougie's masturbation phase – all those bunched-up tissues I used to find under his bed when I was vacuuming.

'Oh Christ,' she says. 'How could I forget? And I was going through the same thing at home with Nathan. I had to take to his sheets with a chisel.'

I've been avoiding Nathan and Ella. I'm terrified that I'll find myself resenting them – their warm bodies; their working lungs; their futures – and I love them too fiercely to risk showing them that. But when Sue and Dan bring them to the house I can't refuse them – they grew up with Dougie, after all. Ella squeezes Teddy to her, and Nathan stands, all big hands and feet, looking awkwardly around the hallway as if searching for a place to put down his sadness.

I'm glad to have them here – I am. I want to hear all about Nathan's share-house, his uni course, and Ella's exams. But after nearly an hour, Nathan starts to cry again. He says, 'Is Gabe going to bring Dougie home with him, when he comes?'

'We can't sort out any of that until they've done the operation first,' I say.

'You mean the post-mortem?' he asks.

I nod. *The operation*: that's how I prefer to think of it, whenever Gabe brings it up.

'And the funeral? When will that be?' asks Ella.

'It's all up in the air at the moment.' It's the same line I've repeated to everyone who asks.

'We could help you,' Nathan says. 'If you want. To organise it, I mean. Heaps of our friends have stories, and photos and stuff, that we could use.'

'Thanks love,' I say, grabbing the dirty mugs from the table and heading back into the kitchen. 'But there're a lot of things we need to sort out first.'

A lot of Dougie's other friends have written or emailed – awkward, stilted letters that their parents probably told them they had to write. *I heard the sad news*. His old friend Tom appears at the door one morning, and cries. I cry too, and give him a hug, but I don't invite him in.

'I have to head out in a minute,' I say. 'An appointment at the hospital. Sylvie – you know.'

I hug him again before he goes. Then I close the front door and lean against it, breathing too fast.

Seventeen days since I got back, and since I gave Sylvie that final letter from Dougie. She hasn't said anything, but I know she will have noticed. This vigilant girl, who used to peel apart her sandwiches to check the thickness of the butter. Who once worked out, by taste alone, that I'd been slipping full-fat milk into her porridge instead of skim. She doesn't miss a thing.

I've fabricated the details of Dougie's operation, and his recovery. I've told her that Gabe's staying with Dougie, and that as soon as Dougie gets the go-ahead from doctors, the two of them will do some travelling together, because Dougie will still need help. They're thinking about going to Florence, I've said.

But if a letter doesn't come soon, she's going to wonder why she hasn't heard from him. She's going to start asking questions.

After I drop Teddy at school, I come back to the silent house. In the study, I open my laptop and hear the wheezy hum of the machine starting up.

Everyone says I should get back to doing more writing. Sue, Gabe, and my sister all keep telling me the same thing: *It'll be good for you*. I haven't shown them the new recipes – the ones that barely make sense, even to me. I don't know whether I'll be able to show them this new project, either.

Closing my eyes, I think of all the letters I've read, and re-read, these last weeks. Like a radio scanning the frequencies, I search my mind for Dougie's voice. I take a deep breath, then another, and start to type.

Gabe

The nights are worse than the days. Sometimes, at night in the little flat, I don't know if I'm crying for Dougie, or Gill, or Sylvie, or Teddy. Or for myself, missing all of them. But I can't leave – there's work to be done. I stay up late, hunched over the laptop, and I read everything I can find about the accident, and about caving, floods, and rescue procedures. I let each tangent carry me further down.

One of the police reports identified the particular brand and type of rope that they used – it's listed in an inventory of items retrieved from the cave, along with 'One (1) purple headtorch (not working)' and 'One (1) Scarpa boot (left foot), unlaced.'

Was his headtorch working before it went into the water? Did Dougie enter the caves with his bootlaces undone, or did it happen later, the water's fingers unlacing them for him?

I order the same rope online. It's £120, and I don't even dare to convert the price into Australian dollars. I don't know how I'll explain to Gill that I need to feel in my hands the same rope that Dougie held.

I take a bus to Covent Garden to collect it.

'There you go,' the man in the shop says, throwing it down on the counter. It's neatly coiled – calligraphic loops. 'Got any good trips coming up?'

'Not really,' I say.

All the way home I'm aware of the weight of it in my backpack. 4kg, the label says – the weight of a baby a few weeks old. I remember how I used to carry Dougie in a sling, his face in my chest, the top of his head tucked under my chin so that I could smell his hair.

Back in the flat, I uncoil the rope. It's stiffer than I'd expected – more unyielding. I run it through my fingers. I fill the sink and submerge the rope, then check how hard it is to grasp when it's wet. I try to coil it again, but I don't have the knack, and it makes an ungainly bundle.

The police pathologist's report, from when they first recovered Dougie's body from the cave, said his hands were clenched. I've learned that this doesn't mean his hands were clenched when he died. Sometimes it happens afterwards – the hand muscles seize of their own accord. I spend a whole night reading scientific journal articles about the clenching of fists. *Cadaveric spasm.* I can't explain why this has become so important to me: were his hands reaching out, or were they clenched?

I go to meet an old friend of Dan's, called Jeremy Gamlin. Dan emailed me Jeremy's contact details and told me that he's a climber and caver who might be able to talk me through some of the details.

We meet in the coffee shop in the British Library. I suggested it because it's one of the few landmarks in London that I know, but I regret it now I'm here, surrounded by students, all around Dougie's age, with their laptops and coffees.

Jeremy and I queue up for drinks, and there's a minute or two of fussing and rearranging of trays and teapots and saucers before we can really talk, and it seems too big a leap to go from *No, I insist, let me get this,* and *Did you want milk?* to talking about how Dougie drowned.

'This is the kind of rope they were using.' I pull it from my backpack. The rope smells of damp, and looks incongruous here in the café. '10.6 millimetres thick. Sixty metres long. I bought the exact same one.'

'Is that important?' Jeremy asks. 'I read the report you forwarded me, and a few of the newspaper articles – I didn't see anything about the rope failing? They were using that for the ascent back from Cavern 3 to 2, right?'

'The rescuers found the rope intact. But I just want to understand how it all works.' I hesitate. 'I'm trying to get the full picture.'

He nods. When we first shook hands he'd told me, 'I can't imagine what you're going through.' The thing is, I can't imagine it either. I'm in the middle of it, and I still can't imagine it, can't grasp the shape of it.

'I did a bit of Googling,' he says, 'after Dan got in touch. The group your son was with, they were legit operators, not some cowboy set-up. They have a good safety record, until this. All the paperwork that you'd expect.'

'If they were so well qualified, why did they let it all go wrong?'

He grimaces slightly, folds his hands together and then unfolds them again. He hasn't touched his coffee. 'Every time you go into a cave, or up a mountain, it's a risky environment. A good instructor can mitigate the risks – control certain factors. But there are always going to be elements outside their control. Weather; rockfalls; stuff like that. It's not necessarily a case of human error.'

Rocks don't make errors, I think. *Weather doesn't make errors. People do.*

'The guy in charge – Phillip Murphy – why didn't he check more carefully?' I ask. 'How could he not have realised there'd been too much rain that night?'

'It was a bad combination. Heavy, localised rain upstream. Then the spill over that reservoir wall. So much can change so quickly – there's a reason it's called a flash flood. The guide made a judgment call.'

'And he got it wrong.'

'Clearly.' He holds his hands wide, like he's offering me their emptiness. 'And if he'd done his prep, he should've known about the rains overnight. My bet is that he did. And he would've assessed the water levels on entry. But he couldn't have known about the reservoir. And the Smith–Jackson System – it's not known to flood. The reservoir was the game-changer.'

'He should have known,' I say. 'His website said he'd guided groups there for at least eight years.'

'There hasn't been a flood like that. Not in eight years. Not ever, from what I can tell.'

'I can see that,' I say, impatiently. 'And I'm not looking to sue – I'm not after money, nothing like that. I'm not even trying to place blame. We just want to know what happened. My wife and I—' I stop for a second. Is it fair, dragging Gill into this, when I know it's only me? 'We just want to understand what happened to Dougie.'

'I can understand that,' he says. 'I'm just not sure what I can clarify for you. What exactly are you looking for?'

I go to the hospital every morning, to see Dougie. The various chaplains all know me now, so there isn't much preamble. They have Dougie ready in the little room, and I go in and look at him for half an hour.

'You can talk to him, if you want,' the chaplain suggests one day. 'Some people find it helpful.'

I try it, but I know she's in the adjoining room and I feel embarrassed. All I manage is his name, in a whisper: *Dougie. Dougie.* I say it so many times that the name starts to sound strange to me, and it becomes just a noise, rather than a word. Dougie's death keeps slamming me up against the hard limits of language.

On the other side of the world, Gill is making her own daily hospital visits. I suspect hers are nearly as silent as mine – Sylvie hasn't spoken properly to either of us for a long time. Her silence is harder to bear, in some ways, than Dougie's. His silence isn't directed at us. It's not a choice, or a weapon.

I ought to be at home to navigate Sylvie's silences with Gill. I ought to be there with them all. But how can I leave Dougie here alone? How can I abandon him when there are still questions unanswered, his story unfinished? The inquest hasn't even been scheduled yet, and the post-mortem keeps being delayed. I've been in London for nearly three weeks before Heather from the coroner's office finally calls to tell me that it's booked for the next afternoon.

In the hospital the next morning I stare at Dougie extra hard, trying to commit him to memory. The bruising on his face has darkened since the first time I saw his body. This is what I'm going to remember: not my living boy, but this, the tenderness of bruises, and the perfect stillness of a face without breath.

I squeeze his hand, unyielding and cold, and linger beyond my allotted half hour, until the chaplain comes into the doorway and gives a polite cough.

I want to say something to Dougie, but I don't know what words would fit. Gill's always been the one who's good with words. She's the writer; she'd be able to say all the things that I can only feel. I need her to tell me how I'm feeling. To explain it to me, so I can say the right things to Dougie. But Gill and her words aren't here. It's just me and Dougie, and he can't tell me anything.

Back in the flat, I keep looking at the clock. Ten o'clock. Eleven o'clock. Noon. I'm not allowed to be there, but I've researched every detail of the post-mortem. I know better than to tell Gill this, but in the last few weeks I've read webpage after webpage about how post-mortems are conducted. I learned about the central incision down the front of the body. The cut's shaped like a Y, so that they can get to all the main organs. Heart, lungs, stomach. I read about the examination of the stomach contents. The second incision at the back of the head, so that they can take off the top of the skull and remove the brain.

When Dougie was a baby, he used to fall asleep on my shoulder when I burped him after a feed. Now, if I close my eyes, I can still feel that weight. More than nineteen years ago, but my body remembers. Standing in the kitchen, I find myself leaning my head to the side, against his little body that isn't there.

They call me at four to say that it's done, and the body released into the care of the funeral home. We chose a firm close to my flat in London, and I walk there the next morning. I'm met by a painfully courteous young man in a dark suit, who shows me to the room where Dougie is waiting.

The coroner's assistant was telling us the truth – Dougie doesn't look different after the post-mortem. I expected to see some change – a formlessness in his features; some clue that his scalp has been peeled off and put back on. But they've done a good job. He looks no worse than when I last saw him, in the hospital. He's still recognisably Dougie, though still recognisably and unmistakably dead.

The cremation is later today. When I spoke to the funeral director yesterday he said I could be there, and I was surprised to hear myself say no – I'd argued, after all, for the right to attend the post-mortem. But if I were at the cremation, I wouldn't trust myself to let go.

The young man clears his throat. 'I'll leave you alone,' he says, 'to say goodbye.'

I step closer to Dougie. *Goodbye* is a word you use all the time – something you say before you go to work, or pop out to lunch. An ordinary word. It has no place here, in this funeral parlour on the outskirts of Holloway. There should be new words for this. New languages, made of holes and silence.

'Goodbye,' I say, because even though the word isn't enough, it's all that I have.

Yesterday I consigned him to the post-mortem; today I'm sending him into the incinerator. Can a blade be an act of love? Can a furnace?

Gill

It's midnight here when they cremate him. Gabe calls me.

'Sorry,' he says. 'I know it must be late.'

'It's not as though I'd be sleeping otherwise.' There's a pause. 'Do you think it's happening right now?' I ask him. 'Do you think it's over?'

I'd imagined that I'd know – that I'd feel something, like Jane Eyre hearing Rochester's cry for help. But I didn't sense anything when the cave flooded, and I sense nothing now.

'They'll call me when it's done,' he says. 'They promised. But it won't be for a while.'

'Okay.' So we wait together, our silence stretching between us, a net to catch the dark. After a while he says, 'Do you remember when he was a baby and his wrists were so fat it looked like he had screw-on hands?'

I nod, even though Gabe can't see me. I'm remembering the cookie-dough texture of Dougie's baby flesh.

'Are you there?' Gabe asks.

'That thing he used to do with his eyebrows, when he was angry?' I say, keeping my voice low so I don't wake Teddy. 'You know?'

'That scooter he made us drag everywhere?'

'He and Papabee and the brandy, that Christmas?'

He doesn't need to say any more than that, because his stories are my stories too. So we're just listing things, now, faster and faster, each one a question: *Do you remember? Do you remember it too?*

'I suppose I should get off the phone,' Gabe says. 'For when they call.'

'OK.'

'Are we going to get through this?' he asks.

I don't say *yes*, because I understand that on a night like this, every word is a promise.

'We'll try,' I say.

I'd say sorry for not writing for so long, but for once I have a rock-solid excuse. (I'm going to be playing the broken leg card for a long time, so get used to it.) I guess by now Mum and Dad will have filled you in on everything that happened. It was about as grim as you'd expect. Quite lucky not to remember much of it, to be honest (hooray for shock and hypothermia!) – and probably lucky to get out of there with just the leg thing. Definitely won't be signing up for another caving trip anytime soon...

It used to be him imitating me. Dougie was a good mimic – the natural performer. He did a great Papabee, and a pretty good Gabe. But he impersonated me more than anyone. He'd yank his voice up an octave and mimic the martyred cry that I used to do when the kids were slow to help. *'I'll do it,'* he'd screech, huffing around the kitchen slamming drawers. So many phrases that I never realised I overused, until I heard Dougie echoing them back at me: *Use your brain! God give me strength! Ask your father!*

My turn, now, to be the mimic.

I couldn't sleep after saying goodbye to Gabe, so I tiptoed to the study in the dark and set to work again on the letter. I'm surprised by how much I enjoy it. All the exclamation marks and digressions that Sue ruthlessly cuts from the drafts of my recipes and columns, I allow myself now. And I hear his voice – his loud voice, equal parts enthusiasm and sarcasm.

> *I could work, in theory, but it'd be bloody hard on crutches, so I'm still on paid leave. Dad reckons the school's SHITTING themselves in case we sue. Plus, apparently there's going to be some kind of insurance pay-out, because it happened at work. If I could've persuaded them to cut the leg right off I would've got a cool 100K...*

As always, there's truth inside the lie – apparently there is going to be some money. Not from the school itself, but their insurer. Last week Gabe emailed me some documents, including a neat list of amounts payable for various injuries incurred in the course of work. *Loss of a toe: £9,000. Loss of finger (non-dominant hand): £18,000.* I'd opened it, and glanced quickly down the list. There, at the bottom: *Death.* I slammed the laptop shut.

It's taken me days to write this letter. I need to get the details right. I need to prove to myself that I can capture his voice. His unfeigned enthusiasm, and all those endless parentheses.

> *So my summer travels have started earlier than planned – as soon as we got the all-clear from the doctors, we flew to Florence to start the world's least rock'n'roll gap year travels: me, my crutches, and Dad (not exactly the way that I expected my holiday to go!). But Dad's been a champ, and God knows how I would've managed without him...it'd be one thing to join up with mates from school for a bit of travelling, like I'd originally planned – but another to ask them for help every day when I need to shower with a full leg-cast! (Let us never speak of this again! SERIOUSLY.)*

Dad might cramp my style a bit, but there's another thing that softens the blow: we're staying in way nicer places than I would've stayed in otherwise – Dad says he's too old for hostels – AND he's paying for almost everything – so maybe travelling with the old man isn't so bad after all. There are moments (like at the buffet breakfast at the hotel today – FIVE trips back to fill my plate!) when breaking my leg begins to feel like the best decision ever.

Did the Uffizi Gallery yesterday – queues were ridiculous and I would have been tempted to bail, but Dad was keen. Apparently queues are ten times worse in the summer holidays, so that's another win for the broken leg, which meant we could start travelling early – result!

Today: the Duomo (big main church – looks like St Paul's in London, but on steroids), and we decided (probably stupidly!) to try to go up the tower – 463 steps! We left my crutches at the bottom and I did it by leaning on Dad. Took ages (and A LOT of grumpy tourists queueing behind us), but worth it – the view from the top was amazing.

I check all the details. I read articles and travel blogs about Florence, to check the number of steps. I remember being there myself, twenty-five years ago: me and Gabe, young and invincible with love and the heat of that summer. The sweat on the back of my knees when we climbed the Duomo. Emerging from the cool of the narrow stone steps to the shameless heat at the viewing platform at the top.

Bloody hot here. Dad got sunburnt on the top of his head – said last time he was in Florence (back when the dinosaurs roamed the earth) he had hair (hard to imagine, I know).

Every night when Papabee, Teddy and I watch the SBS world news, I check the global weather report for the temperatures in Italy. It's so hot there – summer coming early. I picture Dougie in the crowded street, squinting into the Florentine sun as he looks up at the obscene bulge of the Duomo. He's more real to me, that Dougie, than whatever remains after the cremation. I can see him clearly, sitting on the steps around the edge of the Piazza della Signoria. There's a stain on the front of his t-shirt from where he and Gabe had gelato on the Ponte Vecchio. I can feel the glare of the sunlight coming off the polished stone steps.

The envelope is the most complicated part, because it has to be handwritten, not typed. I cut out the address from one of his previous letters to Sylvie, slip it inside a blank envelope, lay it on the brightly-lit iPad screen and then trace over his writing. It takes me two goes to get it right, so that the handwriting doesn't look hesitant. I've ordered Italian stamps online, and an ink-pad and mail franking stamp too. I know Sylvie probably won't even look at any of this, but I want to get it right. For two nights I sleep with the envelope under my mattress, like a teenage boy hiding porn. When I take it out on the third day, it's convincingly flattened and creased.

I remember helping Dougie make a pirate map for a homework project when he was in primary school: burning the edges and soaking it in weak tea to stain it brown.

The things we do for our children. The things we do to our children.

I make sure to bundle the letter in with some other things – a handout that her history teacher emailed me, about the Russian revolution; a newspaper clipping about the band Augie March, because she and Dougie used to listen to them all the time; a Philip Pullman book I bought for her at a second-hand bookshop.

In the ward, I hesitate for an instant before I pass them to her. It's one thing to keep the truth from her – we've been doing that ever since Dougie died, more than three weeks ago. But this is different, and tangible. In this artfully aged envelope, the lie has been committed to paper.

'These are for you,' I say, and hand the bundle over, and put the daily container of food on her bedside table.

She tosses the book down on the bed. 'I've read that one,' she says. 'Sue lent it to me last year.'

I pick it up again. 'Oh well. Maybe Teddy will enjoy it in a few years.'

She shrugs and puts the rest of the papers on the bedside table without looking at them. When she turns, her shoulder blades protrude. It hasn't occurred to me before that there's a reason they're called *shoulder blades*. That *blade* smuggled in, disguised as a metaphor, so familiar that I never noticed it at all, until confronted with the sharpness of my daughter's back.

I don't say anything about the letter. When I leave, the bundle of papers is still sitting untouched beside the bed.

The next day I try to keep my voice casual. 'What's the news from Dougie, in the letter?'

'You've probably heard it all already from Dad,' Sylvie says.

'I bet they have a different perspective. I hope Dad's not dragging Dougie into every church in Italy, like he did with me.'

She's turning away. She says nothing at all.

I never thought that I'd be grateful for the awesome self-absorption of the anorexic. But she makes the lie easy for us. She's too busy obsessing over herself to have time for anyone else. She isn't going to scrutinise me, or Dougie's letters. She's given us our alibi herself. She's given us our alibi: herself.

She's wearing a jumper that Dougie used to wear – a big grey V-neck, the wool all pilled now, unravelling at the wrists. From spending so much time in bed, she has a slightly balding spot at the back of her head, like a baby. Her skin is grey, and her lips are blue-rimmed and flaking.

Since Sylvie got sick, I see girls like her everywhere. It's like a kind of Wi-Fi that's been turned on in me, alert to those desperate girls and women. Some of them aren't even thin, but I can still tell. I notice the ones in cafés who shift their food around on their plate, and take forty minutes to eat a bowl of soup, leaving the bread untouched on the side. The ones who eat but then excuse themselves after each course, and go straight to the toilet. They're all around, these women, walking stiffly through their own lives, vigilant as ghosts. I put today's container of food on her bedside table – spanakopita, the layers of pastry like geological strata. I'm close enough to her now to smell her awful reek, like boiling whale blubber. It's the smell of protein wastage, fat burning. Ever since Sylvie got sick, I can't render fat from steak without gagging, because the smell is too close to Sylvie's breath. It reminds me of that old joke – the kind that Dougie would have called a Dad Joke:

'My dog's got no nose.'

'How does he smell?'

'Terrible.'

Now, as I sit back, I think: *My daughter's got no fat. How does she smell? Terrible.* I wish Gabe were here. We'd drive home from the hospital and close our bedroom door and I'd tell him my stupid joke and he'd understand.

'Has Dad called you lately?' I ask Sylvie.

I've warned Gabe about the letter, and told him what to say. Him and Dougie negotiating Florence's cobbled streets together, Dougie impatient on his crutches. Gabe sounded tired, but he didn't disagree with me. Didn't even blame me, when I told him I'd read Dougie's old letters, though I could hear the hesitation in his voice.

'Honey,' he said. 'Jesus. I know how much you're missing him' – and the *but* that was about to follow never came because I didn't let it, launching instead into the details of their travel.

'He rang yesterday,' Sylvie says. 'Said they're going OK.'

I feel a surge of gratitude to Gabe.

There's a pale stain on the right shoulder of Sylvie's jumper – probably some of the liquid food leaked when the nurses were flushing her feeding tube clean.

'Here,' I say. 'That jumper's grubby. Give it to me and I'll wash it.'

'I'm cold.'

'You're always cold.' That's why her skin's covered with a hazy layer of fur, standing out from her goose-pimpled skin. It's the body's response to having no fat to insulate it. 'Put your dressing gown on, then.'

'Fine,' she says. 'But bring it back when it's dry? It's my favourite.'

'I'll bring it back tomorrow.'

She makes sure the disconnected tube is tucked out of the way behind her ear, before she pulls the jumper up over her head. Her pyjama top rises with it, exposing her stomach and her bra – a tiny crop top, baggy over her absent breasts.

There's a drought on the mainland, the news each night full of pictures of bones in the red dust, and starving cattle, like hammocks of skin slung between bones. That's what I think of, when I see the jarring angles of Sylvie's hipbones and ribs.

She yanks her top down, but she caught me staring. And my face must show what I feel, because she looks angry, not just embarrassed.

'Jesus Christ,' I say. I know it's not fair to feel proprietary about her body. It belongs to her, for all that it grew in me. But I can't help this swell of disgust, and anger, and terror, all at once, when I see what she's done to herself, this ruined body, when Dougie's body has only just been dissected and burned.

'Nice, Mum,' she says. 'Really nice.'

'What do you want me to do?' I don't recognise my own voice – the shrillness in it. 'Do you want me to pretend that this is OK? Are you proud of what you've done to yourself?'

Sylvie

'Are you proud of what you've done to yourself?' Mum asks.

Proud. Proud?

See this bit here, where my hipbones poke out? I run my hands across the bones maybe fifty, sixty times a day, to check that they're still there. To measure them with my fingers, and see if they stick out more or less than yesterday. I wrap both arms around myself and strum my ribs like the strings of a guitar.

Proud?

I'm hiding. I'm hiding in these clothes – that old jumper of Dougie's, so big that the sleeves hang right down over my hands, and the neck falls off one shoulder. I'm hiding in this body, this pyre of bones.

I'm hiding. Don't look at me. Look for me. Don't look for me. Look at me.

I hold Dougie's letter. Since he went away, I always picture him at the Neck, because at the Neck we're all most ourselves, and Dougie most of all, always the first into the cold water, the first to catch a flathead from the dingy.

The Neck isn't a safe place – perhaps that's why we love it. In summer, the air is tight with bushfire smoke, and tiger-snakes unravel themselves to stretch across the hot gravel of the driveway. Something moves at the edge of your sight, and maybe it's just a bird setting the long grass shaking, or an echidna following its snout along the dirt, but you speed up anyway, sprinting towards the open places, the cleared roads. The sea is always watching, with its rips and its spiteful waves. The tide comes in quick, and can turn the headland into an island if you're not careful.

The Neck doesn't forget. It remembers the white invasion, and the decades of murder and violence. The attempt to corral Tasmania's entire indigenous population onto the natural prison of the Tasman Peninsula, beyond the Neck. The penal colony at Port Arthur, and then the shooting in 1996. The savage beauty of the whole peninsula.

If a child went missing at the Neck, you wouldn't find them half a day later, asleep in a grass meadow, like the children in fairy-tales. It isn't that kind of a place.

What would have happened, that summer at the Neck, if I'd tried to talk to Dougie? It was so hot that year. The wind smelled of fire – something was always burning, that summer. The water in the tanks was running low and the grass was scorched brown, except for one green patch where we hosed down our wetsuits. When I climbed the tree behind the house, black cockatoos took to the sky with their terrible human screams.

Teddy

When Dad's dad, Papa J, died a few years ago, people kept saying, *I'm sorry for your loss*, which made it sound like we'd left him on the bus or something. But he wasn't lost – we knew exactly where Papa J was: in a hole at the cemetery near his house in Sydney.

They had to use a digger to fill in the grave. We weren't meant to see that bit; after the speeches part of the funeral was finished and they'd put Papa J's coffin down into the hole, the priest walked us all to the car, so we could drive to the wake. But I looked back, while Mum and Dad were hugging people and talking, and I saw the gigantic pile of dug-up earth, with a tarpaulin stretched over it and held down with bricks on the corners. I saw the digger parked around the side of the toilet block, and a man in a bright orange vest standing next to it, smoking and looking bored while he waited for us to go. That's how I learned how much earth it takes to bury somebody: a whole digger-load.

We're not burying Dougie. Mum said she and Dad decided to have him cremated, because it's what he would have wanted. I don't think Dougie would want any of this – but I know why Mum and Dad aren't ready for the digger-load of dirt. A digger-load of dirt is too heavy to be anything except real. You can't ever take it back.

Dad Skypes us, the day after the cremation, and I ask him to show me what Dougie is now.

'It's not much to see, love,' Dad says, at the same time as Mum says, 'I've got to watch the risotto,' and goes back to the kitchen.

Dad goes off screen for a minute, and I hear him shuffling things around, then he comes back with a grey box, only as big as a PlayStation.

'What's it made of?' I ask.

'Polystyrene, I think.' He holds the box closer to the camera. It looks the same kind of stuff that an eski's made of, or the boxes of ice at the fish shop. Like if I pressed my fingernail into it, I'd leave a mark.

'Can you show me the inside?'

'It's all sealed up, Tedster.' He turns it sideways to show me the sticky-tape round the edge of the lid. 'I reckon it's best to keep it that way for the trip home, don't you think?'

I picture the box coming open on the plane, the ashes tipping everywhere when somebody opens the overhead locker. Bits of Dougie falling all over strangers.

'OK,' I say. 'How much does it weigh?'

Dad picks up the box again in both hands. I like that he takes my questions seriously. 'Not much,' he says. 'About the same as a great big dictionary.'

'Paperback or hardback?'

'Hardback.'

'OK,' I say again.

I think for a long time about that little grey box. I don't feel like Dougie's really inside that box, the same way time isn't really inside a clock. But if Dougie isn't in there, where's he gone?

When Dougie went into that little box, I thought the main bit of his dying was finished. I was wrong.

Nobody tells you that being dead just keeps on going. Of course I knew that already – I knew that once you're dead you're dead for good. But I didn't really get what it means – that now Dougie's dead, he's dead every day, always, and that means every single day is another day I walk past his closed bedroom door and think, *Still dead*, and get the milk out and see the photo on the fridge of Dougie at his grade 12 formal and think, *Still dead*. I never knew that even his old basketball, going flat in the corner of the driveway, would make me think, *Still dead*. Nobody ever tells you how much *Still dead* keeps happening.

I start to think maybe the problem is that we haven't had a funeral. I remember Papa J's funeral – Dougie looking sweaty in a tie, and Sylvie sitting next to me and crying, her hand scrunched tight around a tissue, which she ripped into a hundred little pieces.

I didn't cry that day. Papa J didn't feel much like a grandpa. He didn't feel much like anything because he hardly ever visited, and when he did, Sylvie was always his favourite. Grown-ups aren't really supposed to have favourites, or if they do, they're supposed to pretend they don't.

The only other funeral I've ever been to, apart from Papa J's, was for our goldfish, Spotty. He was our first goldfish to die, and we did a big funeral for him. We dug a hole in the garden, Dougie glued two icy-pole sticks together to make a cross for the grave, and Sylvie gave a little speech. I played 'Jingle Bells' on my clarinet – Dad said it should have been 'The Last Post', but I don't know that one, so I did 'Jingle Bells' instead.

But goldfish die all the time, it turns out, and they're actually kind of boring, so it was hard to be upset. By the time the last one died, a year go, Dougie just scooped it out of the tank and chucked it out the window into the lavender bush, and we hoped SausageDog wouldn't find it.

If I were Goldfish-Teddy, the whole world would end at the edges of my glass tank. And the tank would be enough, and the plastic castle would be enough. The stones on the bottom too. And because goldfish don't remember anything, it would always be now, and every day the same: water, tank, rocks. Water, tank, rocks. There'd be no remembering, and no surprises. And nobody could keep secrets from Goldfish-Teddy, because I could see through everything, a world made of glass and water. The light would come straight through.

I keep waiting to get used to Dougie being dead, the same way we all got used to the goldfish dying. I wait and wait, and when Mum isn't watching, I even test myself, by taking Dougie's photo off the fridge and staring at it, to see if it still makes me feel the same. It does – even after three weeks. It feels like a dream of falling, without the bit where you wake up knowing it was just a dream.

So I decide to do my own funeral for Dougie, so that his dying will have a finish to it. It'll have to be a secret funeral, because Mum doesn't ever seem to want to talk about Dougie any more. I don't want to tell my friends, not even Alasdair, because I'm worried they won't get it, because none of them have got dead brothers or nearly-dead sisters, so how could they understand about the Boneyard? And I can't tell Dad, either, because whenever he calls he asks me how I am, and I say, *Fine*, which is partly true and partly not true, and if I tell him about the funeral he might realise the not-true bit. And obviously I can't tell Sylvie, because not telling Sylvie anything about Dougie is my main job now.

So the only person I invite to the funeral is Papabee. He's the very best for secrets. When you're the youngest, like me, you don't get to have many secrets. The big kids are always quicker, smarter – they work everything out. I wear their hand-me-down clothes and I hear their hand-me-down stories, and if I ever have a secret, they're already there ahead of me. Like when I was six and I whispered to Dougie my big exciting secret, that I'd worked out that Santa isn't real, and he just said, 'No shit, Teddy,' and didn't even look away from his computer game. But Papabee's the very best at secret-keeping, because he forgets everything, so when you put a secret in him it stays there.

I make a cross out of icy-pole sticks, to mark the grave. I don't believe in God, but I do believe in crosses because I've seen them in lots of places. If I was going to believe in God, it'd have to be a God that I could see and feel, solid like a wooden cross. It'd have to be a God real enough to give you splinters.

Jesus is supposed to have died on a cross, and then he was dead in a cave like Dougie but came out again, alive. So I believe in caves, and not Jesus. And I don't believe in miracles like turning wine into water, or Jesus coming back to life. I only know about little miracles, like how you can float on the top of water. Dougie taught me that. In the sea at the Neck he put his hand under the back of my neck and his other hand under my knees and said *Go on, Teddy, just lie back.* So I did. Every time you float it's like the water's saying: *Trust me,* and then you do, and it does catch you, it actually does, every time like an actual miracle or some kind of trick or maybe it's the same thing.

I don't have anything to bury at the funeral, because Dougie's still in the box with Dad in London. But I think about the digger-load of dirt at Papa J's funeral, and I decide that maybe it's the digging and the dirt that counts, not what you bury. So on Saturday morning, when Mum's visiting Sylvie, Papabee and I choose a spot under the bushes at the very back of the garden, where Mum won't notice, and I use her trowel to make a hole, as far down as I can dig, until the ground gets too hard. Then I pat all the dirt back down, and poke the little cross into the top.

'Do you want to say something about Dougie?' I ask Papabee.

'Absolutely,' he says. 'Charming boy. An excellent chap, and solid spin bowler.' He looks around. 'Will he be joining us shortly?'

'Sort of.' I think of the box that Dad's going to bring home. Then I play 'Jingle Bells' on my clarinet, like at the goldfish funeral.

'Very festive,' says Papabee. 'A merry Christmas to you, dear boy.'

I squeeze his hand, and don't tell him that it's June. We stand like that for a long time. There are thin pink clouds resting on the mountain. I hold my clarinet in one hand, and Papabee's hand in my other one, and I try to fit it all into myself: this big sadness, bigger than the mountain, bigger than the sky.

Gabe

Heather from the coroner's office rings. 'I was hoping to talk you through the post-mortem results,' she says.

There ought to be a different ringtone for this. It doesn't seem right that a call to discuss my son's dissection can be announced by the same jaunty, generic ringtone as if it were Gill calling, or a market-researcher.

'Is now a good time?' Heather asks.

What would be a good time, I wonder, *to hear my son's post-mortem results?* I don't say it, of course. I make the usual polite noises. 'Yes, go on – please.'

'I have to stress that these are only the preliminary findings. Toxicology results will take a few weeks, as you know—'

'I know.'

'So what I've got today are the main items. I'll be emailing the results through to you shortly, but I wanted to talk them through with you first. Nobody needs something like this just landing in their inbox.'

When all this is over, I'll write her a card, to thank her for all these small acts of thoughtfulness. Then I realise: this is never going to be over.

'Not surprisingly, there was evidence of a pulmonary oedema,' she says, 'which is fluid in the lungs. That's consistent with death by drowning.'

'Like we expected, then.'

She pauses for a moment. 'It's not quite that simple, I'm afraid. It's not common, but there are other things that can cause pulmonary oedema. Head injuries, for example.

185

A serious head injury can bring about pulmonary oedema over the next few hours.'

'He didn't have a few hours.'

'We don't know that for certain, Mr Jordan. His body wasn't recovered for thirteen hours after the flood. The police pathologist took his temperature then, but, in water, the body loses heat about twice as fast as it otherwise would. And the cold water also simulates rigor mortis, which is another indicator that's used to assess time of death. In those conditions, there's no way to accurately confirm the time he died.'

'But you heard what the guide and the others told the police: the water came up fast. You can't tell me that he was alive for long enough for fluid to build up in his lungs.'

'Drowning seems the most likely explanation, I agree. But we can't exclude the alternative – that he might have been alive for some time longer. His body was recovered from a different cavern, deeper in the cave system. If he was alive when he was carried or swam downstream, then there could have been some higher ground, or an air pocket, somewhere. And the coroner has to explore the possibilities, because there could be implications, in reviewing the response, and the approach of the rescue teams.'

'Are you trying to tell me that he didn't die quickly?'

'As I've said, the particular circumstances of Douglas's death make timing extremely difficult to confirm.'

'What exactly are you saying?'

'It's up to you, Mr Jordan, how much you want to go into this.'

'I want to know.'

'I'm afraid that a number of the injuries appear to be ante-mortem.'

'Before he died, you mean?'

'Exactly. The small abrasions on his hands were certainly ante-mortem. But the forensic pathologist also flagged the wounds at the back of the head – the report says: *Two jagged contusions, measuring 80 and 120 mm, each with surrounding subdural haematoma.* That's bruising – bleeding under the skin. That's consistent with an injury that's happened before death. It's distinct from lividity – the discolouration that you might have seen on his face.'

'The chaplain at the hospital said something about that.'

'That's right,' Heather says. 'Lividity is from blood settling, after death. As with most bodies retrieved from water, Douglas was found face-down.'

There's a rustling of paper.

'There was only one actual fracture,' she says. 'The femur – though it wasn't possible to ascertain whether this happened before death.'

'Femur – that's leg, right?'

'Sorry, yes – the upper leg.'

'The broken leg – which one is it?'

Another pause, another rustle of paper.

'Right leg,' she says. 'Why?'

'Nothing.' I have to consciously loosen my jaw so that I can speak again. 'Go on, please. There must be other clues? Other things the doctor could tell?'

'Nothing conclusive. Some of the things that they'd normally look for, to indicate drowning, were made irrelevant by the fact that the body was submerged for so long.' She goes on – something about water in pleural cavities, and diatoms in the bone marrow. But all I can think of is Dougie's broken leg, and our lie.

'We'll get the diatom test back next week,' she says. 'But as I said, it won't be conclusive.'

'So you're telling me you still don't know how he died.'

'I'm saying we can't know for certain.'

'But his death wasn't instant. Is that what you're saying?

187

There was time – enough time for those head wounds. Perhaps the broken leg too.'

'It seems that way,' says Heather.

Gill. How can I tell her this? How can I even raise the prospect of him huddled there, perhaps for hours, injured, with the black water rising? If there was some kind of hidden cave or air pocket, some ledge, I have to keep it from Gill. Dougie didn't survive that place, and nor will she.

I ring her as soon as my breath is steady enough. I talk her through the results – head injuries; signs consistent with drowning – but not the details. I've been worried that she'll ask questions, see through my vagueness, but she asks nothing. This is how it goes, us handing each other lies like a children's game of pass-the-parcel: me concealing things from her, and her from Sylvie.

'There's one other thing,' I say.

'I don't know if I can hear any more,' she says. 'Please.'

'Listen,' I tell her. 'You were right about his leg.'

'What do you mean?'

'He did break his leg. The same one: the right leg. The thigh bone, too. Just like you told Sylvie.'

A long silence.

'Are you still there?'

'Yes,' she says.

'What does it mean? How did you know?' There are 206 bones in the adult human body, Teddy proudly told me last year, when he learned it at school. 206. Of all those hundreds, how did Gill pick the right bone? Did our lie invoke this?

'How did you know?' I ask again.

Gill

Of course I knew, I think, after Gabe has said goodbye. His news about the broken leg hardly even surprised me. I wanted to say: *I told you already.* Dougie's my son. I made those bones – they grew inside me.

The best lies are close to the truth. My own lie to Sylvie just got closer.

And it's working. When I go to the hospital the next morning, Sylvie asks me about Dougie again. Before, a whole visit could pass without her saying a word.

'Dougie OK?' she says, her book still on her lap.

'Better every day, Dad says.'

'How much longer will he stay over there? Dad, I mean.'

'As long as Dougie needs him. Work said Dad can work remotely for a while.' That's true enough – his boss has been great. There it is again, that neat mix of truth and falsehood. 'And Dougie couldn't travel alone – not the way he is right now, that's for sure.'

She nods and looks back down to her book.

I'm a good liar – she's made me one. *It's only for a few days*, we said to her, when she first went into hospital. *We'll find a way to help you. You'll be better soon.* Did I believe that, then?

She has no way of finding out, I reassure myself, as I walk back to the car. There's no internet in Paediatrics 3, and no phones except the ward landline, supervised by the nurses. Not even fresh air can get into that ward. Louise and the rest of the medical team have agreed not to say anything until Gabe's back. The anorexic patients are kept separate, to stop them from competing with another. And Sylvie doesn't really have friends any more, who could visit her and give the game away. Her friends from school all drifted off, after the first year or so of her sickness. I can't blame them. Three years is a long time, and never more so than in your teens. Even Sue's daughter, Ella, who's more family than a friend, now only goes to the hospital very occasionally, always with Sue. I suspect Sue drags her in, and while I appreciate the effort, I don't blame Ella for her reluctance. The girl in the hospital bears no relation to the girl Ella grew up with.

I see Sylvie's friends from school sometimes, around town, holding hands with boyfriends, texting on their phones. They've rolled their uniform skirts at the waist, to make them shorter. They always look guilty when they see me.

'Hi, Mrs Jordan,' they say, shooting a look over my shoulder at the waiting cluster of their friends. 'How's Sylvie?'

'Oh, you know,' I reply. 'The same.'

Sometimes they make vague promises to visit her in hospital soon; sometimes they offer excuses: 'Sorry it's been ages. I've been so busy with school. And hockey.' I never prolong their awkwardness – I've learned to smile broadly and make an excuse of my own, and dash off. It isn't their fault. What would they talk about, now, with Sylvie? Their lives don't intersect in any way. Sylvie's cut herself off from all of that. From everything, and everyone.

Her closest school friend, Esra, visited Sylvie a lot in the first year. Then I came across Esra in the hospital corridor after a visit, crying, facing the wall, her face pressed against a poster about shingles vaccinations. I stopped, unsure whether she'd want to be seen, but she turned before I could make a choice. She stared at me, wiping her cheeks with a fist balled inside her sleeve.

'It's all right,' I said. 'Sweetie. It's all right.'

She shook her head. 'It's not though, is it.'

I exhaled. 'No. But it will be.'

'But what if it's not?'

We stared at each other, under the merciless fluorescent lights of the hospital corridor. She wiped her face again, I squeezed her shoulder, and she left. I never saw her again, after that.

Sue calls on Thursday. 'We're going to the Neck on the weekend. D'you want to come?'

'Sorry,' I say automatically. 'We can't make it.'

'You wouldn't even need to drive. Ella's at music camp for the weekend, and Nathan's got some party at his flat. So it's just me and Dan. We can fit you and Teddy in our car. Even Papabee, if he's up for it.'

Teddy would be alone in the boys' room, underneath Dougie and Nathan's empty bunks. No footsteps creaking above us at night from the girls' room upstairs – that will be empty too. Draped over a railing in the laundry, Dougie's wetsuit, with the shape of his body still in it.

'I don't think I should be away from Sylvie for that long,' I say.

'Nonsense. It's two days. We'll be an hour's drive from the hospital. She'll understand you need a break. And it's not like she talks to you anyway.'

'I'd like to come. I'd love it. But I—'

'It'd be good for Teddy,' Sue says, cutting me off. 'He can have a last swim, before real freezing weather settles in. We can take the boat out, do some fishing. He hasn't been down there for ages. He can bring a friend if he wants. That weird kid with the eyebrows?'

'Alasdair,' I say. 'But we just can't this weekend – sorry.

And I have to dash – got a meeting with the dietitian at the hospital in twenty minutes.'

It doesn't matter that what I said about the meeting is true. Sue still knows me well enough to know that I have slammed the conversation shut like a door.

I close my eyes and picture the Neck. Even though it's months since I've been there, I can still see it perfectly clearly. I could assemble the beach, grain by grain, stone by stone, each in its rightful place. Set every bleached limb of driftwood into its proper location on the sand.

Just down the road from the house is the tessellated pavement. It's famous – in summer, tourists are decanted from huge coaches to take photos and leave again. The plateau of stone lies almost at sea level, and through some geological quirk it formed into a grid of squares, a game of hopscotch that reaches all the way to the sea. I've always loved the tessellated pavement, its strict geometry. When the tide goes out each square becomes its own small, sharply delineated pool. When the kids were younger we could spend hours there, the children squatting over the rock pools, or jumping from square to square.

Once, at the Neck, Gabe caught me licking my own wrist.

'What are you doing?' he asked, laughing.

'I can taste salt,' I said. I hadn't even swum that day. It was just the Neck, the beach, the salt air. 'Try it.' I held out my arm to him, and he did, his tongue warm on my skin.

'I always love your recipes,' he said, moving his kisses up my arm.

Some days, Dan drove the trailer down to the beach with the dinghy, and we took the kids out fishing, padded and fat in their bright orange life jackets. On those nights we'd eat the flathead they caught, always too small to be satisfying, and full of long pine-needle bones. Sometimes the kids would gather mussels, wrenched off the rocks at low tide.

They were my favourite meals of all: no good for recipes, because they're too simple. To capture meals like that, the recipe would need to begin at dawn, with the loading up of the trailer. The sand in everything, even the beds and the sandwiches. The recipe would have to include all the noises: the sound of the kids riding their bikes in circles around the barbecue while Dan and Gabe cook; the radio propping open the kitchen window so they can hear Radio National. The sound of tennis balls pinging off the water tanks when we play cricket round the side of the house, and everyone yelling *Sausage!* in unison when somebody hits a four and Sausage gets carried away and harries the ball all the way into the blackberry bushes that grow out of control along the edge of the property. The recipe would have to include what comes after the meal, too: the washing up, and the board games, and those moments when the kids are asleep, or at least out of earshot, when we finish the half-warm bottles of white wine, and I lean into Gabe and smell the sea and the barbecue smoke on him.

I should have tried, somehow, to write a recipe that could fit in all of that. But I didn't know how – and now that's all finished with anyway. I can't imagine ever going there again.

When Sylvie first got sick, I wondered what we'd done to deserve so much suffering. Now, after three years of her sickness, and with Dougie gone, I look back on all those years at the Neck, and I wonder how I ever dared to think that we deserved so much happiness.

I can't write a recipe to capture those days at the Neck. Instead, I keep writing my own secret recipes. I serve them, daily, to Teddy and Papabee, but their titles I confide only to my notebook. *Roast beetroot salad for the week after your son's post-mortem results are released. Three simple soups for*

the days immediately following your son's death. My job has always involved writing recipes for particular occasions. If I went through my old books, or the box where Gabe keeps all my newspaper cuttings, the titles follow the same pattern: *Casseroles to warm the winter evenings. Three seasonal salads to put a spring in your step. Quick weeknight eggplant pasta.* So these new meals aren't such a change – it's just that the occasions are different.

I think these new recipes might have started with the sweet tea that everyone kept offering us, in those first days. *For the shock*, they all said. We must've drunk gallons of the stuff. It didn't make any difference, as far as I could tell, but the ritual of it got me thinking about the ways people have always had recipes for specific days, particular milestones. Christmas pudding; wedding cakes; my friend Esther making challah bread each Thursday, for the Sabbath. The startling red of Tiet canh, blood soup, when Gabe and I were once in Vietnam at Lunar New Year.

So I navigate these formless days with recipes. I cook for Teddy and Papabee, and for Dougie and Sylvie and Gabe, who aren't here to eat what I make. I cook and I write and I cook and I write. *Quiche for the day after your son's cremation. Cake for your daughter's birthday, which she will not eat.*

Teddy

Before I go into the hospital, I try to remember all the things I'm not supposed to know (Sylvie trying to kill herself; the twenty per cent) and all the things I'm not supposed to say (Dougie being dead; the secret funeral; Mum making more and more weird food at home). I go through the ward and count the rexiles: four today. Four's bad: it's better when there are more, because of the twenty per cent.

Sylvie doesn't say anything except for 'Hi,' which is bad, and boring, but also a relief, because at least that way I don't have to tell her any lies. She's wearing a singlet and pyjama trousers, and when she turns around to get another book from the bedside table, her back shows all the bones and the tight strings where muscles used to be. Dad took the back off his old watch once and showed me how it worked, all the little metal cogs and bits. Sylvie's just like that now – all the inside bits on the outside.

A nurse comes in, and Sylvie holds out her arm for the blood pressure machine without even being asked, because it happens every few hours. The nurse says, 'How's school, Teddy?' to me, and 'That'll do nicely' to Sylvie, when she's checked the machine. After she's written down her notes and gone, the silence feels even bigger than it did before.

I go into the bathroom. I don't even need a wee – I just go there because I want a break from Sylvie, because her not-talking gets very noisy. So I go into the bathroom and sit on the loo for a bit. Then I feel bad about hiding from her in the bathroom – *it's not her fault she's sick*, Mum and Dad and the doctors are always telling me. So I decide to write her a message, something she can find later, as a surprise, and because there are things I can say in writing that I can't say when I'm in the room with her and all her bones. I take her toothpaste, smear some on my finger, and squish it against the mirror. I wait for a while, wondering what to write. *I love you*, maybe, but she knows that already, and I'm embarrassed to imagine nurses or cleaners reading it if they go into the bathroom. I want to tell Sylvie something she doesn't already know. And not one of the things that people kept writing in cards, the first time she went into hospital. *Get Well Soon. Thinking of You. Sorry to hear you've been unwell.* There weren't any cards, the second time, or the time after that, or the time after that. People ran out of things to say – all the easy words were used up.

I stand in front of the mirror and try to think what words Sylvie actually needs. I want to write something that's true. In the end, I write: *Don't die.* I really mean it. And it's short, which is good because making the letters on the mirror is harder than I thought, and I've used up half a tube of toothpaste by the time I get to the *e.* I feel bad for the cleaners, knowing they'll have to scrub the mirror clean, but I hope they'll understand. This isn't graffiti like at school: *JT WAS HERE* or all the cocks and balls scribbled on the lockers. This is important. You only have to look at Sylvie, wearing her bones on the outside, to see she needs this message.

When we visit the next day she doesn't even say whether she saw it – she doesn't say anything. Mum and Papabee are with me so I'm embarrassed to ask and, anyway, Sylvie's still busy not-talking.

Gabe

When I did my PhD in fluid mechanics, I wrote a whole chapter on egg whites. Then I met Gill, and she used to joke that my egg whites chapter was proof that we were suited: *We're both food writers, basically,* she said. I liked the idea, but I knew it wasn't true. I was never interested in the eggs themselves. I was interested in the forces: the shear rate; the viscoelastic properties; the way that egg white can simultaneously behave like a fluid or a solid. I liked the clarity of the scientific model: hypothesis; experiment; results.

Later, I got a job as a research physicist. It's never made me much money, but it's always been interesting work, with good people. Hypothesis; experiment; results. When the kids came along, with their endless questions about how things work – *Why does rain fall down and not up? What makes the wind blow?* – I enjoyed being able to give them real answers.

But I don't know how to disassemble the events of Dougie's death and make them into an answer. I go back to the British Library, and spend hours researching water catchment areas; runoff; the different absorptive capacities of limestone and clay. I go to the Wellcome Centre Library with the print-out of Dougie's post-mortem results, and spend hours translating them into a language that I can understand. The Centre has an exhibit about the human body, and one of the glass cases holds a pair of cross-sectioned lungs. I stand there for an hour, maybe more, trying to picture the bronchi and bronchioles filling with water. I think of what Teddy asked me about the box of ashes: *How much does it weigh?* I wish I could reach through the glass and pick up those lungs and feel their lightness. Compare them with a waterlogged pair. Heft the difference in my hands. Hypothesis; experiment; result.

I'm supposed to be working – my boss has been sympathetic, but there's a limit, and I can't afford to take any more unpaid leave. I do just enough work to stay on top of things, but my real job now is Dougie. I don't sleep much. I take my laptop to bed and spend the night descending into the endless caverns of the internet – meteorological archives; articles from scientific journals about diatoms, the algae sometimes found in the bone marrow of drowning victims; potholing club message boards where cavers argue about the relative merits of different brands of gear. I buy a cheap inkjet printer, a pile of papers mounting next to the toaster.

People talk about 'heavy rain', but I'd never really understood how heavy it can be. In article after article, I learn the heft of water, the solid weight of rainfall. A cave system has what's called a 'gathering ground' – a catchment area from which water will run into the caves. A single inch of rainfall adds up to 27,154 gallons for each acre. Above the limestone karst of the Smith–Jackson caves, the soil is clay, which means it doesn't soak up much rain. Instead, it shrugs off water like an oilcloth. The gathering ground for the Smith–Jackson System is at least 1,700 acres. The nearest Meteorological Office station records that between midnight and 2am on the morning that Dougie died, 1.4 inches of rain fell. That's 64,626,520 gallons. Add to that whatever water spilled over the lip of the Lipscombe Reservoir – thousands of gallons, conservatively. And all that water – all that weight – had to go somewhere. It found its way down, easing through gaps and cracks, coaxing open fissures in the earth, until it poured into the Smith–Jackson System.

So I learn that Dougie's death didn't happen in the caves at all. It happened upstream, hours earlier. It happened between four and four forty-five that morning, when the wall of the reservoir was breached, and the spilled water began to soak through the layers of rock towards the caves. By five that morning, while Dougie was still sleeping, probably in bed with Rosa, his death had been decided. At eight am, while they were on the coach heading towards the caves, his death was already a done deal.

Or maybe it happened earlier: when the rain first began to fall on the reservoir at midnight; when the wind turned northerly the day before, driving the thick band of clouds down from the Pennines. Or earlier: when the school decided on the excursion; when Dougie decided to take a year overseas; when an engineer decreed the height of the reservoir wall. It becomes a *reductio ad absurdum* that takes me all the way back to the moment Dougie was born, his birth containing his own death.

And the question I'm grappling with has become one of those simple maths problems from primary school: *If a coach arrives at a cave with twelve passengers, and leaves with eleven, what is X? If a family has five members, and one is in hospital and another is dead, how many people are in the family?*

Much as I hated the idea of a post-mortem, it still isn't enough. I want them to get the excavators in, take the whole cave system apart. I want every adult and child on the trip interviewed, twice, by the police. The coach that took them there dismantled, piece by piece. Each rope untwisted to its separate filaments. The water strained, each pebble counted.

At first I email articles and links to Gill, sometimes several times a day. *This one's interesting re the speed of flash floods*, I write. *See the link for the cached BBC weather report.* But

Gill never mentions them, and when I ask her, she's vague.

'I haven't had a chance to get to them yet,' she says. 'Had a meeting with Sylvie's cardiac specialist today. And I haven't managed to do a sweep of Papabee's flat for at least a week – God knows what's growing in his fridge by now.'

I ought to be there to help her. She's doing it all herself: scrambling to stay on top of hospital and school runs; feeding Teddy and Papabee and not feeding Sylvie; and also somehow staying on top of her own work, and the increasingly elaborate lie.

It's been three and a half weeks, and we still haven't told Sylvie the truth. Worse than that: Gill's told her Dougie and I are travelling together. She's given Sylvie a letter that's supposed to be from Dougie. The lie is growing bigger and I can hardly keep up.

'You've left Florence by now, OK?' Gill says to me. 'Remember that, when you call her. I'll put it all in the next letter. You've taken the ferry across to Cephalonia. It's been hot there – high-twenties every day.'

I look around my cramped flat, the white-grey London sky outside.

'Is this mad?' I ask her. 'Is this whole thing mad?'

The whole situation seems so far-fetched already – Dougie dead; Sylvie in hospital; me on the other side of the world with my son's ashes in a box – that I can't tell any more what's normal, what's acceptable.

'Are we making it more complicated than it needs to be?' I ask.

'I don't know how to make it simple, if *simple* means Sylvie dead.'

I can't argue with that. *Sylvie dead* stops all debate. It's the place that my mind won't allow itself to approach.

'You should ring her tonight,' Gill continues. 'She misses you, you know.'

Does she? Is Sylvie even capable of thinking beyond herself, that ever-shrinking orbit of her attention? It's the nature of anorexics to be self-absorbed. If anyone could have got through to her, it would have been Dougie, but his letters went unanswered.

'I'll ring her tomorrow,' I promise Gill.

Every few days I call Sylvie on the ward phone, but the conversations are always stilted. She didn't want to talk to me when I was at home, and my being here hasn't changed that. She asks about Dougie, and I keep my replies brief, not wanting to sink deeper into the quicksand of the lie. 'He's on the mend,' I say. 'Leg still really painful, but he's not whinging too much.' I have excuses prepared in case she asks to speak to Dougie: *I left him in town when I came back to the hotel – even with a broken leg, he's got more energy than me!* Or: *He's not up yet – he was drinking with some Canadian lads we met last night. God knows what time he came in.* But I don't need any of my excuses – she hardly talks at all. Calling her from England is mainly a very expensive way of talking to myself.

'I miss you, sweetheart,' I say to her. I wonder whether it's really her I miss, or just the girl she used to be before she got sick. Before she began hating us for refusing to let her die.

'I should go,' she says. 'I think somebody else wants the phone. Tell Dougie hi from me.'

The truth is that I don't look forward to those phone calls any more than she does. I picture her bony hands holding the phone, but it's Dougie's hands I'm seeing. I'll do anything to keep her alive, but it's even more painful now that I've seen the scratches and the broken fingernails on Dougie's hands that show how hard he fought to live. He won't get to do any of the things that he planned, or that I imagined for him. The Engineering degree he was going to start next year, and the career that would follow. Marriage, maybe, and kids. All of it.

Staring out the window, with the phone in my hand, I realise that I no longer have those sorts of hopes for Sylvie. My thoughts never get beyond the next weigh-in, the next ward-round. I don't wish for great things for her any more – just more days.

*Roast beetroot salad for the week after
your son's post-mortem results are released*

Preheat the oven to 190°. Set one beet aside, and
chop the others into hefty chunks. In a roasting
tray, stir the chopped beets with sea salt and a
liberal dousing of olive oil, and roast for about
40 minutes, until they're sticky and seeping with
black juice.

Drain the preserved lemon well and dice finely.
Toss with the roasted beets, throwing in a
handful of roughly torn basil. Add a good dash
of balsamic vinegar, half a teaspoon of ground
coriander, and ground pink peppercorns (add
more than you think you need, if only for the
satisfying rasp of the grinding itself).

Take the single beet that you left unroasted, and
a large radish. Slice them into rounds, as finely
as you can, to scatter on the salad. You can use a
mandolin, if you have one. Otherwise, just slice
them as thinly as your knife and your courage
permit – thin enough that if you press your
finger against a sliver, you'll see your fingerprint
through the radish's translucent flesh. Don't
think about scalpels.

Gill

When Teddy's asleep I settle down in the study to write the second letter.

I've hardly written any letters for years – these days it's all emails, or texts, or cards on special occasions. For years Gabe and I even resisted doing a Christmas round-robin letter. We used to roll our eyes reading those middle-class litanies of achievements, the boasts disguised as self-deprecation.

> *This year Clem sat his grade 6 clarinet exam, and we were proud (and relieved!) that he received an A, as he didn't seem to do much practice! Lucinda is representing Queensland in the Under-18 netball team, and next year will be Head Girl – now, if we could only persuade her to tidy her room...*

After Sylvie and her sickness had swallowed up the last of our free time, we finally gave in, but we tried to keep our Christmas letters short: important news, one or two anecdotes. I used to find myself staring at my laptop screen and envying those other families with their normal news, their normal lives. For three years, our main news was that Sylvie was doing her utmost to die. *Sylvie remains unwell*, I used to write, *and is still in hospital, but we're hopeful that next year will be better.* How could any letter ever tell the truth about that?

These new letters are easier. I open a fresh document and start.

Dear Sylve,

*The rest of our time in Florence was great. Went
to the Galleria dell'Accademia. Kind of funny to
queue up for so long to see the statue of David
when literally every shop and street stall is selling
magnets and postcards and assorted David crap
(resisted temptation to buy Mum a novelty David
apron with fig leaves over his junk). Thought I'd
reached David-saturation-point – but actually it was
pretty amazing when we finally got to him. Crazy
how Michelangelo managed to make marble look so
much like flesh.*

*Then: south on the trains (thank God for podcasts –
can only admire the view for so long...) all the way
to the bottom of Italy and across to Greek islands.
Arrived at Cephalonia this morning, after a whole
night on the ferry from Brindisi. Two American
guys on the boat had guitars (I learned at Easter
that anywhere there are backpackers, there's always
at least one guy with a guitar, who usually can
play Stairway to Heaven and nothing else...). We all
stayed up most of the night (not Dad, obvs) out on
deck.*

*Coming towards the islands, the colour of the water
is ridiculous. Makes the water at the Neck look like
dishwater!*

I check the ferry schedules online, and download the train
timetable from Florence to Brindisi. I know Sylvie has no
way to check any of this stuff, but it matters to me. I need to
get this right. I even dig out our old atlas from the bookshelf

in Sylvie's room, and trace the journey down to Brindisi, in the heel of Italy's boot, and then across to Cephalonia by sea. Trailing my finger across the map, I close my eyes and feel the slight churning of the ferry's engine. I taste diesel fumes and salt.

Gabe

The doorbell rings. At first I can't even place that loud buzzing sound – in my weeks here, nobody's rung the bell for this flat. I've had no deliveries, no visitors. The insistent buzzing comes again, before I work out that it's the doorbell and run down the three flights of stairs.

It's Rosa, Dougie's girlfriend, holding her good arm up across her forehead to keep the rain off her face.

'Hi,' she says.

'Rosa.' I pause. 'How are you?'

A few raindrops have settled on her eyelashes – or she's been crying. She's no longer wearing a sling, but her injured arm is still encased in plaster.

She shrugs. 'You know.' She gestures over her shoulder at the rain. 'Wet.'

'Sorry. Come in – please.'

She follows me up the stairs to my flat. In the living room I go to help her off with her jacket, given the cast on her arm, but she doesn't notice, or pretends not to, and manages it herself, clumsily. She tosses the jacket on the table, and I think of all the hundreds of times that Gill and I used to pick up Dougie's school blazer from wherever he'd chucked it when he came home.

'Can I help you with something?' I sound like a waiter, or a salesman in a car showroom.

'I don't know. Probably not. I was out this way, so I just thought I'd come. I wasn't even sure if you'd still be here.'

'I'm staying until the inquest,' I say. 'Things to do. You know.'

She nods, and I wait. But she doesn't seem to want to

talk – about Dougie or anything else. She walks around the living room picking things up and putting them down again.

'These aren't my things,' I say. 'All the stuff – it came with the flat.'

Am I worried that she'll judge me for those generic trinkets – the Ikea prints on the wall; the mirrored lamp; the tacky coffee table book called *Cats of the Greek Islands*. Actually, I like that book. I like flicking through it, imagining a world in which something could be as simple as that. A cat. A blue painted door. A pot of geraniums.

'Oh shit,' she says.

She's looking at the rope, roughly bundled on the couch. At first I think that it's freaked her out because she doesn't want to be reminded of the flood. But she's looking from the rope to the ceiling, and back again, and I see the exposed beam up there and realise what she's thinking.

'Christ,' I say. 'It's not for that.'

She's taken a step back, towards the door. 'I mean, I know it must be hard. I get it – I do. It's hard enough for me. And when it's your son – I can't imagine. But—'

'Jesus, no, I swear. I'm not planning on topping myself.' I'm laughing now, because it's all so absurd, having to reassure this girl, whom I hardly know, that I'm not actually going to kill myself.

'That's for the inquest,' I say. 'I ordered the same rope that they used in the cave – for research.'

I'm not sure whether this explanation is reassuring. Rosa stands with her good arm crossed over the cast, her eyes still shifting between the rope, the beam and me.

'I'm trying to find out all the details of what happened,' I continue. 'What went wrong.'

'How does that help?'

'Knowing the details?'

'No,' she says. 'Though that's another question, I suppose. But the rope – how does that help?'

'It gives me a feel for what happened. Literally, I suppose.'

She nods and moves a little further into the room. 'You're sure the rope's not for anything else? You promise?'

'I promise. I couldn't do it to Gill and the other kids, for one thing.' It's true. That's the relief and burden of family. 'Anyway, if I were just going to hang myself, I'd get some cheap rope from a hardware store. Not that one – that particular rope cost me a fortune.'

She's close enough to the rope now to flip over the price-tag, still tied around one end of the rope, and makes a whistling shape with her mouth. 'Worth it?'

'Who knows?' I want to take the rope from her, hide it away somewhere, but the couch is between us, and it's too late. 'Sorry – I wasn't expecting you. I wouldn't have had the rope out if I'd known you were coming. I'm sure you don't want to be reminded.'

'It's OK,' she says, a bit too quickly. 'I don't remember. It doesn't remind me of anything.'

'Why are you here?' It sounds more abrupt than I'd intended, so I add, 'Do you want tea? Or coffee?'

'Tea would be nice. Thanks.'

I put the kettle on, and its loud rattle takes the edge off the silence. She sits on the arm of the couch, but she's still staring around the room, not hiding her curiosity. Her eyelashes are white, her eyebrows too. Skin white and blue like the inside of an oyster shell.

Why did Murphy save her, and not Dougie? It's a question I've tried not to ask. Perhaps she was closest to the exit. Perhaps Murphy saw she wasn't as strong a swimmer as Dougie (all those years at the Neck, in and out of the sea). Maybe because she's a woman – does that old seafaring rule about women and children apply to caving? I don't know –

209

don't want to know, because then I'd have to admit to myself that I wish it were her in the box of ashes, and not Dougie. And that seems a terrible thing to think while she's sitting here, so small and pale, her arm still in a cast. *None of this is her fault*, I remind myself.

'I don't really have anything else to do, at the moment,' she says. 'You know – while I'm off work.' She looks at me. 'Do you mind me coming here? I mean, are you busy?'

I'm not sure how to answer that. It's true that emails are mounting in my inbox from work. Then there are those other tasks that are harder to explain: maps to scour, and articles and meteorological forums to read.

'Not really,' I say, opening the box of tea bags. 'Not right this instant, anyway.'

'Is this normal?' she asks, once I've brought the drinks to the coffee table. She gestures at the rope. 'I mean, do you have to do this? Isn't this the police's job?'

'The coroner's, actually,' I say. 'But I just want to be sure—' My voice trails off. I change the subject. 'How are things at the school?'

'You know they want to name a boat after him?'

'The headmaster told me.'

'So what do you think?' she asks.

'Honestly? I don't really care. It doesn't seem important. I suppose if it makes them feel better, I don't mind.'

'I think it's a stupid idea,' she says. She swings her legs, kicking her heels against the couch. 'A boat, for fuck's sake. It's bad luck, for one thing. I mean – he drowned.'

I smile, but she apologises anyway. 'Sorry. Do you find yourself making bad jokes like that, since he died?'

'Dougie would say my jokes have always been bad. You know: *Dad jokes.*'

'I don't seem to find anything very funny any more. Except for inappropriate things that probably shouldn't be funny, like the idea of those honking poshos at the school naming a boat after Dougie.'

I put down my mug. 'What was he like?' I ask her.

'You're asking me? He was your son.'

'I know. And I know what he was like at home. But over here – what was he like? With you?'

She's quiet for a long while.

'He was full of energy. He always wanted to be doing something. Sometimes on weekends I wanted to just take it easy – you know, watch TV and sleep in. Maybe go to the pub. But he always wanted to go somewhere, see something. Go to Bristol, go to Bath, go into town. It made me feel lazy.' She bites down, hard, on her bottom lip. 'I don't know if it was because he knew he was only here for a little while—' She shakes her head immediately. 'Not like that,' she says, watching me. 'I just meant, he knew he was only in England for a year. I don't have any crazy idea that he knew what was going to happen. I don't believe in any of that stuff.'

'I don't either,' I say. 'Though since he died, I'd quite like to. I get it now, why people suddenly turn religious.'

I've always liked churches – I never believed in any of it, but I like the architecture, the paintings, the history. When Gill and I travelled around Europe together in our mid-twenties, I used to drive her crazy, wanting to go inside every old church that we passed. I used to like craning my neck back to stare at the stained glass, and squatting to read the gravestones used as flagstones in the aisles.

Here in London, I've spent a long time sitting in the front pew of the empty church near High Barnet station. Yesterday I even slipped fifty pence into the locked box at the side to buy a candle to light. I don't believe in prayers, but I lit the tiny tea-light candle anyway. I wasn't sure how long to stay and watch it burn; how long I'd have to wait before I'd had my fifty-pence worth of comfort. I think of Rosa's question about the expensive rope. The boat that the school wants to name after Dougie. The price of our consolations.

'What about you?' I ask. She's sitting with both hands wrapped around her mug, holding it in front of her like a begging bowl. 'How are you doing, really?'

She scrunches her nose. 'You've got your own things to deal with.'

'We're dealing with the same thing, aren't we? More or less, anyway. I think Dougie probably would have wanted me to help, if I could.'

She stares straight back at me. 'I could say the same thing. But what are we supposed to do?'

What can anyone do, with death? That's what makes it death: the incommensurability of it. It's done, and nothing she or I can do can make any difference to that hulking fact.

I'm thinking of the candle in the church. I'm thinking that maybe that's what prayer is: what we do when we don't believe, but we do it anyway.

'They're offering me therapy,' Rosa says. 'At the school. But it's with the matron. She's qualified as a therapist too, apparently, but it's too weird trying to talk to her about Dougie, when usually she's the one I'm sending kids to if they've been scratching their heads and I need her to check for nits. I have to see her in the dining hall every mealtime, slurping her tea. I can't talk to her about any of this stuff.' She looks around the room again. 'I'd much rather be busy. I feel like I might be going crazy, just hanging around the school. And the whole place will be shut up in a few more weeks, when the kids go home for the holidays.'

I hadn't thought about that. The holidays are different in England, like the seasons. At home it must be getting cold now. Teddy will be wearing his winter uniform, the sleeves of the jumper too long, like all the rest of his hand-me-downs from Dougie. Papabee will be leaving a trail of gloves and scarves wherever he goes. And to Sylvie it will make no difference – there are no seasons in Paediatrics 3.

I offer to take Rosa out for lunch. There's no real food in the flat – I've been living on toast, mainly. We wander down the High Street until we find a small Turkish place and we order mezze. It means we have to share everything, all those little bowls of hummus and tabbouleh.

She orders wine – a carafe of the house rosé, which is terrible, and which she seems to enjoy. I remember being young enough to enjoy bad wine. Today, I drink it anyway. I don't think I've had a drink since Dougie died, and it doesn't take much to make me feel drunk.

'Do you mind if we get more?' she asks, lifting the empty carafe.

'You don't need to ask me.'

I like seeing how Rosa eats. She rips up the flatbread with her hands and digs in until the table between us is littered with small empty bowls, scraped clean of hummus. She gnaws the olive stones clean. I think of Sylvie, and the time I watched her cut a single grape into six pieces and pick at them for forty minutes.

'Have the police or the coroner been in touch with you again?' I ask.

She nods, still chewing. 'Yup. A few times.'

I wait, but she doesn't say anything else. 'What do they want to know?'

'Everything,' she says. 'What happened.'

'And what have you told them?'

She puts down her glass. 'You can just ask me directly, you know. You don't have to edge around it like that. Just ask me if I remember what happened.'

'OK. Sorry. Do you? Has any of it come back?'

'A bit.' She picks up another piece of bread, then puts it down again. 'The weird thing is, I thought the roof had collapsed. I didn't realise the water had gone up. It happened so quick – one minute we were in knee-deep water, and the guide said he was going to take the kids back. Then, when he was gone, Dougie and I were suddenly lifted up and crushed against the roof. My head was scraping on the roof of the cave. So at first that's what I thought: that the roof had come down. I couldn't work out why it had stopped, just above the water – why it hadn't come all the way down.'

She's twisting her yellow paper napkin around and around itself until it's a fraying rope.

'We had a couple of inches of air – that was it. And my headtorch was gone – it was knocked off, by the roof I guess, and it was under the water, shining somewhere on the other side of the cavern.'

I think of the police inventory: *One purple headtorch (not working).*

'Did Dougie's torch still work?'

'I think so. I can't remember. But I think it must have, otherwise I couldn't have seen him. That's right, isn't it? That must be right. Because I could see him.'

'And what did you see?'

Another pause.

'He was just like me. Face pressed up against the roof, and trying to look around. We could still stand, but only just. He—' She stops for a second. 'He grabbed my hand. Or I grabbed his. I don't remember. But we were holding on to each other.'

'Then?'

She swallows.

'That guide – Phil – came back the way he'd gone. He sort of bobbed up right next to us. He looked at us, just for a second. Then he grabbed me, shouted, *Hold your breath.*

And he pulled me through the passage out.'

'Did he say anything to Dougie? Or you – did you say anything?'

She shakes her head impatiently. 'You don't know what it was like.' She's dropped the napkin now but her hands are still busy, clawing at the air in front of her – trying to carve a space in it for this story. 'There was no time, no air. Our faces were pressed against the roof. It was nearly totally dark – just Dougie's headtorch, and then Phil's.' Her voice is rising. 'And the water was loud. I never thought water could be so loud.'

I try to picture it: Dougie's face against the cavern's roof, under the glare of his headtorch.

When we leave the restaurant I'm shocked by the brightness of the day. It's only two pm; the city is going about its daytime business, but I feel like I've emerged from an underground cavern, not a cheap restaurant.

I walk her to the tube station, and we say goodbye. I wonder whether we'll hug, but we don't. I watch her making her way down the crowded stairs. She holds her body awkwardly, a bit sideways, so that nobody can jolt the injured arm. I watch until I can't see her white hair any more.

Gill

I get called in for another meeting with Louise, Sylvie's doctor, in her tiny office.

'You and Gabe still haven't told her about her brother?'

I used to like that Louise usually gets straight to the point. These days, I'd be grateful for a little prevarication.

'We agreed to go along with this for the initial period,' she continues. 'Just while Gabe was away. To buy you some time to get on top of things.'

'He's still away,' I say quickly. 'Until the inquest. It could be months.'

'It's been nearly four weeks already,' she says. 'How long do you plan on lying to Sylvie?'

I bridle at the world *plan*. None of this has been planned. I'm just scrambling to keep my daughter alive.

'Not lying,' I say. I'm thinking of the broken leg. The truths that only a mother knows. The lies that only a mother can tell. 'Just not telling her. Waiting until she's well enough to handle the news.'

'I have to act in the best interests of my patient,' says Louise. 'You know that.'

Her patient. My daughter. Today Sylvie was wearing a singlet with thin straps. Her shoulder blades jutted out like the small wings of a gravestone angel.

'Is it in Sylvie's best interests to kill herself?' I say. 'Because we both know that's what'll happen if she hears this news.'

'Not necessarily,' Louise says.

'Oh, come off it,' I say. 'This whole thing started not

long after one of her grandfathers died. And look what happened after Katie P killed herself.'

'That was two years ago.'

'And she's so much better now, is she?' I jerk my head towards Paediatrics 3, down the corridor. Sylvie's in there with the tube up her nose, her left arm cross-hatched with scars, and her organs even more wasted than at her last suicide attempt.

'You said *Not necessarily*,' I say. 'A moment ago, when I said Sylvie will kill herself. I need more than *Not necessarily*. It's her life we're talking about. *Not necessarily* isn't going to cut it.'

'We have measures in place to keep her safe.'

'For how long? How long can we watch her for?' My voice is shaky and too high. 'She can't stay in a secure ward forever.'

'You can't lie to her forever.'

'If you're saying you're going to tell her, we'll take her out of the hospital.' I stand, snatching up my handbag and coat. 'We'll take her out of here – find a private clinic. Or a hospital on the mainland—'

'Sit down, for God's sake,' Louise says.

I slump back into the chair, holding my bag across my chest. Louise leans towards me. 'We want to be able to continue working with you and Gabe, as a team, to help Sylvie. It's not in anyone's interests for me to alienate you, or to have Sylvie removed from here.

'But you need to understand: if you keep lying to her, there're going to be consequences in the long term. I understand why you're doing it. Yes, Sylvie's weak at the moment, mentally and physically. But when you finally do tell her, the grief that you're trying to avoid will still come, and it'll be complicated by resentment and anger towards you.'

In the parallel vertical lines between Louise's eyes, I recognise some of my own tiredness.

'Look,' she says. 'I understand that you're trying to protect your daughter. I don't necessarily agree with your choices about that. But I'm not sure it's even relevant, to be honest. She's in no fit state to face the underlying psychological issues – let alone her brother's death. Right now, my pressing concern is keeping her tube in, and keeping her stable.'

I nod. This is the Catch-22 of this disease, the problem that Gabe, her doctors, and I have circled for more than three years. It's a mental illness with physical symptoms. Terrifying as the physical aspects are, they're almost irrelevant. But that doesn't mean that they can't kill her.

Louise continues. 'We can't address the mental stuff – any of it – until we get the physical stuff under control. If we don't treat the malnutrition, she's not capable of rational thought. The brain doesn't work when it's starved. All we can do is feed her up, try to get her to a point of rationality where we're in a position to tackle the psychological issues. And that will include coming to terms with her brother's death.' She leans back in her creaky office chair. 'To be perfectly honest, my realistic assessment of this ward's value – the value of my work here – is that we keep these girls alive until they're ready to start actually doing the work of getting better.'

I feel a wave of sadness for Louise. She's a good doctor – an excellent doctor. She's one of the reasons Sylvie's survived this far. It's awful to hear her give such a bald assessment of her life's work.

'What we do here has its limits, but it's not nothing,' she goes on. 'We give them some strategies to cope with food; we try to get them to start the process; we let them know what support's available. But until they're ready, all we're doing is keeping them alive.'

'So you won't tell her about Dougie?' I ask. 'For now?'

'For now,' she echoes.

I'm halfway out the door when she calls after me. 'Sylvie's a highly intelligent young woman.'

Young woman, not *girl*. I must stop thinking of Sylvie as a girl. She's nearly eighteen, for all that she's starved her body back to pre-adolescence.'Yes,' I say. 'She's always been like that.'

'I can imagine,' says Louise. 'So don't underestimate her.'

I take up the knife. The leg of lamb is so heavy that when I drop it onto the chopping board the whole counter shakes.

I make deep incisions all over, to stuff the garlic cloves into. There's a violence in the stabbing, and a tenderness in the filling. I don't know if I'm destroying something or making something, and sometimes it's both, and sometimes it's neither. The meat is slick with white fat and leaves a film of grease on my fingers. Before roasting, I rub the meat with sea salt, oil and pepper. I relish the sharpness of the sea salt on my skin.

Louise can't understand that I've been lying to Sylvie for a long time. Parents lie – it's our job. *A kiss from Mummy will make your knee all better. Sticks and stones may break your bones, but words will never hurt you.* Then the lies get bigger: *We'll find a way to get through this. The doctors know how to help you. I'm fine.*

Lying to Sylvie about Dougie has become normal now. Anything becomes normal, if it lasts long enough – Sylvie's illness taught me that. When she went into hospital, it became normal to have the hospital ward's number saved as a favourite contact in my phone. Normal to know that there are sometimes parking spaces in Argyle Street, around the corner from the hospital, and that the quickest way up to Paediatrics 3 is to go past the oncology clinic and take the fire escape stairs, instead of waiting for the lift.

So when people used to say to me, *I don't know how you do it*, the answer is always that I don't know either. You just do it: you learn what needs to be done, and you do it, and you keep doing it because you don't have any choice, and because this is your life now.

Teddy

Mum puts the tray of lamb in the middle of the table. It's huge – so huge it looks wrong.

'Goodness,' says Papabee. 'What a marvellous sight.'

For the first week or two after she came home from London, Mum would mainly cook late at night, or she'd make something and then I'd find it in the bin. Sometimes she'd serve up dinner so spicy I couldn't eat it, even when I mixed in half a tub of yoghurt. It didn't really matter – so many people dropped off food after Dougie died that there was always something to eat. But the Death Casseroles ran out eventually, and maybe that's a good thing, because even though Mum's cooking's still a bit weird, at least she's making stuff we can eat again.

She cuts the meat and drops slices on my plate – *slap, slap, slap*. She stops and looks up at me. 'How hungry are you, love?'

I stare at that huge piece of meat. Behind it, the other half of the table's empty, where Sylvie, Dad and Dougie used to sit.

I'm already pretty full from biscuits at Papabee's this afternoon. But I know how Mum's hands hang on so tight to her knife and fork while she eats and pretends not to watch me. Pretends not to count the bites.

'Starving,' I say, and Mum smiles. More meat lands on my plate. *Slap, slap.*

Sometimes my tummy gets hard and sore, from always saying *Yes please* and *Starving*. But I want to show Mum I'm different from Sylvie. I want to show her that she doesn't need to be afraid. And I want the edges of my body to go out, where Sylvie's go in. I want to be too full to have any room left in me for secrets.

In my room after dinner I get out the things I keep hidden in my drawer: the envelope of my Papa J money, and the photo of Sylvie grinning. Both the wrong price – either not enough, or the wrong thing altogether. I open the notebook with the list of all our family's private words in it. I lie on the floor and chew the end of my pen, and try to write down more of the words, because if I can't figure out the right price for Sylvie's story then all the words will be lost for good.

Mum pops her head through my bedroom doorway.

'Bedtime in five minutes,' she says. 'Want me to read you a story?'

She's got a tea-towel over her shoulder. It's an old one from the market, and because it's folded in half longways, instead of saying, *ENJOY BEAUTIFUL TASMANIA* it just says:

JOY

FUL

MANIA

Dougie would've understood why that's so funny. He would've laughed a lot, I reckon.

'I'm OK without a story tonight,' I tell Mum. I want to work on my list instead.

'What're you up to?' she asks.

I put my arm across the page of the notebook and try to make it look like I'm just leaning on it.

'Book report for school.' I don't want to explain about my list of family words, because it sounds silly when I say it out loud. It's not silly though – it's serious. As serious as a flood, or a digger-load of dirt.

Everyone has their own little superstitions. Even Mum and Dad do it: saying *Bless you* when somebody sneezes;

counting magpies. *One for sorrow, two for joy.* My list, and my prices for Sylvie, are just the same. I don't think I could stop even if wanted to. It's a little bit habit, a little bit fear.

'Need a hand with it?' asks Mum.

'Nope,' I say. 'Thanks.'

'Good old Teddy,' she says, walking away. She calls back, 'Five minutes, OK? Remember to brush your teeth.'

I close my notebook, and tuck it back under the jumpers in the drawer so nothing shows. I know what *Good old Teddy* means. It means not sick, like Sylvie, and not dead, like Dougie. 'Thank God for you,' Mum says to me sometimes, kissing me on the head, and I know it's meant to be a good thing. *Good old Teddy*. But I'd like to be something, instead of just being *not* something.

And I know how. When I showed Sylvie that photo – the last one of her smiling – she said *Thirteen and a half.* Every day since then, I've tried to figure out how to use that number to find out the price of her story. Once, I watched a TV show where the detective could tell what time a guy was shot because the bullet smashed a clock on the wall too, and it got stuck at that exact time. I think Sylvie is a bit like that. Something happened when she was thirteen and a half, and her whole life stopped like a smashed clock.

Gabe

The next morning the doorbell rings again.

'I have croissants,' Rosa says, instead of hello. She holds up a brown paper bag with her good arm, and heads past me up the stairs before I even reply.

After that, she comes nearly every day. She never rings or texts, and we never make any plans, but about eleven she shows up, straight from the station. I've got into the habit of making sure I'm there. I get up early, work on the laptop for a few hours; pop out for coffee in the Turkish café down the road, but always make sure I'm back for when the doorbell rings. Sometimes she stays for an hour, sometimes four. If we get lunch, she always orders wine, and I always drink it with her. She doesn't talk any more about the cave, and if I ask her, she changes the subject, pours more wine.

'Rosa comes here pretty much every day,' I tell Gill.

'That poor girl,' she says. 'What for?'

I don't know the answer. I only know that it's begun to feel like part of my daily routine: *Reply to work emails. Research the cave's catchment area. Let Rosa in.*

Often we barely even talk. For hours at a time she lies across the couch and scrolls through her phone, while at the table I concentrate on stuff for the inquest, forms for the repatriation of the ashes, paperwork from the school's insurer. I never imagined that death would involve so many forms.

On all the paperwork relating to the inquest, I'm referred to as a *P.I.P.* The first time I encountered the term, I had to ring Heather at the coroner's office to ask what it meant. '*A*

Properly Interested Person,' she said. 'You know: immediate relatives, partners – that kind of thing.'

How close to Dougie do you have to be, I wonder, to count as a Properly Interested Person? Does Rosa count? How far would somebody's interest have to go to be considered *Improper*? If I spend too many hours researching cadaveric spasm, or staring at maps of the cave system, will I cross that line? Have I already? And if I cease to be a P.I.P., what new, uncharted territories of love and grief do I enter then, beyond the remit of the inquest and its acronyms?

Gill rings in the middle of the night.

'Is it Sylvie?' I say, before I've even fumbled the lamp on.

'No, she's fine. I mean, not fine, but – you know. The same.'

'Is it Teddy? What's going on?' My mouth is tacky with sleep. 'It's three in the morning here.'

'I'm sorry. I didn't even check the time. I just – I had an idea.'

I wait.

'It's Rosa,' Gill says. 'What if she's pregnant?'

'I don't think she is.'

'How could you know?'

'Because she's twenty-one or twenty-two years old. Because he was nineteen, and they were both sensible.' What I don't say: *Because two days ago, she drank five glasses of wine at lunch with me.*

'But what if she is?'

For the last couple of years, that had been the nightmare scenario: Dougie getting somebody pregnant. Every parent of a teenage boy worries about it. We'd given him the talk about safe sex – us even more embarrassed than him, though it was a close thing.

But now Gill's voice sounds hopeful. 'I'm just saying,' she continues. 'It's not impossible.'

'I suppose not.'

'We could help her with the baby. Maybe even raise it if she didn't want it. Maybe that would be better, after all – she's so young. She wouldn't want it – what would she do? So we'd raise it. Dougie's baby – can you imagine?'

'Not really,' I say, and it's a lie, because I can imagine it, but I don't dare let myself.

'Rosa would need a lot of support,' Gill goes on. I slump back down on the pillow, and she keeps speaking, her voice faster than usual. 'And even if we raised the baby, she'd want close contact, of course. And we'd want that too – for the baby's sake, and ours.'

She keeps on talking, but after a while it becomes clear that she's also been listening to all my silence.

'Do you think it's a mad idea?' she asks.

I exhale slowly. I don't think she's mad. I think of my candle in the church. If Gill's idea is madness, then it's the madness of prayer.

'Love,' I say. 'We're pushing fifty. Sylvie's in hospital, Teddy's approaching his teens, and Papabee's getting more hopeless by the minute. The last thing we could handle is raising a baby. And there is no baby.'

Gill doesn't try to argue with me. Instead, she speaks very quietly. 'Just let me have this. Just for tonight, OK?'

So I listen, while she tells me how it would be.

'Rosa might even want to move to Australia,' she says. 'A fresh start might appeal, after what she's been through. Or she could visit a few times a year. We could help her with the airfare.'

I think of how Teddy used to love having Papabee read him stories before bed. I listen to Gill until she's run out of words, and then we're silent together.

She breaks the silence first. 'Will you ask her?'

'I promise,' I say into the dark.

When I open the door to Rosa the next day, she raises her left arm triumphantly. The cast has gone.

'They took it off yesterday.' She rotates her bare wrist and wriggles her fingers. 'The doctor says it's fine.' The skin of that arm is pale, and slightly puffy. I think of Dougie's body, his waterlogged skin.

'That's great.'

'Aren't you going to ask me in?' she asks.

'Let's go out,' I say. 'Get a coffee. My treat.'

She shrugs, already turning and heading back to the street.

I follow her to a chain café on the corner. I hate this place, and its overpriced, massive, milky coffees, but today I don't mind. If I'm going to ask her this question, I don't want to do it in the flat where Dougie's ashes are on the bedside table.

Rosa sits opposite me. She's beautiful in the way that all young people are beautiful – the newness of their skin; the novelty of their bodies. She's beautiful in her own way too – her startling paleness; the candour of her freckles. It's ugly to admit to myself that I'm noticing these things.

'Gill asked —' I hesitate. It had sounded outlandish enough last night, in the dark, between just me and Gill. Now, in the echoing noisiness and bright lights of the café, it seems even more absurd. But I made Gill a promise. And I have my own curiosity too, I have to confess. 'Gill asked if there was any chance – I told her it was extremely unlikely – but she wanted to know—' I clear my throat. 'We wanted to know whether there was any chance that you might be pregnant. That you might be carrying Dougie's baby.'

She snorts. 'Are you serious? Jesus, Gabe, no.' The pity on her face is worse than her outrage. 'I'm sorry. But no way. That was never an option. Of course not.'

'So you're sure?'

'You want the proof? You want to dig around in my bathroom bin for the used tampons?'

I wince. The woman at the nearest table looks across, then looks quickly away.

'You're embarrassed because I'm shouting about tampons? You should be embarrassed that you want to turn me into some sort of incubator for your dead son.'

'I'm sorry. I'm so sorry. We just —'

'Look, it's OK,' she says. 'I thought about it, too. For about two seconds, before I realised it was completely insane.' She shakes her head. 'I don't want to have a baby. I'm twenty-two. I'm probably about to lose my job. I only knew Dougie for a few months. It would've been a terrible idea, even if he were still alive. Even if I'd been pregnant, I couldn't have kept it.'

'Gill and I could have helped. We would've helped.'

'I don't want a baby,' she yells. 'I don't know if I'm ever going to want a baby. Let alone to my dead boyfriend.' Then, more calmly, she asks, 'Do you really want to argue about a hypothetical baby?'

'No,' I say. 'Not at all. It was stupid of me.'

'I don't blame you for clutching at straws,' she says. 'But it's my whole life you're talking about.'

'There isn't a baby,' I tell Gill when I ring that night.

'I know,' she says. 'Of course there isn't. And it was probably a mad idea anyway.'

She sounds surprisingly chirpy. It doesn't reassure me.

'How's the book going?' I ask her. 'Doing much writing? Anything new?'

'It's going,' she says, and offers nothing further.

'Have you shown any of it to Sue yet?'

'Not yet. One day soon.'

I'm on the wrong side of the world. She needs me, and Sylvie and Teddy too. How can I be here, when Teddy's there, with his bony knees and his obsessions and his small hands? But when I think of Teddy's hands, I can only picture Dougie's at the same age – his always-grubby nails, and the lump on his right thumb-knuckle from where he sucked it until he was nine. Who will take Dougie's cold hand now and guide him through the inquest, if not me?

I miss Sylvie and Gill and Teddy – I miss them so much it feels like I'm wearing my skin inside out, all the nerves exposed. But when I wake, gasping, from dreams of water, it's Dougie's name that rises from my throat like my final breath.

Teddy

When we're tidying up after dinner, Mum trips over Sausage and shouts, 'That bloody dog!'

Since Dougie died, and Dad went away, Mum's started calling SausageDog 'That bloody dog' even more often. She did it yesterday afternoon, too, when she found another hole that Sausage dug under the fence to chase next door's cats. Even from my room, I heard her yelling, 'That bloody dog.' Sausage was sitting next to me on my bed while I did my geography homework, so I squished his long ears down, holding my hands over them so he wouldn't hear her.

SausageDog's not the only one whose name has changed lately. Lots of names have changed, since Dougie died – Dougie's name, most of all. Before, he was always Dougie, except for school reports or if he was in big trouble, when Mum would shout *Douglas Benjamin Jordan,* or *Young Man.* After he died, he somehow turned into Douglas. There's a whole pile of papers that Mum's shoved into a corner of the study – stuff from the insurance company, and the coroner, and the airline – and none of them are about Dougie. They're all about *Douglas Jordan*, or (even worse), *The deceased.* Even Mum and I hardly say his name any more, and when we do, it comes out strange.

When I was six or seven I remember looking at the first baby tooth I ever lost, and trying to work out whether it still counted as a part of me now that it was in my hand. Since he died, Dougie's name is like that tooth: it isn't attached to him any more, so I don't know where it belongs, or what to do with it.

I didn't realise how slippery names could be, until he went into the cave as Dougie and came out as Douglas. Mum's started calling Dad 'your father' a lot more, instead of Gabe. And Sylvie often doesn't answer, no matter what name you call her. She just turns her head the other way, and says nothing. Mum's still Mum, but I don't always recognise her, this lady who shouts at the dog and goes quiet halfway through conversations, and cooks late at night so that when I have nightmares about a cave flooded by a digger-load of dirt, I wake up to the smell of her cooking in the dark, and my fear smells like onions and garlic.

Sylvie

Mum brings me a container of roast lamb. Whole garlic cloves, soft and white, roll around in the tub like little blind eyes. She puts it on my bedside table, balanced on top of my books.

Mum's always making things. I do the opposite. See: I unmade my whole body.

I used to look like Mum. Everyone said it: *You're the spitting image of your mother.* They don't say that any more.

I haven't told Teddy that I found his note, written on the mirror in toothpaste: *Don't die.* I'm too much of a coward to say, *I saw your message.* I'm too much of a coward to obey it.

Once, when I still lived at home, I watched a nature documentary with Teddy and Papabee. It showed how some animals signal that they're poisonous. The garish acid-yellow on the back of the poison dart frog is a warning: *deadly.* The striking bands of the coral snake, announcing to predators, *Poison; don't touch.* I saw it myself at the Neck, once, when Ella and I startled a tiger snake on the path down the beach. It reared up and flashed us its acid-yellow belly. We ran.

I look down at my body. The bones of my elbows, sharpened and conspicuous: *Stay away.*

Gill

'How long can you keep this up?' Sue asks me. 'It's been more than a month. You know you need to tell her.'

It's colder now – with the end of June, winter has slouched its way over the mountain and settled on the city, and Sue and I are inside, SausageDog on her knee for warmth.

'I know.' I take another sip of my wine. 'But I can't.'

It's that simple.

Things I can do, just about: take this breath, and the next. Drive Teddy to school, and cook dinner for him and Papabee every night. Email my articles to my editors twenty minutes before each deadline. Make it to the hospital every morning and most afternoons.

Things I can't do: tell Sylvie that her brother is dead. Watch her die too.

'What about Teddy?' says Sue. 'It's asking a lot of him, to keep it from her.'

'I know.' Poor old Teddy. Good old Teddy. He learned, right from the start, to get by on the amount of attention that was available to him, which was never much – the big kids so noisy and mobile and demanding, compared with this unexpected baby. We had no time, and no money. I'd published my first two books, but they hadn't sold well, so when Teddy was a few months old I was already back to taking shifts in restaurant kitchens to make ends meet, breast-milk leaking through my chef-whites and leaving yellow stains.

When Teddy first taught himself to crawl, he could only crawl backwards. One day we realised none of us had seen him for fifteen minutes, and eventually we found he'd reversed himself under the dining room cabinet and got stuck. Dougie or Sylvie, at that age, would have screamed blue murder, but when we found Teddy he was just waiting quietly, playing with dust balls.

'Don't worry about Teddy,' I tell Sue. 'He understands why we have to do it. And he'll be OK. He always is.'

The sea in Cephalonia is just ridiculously stunning – so clear it's basically showing off. But having the cast means no swimming, which is shit – getting tired of sitting on the beach watching our stuff while Dad gets to swim! Getting v fed up with the leg thing by now. Any benefits of the cast (sympathy from old Greek ladies; getting a seat on crowded trains) are well and truly outweighed by the stink of sweat-soaked plaster – a real olfactory delight (Dad calls it 'the old factory situation' – vintage Dad Joke). And with no swimming, the heat is hard work. At any given moment I'm itching in at least three different ways (sunburn peeling; mozzie bites; sweaty skin under the cast, which is a special kind of torture because there's no way to get at it).

So overall this bit of the trip has been kind of great, and kind of frustrating. Sort of feels like I'm having two trips: this slightly weird one, with Dad and the cast and my crutches, and at the same time, in my head, imagining the trip that I would've had if I'd never gone into the bloody cave. I keep picturing being here with Rosa instead, like we'd planned (Dad's got many strengths, but looking great in a bikini isn't one of them). Anyway, sorry to complain – I know I'm lucky to have Dad helping me out, and I know that even this version of the trip is still a lot more exciting than Paeds 3. We'll come here together one day, when we can both make the most of it.

Yesterday we went out on a little boat to Ithaca – the smaller island nearby. It's meant to be the place from the Odyssey, which I bet you've read. Don't tell Mum that we just went to beaches and a taverna, instead of doing any of the cultural stuff (in our defence, we only had a few hours there). Had lunch at a taverna that's literally on a jetty – having a beer there while dangling my good leg in the water did make me feel like a bit of a dickhead for moaning about the annoying stuff.

I lick the flap of the envelope and seal it tight. For the next half hour the gluey, chemical taste lingers on my tongue. Dougie's voice lingers too – my mouth full of it. *Don't tell Mum. A bit of a dickhead. If I hadn't gone into that bloody cave.* Phrases from this letter echo among fragments from his earlier letters. *I miss the Neck – miss being in the sea. They're OBSESSED with potatoes. Try not to freeze out the parentals. Dad says he's too old for hostels.* I can't tell, any more, which are his words and which are mine.

Gabe

Gill rings.

'You've been in Cephalonia,' she says. 'The two of you went on a boat trip around Ithaca. But it's hot, and he's frustrated that he can't swim, with the cast.'

Always the water. I can't get away from it.

'And then we're headed to Sicily, right?'

'It's all in the letter,' she says. 'I'll email you a copy. Make sure you read it before you call Sylvie.'

I might tell myself that it's Gill writing the letters, but I'm lying to Sylvie every time we speak. I'm not just implicated – I'm neck-deep.

When Sylvie went into the hospital, Dougie started coming out of his room with red eyes, looking like he'd been chopping onions.

'Is he smoking weed in there?' Gill whispered. But there wasn't even a whiff of cigarettes, let alone weed. It took us a few days to realise that Dougie had just been crying.

He and Sylvie had always been a team. Whenever I walked past Dougie's room, after dinner, they were talking, laughing, arguing, him on his bed and her lying on the floor with her feet up on his bookshelf. Before Dougie's voice broke, there were times that I couldn't tell which one of them was speaking, because they shared the same inflections, the same secret language of shared jokes and references and irritations.

Then she was in hospital and he was left behind, one half of the big kids. We tried to talk about it with him, and he was about as responsive as you'd expect a sixteen-year-old boy to be.

'I'm fine,' he insisted.

'If you don't want to talk about it with me or Mum, what about a counsellor?' I asked. 'Or one of the teachers at school?'

'I literally can't think of anything worse,' he said, and went back outside to play basketball.

He and I still played cricket in the backyard on weekends. We had an ongoing list-game that we'd been playing ever since he was big enough to hold the cricket bat. We took turns to come up with prompts, in between each ball.

'Top five one-day bowlers.'

'Top five concept albums.'

'Top five stories that Papabee's repeated most often.' (My turn. 'Don't tell Mum,' Dougie said.)

'Top five Jason Statham films.' (His turn. 'Is he the bald one?' I asked.)

'Top five reasons Sylvie won't eat,' I said one day last year, when it was my turn to bowl. As though I could ambush him with the question, like a reverse swing ball.

He stopped. 'It's not a game, Dad. Jesus.'

'I know,' I said immediately. 'I just thought – I don't know. I thought we could talk about it.'

'This isn't some clickbait article.' He let the ball drop. '*Top Five Reasons Your Sister's Dying. Number Three will blow your mind!*'

I watched the ball roll against the house, among the flowerpots. 'You know that's not what I meant. I just mean – you know her better than anybody. And I thought we could talk about it.'

'Do you and Mum really think that if I knew something, I wouldn't have told you already?'

'I just thought it might help to talk. That's all.'

'Help who?' He didn't wait for an answer. 'I have homework,' he said, and went inside. The cricket bat lay where he'd dropped it.

Three months later he boarded the plane for London. I wondered whether he'd planned his gap year as a way of running away from her, or from us.

I ask Rosa if she wants to come with me to the caves. She's lying on my couch reading something on her phone, while I work at my computer. When I ask her, she snorts. 'You must be kidding.'

I understand. She was there – she doesn't need to go back to the caves to understand what happened.

But I do. I hire a car and set off the next morning. It's been raining since dawn, a resolute grey drizzle that seems very British. The drive takes about ninety minutes, after I've left the traffic of London. I follow the sat nav down a long, unsealed road that ends in an empty car park, puddles starting to settle in the gravel, below the tumbled stone cliff.

The entrance to the cave is narrower than I'd expected – a low black gap in the cliff face. You would have to crouch to enter, but it's all I can do to touch the wet stone wall. I lean close to it and the stone, rough as sharkskin, brushes my cheek.

By the entrance to the cave, there's a small wooden shelter, no bigger than a bus stop, open along one side. Inside, a noticeboard gives cursory information about the cave system. And on a shelf, with a Biro attached by a string, is a logbook. Above it, a sign on the board says: *All parties to sign in and out, noting destination and any other relevant information.*

Why wasn't I told? The police and the coroner's office haven't mentioned this.

I flick through the book, until I spot the date I need: *13th May 2016*. The lower half of the page is crowded with the details of the various search parties:

> *J. Lewis + 4, entering 11, out 11:10 (can confirm: not safe to proceed beyond cavern 2)*
>
> *J. Lewis + 4, in 1400. Out 1445 (as above – water still too high)*
>
> *P. Hawley + 4, entering 7pm. Out 8:25pm. Water receding; made it as far as Cavern 3.*
>
> *D.I. Preston + 6. Entering midnight. Out 3:45am (body retrieved)*

The handwriting is rushed, the later entries probably written by the light of headlamps through that long night.

Further back, at the top of the page, in neater writing:

> *13th May 2016. P. Murphy and T. Wan + 10 – entering 10am; heading for cavern 3.*

Then Dougie and Rosa's names, both in Dougie's handwriting:

> *D. Jordan, R. Campbell*

Below, they'd let the kids sign their own names, in their careful, childish writing. These kids were barely older than Teddy. One of the girls, Miriam Abiola, has topped each *i* with a little love heart. I look at her name for several minutes. Would I have swapped her death, or any of the other children's, for his? I don't have an answer – at least, not one that I can admit to myself.

Then, in the *Out* column, in different handwriting: *11:10 P. Murphy + T. Wan + 9*

There it is again, that maths sum, at once perfectly simple and impossible to grasp: If twelve people go into a cavern, and only eleven come out, what remains?

I spend a long time looking at the entries. Several times, I run my finger over Dougie's handwriting. The rain is heavier now. I watch it dent the shallow puddles in the gravel of the car park.

Before I close the logbook, I turn over to the previous page. From the days before the flood, various standard entries, where the numbers *in* and *out* tally. But at the bottom, there's another entry with the same date as the flood. I check it, then double-check it: *13th May*.

My hands are shaking when I call Heather at the coroner's office.

'Do you know about the other logbook entry?' I demand. 'Somebody called M. Calvert – they didn't give their full name – signed in for a group of three. They signed in at nearly nine that morning, more than an hour before Dougie's group. Then signed out again, twenty minutes later. *Water underfoot at Cavern 1 – not tempted today.*'

'The police gave us copies of the relevant pages of the logbook,' she says. The rain is loud on the tin roof of the shelter, and I can hardly hear her.

'And? That's it? You don't think it's important, that somebody an hour earlier noted that it was already flooding?'

'They didn't say anything about flooding. They said there was water in the first cavern.'

'Isn't that enough? It was obviously deep enough that they decided not to go in. And Murphy, the guide, would've seen that.'

'If he read the previous page.'

'Why wouldn't he? He should've done.'

'That's something that the inquest will be exploring, Mr Jordan. I can't pre-empt the coroner's findings.'

The rain thickens on the drive back into London, headlights flaring and receding beyond my windscreen wipers. The downpour turns my car into a box of noise. I'm thinking about this Calvert. What did he see, and what does he know?

Halfway home, I pull over and ring Rosa.

'Where are you?' she asks.

'I don't know. A truck-stop somewhere on the M1. Listen: how much water was underfoot at the entrance, when you first went in?'

'I'm not sure. I wasn't looking – I didn't know it was something I was supposed to be looking out for.'

'But was it wet? Can you remember?'

She's silent for a moment.

'I was wearing these boots that the guides gave us. Big ugly things. I remember being glad I had them on, early on in the cave. I remember looking down and seeing the water near the top of my boots, and thinking I'd have been freezing if I'd worn my trainers.'

'How far into the cave? Was it in the entrance, or the first cavern?'

'I don't know.'

'Try to remember.'

'Gabe, I'm trying.'

That night, back in the flat, I print out the photos that I took of the logbook entries. *Water underfoot.* I keep thinking about the guide who led Dougie into the cave, despite that water. *Phillip Murphy. Goes by Phil,* the police liaison officer had said. *Phil,* the man who saved Rosa and left Dougie to die in the dark.

Two weeks ago I asked the police liaison officer if I could meet with Murphy. He got back to me the next day, told me Murphy's lawyer advised him not to meet with me. I know why. Just like the school, he has to be careful not to admit liability.

I could reassure him that we're not interested in suing him, that I just want to find out what happened – but I don't know if that's true. Once, I would have said that Gill and I aren't the kind of people to sue. I would have said that we know that suing would never bring Dougie back. But that was then.

Now, I'm still pretty certain that I won't sue Murphy. But I think often about the grotesque asymmetry of him being alive, while Dougie is dead. In the dark, when I dream of water and wake choking on air, I remember that Dougie's gone, and I think of Murphy, and what it would be like to kill him.

Teddy

On the way up to Papabee's flat I see Sharon-Over-The-Road.

'You should have another baby,' I say to her. She has a little girl called Alison who Sylvie used to babysit, before she went into the Boneyard.

Sharon-Over-The-Road laughs. She's unloading the shopping from the boot of her car, and trying to keep hold of Alison's hand at the same time. 'God, no way. One's enough for me, thanks, Teddy.'

I wait until she's stopped laughing. 'You should though,' I say. 'Seriously. Then if one dies, you'd still have another one.'

Sharon's smile goes away, and she gets that look in her face that the teachers all had at school in those first few days after Dougie died.

'Oh, Teddy,' she says. 'You mustn't think like that. That's not how it works.'

I don't say it, because she looks upset, but I'm thinking: *Yes it is. Dougie was alive and now he's not. That's exactly how it works.*

I try with Mum too, later that day. 'Are you going to have another baby?' I ask her.

'You must be joking,' she says. She's folding clothes and I watch her hands, folding my school t-shirts so quick and neat, the same way she folds filo pastry when she makes spring rolls.

'But you liked having three children, right?'

She puts down the t-shirt in a pile and swallows really slowly.

'I loved it,' she says.

'So have another one. I know it won't be the same. But at least you'd still have three kids.'

'I'm too old. It's too late. And anyway, your father would have to be here for that.'

That makes me go quiet, and not just because she's called Dad 'your father' again. The idea of Mum and Dad having sex is horrible, even worse than when someone on TV takes their clothes off when Papabee's in the room.

Mum touches the side of my face. 'I can't do it again, love,' she says. I don't know if she means, *I can't have a baby again*, or, *I can't lose a child again*. Maybe both. Since all the names started to change, everything means at least two things.

If I can't find a way to save Sylvie, then everyone will fall out of their names for good. *Sister in the hospital, brother in the water*. Already it feels like our names are broken, and our private family words too. This must be what it feels like to be Papabee, when words are never where you left them.

'Were you at Papabee's all afternoon?' Mum asks at bedtime. Papabee's gone home, and she's sitting on the edge of my bed.

This is one of those times when what she says isn't what she means. What she means is: *Why didn't you go to the hospital?*

'Yup,' I say. 'We played dominoes. I won twice. Then I let him win once. And then he actually won once.'

Mum pulls the doona up higher, so it's tucked right under my chin, and she rubs her thumb against my shoulder.

'It's great that you spend so much time with Papabee,' she says. 'But it's important to spend time with your sister too. She needs at least some parts of her life to stay normal.'

'I went in yesterday.' That's true – I make sure I go in at least two days a week after school, and on weekends too. But until I find the next price to give her, I don't like going there. There's nothing normal about those visits. It's just me sitting in Paediatrics 3 trying not to stare at the tube coming out of her nose, and trying not to say anything about Dougie – and that's not normal at all.

'You used to go in more often, that's all.'

'She never wants to talk,' I say. 'It's boring.'

'I'm not having this conversation, Teddy. She's part of this family, and we're not leaving her alone in there just because she has a disease.'

'What am I supposed to say to her?' I can't think of things to say to Sylvie, when I'm concentrating so hard on all the things that I can't say to her about Dougie.

'I don't know. Nothing. Take a book, if you want. You can just sit with her.'

So after school the next day I take my homework with me into the hospital. I count the girls (ten today – that's not bad; eight of them will get to live). Sometimes Sylvie says *Hi*, sometimes she doesn't. Today's a *Hi* day, but then she stays quiet. I don't know whether or not she's glad that I'm there. She doesn't give away any clues. She doesn't give away anything.

And I'm trying so hard not to give away any clues either. I sit here with my maths assignment on my lap, but instead of focusing on diameter and circumference, I'm thinking of all the ways that I might accidentally let the secret out. I get tired, worrying about all the ways that I might get it wrong, and then Sylvie would die, which would kill Mum and Dad too, all of them going down dead, *one, two, three,* like dominoes going down *clack clack clack* on Papabee's coffee table.

So many ways for me to make it worse. And only one way that I can make it go right: get the price for Sylvie's story, and save her myself.

Sylvie

In Dougie's latest letter he complains about the heat in the Greek islands. I can't imagine ever being hot again. I'm always cold. My fingernails have been blue for years.

Now the weather outside matches my chilled body. Teddy visits with a puffy jacket over his school uniform, his scarf wrapped halfway over his face, and his hands chapped and red.

At the Neck the tessellated pavement will be slippery and slick, and the puddles of the gravel driveway will have a crust of ice. The possums in their winter fur will chase each other across the tin roof of the house. At the edge of the beach the marram grass will be tipped with frost, and the gum trees will stand, grey-white sentinels, on both sides of the road. Deep in their burrows, the mutton-birds will be thick with fat. The tides will eat the beach and spit it out again.

At the Neck I learned not to trust time. I was a girl, and I was busy finding crabs in rock pools and climbing trees and laughing at Dad's bad jokes and suddenly I was something else: a woman. We were playing Classic Catch at the beach – me and Dougie and Nathan and Dad and Papa J – and Dougie lobbed the ball way up high and I jumped up for it and my right boob popped out from under my bikini top. My boobs were still only tiny, and I didn't realise, and I was standing there, waiting to throw the ball back, but they'd all stopped, and except for Teddy they were all looking away. Dad said, 'Sylve, love—' and I said, 'What?' and Nathan made an awkward gesture towards his own chest. Teddy laughed and said,

'Your boob, dummy,' but Papa J and Dougie and Dad were all still looking away, as if it were something shameful. As if I were something shameful.

This is what you need to understand: when I stopped eating, I wasn't trying to become beautiful. I was trying to get away from my beauty. It was too heavy. I wanted to step out of it – leave it behind me like clothes on the beach.

Gabe

M. *Calvert* from the car park logbook at the caves turns out to be a woman, and I chide myself for having assumed that somebody leading a group of cavers would be a man. Ten minutes on Google – *M Calvert potholing; M Calvert Buckinghamshire* – and there she is: Meredith Calvert, architect at a firm in Milton Keynes; Facebook account (locked); a captioned photo of her at the Chiltern Hills Potholing Club's annual pub quiz.

I email her work address.

Dear Ms Calvert,

My name is Gabriel Jordan and my son Douglas was the young man killed in the floods at the Smith–Jackson caves in May. I've recently become aware of your entry in the logbook from earlier that day.

I understand that it might seem strange that I'm contacting you – please forgive the intrusion. I'm sure you'll understand that my wife and I are keen to find out any information that can help us to understand what happened. I'd be extremely grateful if you'd be kind enough to meet me, to discuss what you saw that day. Equally, if you could put me in touch with the other members of your group, it would be very much appreciated.

I'm currently in the UK to sort out my son's affairs, so am free to meet you any time and place that suits you.

Yours sincerely,
Gabriel (Gabe) Jordan

Gill wouldn't have used *understand* twice in one paragraph. She's always been better at crafting words than I am – it's her job. But I haven't even told her I'm trying to contact Meredith Calvert.

I put 'Smith–Jackson potholing accident' in the subject line, and wonder if that will be enough to stop my message being consigned to the Junk folder.

Meredith emails back that same night.

> *Dear Gabriel,*
>
> *I'm so very sorry about what happened to your son.*
>
> *I'm not at all sure that I will be able to help you, but I'd be happy to meet.*
>
> *There's a café called Brass Bear near my work on Hepburn St (Milton Keynes) – it's not far from the station, so should be easy for you if you come by train. We could meet there for coffee at 2:30pm on Friday, if that suits you?*
>
> *Best wishes,*
>
> *Meredith*

I tell Rosa I won't be at home all day on Friday. I'm so worried about being late that I catch an early train from London and arrive at the café forty minutes before Meredith is due. When she finally enters I spot her straight away, looking around and holding a big bag across her body. She's about my age, with curly brown hair, cut shorter than in the photo I saw online. She keeps fidgeting with her bag.

'I can't stay long,' she says, after the initial handshake and introductions. 'Sorry. It's bad timing – busy week at work.'

'I understand. Of course.'

She nods sharply, twisting the handles of her bag.

'I kept thinking about what happened to your boy,' she says, when we've sat down at a table in the corner. 'I couldn't believe it when I heard the news. It's awful.'

If I told her the truth I'd say, *Yes, it's as awful as you think. Worse. It's the very worst thing*. But I'm learning that one of the burdens of grief is that you want to shield others from it – so I say nothing, and just change the subject.

'The potholing world isn't that big, I expect,' I say. 'Do you know this Phil Murphy, the leader of the school expedition?'

She shakes her head. 'I've never met the guy. I don't do that much potholing these days, and a lot of what I've done was overseas anyway. I know people who have met him, though, from the club.'

'And?'

'And what? You want me to tell you what some other people think about somebody I haven't met?'

'I suppose so,' I say. 'I know it's only hearsay. But this isn't a court – nobody's on trial, least of all you. I'm just desperate to find out whatever I can.'

She shrugs. 'Fine. They like him. A friend of mine even worked for his company one season, a few years back. Apparently Murphy's a nice guy. My friend had no complaints.'

'So why did he go in? It was nearly an hour after you'd turned back. The water almost definitely would've been higher. But he took ten kids in there.'

'I've got no idea why,' she says. 'Or what it was like when he arrived. Look – I really have to get back to work soon.'

'Please – just a few more minutes? You said, in the logbook, *Water underfoot at Cavern 1*. How deep was it?'

'I've thought about that constantly. Honestly, I don't know. It was splashing, but not like we were wading. It wasn't hard work – it wasn't *deep*-deep.'

'But too deep for you to want to go in.'

'I didn't say it was dangerous. I just didn't fancy it. I'm not some kind of hardcore, intrepid, outdoors warrior. I just wanted a few hours, a nice morning's potholing with my kids.'

'They were the other two people in your group? Your kids?'

'I say *kids*,' she laughs. 'They're bigger than me – seventeen and nineteen, now. But you know what it's like—' She stops herself, appalled.

'I get it,' I say. 'They'll always feel like your babies, right?'

She moves on quickly. 'That's it. And I don't get to see much of them, these days. They live with their dad, and Gordon – the oldest one – he's at uni now. But they came down for my birthday and we wanted to do some potholing together, like we used to.'

'Could I talk to them? Just in case they remember anything else?'

She shakes her head again. 'I think it'd be best if you didn't. I don't want them dragged into this. And David's doing his A-Levels – he's got enough stress on his plate.'

I'm getting used to this – the fear that tragedy is contagious. I don't even blame her. If there's one thing I can understand, it's that fierce desire to protect your children.

'But I've asked them, I promise,' she says, rushing to fill the silence. 'I've asked them to think about it really carefully. And they don't remember anything more than what I've told you. And the police asked all three of us the same thing, about the water level.'

I'm relieved to hear that the police have at least followed up the lead.

'Had you ever seen it that high before?'

'I don't know. A couple of other times there was water underfoot. But that was with friends who were more experienced than me – not with my kids. It wasn't my call to make, those times. But that day, I was in charge. I didn't want to wade in with the water that height, and rising.'

'Rising? You didn't say that in the logbook.'

'It's not my job,' she snaps. 'I'm not the weatherwoman. You said nobody's on trial. I didn't even have to write as much as I did. Time in, time out – that's all that I needed to put in the book.'

'Sorry,' I try again. 'Of course, that's quite right. I know it's not your responsibility at all. But it's important – you thought it was rising?'

She's flustered now. 'I don't know. Did I say that? I don't know for sure. I guess it was just a feeling? I wasn't in there for long enough to notice a change. But I hadn't seen it that deep before, so I guess I figured—' She stops, closing her eyes for a second.

'Look. I don't know why I said *rising*,' she says. 'If I'd known you were going to cross-examine me, I'd have thought more carefully about my words.'

'I'm sorry,' I say again. I'm getting this wrong. 'I really didn't mean to make you feel that way. I'm not here to interrogate you. I'm just trying to figure out what happened. It's my son.'

'I know.' She's gathering up her things, pulling her coat off the back of her chair. 'But I can't help you any more than I already have. I told you: I went in, there was water underfoot, so I left. I'm not part of this.'

She puts on her coat. 'I'm so sorry about your son.'

I nod. 'Dougie. He was nineteen years old.'

'I remember that,' Meredith says, pausing with her coat half-zipped. 'I read it in the papers.'

She hoists her bag onto her shoulder. 'I have to go. I'm sorry.'

When she's gone, I'm left with my untouched coffee and that bare sum: Murphy led a group of twelve into the caves, and eleven came out. An equation I can't solve, except for one variable: Murphy.

It isn't hard to find his address. It takes less than five minutes online. His guiding business is a limited company, and he's the sole director, and it's registered to a residential address. Part of me wishes it weren't so easy. If it had been harder, then I wouldn't have to choose what to do next.

For a long time, I stare at the address on the screen. It's in Potters Bar, just beyond London's northern edge. *24 Hetherington Close*. It sounds very suburban, very English. Very distant from all the things that I know about Murphy: the caves; the flood; the look on his face in that one newspaper photo. I've stared at it hundreds of times: it shows Murphy sitting in the open door of the back of an ambulance, a tinfoil blanket around his shoulders. He has scratches on his hands, and wet hair, one hand to his head, and his mouth is hanging open, a perfect oval, like the perpetual scream of a cartoon ghost.

Cauliflower florets with saffron rice, for when your husband has been gone for five weeks

Slice the cauliflower into inch-thick steaks, like a cross-section of a brain. Drizzle with oil, scatter with sea salt, and roast at 200° for 30 minutes.

Count out six saffron threads. You don't actually need to be this precise, but I find the process calming. I like picking them up, one by one, with the tips of my fingernails.

Drop the saffron into the pot of basmati rice when the liquid has almost cooked away. If you have a glass lid for your pot, you can watch the orange unfurl through the rice as it boils, until the rice is an almost indecent shade of orange.

While the rice is cooking, use a fork to toss together a thick paste of the crushed garlic and almond slivers, a tablespoon of olive oil, and a handful of coriander, finely chopped. Add a diced red chilli too, scraping out the seeds first – you want the chilli for colour rather than for intensity. Fry the paste on a low heat, throwing in a couple of anchovy fillets. They'll melt away entirely, but their taste will stay. I've been thinking, lately, about how things can linger. About what remains.

When the garlic is softened, turn up the heat a little and briefly sear the roasted cauliflower florets in the paste, until each side has a crispy coating. Serve with the rice (you can stir in a knob of butter, or some sesame oil, for extra decadence), and garnish with orange nasturtium petals, surprisingly peppery.

(Don't use those tiny tins of anchovies – the miserliness of them goes against the whole spirit of this dish. Don't even use those skinny jars with only a dozen fillets. Get a big, fat jar from a Mediterranean deli and ignore any nonsense about 'discard three days after opening'. One jar will last you for months. The trick is to keep the anchovies submerged in oil – top up the oil if necessary. Whatever you do, don't let the air in.)

Gill

At five weeks, when it's become clear that Gabe's not going to be coming back any time soon, Sue says, 'At least you can cook all the things he doesn't like. Mussels every night.'

Sometimes, at the Neck, the kids would pluck mussels from the black rocks in the shallows, and I'd cook them in white wine broth. Gabe always screwed up his whole face. 'It's the texture,' he'd say. 'Like chewing somebody's gums.'

Now he's gone, I'm surprised to find that instead of cooking mussels, I catch myself wanting to cook the things that he enjoyed most. He's always liked saffron, which I used to find cloying; since Gabe left, I start adding saffron to things. Those velveted orange threads cost more, per ounce, than gold – but once I start, I can't stop. I add saffron to smoked haddock and potato soup, and watch it gradually turn jaundiced. I make a lemon tart with saffron and pistachio cream.

I'm plotting the next stage of Dougie and Gabe's trip: Sicily, where saffron's a common ingredient. I want to taste that decadent golden flavour while I plan the letter.

I serve Teddy and Papabee saffron rice with cauliflower, the rice the colour of a workman's high-vis vest.

'Good Lord,' says Papabee.

'Why's everything orange?' asks Teddy.

The answer is: *Because I miss your dad,* but that isn't a straightforward answer, and it would begin a conversation that I don't know how to end.

'I like it,' Teddy says, not waiting for my response. 'It looks cool. Can we have a blue dinner one day? Or purple?'

Dougie and Gabe are in Sicily now. The air is so hot that the whole island smells of rosemary and lavender, and the hot-wood smell of a sauna. In the hilltop town of Erice, Dougie sits on some shady steps to rest his leg, the grey stone surprisingly cool beneath him.

> *Food here is the best. We're living mainly on arancini, these rice balls that they sell everywhere (Dad doesn't find my 'balls' jokes as hilarious as I do...). Have learned not to translate what things are made of – was loving these sandwich things at the station in Palermo, then I used Google Translate and apparently they're made with 'Pork spleen' (not even exactly sure what that is, to be honest, but not brave enough to Google further...). Have learned my lesson: just eat, and don't ask questions.*

> *We came up to Erice on a cable-car from Trapani, swaying like mad in the wind (worse than Papabee's driving!). Amazing views from here but they're kind of pointless because half the time the whole town is covered with cloud. The locals call it 'Kisses of Venus' (sounds better in Italian – everything sounds better in Italian) which is a v v romantic way of saying it's grey and you can't see a thing.*

Teddy yells from the living room. 'Mum! Dad's on the phone!'

'Tell him I'll call him in a bit,' I shout back. 'Just in the middle of some work.'

> *Last week we went to a few beaches – even though*

all I can do is kind of hop around in the shallows.
Beaches are different here anyway – lots of crowds,
and people selling stuff, and deck-chairs that they
charge you money to sit on. Makes me nostalgic
for the Neck, even though I don't miss the freezing
water.

When I'm finished I slip it under my mattress for a few days, to get the envelope less pristine before I give it to her. And I like to know the letter's close to me as I lie there. I sleep above it like a bird roosting on an egg.

Gabe

Gill doesn't ring back. I lie on my bed in the dark, one hand reaching out to rest on top of the box of ashes, and I try speaking to Dougie, like the chaplain at the hospital suggested. I try to imagine that we're in the backyard again, the cricket ball in my hand.

'Five best strikers in the Premier League?'

'Five things that made you fall in love with Rosa?'

'Five thoughts that went through your mind when the flood came?'

All I get is the blinking of the clock radio's luminous dial, and five different kinds of silence.

I'm beginning to suspect that this grief of mine is selfish. I ought to be grieving for him – for everything he won't ever have a chance to do, or to be. But I can't help grieving for myself, too – for the days and years with him that I've lost. I make so many wishes: I wish that he'd never come to England; that he'd never gone on the caving trip; that it hadn't rained; that we'd never let him drop French in grade 10, and then he might have gone to France for his gap year instead.

Since Sylvie got sick, and Dougie died, I'm learning that every wish is the same: *more time*.

When Gill rings back the next day, she launches straight into telling me about the latest letter.

'Sicily now, remember,' she says. 'I'll give it to her in a few days. I've emailed you a copy.'

I don't know how to tell her that I can hardly bear to skim the letters she emails me. They're too uncanny. It's like hearing Dougie's voice through a wall, muffled and just out of reach.

I feel closer to Dougie when I listen to Rosa's stories about him.

'Did he tell you about the shampoo?' she asks, when she's here later that morning. She's sitting on my windowsill, her shoes off. There's red polish on her toes but it's flaked and picked away. It makes me nervous when she sits next to the open window like that, three floors up, but I know I'm being paranoid. And I'm not her father.

A lot of her stories start the same way: *Did he tell you...*

'No,' I say. 'Tell me.'

'You know he had to share a bathroom with the senior boarders? One of the students, or maybe a few of them, kept using his shampoo. It wasn't a big deal, but it was annoying. Like: they're all loaded, and he was scrimping and saving so he could travel in summer. He tried writing his name on the bottle, but the shampoo kept going down. And you know what he was like about his hair.'

I nod, remembering watching the hospital chaplain apply the hair-gel.

Rosa hops down from the windowsill and crosses the room to sit on the arm of the sofa. She always does this – sits everywhere but on a seat. She sits on the floor, leaning against the sofa; she perches on its arm. She moves about my flat like it's her own. I should give her a key – she's here every day anyway. The school's shut now for the long summer holidays, and she's still in limbo about what she'll do afterwards.

'I hope he wouldn't mind my telling you this.' She hesitates. 'It's pretty gross.'

'Jesus,' I say. 'How bad is it?'

'Oh well, not much Dougie can do about it now.' She laughs bleakly. Then she leans forward, grinning, hands clasped together. 'He pissed in the shampoo. Waited until it was half-empty and topped it up with pee.'

I wrinkle my nose, but I'm grinning too.

'Did anyone use it?'

'Yup. And the kid complained to the housemaster, and Dougie got hauled into Overton's office. Big trouble – the whole works: *deeply inappropriate; we expect better of you,* blah blah blah. Dougie tried to say, *Well, it was my shampoo after all, I should be able to do what I like with it,* but Overton wasn't buying it, and Dougie made it worse because he couldn't stop laughing.'

Overton hadn't mentioned this. I can't blame him – it hardly fits with his narrative. *An immeasurable contribution to the school community,* he'd said to me. But I can recognise Dougie in Rosa's story: the impulsive plan. And that teenage-boy mindset, with the penis as the solution to everything. *What did you think would happen?* I want to ask him. And I want to laugh with him over the idea of some spoilt rich kid lathering his floppy hair with Dougie's piss. I want to say to Dougie, *I promise not to tell your mother.*

But he never told me, either, and he's gone now. It's just me and Rosa, and the traffic sounds coming in the open window.

I hire a car again, and drive to Potters Bar. I'm not even intending to go to Murphy's house – I tell myself I'll just have a look around, get a feel for the area. I cruise his suburb, then circle his block a few times, slowing when I reach his street. I scan for house numbers, driving so sluggishly that I stall the unfamiliar car. I imagine what Dougie would say:

Smooth, Dad. Really stealthy. The car coughs back to life, and then I ease to a halt when I spot number 24. It's a bungalow on the corner of the block. The garden's neat enough but not fancy – the lawn mown, but nothing in the flowerbeds except some overgrown agapanthus, the first of the purple flowers daring to show.

For an hour I sit in the car. I'm not waiting for anything – I just don't know what to do next. Then the door of the bungalow opens, and Murphy comes out.

I've only seen him in a handful of online photos, half of them taken on the night of the flood, his face distorted by dirt and flashlights and shock. But I know him straight away, even though his hair looks longer now. He's tall, with wide shoulders. He's wearing running shorts and a singlet, and as soon as he reaches the pavement he breaks into a jog.

I lower my head as if I'm examining my phone, and keep my face down until he's passed my car. I force myself to calm my breathing. It was stupid of me to assume the house would be empty in the daytime. Where else would he be? His guiding company has shut down, probably for good. For the first few weeks, the website had a holding message on the home page: *We regret that we are on hiatus as of May.* Then the site was taken down altogether – each time I check, I get the same dead-end message: *Server not found.*

He speeds up. I wait until he's nearly at the corner before I pull out and drive slowly behind him. I stall once again, and hear Dougie's snort: *Basically James Bond, you are.* I follow Murphy for two blocks, but there are no other cars around, and I feel conspicuous. He turns right and jogs across the road, not twenty metres ahead of me. My foot's already on the accelerator. It would only take seconds to hit him.

I let him go, watching his calf muscles bunch and contract as he strides up the hill.

What's the point of all those muscles, I think, *if you couldn't even save my son?*

At home, I pick up my phone to call Gill and tell her what I've done, then I drop it back onto the counter. I'm afraid she'll be angry with me. I'm angry with myself. The policeman and the coroner's office have both said I need to keep away from Murphy.

And Gill's got enough to worry about. When we talk, she's always distracted. I recognise the exhaustion and fear in her voice because I hear it in my own. I don't know if it helps, those snatched conversations that we have; her running through the travels I'm supposed to be going on, and me running through my research. I don't know what we're offering each other but our own fears.

Sometimes, in my cramped bedroom in the London flat, I turn on the electric blanket for the side of the bed that would be Gill's. It's already too hot at night here, but I like the vague warmth of it, the heat coming from the other side of the bed as if she were sleeping there. I lie there in the dark, Dougie in a box on one side, imaginary Gill on the other.

There's still at least a month until the inquest. I'm afraid that all my research is getting me nowhere, when I should be at home with my family. Am I failing them, by being here, or would I be failing Dougie by leaving while there are questions still unanswered? I'm scared that I've achieved nothing, and now, after seeing Murphy, I'm scared of what I might do.

I call Gill.

'Maybe I should come back,' I say. 'I'm not getting anywhere here, really. I'm not doing anyone any good. And it's not fair on you. Maybe it's time to end all this. I'll bring Dougie home. We'll tell Sylvie the truth.'

There's a long pause.

'No,' she says, finally. 'We're managing OK here – don't worry. You have things you need to do. One of us needs to be there for the inquest. For Dougie.'

Gill

I hang up and hold the phone for a while in both hands. Of course I want Gabe to come home. I miss the sound of his voice talking to Teddy, and his patience with Papabee. The clattering of his laptop when he's working. He never learned to touch-type properly, so he jabs at each letter using only his index fingers, each keystroke a loud clatter. It used to drive me crazy, and now that it's gone I miss it.

But I just need a bit more time.

I give Sylvie the next letter, in a bundle along with a sheet of essay questions that her geography teacher emailed me.

'Everyone else can just Google the answers,' she says, glancing at the homework. 'D'you know how much harder it is without the internet?'

'If you feel like getting better and joining everyone else out there' – I gesture beyond the hospital window – 'you go for it.'

She hasn't mentioned the letter. It's the fourth one, and tracing Dougie's handwriting for the address gets easier every time. But I think of what Louise said to me: *Don't underestimate her.* I worried that the first letters were too pristine, so for this one I poured myself a glass of beer, letting the head froth over a little, and sat the glass on the letter, leaving a pale stain, nearly invisible. Then I poured it down the sink – I've never liked beer.

She doesn't open the letter while I'm there, but I notice that she holds on to it, turns it over, then turns it over again.

I ask her about the book she's reading (Emma Donoghue's

Room); I tell her about how Papabee picked Teddy up from school the other day wearing one black shoe and one brown. She remains stalwart in her silence and my voice sounds strained, so I stop, and try to keep my hands still. I watch her, holding the envelope, and catch her glancing at me.

'Is Dad OK?' Her voice startles me.

'What do you mean?' I say quickly. 'Of course he's fine. You've spoken to him, haven't you?'

'Yeah,' she said. 'He called again yesterday. But he was kind of quiet.'

'He's busy with Dougie, love. I know they're having a lot of fun, but it's not easy for Gabe, helping Dougie get around. He's working, too, remember – trying to keep on top of work stuff from over there. And anyway, he knows Dougie's been keeping you up to date with everything they're up to.' I point at the letter, still unopened in her hand.

'You'd tell me, wouldn't you?' she asks. 'If there was anything wrong with Dad? Or if there was something wrong with you and Dad? If you were getting a divorce?'

I laugh, and it's genuine. I feel drunk, giddy with relief that she's so far from the truth. 'Darling, I promise you. Dad and I are fine. He's only there to take care of Dougie.'

'He's been gone for a long time,' she says. 'Six weeks. So I just wondered.'

Six weeks. I'm so delighted that she's counting something other than calories or kilograms.

'We're fine,' I say, 'He's a bit knackered, but I think he's still having the time of his life, to be honest.' I picture it again, the two of them on Cefalu beach in Sicily, Dougie brown and Gabe pale. Dougie's leg-cast propped on a rolled-up towel.

Sylvie's belief only makes it more real. I can see the blue and white stripes on the towel; the skin on Gabe's bald head peeling slightly; the way Dougie sweats on the bridge of his nose, where his sunglasses sit.

Teddy

Thirteen and a half. That's what Sylvie said when I showed her that photo of herself. That means she would've been in grade 7 or 8. So on Sunday morning, when Mum's in the hospital and Papabee's reading in the living room, I go through the photos in the study again, one last time. There's the beach at the Neck, with Dougie and Ella sitting on the same towel. Me with a certificate from the school spelling contest, two missing teeth making a big gap in my smile so my face looks like it's not finished. Sylvie in a pair of black leggings and a black and white striped shirt, ten times too big for her, after the school play.

It was *King Lear*, and Sylvie was the Fool. Mum and Dad went both nights the play was on; Papa J even flew down from Sydney just to see it.

'He didn't come down for my nativity play,' I said, when he arrived.

'Sweetie,' said Mum. 'You were Camel Number Four. It's not the same.'

I was only seven or eight, but Mum and Dad still made me go and watch Sylvie's play. Most of it was boring – I couldn't understand the words, even though Mum spent ages beforehand explaining the story. When they squished out that man's eyes, they had fake eyeballs that looked really real, and one of them rolled across the stage to the front, near where we were sitting, and for the whole rest of the play it sat there, staring at me, and I stared back. Afterwards, when Mum and Dad asked me if I'd liked the play, all I could think of was that eye. Now I wish that I'd watched more carefully. I should've been watching Sylvie.

The school play's always at the end of the year – it must've been around December. By the end of the summer after that, Papa J was dead, and Sylvie was in hospital. So much changed, so quickly. Had her sickness started yet, while she was in *King Lear*? I didn't pay much attention to her then – why would I? She was just my sister.

I do remember how Sylvie looked, with her make-up on for the play: half of her face painted white, and half black. I remember Papa J giving her a hug after the show and she turned her body sideways, like she was already trying to disappear.

I stand in Sylvie's bedroom doorway for a second before I go in. It smells like rooms always smell when they're shut up for a long time: dust, I suppose, and old air. On her bookshelf the books are squished in, not just standing up but also lying down sideways across the top, filling every gap.

I find *King Lear* on the top shelf, between a French textbook and a book called *Wolf Hall*. I pull out the play – the pages are all crackly and wavy along the bottom, like Sylvie dropped it in the bath, and lots of the pages have the corners bent down (Mum tells me off when I do that).

I lie on my tummy on my bedroom floor and flick through the whole thing. Sylvie's gone over all the Fool's lines in bright yellow highlighter. I find every yellow bit and read every single one of the Fool's lines. I'm hoping for some big, obvious clue, like a note in red pen, written in the margin, to explain everything. But there's nothing like that, and sometimes Shakespeare makes English seem like a language I don't speak:

> *She'll taste as like this as a crab does to a crab.*
> *Thou can'st tell why one's nose stands i'th' middle*
> *on's face?*

Why to keep one's eyes of either side's nose, that
what a man cannot smell out, he may spy into.

It's all like that: nearly everything that the Fool says is riddles and nonsense, hiding in old-fashioned words. I read until the stripes of the carpet have pressed perfect stripes into the skin of my elbows, and I still haven't found any secrets.

There are some parts where I feel like I can spot a bit of Sylve in the Fool, or a bit of the Fool in her:

Have more than thou showest,
Speak less than thou knowest.

But that doesn't help me work out what it is that she *knowest*. It only tells me that maybe when she was learning all those lines, and saying them on stage every night, they got inside her, like the flu or chickenpox.

That's when I notice that the Fool's lines aren't the only ones Sylvie's marked. With a pencil, she's underlined other things too. I go through it again, every single page, checking what she's underlined, and I see that she has left me a clue after all. The underlinings aren't random. There's a pattern.

Sylvie

When I first read *King Lear*, in Mrs Robson's class in grade 8, I remember thinking, *Why would you show this to a classroom of teenage girls? Don't you realise what you've given us?* Mrs Robson leaned against her desk at the front of the class to read the first scene out loud, and when Cordelia uttered her first *Nothing*, I looked around the classroom and couldn't understand why everyone else wasn't feeling what I felt. Everyone looked completely normal. Janet Paterson was painting her nails with White-Out; Faizah and Kelly were passing notes. I looked at all of them, and then back at the book. 'Nothing,' Mrs Robson read. And I thought: *This isn't a book, or a play. This is a grenade.*

That's where I learned about *nothing*. I learned to be Cordelia, stoppering her mouth.

I read *Lear* again and again. I read it until the corners of the pages were dog-eared, and the paper along the bottom was crinkled from reading it in the bath. I got a part as the Fool in the school play, and I learned everyone else's lines as well as my own. I read it on the bus, and I made Mum take me to a bad am-dram performance in Cygnet. I read it when I should have been studying French, and when I was meant to be sleeping. *Nothing,* I said out loud to myself, under the covers. *Nothing will come of nothing.*

I always knew that Gloucester's eyes being gouged out isn't the most violent part of the story. It's Cordelia, and the way she does violence to language. She's the one who stills her own tongue, refusing to come to her own defence. She speaks loudest with her silence – louder than her sisters, or her father; louder than the storm. It's her silence that sends Lear mad. *Nothing*. The audacity of it. I'd always been a good girl: a straight-As, polite, wanting-to-please girl. It hadn't occurred to me, until Cordelia, that I was allowed to say no.

After *Lear*, I worked my way through all Shakespeare's plays. Reading *Othello*, late at night, I misread a line. I was in bed, half asleep, and when Othello says, 'Silence that dreadful bell,' I read it as: 'Silence, that dreadful bell.'

In my tired state I had to re-read it twice to make sense of it. I never liked the real version as much as my accidental one. I recognised something in 'Silence, that dreadful bell.' I understood how noisy silence could be, just as I understood how *nothing* could be a verb.

But these days, I think less about Cordelia, and more about Lavinia, in *Titus Andronicus*. I keep coming back to her. Unlike Cordelia, Lavinia doesn't choose her silence. She is silenced with a blade – her tongue chopped out at the root, her hands hacked off.

Is this what I've been doing, all this time?

I have hacked out my own tongue.

I have been here, alone, ringing the dreadful bell of silence.

Gill

I slice mushrooms, to bake with tomatoes and polenta. I speed up until the knife on the wooden board is a metronome, set too quick. So fast that I'm daring something to go wrong.

I can't stop writing my new recipes. They're not really about Dougie and Sylvie; they're about what's left after they've gone. About our house, crowded with all its absences.

That night, on the phone, I tell Gabe I'm writing more than ever.

'That's great,' he says. 'I'm so glad. And it'll do you good.'

He's always been like that: excited for me. Cutting out all my newspaper columns; recording me any time I was on the radio. Somewhere in the shed we still have a shoebox of cassette tapes, even though I don't think we even own a tape player any more. Gabe's handwriting on each label: *Gill – ABC. Do Not Tape Over!*

The next day, after I've been to the hospital, I finally email some of the recipes to Sue. She texts me within forty minutes. *Are you in? I'm coming over.*

She has a stack of papers in one hand as she comes up the front path.

'I can't sell this to a publisher,' she says, putting my recipes down carefully on the kitchen counter while I pour the gin. 'You know that, right?' She gestures at the pages. 'You can write stuff like this and you know I'll always be happy to read it. And if it helps you, great. But I can't sell this. People will think you've gone mad.'

I nod. 'It's not really for selling.'

She grabs a page at random. '*Soufflé for the day your daughter's weight reaches a new low.*' Another page. '*Quiche for the day after your son's cremation.* This isn't a book. It's a therapy session. Which is fine, as long as you don't want to, you know, keep making a living from selling your writing.' She fishes through the pages and yanks out the saffron and cauliflower recipe. 'You have to pay for all this bloody saffron, for one thing.'

We both laugh, but she's still got an eyebrow raised.

'Have you called that man yet?' A few weeks ago, she gave me the number of a therapist that her sister recommended. 'Natasha says he's really good,' she continues. 'Sensible. No Enya music, I promise. No dolphin wall-hangings.'

The phone number's been sitting on a Post-it note by the phone for weeks. At some point I propped a shopping list over the top of it. *Loo paper. Teddy's muesli bars. Saffron. Washing powder.*

'Maybe this is therapy enough,' Sue says, sweeping the recipes into a rough pile. 'But it couldn't hurt to see a professional.'

'Probably. I'm sure you're right. But when? When would I find the time?'

I'm glad Sue's been honest with me – and I didn't ever expect that these recipes would make a viable book. But I also know it will make no difference – I'll keep writing the recipes. I don't have any choice.

When she's gone, I get back to work on the latest letter.

> *After Sicily, Rome's a bit of a shock to the system –*
> *it's crammed with traffic and noise and people and*
> *heat. And all v unmistakably Italian – in a tiny alley*
> *yesterday we saw a café where people literally drive*

*up to the counter on their Vespas, slam down a shot
of coffee from the counter, and drive out. Like drive-
thru McDonald's but a million times classier.*

*We did a tour of the Colosseum yesterday – usually
guided tours are my idea of hell, but I'll admit that
this one was worthwhile. Surprise twist: apparently
heaps of the ancient statues, buildings etc. actually
used to be painted really bright colours – we all just
picture them the colour of faded sandstone because
that's how they look now. (If you already know this,
please pretend you don't – I want to be the smart
one for a change.) Am looking forward to being
a massive bore who smugly points out errors in
historical films from now on...*

*Heaps of stray cats around Rome (Teddy would love
it) – they're extremely cute but Dad said I shouldn't
pat them in case they have fleas, which led to a
classic language barrier moment at lunch yesterday.
Me to the waiter at the outdoor pizza restaurant:
'Can you touch the cats?' Him (v enthusiastic) 'Oh
yes! Yes!' (Runs inside, comes back a moment later
with a broom and starts trying to hit the cats and
chase them away down the street.) Anyway, Dad's
probably right about not touching the cats – fleas in
my cast would be a new low.*

I can picture him: skin brown all over, even the toes where
they emerge from his cast – and then the stark white flesh
underneath the plaster, smelling like an old Band-Aid.

*At times Dad and I've come fairly close to wanting
to kill each other (in the year of our lord 2016,
does he really need to have the key-strokes sound*

*turned on in his phone? REALLY?), but we've also
had some really great chats. You know he worries
about you all the time, right? (Even with my
broken leg, you're still stealing my thunder.) Mum
too, obvs. But you know that already. Go easy on
them, yeah?*

*Anyway, enough of the soppy stuff. Day after
tomorrow we're off to Paris...*

When the hospital rings, I'm squatting on the grass in the
backyard, with a black plastic bag on my hand, like a glove,
to scoop up a shit that SausageDog's just deposited. I have
my phone in my pocket – this is what you do, when your
daughter lives in the hospital. You take your phone with
you to the garden, and to the loo. When you have a shower,
you balance your phone on the towel-rail where you can
still hear if anyone calls.

I drop the poo bag and fumble to answer the call. *There's
a limit*, I think; *I can deal with dog shit and calls from the
hospital, but not at the same time.*

'Should I come in?' I say, as soon as I recognise Louise's
voice.

'No need,' she says, quickly. 'It's not bad news.'

My stomach wants to unclench, but I don't trust Louise's
words. It's never not bad news.

'Is it her blood pressure again? The cardiac guy said—'

'Honestly. It's nothing to worry about. Good news, in fact.
I thought you'd like to know.'

I wait.

'Nothing momentous,' Louise says. 'We both know that's
not how this works. But she's drunk a Sustagen, two days in
a row. Voluntarily.'

Sustagen, that viscous beige fluid that the hospital uses
as a food replacement. 249 calories in each carton (Sylvie's

made us all into experts). We buy it in bulk when she comes home – a shelf in the fridge is still full of Sustagen from the last visit, when she only lasted a few days before being readmitted.

'She didn't say anything when I was in yesterday, or this morning,' I say.

'I'm not surprised – on some level, she's ashamed. But today she asked the dietitian how long she'd have to keep it up to get the tube out.'

'How long would that be?'

'Let's not get ahead of ourselves,' Louise tells me. 'She'd have to manage more than one Sustagen a day. I'd like to see her coping with some solids, too, and maintaining at least her current weight. So we're still talking a good while, and I wouldn't want us to count our chickens. But it's the asking that seems positive to me. It was off her own back. Taking some ownership of the process – I see that as a really positive sign.'

I can forgive Louise her brief lapse into psycho-jargon. *Taking some ownership of the process.* Today, I can forgive anyone anything. After I thank Louise I pick up the dog poo, and even the warmth of the bag in my hand feels like a benediction.

I ring Gabe as soon as it's dawn in London.

'That's brilliant,' he says. 'Jesus. Really brilliant.'

'It's only been two days.'

'I know. But still – it's better than nothing.' Sylvie has trained us to be grateful for such small things. Two days, two cartons of Sustagen.

His voice is hesitant. 'Does this mean we should think about telling her?'

'Are you out of your mind? You want to derail this, just when she's showing some signs of progress?'

'Of course not. That's the last thing I want to do. But lying to her—'

'We're keeping her alive,' I say. 'That's not the same thing.'

What if it is, though? What if it's exactly the same thing? What if the only way to keep my child alive is by lying to her?

Gabe

'Anyway,' Gill says, 'remember you're heading for Paris shortly. Rome's been a bit much, but he loved the Colosseum. And cats – there're cats all over Rome.'

'Listen,' I say. 'Maybe we don't need to do this any more. If she's doing well, maybe we need to try trusting her.'

'Trust her? How?'

I know what she means. We have to have Sylvie fed through a tube because we can't trust her to keep herself alive. Since the first suicide attempt, we've had to keep the knives and the medicines in a locked box whenever she's allowed home. How can we entrust her with Dougie's death, and our grief? In her hands it will become a weapon, to be turned against herself.

Gill's shouting down the phone now, through sobs. 'I've been working so hard to keep her going. To make sure this whole thing doesn't fall apart. And just when it's working, you want to risk telling her?'

'I know how hard you've been trying.' I do. I know she's done what I can't bring myself to do, which is to step back into our lives, and to keep going. She hasn't had the luxury of indulging her grief, the way I have. But this lying to Sylvie can't be right. I'm afraid of what Gill's doing. I'm afraid for her.

'Don't you trust me?' she asks.

'I love you.' I don't know if that's the same thing.

Two years after Sylvie was first admitted to hospital, I said to Gill, 'It'd be easier if she had cancer. Then, at least, we'd all be on the same side.'

It's not something that we could say in public. Nobody would dare wish that on anyone, let alone your own daughter. And we saw them in the hospital all the time – those poor kids, bald and eyebrow-less, faces puffed with steroids.

Nonetheless, it's true: this illness sets us against her. Sylvie hates us for refusing to let her die. She resents us the same way that she resents the nasogastric tube that keeps her alive. 'How dare you?' she screamed at us, once, when we were driving her back to the hospital because she hadn't maintained her weight and her lips had started to turn blue again. 'How dare you?' she yelled again and again from the back seat, while Gill gripped the steering wheel. In Sylvie's last year at school we'd gone to watch her in a production of *King Lear*; now her clenched, furious face in the rear-view mirror made me think of what faithful Kent says about Lear's death being a relief: *He hates him / That would upon the rack of this tough world / Stretch him out longer.*

We stayed at the hospital while they re-inserted her tube. The first time, she yanked it out again straight away. The second time, they sedated her. That was the night, on the drive home, that I said to Gill, 'It'd be easier if she had cancer.'

'Don't ever say that,' Gill said. 'How can you say that?'

It's my job, you see, to tell the truth, and it's her job to hate me for it.

It's barely dawn; Rosa won't be here for hours. Outside, the buses are grinding down High Street. It's warm already; exhaust fumes suspended in the humid air.

I get a glass of water. On the kitchen bench, by the sink, is a knife block. The medium knife is a good size:

small enough to fit in a pocket, but not too small to sink deep. It feels right in my hand. And I'm not going to be slicing anything. Just one sharp jab, upwards, under the ribs. I've Googled it. I've even practised it, standing in the kitchen feeling like an idiot.

When Rosa comes, around eleven, she makes herself tea. I've left the knife on the counter and she picks it up automatically, turns it over to see if it's clean, then slips it back in the block. I act as though nothing has happened. Nothing has happened, yet.

'What are you working on today, Sherlock?' she asks, throwing herself down sideways on the couch, her legs dangling over the arm.

'I'm trying to put together a clearer timeline. The ambulances weren't there until 1208 – that's thirty-eight minutes after they were called. I drove the route myself, from that same hospital, and it only took me eighteen minutes.' I did it this week, in a hire car. Twice, to be sure. 'And I don't have a siren.'

'Would it have made any difference? They didn't find him for hours.'

'There's an NHS guideline – it's supposed to—'

'Would it have made a difference?' she interrupts in a flat voice.

'Don't you want to know?' I wave at the papers in front of me. 'Don't you want to work out what happened?'

'I don't need to work it out. I was there, remember?'

While she doesn't like to talk about that day, she's happy to talk about Dougie. *Did he ever tell you...* she says, and I stop whatever I'm working on and listen. Sometimes, when she's gone, I write her stories down. Not for the coroner – this is just for me. And for Gill, and Teddy, and even for Sylvie, one day, when we tell her the truth. I scribble my summaries of Rosa's stories:

Prague (Easter) – they forgot the code to get back into the hostel and D climbed up to the second floor and tried to get in through the balcony; got the loop of his jeans stuck on the railing and an Israeli guy inside had to rescue him.

At the school – he was meant to be helping the matron in the laundry and he washed a whole load of uniform jumpers at 60° and they all shrank; said it was a great result because they never got him to do laundry again.

He and Rosa downloaded all the old Miss Marple movies (the ones with Geraldine McEwan) and binge-watched the whole series over a few weeks. R says D was 'really into them'.

'I liked that he enjoyed weird stuff like that,' Rosa said with a shrug. 'Not a jock, even though he did so much sport. It was refreshing – a lot of the male teachers are really macho. Sometimes the staffroom felt like a big sausage-fest.'

When she uses terms like that, I'm reminded of how young she is. How old I am. The only thing that we have in common is sitting in a small grey box in the next room. Why does she keep coming here? Why am I so glad that she does?

I want to call Gill and tell her all Rosa's stories about Dougie. But Gill doesn't want to talk about him, except for the details of the letters she's writing. I understand why – it's too raw, and she's working too hard to maintain the secret for Sylvie. But because I can't talk about him properly except with Rosa, it's as if his life has become the secret, rather than his death.

In the late afternoon, when Rosa's gone, I practise again with the knife. I rehearse the movement, slipping my hand from my pocket and bringing the blade up hard, like a punch but with the knife gripped tight in my fist.

What I don't practise is what happens after that. I don't practise trying to put the knife back in my pocket, or running away. I can never think beyond that moment: the grab with the other arm, and then the strike. I can't picture the man bleeding, or dying. I'm not even sure that I want to. It doesn't make any difference. I can picture Dougie, drowning in the dark. That's enough. There has to be a price paid for that. Twelve went into the cave, and only eleven came out. That equation has to be balanced.

I turn the knife over again. *Don't you trust me?* Gill asked me on the phone. Do I trust myself?

Teddy

Going into the ward this time, I don't get nervous when I walk past all the other rexiles' rooms. I don't count how many there are. I don't even look at them. This time I know what I'm doing.

I pull the curtains shut around Sylvie's bed, and hold up the *King Lear* book so that she can see the cover.

'You were the Fool,' I say. 'How come you've underlined all Cordelia's lines too?'

She takes a deep breath in and lets it out slowly. The tube shakes when she breathes. I try not to look at it.

'Have you even read it?' she asks.

I nod. 'And I watched you do the play, remember?'

Somebody walks past her door, footsteps going *squeak squeak* on the shiny floor.

Sylvie keeps her voice quiet. 'Yeah. But did you understand it?'

I shake my head. 'Not most of it. But in the Cordelia bits, there was a lot of stuff about *nothing*.'

If *nothing* is Sylvie's answer, what's the question? And can you catch silence from a book?

'What are you playing at, Teddy? Why do you keep bringing me this stuff?'

I don't want to lie to her – all my lying is used up with the Dougie lie.

'I'm trying to find the answer,' I tell her.

'To what?'

What I want to say: *To you.* Instead, I say, 'To all of this.' I wave my arm around at her little room, and the big ward outside it.

'I'm not a problem to be solved,' she says. But she doesn't sound cross. She sounds tired, the same as always, and a bit afraid.

'Teddy,' she says again. 'What are you doing?'

I'm not sure how to explain to Sylvie how it all fits together: these prices I'm looking for, the Lorax, and her. Sometimes things make sense in my head and then when I say them out loud they feel all wrong. In case my own words aren't working properly, I try using that bit from the start of *The Lorax*, about the price you need to pay to hear the story: the coins, and the nail, and the ancient snail shell. I know it off by heart. I say it like it's a nursery rhyme, or a prayer. She still looks at me like she doesn't get it.

'I'm trying to find the right thing,' I explain. 'Special things, so you'll tell me your story. To help you get better.'

'Like your bribe? That money you tried to give me?'

'No. I got it wrong, that time. I was wrong about the photo, too. What I'm looking for, it's not a bribe. It's like a – a price, or a key, or a present. Like I'm treasure-hunting.'

'Does this look like a treasure to you?' She picks up the creased old book.

I shrug. 'I know that if I had special treasures, at least one of them would definitely be a book.' Probably *The Lorax*. Or *101 Dalmatians*.

'What would your other treasures be?'

I'm little, but I'm not stupid. I know she's changing the subject so she doesn't have to talk about herself, or *King Lear*, or how she took Cordelia's *nothing* and built a cage out of bones. Still, it feels good that she asks me something. Since she went into the Boneyard, Sylvie's usually not interested in anything at all. So when she asks me about my treasures, and looks at me seriously like that, it makes me feel like a giant, big as the world.

'SausageDog,' I say. 'Definitely. And my key to Papabee's flat.' Neither of the big kids got one – just me, because I'm the one that goes to Papabee's all the time. Normally I get their hand-me-down things, but that key is just mine.

'The book that Mum wrote for me, when I was a kid, and Dad did the pictures.'

'I remember that,' she says. '*Teddy to the Rescue.*'

'Yup. And my sunglasses that you bought me two Christmases ago.' Because Mum and Dad don't believe in brand-name things, but Sylvie knew I really wanted some Oakley glasses like the cool kids at school, and she bought them for me herself, with some of her babysitting money from before she got sick.

'What else?'

I want to say Dougie's old cricket bat, which still has the marks of his fingers on the rubber grip. But I don't dare to say it out loud to Sylvie because even just thinking about Dougie makes my tongue feel bigger and heavier in my mouth, and I can't risk getting ox tongue again – not now.

'They're good treasures,' she says, smiling at me, and just for a moment, if I ignore the tube, her smile even looks a bit like the smile in the photo that I brought her. Like a real smile, on a real person.

'Any more?' she asks.

'I can't think of any for now,' I say. 'What about you? Are you going to tell me about *King Lear*?'

'There's nothing to say.'

Sylvie

'You were the Fool,' says Teddy. 'How come you've underlined all Cordelia's lines too?'

I can't explain to Teddy about Cordelia and the Fool. How being the Fool is being Cordelia too, and vice versa. Teddy's eleven – he doesn't want to hear me rehash the essay I wrote for Mrs Robson in grade 9 English. He won't get it.

The year I discovered *King Lear*, I read every book in the Shakespeare section of the library. I pored over his plays like I was lost and they were maps. When I'd finished them all, and the poetry too, I read all the criticism I could get my hands on.

And this is what I learned: Cordelia and the Fool never appear at the same time. Some people think it's because they would have been played by the same actor (a young boy, maybe). Some people even say they're meant to be the same person. I don't know about that – but I know there's a link between them. Cordelia's exile made the Fool fade away: *Since my young lady's going into France, sir, the fool hath much pined away.* I know that when Lear holds Cordelia's dead body in his arms, it's the Fool's name in his mouth: *And my poor fool is hanged.*

Perhaps Lear's just using a pet name for Cordelia. Or maybe he's confusing the two – the same way Papabee calls Dougie Teddy, and Teddy Dougie. It doesn't matter. Either way, the two are blurred.

So while I was being the Fool, I was thinking about Cordelia. I was thinking about how she refuses words, and he refuses food, and they both end up dead.

I was thinking about Cordelia's *nothing*, and how it's her salvation and her destruction.

And Teddy, little Teddy, with his treasure hunt, and his head full of books. Holding out my battered copy of *King Lear* as if I'm going to throw up my hands and tell him everything.

He thinks my secrets will come pouring out like coins from a poker machine: *Jackpot.*

He doesn't realise that my secrets will swarm out of me like bees.

PART FIVE

Blue cheese and smoked salmon risotto for when your daughter may be recovering, but you're afraid to believe it

When you add the white wine (or, even better, vermouth, if you have it), bend your head low over the hot pan and take a slow, deep breath. Let that flush of boozy steam coat your face. It might even burn a little. You won't mind.

Everyone knows that the rice in a decent risotto should be al dente, but for this one, I stop at the instant just before. The rice must be firmer than the toasted pine nuts that you'll sprinkle on top at the end. When nothing feels real, you need to hear the crunch between your teeth. If you leave it on the heat for a minute too long, it slips into blandness, the rice going limp. You need to get this right, even if it takes two attempts. You need the rice between your teeth to crunch like sardine bones.

Gill

I stir the rice, and I try not to think about Dougie, or his empty room at the end of the corridor. I stir, and I try not to think about Sylvie and her cartons of Sustagen, or the four crackers that she ate yesterday, according to Louise. I can't allow myself to believe that Sylvie's really beginning to eat again. Hope is a place that I dare not go; if I enter, there will be no coming back.

So I cook risotto instead. I savour the repetitiveness of the stirring, and the patience that it imposes. The stock is absorbed at its own pace, one ladleful at a time. I watch the trails my wooden spoon leaves in the rice, and the way the rice always closes over them again. I envy the rice its reliable forgetting.

When I look over my hurried notes for the recipe, speckled with oil, I see how the handwriting slips between my own and Dougie's.

Sylvie

It doesn't happen just like that. It happens in small steps. First, the Sustagen. Then the foods that I can trust: crackers; Special K breakfast cereal, precisely weighed, with skim milk. Black tea (no milk; no sugar). Sometimes it takes me an hour or two, and the nurses hover nearby, watching to make sure I'm not squirrelling anything away. I'm not allowed to go to the toilet for at least an hour after eating, either, to make sure I keep it down. I do (vomiting's less tempting with a tube in, anyway – that's a mistake you don't make twice).

When Mum comes in, she fishes around in her bag for the latest offering. 'Risotto,' she says, holding up the small plastic tub. 'Blue cheese and smoked salmon, with baby spinach and pine nuts.'

She puts it on my bedside table, and picks up yesterday's container, to take home. Then she notices that it's lighter than it should be. It's only a small container – barely a few spoons full – but it's half-empty. And in our family, we're alert to tiny changes in weight.

She's still holding the container, trying very hard to pretend that this is normal. Teddy's noticed too, and goes to say something, and she shoots him a look. They're both watching me now, which makes it worse.

'Was that cumin, in the sauce?' I ask.

She nods. 'And turmeric, too – just a bit.'

Teddy

After dinner, Mum and Papabee and I watch a quiz show, and there's a bit about how the City of London still pays rent to the queen, because of some leftover law from hundreds and hundreds of years ago. The part that makes me pay attention is the price that they pay her. I even Google it to double-check, after Papabee's gone, and it's just like they said on the TV: *a knife, an axe, six oversized horseshoes, and sixty-one nails*. That's how I know I'm onto something – the London price has got nails, just like *The Lorax*, with its fifteen cents and its single nail. So I know for sure that I'm on the right track.

After that, I think a lot about nails. When Sylvie was younger she did tap-dancing lessons in a church hall in West Hobart, and Mum and I used to wait in the room off to the side. There was a poster on the wall that was a picture of Jesus on the cross and great big letters that said:

IT WAS NOT THE NAILS THAT
HELD CHRIST TO THE CROSS
BUT HIS LOVE FOR YOU AND ME

That picture never made me think about love – only about nails. Every week, I used to sit on the bench right underneath the poster, so I wouldn't have to stare at it. I already knew about Jesus and the nails and the cross, of course – we have RE lessons at school – but up until the poster I'd never really thought about what would happen when a nail goes through a hand.

Even though I haven't seen that poster for years, just thinking about it makes me scrunch my fists up tight. And it makes me think there must be a special magic that has something to do with nails. Jesus, *The Lorax*, and London can't all be wrong.

I'd like to see what Sylvie would say if I went to the shed and got a nail, and took it in to her as part of the price for her story. But they're really strict about No Sharp Objects in the ward. Aunt Amy sent Sylve a pair of silver earrings for her birthday, once, and the nurses made Mum take them home again because they were long and kind of pointy at the end. I get it. I've seen the scars all the way down Sylvie's arm.

Anyway, I have another idea for what the price might be – something even better than nails. I know where I need to go this time. The only problem is that I need Papabee to drive me there, and his driving's getting worse and worse. I didn't tell Mum that he got lost the other day and was late picking me up from school. And I definitely didn't tell her that when Papabee parked outside his flat yesterday he hit the telegraph pole with his back light. I don't want Mum to worry. And I especially don't want her to start talking about Papabee having to stop driving. I want to believe that if love could keep Jesus on the cross, then love can also keep Papabee's Toyota Corolla on the road. Because, this weekend, I need him to drive me a lot further than just back from school.

Gabe

Rosa and I have drunk too much. It's become a habit. She comes around in the late morning; we open a bottle of cheap wine and make sandwiches for lunch; if she's still here in the evening we go to the Italian place down the road and drink their house red with greasy pizza.

This daily drinking isn't like the drinking that I remember from home: the kind of happy, noisy drinking that we used to do at the Neck, Sue and Gill laughing louder and louder and Dan pouring more wine and all of us talking over each other.

This is different. Rosa and I drink like we're thirsty. And even though we talk, it's quieter than those conversations at the Neck. Rosa and I talk around and around the silence that would be there if we stopped talking. The silence of Dougie, who says nothing.

This afternoon, her cheeks are red. I don't know whether it's the heat or the wine we had with lunch. The school's still closed for the summer holidays, the boarders all at home with their families. I picture Rosa walking those long, empty corridors. No wonder she comes here so often.

After today's lunch she sprawls across my couch and flicks through her phone, a glass of white wine on the floor nearby.

'I'm going to look back on this stage of my life as, like, *Rosa Campbell: The Couch Years*,' she says.

'Hardly years,' I say. 'Anyway, cut yourself some slack.'

She doesn't reply.

'Have they said anything yet?' I ask her. 'About your contract, at the school?'

She shakes her head. 'Not yet. I don't know if I want to stay, even if they do decide to keep me on. My sister says I can go and stay with her for a while in Mexico. I'd like to. And my best friend wants to go to Iceland, for a holiday – asked me if I'll go with her. The hot springs, you know? But it depends on what the school decides. Or what I decide. And I sort of feel like—' She pauses, one hand circling impatiently. 'I feel like I'm waiting for something to happen.'

'Maybe after the inquest you'll feel different,' I say. 'Some closure, maybe.'

'Closure,' she says, then says it again in a bad American accent: '*Closure*. What does that really mean, anyway?' She shrugs.

That night, when we're halfway through the second bottle at the Italian restaurant, and I'm telling her that Meredith Calvert still hasn't replied to my email asking her to meet again, Rosa puts down the pizza crust she's fiddling with and says, 'And then what?'

'What do you mean?'

'I mean: what happens next, after you've found out all the answers? Is that going to make it all better?'

'I'm not kidding myself that it's going to bring him back. Or even that it'll make it easier. But it's something I have to do.'

'Who for? For Dougie?'

'What about for you? Don't you want to know?'

'Don't make me your excuse,' she says, picking up the pizza crust again. 'You're not doing this for me. I never asked you to do any of this.'

'I need to do this. I need to find out why it happened.'

'You're still not answering my question,' Rosa says. 'What then?'

In the morning I go to the Wellcome Centre Library again, to read more about subdural haematomas. My bus gets held up in traffic on Euston Rd, and I get back to the flat later than usual. Rosa's waiting there, sitting on the steps that lead up to the door. She jumps up when she sees me coming from the bus stop.

'Where were you?'

'Sorry,' I say. 'Traffic. Why? Everything OK?'

'It's fine,' she says, but she throws her bag over her shoulder and stomps up the stairs.

'You could've texted me if you were worried.' I put the kettle on.

'I wasn't worried. I'm fine.'

But I worry, too, later that week when she has the norovirus and doesn't come. She texts to let me know, but I can't stop thinking about her, there in that huge school with nobody to take care of her. When she comes back on the fourth day, thinner and with dry, flaking lips, I tell her that she needs to drink more water, and while she naps on my couch I go out to the pharmacy and get her some Dioralyte sachets. At dinner that night the waiter at the Italian restaurant says, 'Nice to see your daughter is back,' and neither of us corrects him, because we don't know what we are to each other.

She orders wine.

'Are you sure we should?' I say. 'You're still on the mend.'

'What's the worst that could happen?' she says.

And there's no answer to that, because the worst thing that could happen has already happened. When the wine comes, I pour us both a glass.

That night I catch the train out to Potters Bar. I don't need to check the address – I have it memorised – and I find my way from the station on foot. The streets are wide and mainly empty, and every house has a front garden. It's so suburban and quiet compared to the sirens and constant traffic that

I've become used to near my flat. I stand outside Murphy's bungalow at the corner of the street. A light glows from a rear room. A man with a dog walks past and I pretend to look at my phone until he's gone.

It's nearly nine o'clock now but only just starting to get dark, and the day's heat hasn't dissipated. Another light comes on inside the house. I walk the length of the agapanthus that rim the lawn. There's no sign of any kids: no children's bikes chained to the fence, or play equipment in the yard.

I duck my head as a car's headlights sweep over me. The car slows, then pulls over and parks barely five metres from me. The man who gets out is shorter than Murphy, and has a beard. I pretend to examine my phone again, but he's not looking at me. He strides towards the front door with a briefcase in one hand and a shopping bag in the other. I can even hear his voice, when he calls out as he swings the door shut behind him. Not the words, but the sound of it – the unmistakable *I'm home* tone of someone arriving at the end of a long day. I walk slowly round the corner and peer over the fence to the rear of the house, where the lights are on. There are French doors to the garden, a whole wall of glass looking into the kitchen. Murphy's cooking; the other man's unpacking the groceries. They move around each other easily. They're not talking, but there must be a TV or radio on because they both laugh at the same instant, at something I can't hear.

Does he look happy, or sad? *Devastated,* the newspaper report said. I'm looking for remorse in the way that he fills the kettle, or the angle of his head when he bends to close a cupboard. I've become an old madwoman scrying for messages in tea leaves.

I can't tell what they're cooking – Gill would have worked it out. The thought of her makes me ask what I'm doing here, standing in the dark, staring over Murphy's fence like some kind of pervert. Am I really even here? Or am I in Hobart, with my family, or in Paris with Dougie, as Gill's letters pretend?

Murphy lowers the blinds on the French windows. For a second, as he reaches up for the blind, he's facing me directly, and I freeze. But he's in the brightness and I'm in the twilight, and he doesn't seem to see me. The blind drops. A light goes on in another room, and then off again, leaving the strobing blue light that only comes from a TV. I stay there a while longer, but there's nothing to see.

Am I going to do this? Can I really hurt this man now I've heard his partner call out to greet him? Now I've seen them cooking together in their own kitchen?

It doesn't feel like a choice. It feels like something already marked on one of my maps. It feels like a fact – solid and incontrovertible as the asphalt under my feet. Solid as Dougie's body in the morgue – the unyielding coolness of his skin.

Sylvie

Dad rings, so I have to wheel the drip-stand with my feeding pump to the nurses' station.

'I miss you, love,' he says. 'How are you? You being nice to Mum?'

I make a non-committal sound, and twist around so that the nurses can only see my back. It's night here – it must be morning in Europe.

'Are you still in Rome?'

A moment's pause. 'No – Paris now.' His voice is kind of croaky.

'You sound tired,' I say. The feeding pump whirrs and clicks.

'Feeling a bit seedy this morning, to be honest,' he says. 'Your brother's leading me astray. I'm too old to be trying to keep up with a nineteen-year-old. Too much beer, not enough sleep.' He's silent for a few seconds. 'He sends his love, by the way.'

The first and last time I ever got drunk was with Dougie. It was New Year's Eve at the Neck, and everyone went down to the beach. There were two bonfires – a big one where the grown-ups had set up their deck-chairs and picnic mats, and one further down the beach, where we kids gathered. Nathan had stolen half a bottle of vodka from Sue and Dan, and the rest of us had pilfered wine and beer from the eskis near the adults. I had two beers tucked in the front of my hoodie. They'd come straight from the ice-filled eski and they pressed cold and wet against my stomach. I tried not to clink as I walked.

I pretended to like the taste of beer, until I'd drunk so much it didn't taste of anything. The fire was hot on one side of my face, the sea wind cool on the other. Teddy was snuggled in against my legs, half asleep, while Dougie and Ella and Nathan talked across the fire, the alcohol making all their jokes a lot funnier than they should have been. It was the summer before Papa J died. Ella passed me the vodka bottle and I took another big swig.

Later I threw up and Dougie patted me on the back, kicked sand over the puddle of vomit and fetched me water to drink. He walked me up and down the water's edge until I felt sober enough to face the grown-ups back at the other fire.

Dougie took care of me, even then, when I'd begun not to care about myself. I was already hiding food, and testing the gaps between my ribs with my fingers.

I open his latest letter and read it again.

Gill

I get talking to a young woman in the hospital canteen – we've both ordered the cheese and mushroom toastie for lunch. I see her tentatively prodding her soggy sandwich, and from the next table I say, 'Honestly, I wouldn't bother. I made the mistake of eating mine and I'm regretting it.'

Over tea in Styrofoam cups, she ends up telling me that her boyfriend is upstairs in the reproductive health clinic, giving a sperm sample before starting aggressive chemotherapy that will probably destroy his fertility.

'He doesn't even know if he wants kids,' she says. 'He always said probably not, and I'm not sure either way. We hardly even talked about it – we're only twenty-seven, for God's sake. But suddenly, it's now or never: freeze his sperm before the chemo kills it for good.' With the plastic fork she pushes the flaccid grey mushrooms around on her plate. 'I can't stop thinking about him, up there, wanking over some second-hand porn magazine.' She shakes her head. 'I love him – I do – but this whole sperm thing – in a weird way it's actually been harder than the cancer.'

All through the afternoon I think about her, and that mound of grey mushrooms congealing between the slices of damp toast.

That night I write: *Mushrooms for the day your boyfriend is giving a sperm sample before starting chemotherapy.*

I use smoked garlic, for depth, and sear the mushrooms so they won't be soggy. I add some samphire, for colour, and for the saltiness. I serve it for dinner on crispy sourdough toast, which Teddy complains is too crunchy.

A week later my old friend Esther phones to tell me that her first grandchild has been born.

'I didn't want to upset you,' she says, a bit hesitant. 'I expect all these things must be hard for you.' Her husband died two years ago, after a sudden stroke, so she understands better than most what loss feels like. But tonight, her giddy joy is hard to resist. 'I don't know what to do with myself,' she admits. 'I'm doing laps of the kitchen like a drunk person. I keep looking at the photo they emailed, and crying.'

I cook for her, that same night: *Late-night supper after receiving a phone call to announce the safe birth of your first grandson.* Figs, because that seems suitably fecund. Fattened and warmed in a ginger sugar syrup, with slices of lemon floating like lily pads, the citrus and the sweetness together.

I know that what Sue said about these recipes is probably right. I know that when people buy my cookbooks they're buying an idea, an aspiration: the artfully styled photographs of a kitchen that isn't mine (it's a studio, hired by the publisher). I've always tried my best not to peddle any nonsense: no clean-eating nonsense; no diet claims; no 'this meal will change your life.' But I know how the business works – and I fall for it myself when I buy other people's cookbooks. It's the transaction that we make:

Buy this book and you too could be standing, with good hair, in a shabby-chic kitchen, an egg nestled peacefully on a mound of flour on a wooden table. You'll grind your own spices in a mortar and pestle, instead of relying on out-of-date powdered spices with a layer of greasy dust on the lid.

Buy this book and you too will be the kind of person who keeps your dry goods in glass jars,

each one labelled. Your counter will be covered
with small bowls of ingredients you prepared
earlier, instead of being scattered with unopened
mail, a packet of dog treats, and your son's soccer
mouthguard.

Lately, I don't feel I can participate in that transaction. I look at my life and ask, *Who would want this? Who would want any part of this?*

Buy this book and you too could have a whole shelf
in the fridge devoted to the food-replacement drinks
that are the only thing your daughter will eat.

Buy this book and you too could be crying over the
sink because the taste of maple syrup reminds you
of your dead son.

I'd like to tell Gabe the truth about my new recipes, and what Sue said about them, but I can't bring myself to ring him. He still calls every day, to speak to Teddy, but when it's my turn to talk to him I find myself saying that we're running late for school, or that I need to call my editor about the afternoon's deadline. 'Tell him I'll call him later,' I say to Teddy. 'Give him my love.'

I don't call back later. It's not that Gabe doesn't understand me – it's that he understands me too well. He asks me questions about when we should tell Sylvie, and I don't have the answers.

I know my new recipes – my *batshit recipes*, as Sue's started to call them – will never become a book. But I keep writing them anyway. I've been thinking about *The Book of Common Prayer* that my mum always kept on her bedside table. All those prayers for specific days. *The Thanksgiving of*

Women after Childbirth. Forms of Prayer for the Anniversary of the day of Accession of the Reigning Sovereign. The Order for the Burial of the Dead.

I even email a working title to Sue. *What do you think about this, for a title: THE BOOK OF COMMON FARE.*

She emails back, straight away. *I like it, but this is better: THE COOKBOOK OF COMMON PRAYER. Come over?*

I grab a lemon and drive to her place, and we sit at the outside table with gin and a bowl of olives.

'You're still doing it, then? These batshit recipes?'

I nod, passing her a small pile of paper. 'Turns out I don't seem able to do much else.'

She flicks through a few pages.

'I know they're weird,' I say.

'Yup.' She reaches for another olive. 'I like this one, though – the sperm mushrooms one. I'd cook that.' She gathers the papers into a pile. 'Let me take these, have another look through them. Far be it for me to admit to being wrong, but there could be a salvageable idea in here, among all these weirdly specific recipes.'

'That's the problem, though, isn't it? Most of them are so specific to what's going on for me – they're not going to be relevant, or even interesting, to anyone else.'

She shrugs. 'Pretty sure not many people have had the experience of faking madness while finding a way to kill their uncle and avenge their murdered father – but young Will Shakespeare seems to have done alright out of it.'

'But you're right that it couldn't work as a book,' I say. '*Sperm mushrooms*. It's hardly aspirational.'

She leans back and spits the olive stone into a rosemary bush.

'I dunno,' she says. 'Maybe people don't want a cookbook about a life they aspire to. Maybe they want a cookbook they can recognise themselves in.'

My phone rings. When I see *Hospital (Louise)* on my screen I get a lurch of fear.

'Tell me now,' I say to Louise. I knock over the olive bowl as I stand up. 'Please don't make me wait.'

'It's sort of nothing,' she says. 'Something and nothing.'

'What do you mean?' I'm already grabbing my car keys, gesturing to Sue that I need to go.

'She ran away,' Louise says. 'For about half an hour. But then she came back.'

It's not the first time Sylvie's run away. She managed it last year, despite all the precautions on the ward. Afterwards, when they reviewed the CCTV, it turned out that she'd slipped through the double security doors behind a couple who'd been visiting their daughter. That's all it takes: a distracted nurse, a busy corridor. She was gone for a few hours – a few hours of me and Gabe driving in increasingly frantic circles around town until the police rang us to say they'd found her.

I used to keep thinking, *This must be the worst part*. Each hospital anniversary. The suicide attempts. Then, driving round and round scanning the streets, I thought: *Actually, this is the worst*.

I've stopped all of that now. There isn't any *worst*. Just days, and then more days.

This is how she escaped this time, Louise tells me: if the patients on Paediatrics 3 are doing well, they're given occasional access to an outside area, for some fresh air. It's a small, walled terrace on the first floor, with a few benches and a depressed collection of cactuses. People stand around in hospital gowns or pyjamas, some of them wheeling drip-stands, some of them smoking furtively. This time of year, it's usually empty, nobody wanting to be out there in the cold and the drizzle.

Sylvie's been allowed out there, these last few days, thanks to her incremental progress with eating. And today she got lucky: there was nobody else there, and when the nurse got called away, Sylvie climbed her way out.

'Nobody's ever done it before,' Louise tells me. 'It didn't occur to us that it could be done. Let alone by a patient.' She sounds almost admiring. She says Sylvie must have disconnected her feeding tube, climbed onto one of the benches and heaved herself on top of the wall, then climbed from there across a flat section of roof and jumped down into the car park.

Twenty minutes later, they found her drip-stand in the courtyard, by an empty bench in the rain. They were about to call the police when she walked back in.

Sylvie

Mum charges into the ward, ricocheting between relief and anger. She squeezes my hand, and I try not to stiffen against her touch.

'I thought you were making progress,' she says. 'Jesus Christ. You could've been killed, falling off that roof. And you know you have to be careful with your heart. Scrambling around like that – anything could have happened.'

'But it didn't.'

Everyone's so busy asking me why I ran away. Nobody thinks to ask why I came back.

Mum's right that my body's weak. It took me four goes to climb up onto the wall. I don't have any strength in my arms, and by the time I'd pulled myself onto the top I was out of breath, my pulse drumming its fingernails against my chest. I tried not to think of what the doctors have said about my heart-rate.

I balanced on top of the wall, panting, and checking my right elbow where I'd scraped it on the bricks. Even though it was bleeding, and even though my breath was still coming fast, it was the first time in years that I'd thought of my body as something for doing things with, rather than just something for scrutinising.

When I'd edged to the end of the wall I had to pull myself up again, onto the flat roof. An empty chip packet was blowing across the rooftop.

In Paeds 3 the windows are all double-glazed, and they don't open. I don't know if it's a suicide thing, or an infection thing, but it means that the air's always stuffy and dry. All day, from my bed, I can see the lines of cars moving down Campbell Street, but the windows change the outside world into a silent movie. The only noises are hospital noises: shoes squeaking on the lino; the beeping of monitors; the hiss and whirr of the feeding pumps; the voices of nurses.

Outside, it took a while for my ears to get used to the noise. It was like that moment in an aeroplane when your ears pop, and suddenly you realise that you weren't hearing anything before. I could hear the crackle of the chip packet as it scraped across the bitumen roof, and the deep, distant rumble of the cars below. I closed my eyes and let the sounds come.

Then I crossed to the far side, where I could jump down onto the top of the car park, and follow the stairs to street level. The dark staircase stank of piss, and as I headed out the door I wrapped my long cardigan tight over my pyjamas. It was raining, the pavement dark and shining. I passed the back door of the hospital, skirting a wide puddle with a tideline of cigarettes. It was early afternoon, not too many people around to stare at me as I walked down the street. My pyjama trousers are plain grey; my Ugg boots could pass for actual boots. I let my hair hang over the right-hand side of my face to cover the tube.

Maybe I wasn't trying to get away. Maybe I just wanted to see for myself whether the world was still there, and whether there was still room in it for me.

Mum touches my hair, still wet from the rain outside. 'I just worry about you, sweetheart,' she says. 'You know that. We just need to know you're safe.'

I don't say anything.

'And when you're ready to leave this place properly, I'll be the first to celebrate. You've been doing so well lately. But you can't just run away. You need to get well first. Then you can do whatever you want.' She waves her arm wide, the movement too big for the cramped space of my room. 'Go travelling, like Dougie. Fall in love.' She leans forward, as if we're sharing secrets at a sleepover. 'You know Nathan has a boyfriend now, apparently? Sue told me.'

She's done this before – dangled bits of gossip in front of me like shiny lures to coax me back to the world.

There was a boy my age in Paeds 3 for a while, last year. He was called Will, and even though they try to keep the anorexics separate from each other, he wasn't anorexic, and we got talking in an occupational therapy session. He was in here because he cut his arms so much he almost bled to death. I don't much like talking, these days, but talking to Will wasn't so bad.

'You seem to be getting along well with Will,' Mum said, after she came in one day and saw me and Will talking by the nurses' station.

I shrugged, glad that Will had gone back to his room and couldn't hear this.

'Yeah. He's nice.'

'Nice-nice, or *nice*-nice?' she asked.

Mum and I didn't have any practice at this. Maybe if I'd stayed at home, stayed in school, she and I might've had a chance to get better at this kind of thing. There would have been school dances; maybe dates; bringing boyfriends home, like Dougie used to with his girlfriends. But I've spent those years in Paeds 3 instead, which means that Mum and I didn't have the vocabulary for this situation.

'Just nice, Mum,' I told her.

She asked me a few times, after that, 'And how's your friend Will?' Dad asked too, 'Seen much of Will?' I know the story that they wanted: the story where I would fall in love with Will, and he'd entice me back to normal life. That would have been a nice story: *Girl gets sick. Girl meets boy in hospital. Girl falls in love. Boy helps girl get better. Maybe they heal each other.*

But that isn't my story, and it wasn't Will's either. He had his own story, for one thing, and having seen those scars on his wrists, I'm pretty sure he had bigger things to think about than dating. He got discharged a few weeks after we met, and I haven't seen him since. It's been nearly a year. It's not like he can text me, or email me. And I doubt he'd be keen to come back to Paeds 3 for visits.

Mum's still staring at me. 'Are you planning on doing this kind of escape stunt again?' she says.

I pull my cardigan tighter around my body. The wool still smells like outside – like rain and cigarettes. I want to explain to Mum that it's not going to work the way she used to think it would. It's not going to be a boy that coaxes me back into the world. It won't even be her, or Dad, or anyone else. I want to tell her that what I remember from running away, this time, is the light in the oily puddle. The syncopated percussion of the empty Coke can blowing along the pavement in the street; the reflections pasted onto the dark windows of the office building opposite. That's what I'm learning to find. All of it – all that fierce and ordinary beauty.

Teddy

'Are you sure you'll be OK with Papabee for the whole day?' Mum asks. 'You can come with me to the hospital, if you'd rather.'

'We'll be fine,' I tell her.

She pulls two twenty-dollar notes out of her wallet and gives them to me. 'Here. Get lunch for you both. And tell Papabee he can take you out for ice cream, if he wants. And we'll all do something fun together tonight, OK? We'll watch a DVD – your choice. Anything except *Lord of the Rings*.'

That's because Papabee always gets confused between the different hobbits and keeps asking who's who.

'We'll be fine,' I say again.

It's a Saturday – Mum's going to the hospital, because Sylvie ran away yesterday (which is bad) but came back (which is good) and now they're having a meeting with her doctor and her dietitian and her psychiatrist, all at once. I don't have a soccer game this week, so Mum said I can spend the whole day with Papabee, as long as we're back for dinner. I don't mind – I'm glad. For my plan, I need a long time.

I have to tell Papabee which way to drive. It takes him three goes to turn off the highway and towards the bridge. The first two tries, when I tell him to take the ramp up to the right, he says, 'Absolutely,' but then whizzes straight past it, and we have to do a big loop to get back to where we were. The third time, with me yelling in his ear, he zooms up the ramp without even slowing down and then says, 'There's no need to shout, my dear boy.'

After that I use my phone to navigate, making sure I give him heaps of warning before every turn-off. I've done this drive a million times, but usually in the back seat, arguing with Dougie and Sylve about who's taking up too much room. I've never been in charge of finding the way before.

It takes a bit more than an hour to get to the house at the Neck. I know Sue and Dan aren't here this weekend, because Sue rang to invite us to go with them to one of Ella's violin concerts in town. Mum said no. She says no to everything these days, but I don't mind this time, because Ella's concerts are boring, and I need to come here instead.

As soon as we see the sea I know I've come to the right place. We get to the bit where the land disappears on both sides and it's just the road, sea all around us, and I can hear the gulls doing their yelling, and I know for sure that there are secrets the water knows. When I'm here, I believe extra hard in the particular magic of nails. Here, it feels like if I could just see far enough along the beach, Sylvie would be waiting for me, about to say something, mouth open, her eyes squinched up against the sun.

The driveway gate's open – it's always open – and the house is sitting waiting for us, just the same as it always has. I can hear the sea even from here. The sea is speaking sea language, and the wind is speaking wind language. I haven't been here since Dougie died and I feel a big wave of missing this place, which is also a big wave of missing him.

Sue and the others must have been here recently – there's a beach towel forgotten on the line, and the grass has been cut. I know it's not fair to be angry at Sue and Dan and Ella and Nathan – I've heard Sue invite us here at least twice, even though Mum always says no. But I still hate to think of them coming here without us. I walk under the clothesline and when the wind slaps the towel at my face I yank it out of the way. The broken peg goes *ping* off into the grass and the towel falls on the ground and I leave it there. Papabee doesn't notice.

The fly-screen rattles; Papabee's trying the front door. I know where the key is – on top of the side window frame – but what I'm looking for isn't inside.

'The others will be coming shortly, I expect,' he says. 'Are they bringing Dougie and Sylvie in the other car?'

'That's right,' I say, because it's unfair to tell him he's wrong all the time. Maybe that's why I'm getting good at lying to Sylvie – because I've been doing these little lies to Papabee for so long.

It's sunny – the first sunny day in ages, even though it's still cold. Papabee settles himself down in the hammock, his flat cap pulled down to shield his face from the sun. Sometimes, when we're staying here, I climb in the hammock with him – facing the other way, my head leaning against his legs – and we can lie like that for ages, talking and not talking. But not today. Today I have a job to do.

'I'm just going to check something,' I tell him. 'I won't be long, OK?'

'Indeed,' he says, and his hat goes up and down as he nods.

I go round to the back of the house. Past the water tanks, where there's a bunch of trees, and one tree bigger than all the rest. It's called the Secret Tree, except I'm not meant to know that. Even its name is supposed to be a secret – but the big kids never noticed me, so they don't know how much I see, or how much I know.

I've seen Sylvie and Ella climb up the Secret Tree so quickly it looks easy. But it's different for me: the first branch is way over my head, and when I try to climb up the trunk I scrape the inside of my legs and scratch my arm. Even when I reach the branch it's really thin, and the next one up isn't much better, and under my weight it makes a noise like something complaining. My knee hurts, and my hands are sweaty – if they get any sweatier I'll slip for sure. I think about Sylvie, climbing over the wall at the hospital when she ran away. Was she afraid, like this? Did she hear her blood going *swoosh swoosh swoosh* in her head?

I wish I was Possum-Teddy. Possums don't know about gravity so they just ignore it. I'd go up the tree faster than the big kids, and I'd see in the dark and I'd never want to be anything other than what I am, because a possum is always enough. I could swing from my tail, and stomp on the roof with a noise so loud that you know possums don't have any secrets.

But I'm not a possum, and I'm heavy with secrets, dragging the branch lower and lower and there's a cracking sound too. I wrap my arms around the branch but it's too small and if I fall I'll land smack on my back.

Will Papabee hear me if I shout for him? He's all the way around the front of the house, in the hammock, and he might even be napping by now. Even if he did hear me, would he know what to do? And if I knock myself out, or hurt myself really badly, what will happen to him? How would he find his way home?

I think about Sylvie, and Dougie, and Mum and Dad, and Papabee waiting in the hammock at the front of the house. I unscrunch my eyes and wiggle a bit closer to the trunk, then in a quick scrambly movement I pull myself onto a thicker branch. Two deep breaths, big shaky ones, and then I keep climbing.

Nearly at the top, the hole in the trunk is perfectly round, and just big enough to get a hand inside. This is where Sylvie and Ella used to leave secret notes for each other. Their secret letterbox, except it wasn't secret, because I was watching.

I snap off a twig and poke it in the hole first, swirling it round to try to clear any spider webs. I'm not scared of spiders, but I'm not stupid.

There's nothing there. I don't know what I was expecting. Maybe a diary explaining it all. Or a letter, spelling everything out.

> *Dear Teddy, Thank you for caring about me enough to solve this mystery. This is how you can make everything better...*

But there's nothing in the hole but sticky resin and flakes of bark.

Papabee's still in the hammock, giving little snores. It doesn't seem fair to wake him up, so I climb in with him and we lie like that for a while, together. In my pocket I have a handful of pine needles from the Secret Tree. Both my hands are black with sticky, pine-smelling goo from the tree trunk.

I stare at the sky and try to work out if the swooshing sound I can hear is the sea, or the blood in my ears, still pumping hard after the climb. I decide it can be both.

Papabee wakes up after a while, lifting up his cap and squinting as he smiles at me.

'There you are,' he says. 'I've just been enjoying this splendid view.'

We drive through the skinniest bit of the Neck again, sea on both sides of the road, and I tell Papabee about how, in the olden days, the prison guards at Port Arthur spread rumours that the water was full of sharks, to stop convicts from trying to swim away. I've told Papabee that story a thousand times – we all have – but the nice thing about him is that he doesn't notice. 'You get very good value out of an anecdote, with Papabee,' Dad used to say. So I tell Papabee again about the convicts, and the dog-chain on the Neck, and the sharks. I know the sharks were made-up but I've still thought about them every single time I swim here. All those stories circling in the water, ready to bite.

On the way home we get hot chips from the petrol station, and eat them on a bench facing the water. It's cold, but there are two families mucking about with dinghies. I remember that last summer at the Neck before Sylvie went into the hospital. Dan took us out in the dinghy. I remember Ella diving off the side, and Dougie laughing. Sylvie was watching them.

'What did you two get up to all day?' Mum asks, when we get home.

'We went to the docks in town,' I said. 'Looked at the boats.'

'Did we?' Papabee said.

'The boats, remember? The water?' I prompt him. It feels a bit mean doing this – giving him little bits of truth to make him join in with my lies. I never knew, until Dougie died, how many different kinds of lying there are. And I don't like how good at it I'm getting.

'Of course,' says Papabee. 'A splendid day.'

'Where did you have lunch?' Mum asks him.

'At Mures,' I say quickly. 'Fish and chips.'

There it goes again, that lie machine: give him a little bit of truth, and out comes the lie, like a can of Coke from a vending machine: *Clunk*.

'That's right,' he says. 'Delicious. Excellent chips.'

'Great,' says Mum. 'And I have good news too, about Sylve. The meeting with the doctors went pretty well. They even said it might be time for her to try a home visit.'

When I play fetch with Sausage, sometimes I just pretend to throw the ball. I chuck my arm forward but don't actually let go. At first Sausage used to go rushing off, searching the grass and the bushes. He doesn't fall for it any more, but it took him ages to learn ('He's not exactly one of the great minds of this nation,' Dad said). Now, when I chuck the ball Sausage watches carefully. He doesn't chase after it until he hears it land.

When Mum says Sylvie might come home, I feel like SausageDog. I want to be happy about it, but she's come home so many times. I've learned that, most of the time, it's just a trick. I've learned to wait until I hear the ball land.

Gill

I fold the latest letter and seal the envelope. Dougie and Gabe have caught a cheap flight to Paris, where Dougie's cast has been removed at a walk-in clinic.

It was hot in Italy and Greece too, but this is totally different. Here, all the heat bounces back at you from the pavement and the exhaust fumes, until I don't even mind when Dad suggests ANOTHER museum, because at least there'll be air con. Thank God the cast is off (though I felt sorry for the poor doctor at the clinic here who cut it off, given how bad it smelled!). Now I'm left with one leg that's completely white and skinny, and kind of wrinkly – not a great look! – and doctors said I still need to use crutches until I get some strength back. The scars from the operations are pretty impressive – hoping it's true what they say about girls digging scars.

Today we did the Louvre, and I was kind of dreading it – gallery fatigue definitely starting to settle in (also, in my case, LITERAL fatigue thanks to the crutches). But in the end the Louvre was totally worth it – even worth hauling myself along miles of corridors (the Louvre's like ten normal museums put together. It's the mothership of museums). The funny thing about the Mona Lisa is that everyone tells you so many times that it's smaller than you expect and that it's really underwhelming, so by the time I finally saw it I thought it would be about the size of a postage stamp. Turns out, though, it's actually a decent size, and once I'd squeezed past all the Japanese tourists it was really cool to see it. (No eyebrows! Remember when Ella overdid it with plucking her eyebrows a few years ago and they were basically completely gone?)

Dad's juggling work so has to put in a lot of hours on the laptop, but we usually do some sightseeing stuff in the morning (traumatic flashbacks to him and Mum dragging me out of bed for school!), before it's too hot, and then he works for a bit after lunch, and we get back together for a cold beer in the afternoon and head out again. Still trying to persuade him that we should go to the test match at end of the month if we can get cheap tix back to London, but not sure how the timing will work out (plans still up in air, depending on the leg). I told him I'm desperate to go to Lords and he legit thought I was talking about Lourdes over here in France and started banging on about the architecture of some cathedral there – I think he thought I'd suddenly found religion and was after a miracle cure for my leg? I had no idea what he was talking about – just wanted to watch some cricket. Don't know which one of us was more confused...

Dougie's grown taller. The injured leg is pale, with fat pink scars mid-thigh. His hands are calloused from the crutches, and as he sits on the grass in the Place des Vosges he picks at the thickened skin of his palms.

Yes, definitely taller. I take out the same cookbook that we've always used – *Women's Weekly Children's Birthday Cake Book* – and slide a pencil from the mug by the phone. I place the book just above the last mark on the door frame – *Dougie Jan 2016*. Half a centimetre taller, at least, even if I press the book down firmly on that gelled hair. I hold the book perfectly horizontal and put the pencil to the wood.

'What are you doing?'

Teddy's wandered into the kitchen, one of his soccer socks fallen down and bunched around his ankle.

'Did you measure yourself?' he asks, one hand in the biscuit jar.

I can't speak. The pencil hovers.

'Can I take some for Papabee?' he says, holding up the biscuits and already losing interest in whatever I'm doing. 'He only has boring ones at his place – Digestives, or Scotch Fingers.'

'Sure,' I say. 'Here,' I put down the cookbook and go to the pantry, trying to keep my voice steady – 'take him a whole packet.' I pass Teddy the unopened Mint Slice biscuits. 'But only if you promise you won't end up eating all of them yourself, OK?'

'Promise.' He's halfway down the corridor. 'I'm taking Sausage too,' he shouts, without looking back.

'Back by six, OK?' I call after him.

I hear the front door slam, and the dog's nails on the wooden boards of the verandah.

Leaning my face against the door frame again, I slide down to a crouch. I'm squeezing the pencil so tight I think it might snap. Teddy's voice echoes in my head: *What are you doing?*

'I'm emailing you a copy of the latest letter,' I tell Gabe when he calls.

'Maybe you shouldn't,' he says. 'Maybe we've let this go on for long enough already.'

'Because it's working.'

'For how long? What happens when she finds out?'

'She won't. And she's doing well. Her weight's stable. They're letting her home tomorrow, just for a visit.'

'This letter thing,' he says. 'I'm worried that it's gone too far. I know you're doing what you think is best. But do I have to read the letters? It feels so weird. I'm not sure I want to be involved.'

'You are involved. You're meant to be on this trip with Dougie, for God's sake. You need to know what to say when you ring her.'

'How can this be healthy?' Gabe asks.

'Healthy? It's keeping her alive.'

'OK – perhaps *healthy*'s the wrong word. I don't even know what that means, really. I just mean, what if what we're doing is wrong?'

There he is again: lovely, lovely Gabe, always trying to do the right thing. This is why I married him. This is why I could scream at him.

Why can't he see what the last few years have made of me? This is the awful truth: I no longer have the luxury of thinking about right and wrong. These distinctions are for other people. Morality is the preserve of those who are safe. It's for those whose children are asleep in their homes. Those who have never cremated their sons, and those who don't wake every day wondering if this will be the day their daughter's heart gives up.

It's early afternoon and the sky is beginning to give up on daylight. Patches of snow sit, like dandruff, on the mountain.

In half an hour I'm due to pick up Sylvie from the hospital.

'Just for a few hours,' Louise told me, when she rang yesterday to confirm the arrangements. 'Reintegration. A chance to ease back into non-institutional life.'

Once, we used to get excited about Sylvie coming home. The very first time she was discharged, Teddy made a poster for the front door: *WELCOME HOME SYLVIE!* in big crooked letters. Dougie skipped hockey practice so that he could be there when she arrived.

After the first few attempts, we knew better. We knew what to do: run the vacuum over her room; fill the fridge with Sustagen cartons; hide the sharp knives and medicines in the lockable toolbox. Each discharge lasted one, sometimes two weeks. Every few days we'd go into the outpatients clinic at the hospital to see Louise and have Sylvie weighed. I remember thinking, once, that Sylvie's sheets were due for a wash, and then realising that there was no point, because she'd be back in hospital in another day or two anyway.

Having her at home is always provisional: everything dependent on the next meal, the next weigh-in, the next appointment. When she was briefly home last winter, Gabe and I were worried that she wasn't maintaining her weight, and wanted to take her to the doctor a few days before our scheduled appointment. Sylvie snapped at us, 'You always say that I might not make it to the next check-up, and I always do.'

'Love,' Gabe said quietly. 'You only get to *not make it* once.'

This time she's just coming home for a few hours, and the preparations are different. I have to check the house carefully, hiding every clue about Dougie. There isn't much to hide. The flowers and the casseroles are long gone, and I never put the condolence cards on the mantelpiece – it didn't feel right to display them like birthday or Christmas cards – so they're already in a shoebox under my bed. There's some paperwork in the study – letters and forms from the insurance company and the coroner. I've been avoiding dealing with those forms for weeks; it's a relief to stuff them into the box along with the sympathy cards and letters.

For a long time I stand in the doorway of Dougie's room. There's dust on his hockey trophies, and on the bookshelves. I ought to do something about the dust, if this room's going to be sitting empty for the rest of the year.

I close the door to his room and fetch the car keys. It's time.

Sylvie

In the car, Mum says, 'Do your best to at least talk to Papabee.' She's concentrating on the road, but I can see her sneaking glances at me too. 'I can understand if you don't want to talk to me. Even Teddy gets it, more or less. But it'll break Papabee's heart if you give him the silent treatment.'

'It's not deliberate,' I tell her. 'I try my best.' When I turn my head to look out the window, my nasogastric tube tugs at the back of my ear, where it's tucked out of the way, its stoppered end dangling in my hair like some kind of decoration.

'Papabee's a finite resource, you know,' says Mum. 'He won't be here forever.'

I turn to face her. 'Is there something you're not telling me?' I could swear her fingers tighten on the steering wheel. 'Is he sick? Is that it? Is it cancer?'

'Of course not. He's fine. But he's eighty-one. He's not going to live forever.'

I lean back against the headrest and look out the side window. 'He's strong as an ox. And he eats like one.'

Mum exhales hard. 'Despite your best efforts to die before him, he might still beat you to it and steal your thunder.'

Silence.

'I didn't mean that,' she says quickly. 'I didn't mean to be flippant. You know how it can be – jokes can be a coping mech–'

'It's fine. I get it.'

'Just be nice to Papabee, OK?'

'I get it.'

It's been five months since I was last here. Inside the house, small things are different. They're only tiny changes, but there are lots of them. A new dog bed, replacing the wicker one that SausageDog used to gnaw on. Two potted cactuses on the counter where the goldfish tank used to sit. I have to ask Teddy how to work the new remote control for the stereo.

He's hanging around optimistically, sitting slightly too close to me on the couch, and I know he wants to chat, but I've been away from language for too long. When I try out words in my mind, the letters float apart, and rearrange themselves. Every word turning into an anagram, like the alphabet pasta that Teddy loves. Or loved – does he still? I haven't eaten a meal with him for so long. If I could trust words, I'd ask him what he likes these days.

There's a stripe of dog hair on the thigh of Teddy's left trouser leg, from where SausageDog always rests his chin. On the other couch Papabee has his legs crossed at the ankle; he's wearing odd socks, one grey and one blue. In the kitchen, Mum's chopping something, the unhesitating *chopchopchop* of a proper chef.

I make myself take a long, slow breath. These small things are something. If you notice them, if you gather enough of them, you could almost have enough to call a life.

Down the corridor, Dougie's door is shut. I wonder what it would be like if he were here. I wonder whether I could go in, sit on the floor and lean against the bed, and talk just like we always used to. Whether I could make the words come out right.

But he isn't here. I stand in the doorway of my own room. In the last three years, I've spent maybe five or six weeks here. A few nights, a few times, before my weight got too low, or my heart-rate too high.

Mum's done her best, but if you look closely you can see the clues. The room smells of a mixture of *Spray n' Wipe* and dust. Under the bedside table a dead fly lies on its back, its legs curled inwards. The bedding is the set I chose when I was about ten, with purple and white flowers. Along the top of the dressing table sits my old collection of dolls and stuffed animals.

This is a child's room. A museum. I was fourteen when I last lived here. I have no idea what this room would look like now, if I'd stayed here. Who I would be now, if I hadn't stepped out of my life.

Is this what I've done with my body – turned it into a museum of my childhood?

My body. There's been damage – the kind of damage that doesn't go away. My bones – fucked, probably, after all these years. Louise has talked about it a lot: bone density, calcium. So I have osteoporosis to look forward to. Kidneys and liver have taken a hit too. Fertility: probably ruined, after three years of no periods. Last time Mum asked, Louise said, *I'm not entirely without hope that there may be a chance that Sylvie's fertility hasn't been totally compromised*. I might've missed three years of school, but I know enough to recognise a sentence tied up in the knots of its own qualifiers and double-negatives. So, fertility: fucked too, probably, which doesn't bother me too much at the moment.

It's a problem for later – and I'm only just beginning to be able to imagine a later.

Teddy

All week, I've been trying to get some time alone with Sylvie to give her the needles from the Secret Tree. Every time I've gone into hospital after school, Mum's been there. Now Sylvie's home for the afternoon, but Mum and Papabee are here too and I still don't know how to get Sylve by herself. I'm nervous too, about whether I've got the price right this time. Nervous about what she'll say if I've got it wrong, and also about what she'll say if I've got it right.

I go into my room and open the drawer. Some of the pine needles have stuck to the jumper they're hidden under. I peel the needles away from the bobbly wool, careful not to break them. I get out the notebook, and look through my list of family words. I decide to try some of them out – a little test, to see if Sylvie still remembers.

Back in the living room, I squish up next to her on the couch. She's reading, one hand stroking SausageDog's ear. On the couch opposite, Papabee's humming quietly.

I can't ask her if she wants a *napple*, because she doesn't eat much normal food yet. Instead, I ask, 'Did you notice my big growth squirt?'

'Sure did,' she says, not looking up from her book. 'You're basically a giant, Teddy.'

And even though she's teasing me, because I'm still small for my age, I can't help doing a big smile. I bend down and put my face in SausageDog's fur, right in the doggy stink of him, so she won't see me smiling. And I feel like I'm almost a poem, or an open door. Like I'm about to become something else, and it doesn't even matter what I might be about to turn into, because it's the *aboutness* that matters.

Sylvie gets off the couch and goes to the loo. Mum's coming in from the back door, holding the washing basket.

'When Dougie's back, I'll get him to help me level that patch at the top,' she says, pointing to the end of the garden. 'I trip every time I go to hang the washing.'

'Mum.' I look down the corridor. I can hear the tap running in the bathroom. 'You don't need to do that. She's gone.'

'The bloody dog's had another go at the fence, too,' Mum says. 'Up past the compost bin.'

I don't know if she even heard me.

Gabe

When I call, Gill asks me, 'Did you get the letter?'

'I got it.'

She emailed the latest letter to me yesterday. I read it several times. I can hear Dougie in it – the exclamation marks; the bracketed asides; the appetite. All the details of our travels together. She's good at this. Of course she is. She's a writer. She's his mother.

What I want to tell her: *Stop writing these letters. This has to stop. Write to me instead. I miss you.*

She's still talking. 'When you ring her, remember the letters take at least a week to get here from Europe. So that stuff about Paris is a week old, at least. You're in Barcelona now.'

'How did it go?'

'In Barcelona?'

'No,' I say quickly. 'Sylve's afternoon at home.'

'It was fine. She was OK. Papabee kept asking about the feeding tube again. But apart from that, it was fine.'

'So what next?'

'There's going to be another meeting, with Louise and the rest of the team, to work out a timeline. They're talking about taking out the tube on Friday, if she's still stable and maintaining her weight. I need to make a time to meet with Louise. But I've been busy. There's work, and Teddy, and I'm only halfway through the next letter—'

'It has to stop now, surely? We have to tell her?'

'Coming home's a big change. A big transition. Let's not rush anything. We don't want to derail it now.'

'Gill—'

'I have to go,' she says. 'I've got to call Louise at the hospital before five.'

'Honey—'

'Love you,' she says. 'Love to Dougie.'

She's hung up.

I should get on a flight home. She needs me. Sylvie and Teddy need me.

I look at the box of ashes on the bedside table, sitting on top of a roughly folded map, and a coroner's report about a caving accident in 2005. A picture of Phil Murphy's face, from the newspaper report. I printed it out too big, his bewildered open mouth a cluster of pixels.

I can't go back home until I've finished.

That night I dream that Dougie and I are playing cricket in the backyard again.

'Five things you miss most about being alive,' I say as I bowl to him.

'One.' He makes a neat drive. 'Bodyboarding at the Neck.'

I catch the ball, bowl again.

'Two.' A leg glance towards the clothes line. 'Sylvie.'

I retrieve the ball.

'Three.' This time he hooks it high – I have to run backwards to catch it. 'Teddy. Papabee. SausageDog.'

'That's three things,' I say.

'No it's not – they all go together.'

'Fair enough.' I bowl again. Another drive, but I fumble the catch.

'Four: Mum.'

'She'd have killed you again if you hadn't said that,' I tell him.

We're both smiling. I toss the ball from hand to hand.

'And five?' I ask him.

He hits a sweep this time, bouncing off the wall of the house and into the lavender. Dougie doesn't answer. I wait to see if he'll name me, or Rosa, or something else altogether. I wait for SausageDog to retrieve the ball, but I don't hear him rustling through the bushes. There's nobody else here: not the dog, or even a blackbird in the wisteria vines. Just me and Dougie.

'Five?' I ask again.

I wake. The digital clock gives off its red glow and something outside sweeps a shadow across the ceiling.

Dougie. My deepwater son, drowned in the dark. If he comes to me again in my dreams, he will answer, *You. I miss you most.* And in Rosa's dreams he'll say, *You, Rosa. It's you I miss the most.*

And in his own dreams? They're his own.

The date for the inquest hearing has been set: a month from now. All the statements and reports are now submitted for the coroner's consideration. As a Properly Interested Person, I was entitled to request copies of everything, and of course I did. The whole lot, which Heather at the coroner's office has emailed me.

Heather advised me to keep my own submission to essentials, and not to go beyond my direct experience. Last week, on the day of the deadline, I sent them everything I've compiled over these weeks: the detailed master map of the Smith–Jackson cave system; the reports of the water levels in the reservoir, and the meteorological reports about rainfall in the system's gathering ground. A summary of my discussion with Meredith Calvert, and a timeline of the rescue operation, cross-referenced with comparable operations detailed in reports of similar accidents. An annotated version of the post-mortem results, in which I devote half a page to the state of Dougie's hands, and the possibility of cadaveric spasm, referencing recent articles from academic journals.

'The coroner's office finally forwarded me all the other reports last night,' I tell Rosa, when she arrives later than usual. I point to the papers, carefully arranged on the table. 'Do you want to help me go through all this?'

'I told you,' she says, shrugging off her bag. 'I don't really need to read any of that. I was there.'

She's quiet today, and edgy. She drinks three cups of tea and flicks through her phone. When it gets cool, in the late afternoon, she takes my jumper, which was hanging over a chair, and wraps it around her shoulders like a shawl.

Over dinner at the Italian place she drinks red wine and jumps from subject to subject. She tells me her sister's offered to pay for her flight to Mexico, but Rosa's waiting to hear whether she still has a job at the school. Her parents haven't phoned her – she hasn't seen them since the day after the accident. Another teacher at the school is pregnant, is going to be leaving. Rosa's thinking of moving to Spain – did I know she studied Spanish? (I know) – or maybe Mexico, after all. Or maybe she'll stay.

'Do you feel like everything's–' She raises her hands in the air, holds them there. 'I feel stuck.'

'Your boyfriend died. You went through a horrible trauma yourself. There's all the uncertainty about your job. It's natural to feel unsettled.'

She pours herself more wine, then tops up my glass too. Wine sloshes onto the white tablecloth.

'I still think you should consider talking to someone.'

'I'm talking to you,' she says.

'That's not the same. You should–' I stop myself. I shouldn't be lecturing her on what to do. I'm hardly a model of dealing healthily with trauma.

'Don't be grumpy with me,' she says. 'It's a special occasion.'

'It is?'

'Two months,' she says. She doesn't have to say since what. And she's already turning away, waving down the waiter and ordering a bottle of dessert wine.

It feels churlish to stop her. Two months since she survived. Two months since he didn't.

I pour the sticky wine when it comes. We're both a little drunk.

'I've never actually tried dessert wine before,' she says, wrinkling her nose as she sniffs it. 'I always wanted to try it.'

She drinks, then keeps talking, waving her arm expansively. 'I've been thinking about it, because of the two months thing. I want to try more of the things I've always wanted to do.' She takes another sip. 'Like this. It tastes just like raisins, but to the tenth degree. Like essence of raisins.'

I laugh – she's right. That's exactly what it tastes like, viscous on my tongue.

We walk back to the flat through warm rain. I stumble on the stairs, and she catches my arm. In the living room I make us tea.

'I'd like more wine,' she says.

'That's not a good idea. And anyway, I don't have any.'

I sit on the couch. I should do some work, I think, but she's still here, perched on the arm of the sofa. Then she grabs my hand.

I could let go, but I don't. I hold it.

I bought that expensive rope because I wanted to hold what he held. To feel what he felt. So I hang on to her hand, because that was what Dougie was doing, right at the end.

That's true, but it's not all of the truth. I hold her hand because I want to.

Her thumb runs up my thumb, to the knuckle, and back. I'm looking very carefully at her hand, her thumb, the ragged skin on the side of her thumbnail where she bites it.

She leans down, quickly, and kisses me. She kisses me hard – when she pulls away her chin is red from my stubble.

'I'm not Dougie,' I say.

'I know.' She doesn't even hide her disappointment. But she leans forward and kisses me again anyway.

Of course I kiss her back. Of course it's wrong. She slips off the arm of the couch so she's half sitting on me, and I put my hands to the sides of her face and kiss her with a kind of hunger that's more than lust, though that's there too.

I might try to pretend to myself, later, that I don't want this. That I'm not enjoying it. That would be a lie. I can't believe my luck. This woman – this beautiful young woman, reaching for me. Her hands urgent on the back of my neck, pulling my mouth up to meet hers. She tastes of dessert wine or sadness, or both.

'Stop,' I say. 'We should stop. This isn't right.'

'We're both adults,' she says.

Adults? Oh Jesus. The shame of my old body next to hers. The wispy grey hairs on my chest; my sad old balls, wrinkled as baby birds. And it's not just my body. I'm old in a way that she won't understand for another thirty years. I've buried my parents; I've cremated my son. I've been here for so long.

And I know, too, that I've become that tired, shameful cliché: the dirty old man, lusting after the young woman. I don't kid myself that Dougie's death gives me some kind of free pass for this behaviour. There's no such thing.

She's straddling me now, and I want this so badly, my whole body saying *yes*.

There are so many reasons why this is wrong. Gill. Dougie. But I choose the one that relates to my own pride.

'Stop.' I pull back. 'It would only be because you felt sorry for me.'

She sits back too, looking at me. 'A pity-fuck,' she says.

'A pity-fuck.' I haven't heard the term before, and it sounds ugly and stupid in my middle-aged voice.

'Probably,' she says. 'But the person I'm pitying isn't you.'

Rosa slides off my lap and onto the floor.

'Christ,' she says. 'I miss him.'

'Me too.'

We're both crying. I lean forward and kiss her, once, on the forehead. It's the wrong thing to do – too paternal, when I can still taste her mouth in mine, and my clumsy erection is still straining at my trousers.

'I thought if I did something – anything – I could—' Her hands are raised again, like they were earlier in the restaurant, and then she suddenly splays her fingers, an exploding motion. 'Shake myself out of this stuck feeling. This limbo.'

I nod, and slump back onto the couch. 'I get it. But that's not how it works.'

I've been treating her like a glass bottle in which Dougie might have left me a letter. It hasn't occurred to me, until now, that she's doing the same with me. We would have to break each other open to find any message.

She wipes her face with the back of her hand, and looks up at me.

'There's something I have to tell you,' she says.

Gill

They've taken out Sylvie's feeding tube. Before, I used to have to stop myself staring at it. Now it's gone, I have to stop myself from staring at her bare face. It's still gaunt, the jaw still oddly prominent; I can still see the outline of her teeth through her flesh. But her face is no longer bisected by that line of fleshy rubber, and I stare at her until she squirms and says, 'Alright, Mum – enough. Jesus. I get it.'

When I pass the nurses' station on the way out, Louise calls me into her office, and tells me that she's set a date for Sylvie to come home.

'Are you sure?' I ask.

Louise smiles. 'I'm happy with her progress. We shouldn't count our chickens, of course, but I'm hoping that for once this isn't going to be a one-step-forward, two-steps-back situation.'

Having Sylvie back at home is what I've dreamed of ever since she got sick. But in hospital, I can control what she sees, who she speaks to. No internet, no newspapers. No visitors who aren't on the approved list. Outside the sterile white world of Paediatrics 3, she could find out the news so easily. Her school friends; our neighbours; Mrs P at the corner shop. Any one of them could blow the whole thing, deliberately or by accident. A sympathetic comment – *I was so sorry to hear about your brother* – that's all it would take.

And if that happens, how many steps are there between her and Katie P and all the other dead anorexics? Between her and Dougie, always so close?

I know I can't stop time. That's what Sylvie has spent the last three years trying to do, after all. But my most important job is to keep her safe. I don't know if I can do that once she's off the ward.

'What if she finds out the news before she's ready?' I ask. 'Before Gabe's back to help?'

Louise looks at me for a long time.

'I've told you before, Gill. Don't underestimate her.'

Sue comes over that afternoon, while Teddy's at Papabee's.

'To Sylvie coming home,' she says, raising her gin and tonic and taking a big gulp.

I raise mine too. I've made it too strong; the gin's bitter kick makes me grimace.

Sue puts her glass down. 'You know you're going to have to tell her now, right?'

Outside, a bumblebee butts insistently against the glass of the French doors. It won't stop.

'Not just yet,' I say. 'We'll wait until Gabe's back, for one thing. We don't want to rock the boat, while she's going so well.'

'You didn't want to tell her while she was going badly. It doesn't go both ways.'

'Maybe it does.'

Sue leans forward. She looks nervous. Sue never looks nervous. At the Neck we once found a tiger snake wrapped around the base of the clothesline where the metal pole had been heated by the sun. While the rest of us shrieked, and Sylvie and Ella leaped on top of the outside table, Sue just finished hanging up the beach towels.

'Are you OK?' she asks. 'Really OK, I mean? I mean, of course not – nobody expects you to be OK. But are you above water?'

She stops herself. The clumsy metaphor hangs between us.

I shake my head. 'She's not ready to find out yet, that's all.'

She leans forward and takes my hand. It's partly a squeeze, partly a pinch. 'Look: I love you. I love Gabe, and the kids. You know that. But I can't stand back and watch you mess this up completely.'

'I'm doing my best.'

'I know,' she says, her hand still on mine. 'I got it. I did, at first. And, God knows, I've supported your batshit idea. Because whatever gets you through the day, fair enough – that's what I thought. But the letters, the lying to her – you've gone full-Miss Havisham.'

'You have no idea what I've lost.'

'Nor do you,' she says, sitting back. 'You have no idea. You're trying so hard to keep Dougie alive that you've totally lost sight of him. You can't grieve for him because you're too caught up in all this madness.'

'Why the fuck would I want to grieve for him?' I shout. 'Would you want to? Would you want to grieve for Nathan, or Ella? Or maybe both?'

As soon as I say it, I know it's wrong. Even uttering those words is to cross a line. I shouldn't have invoked her children's names; invoked their deaths.

'I'm sorry,' I tell her. 'But you don't know what it's like.'

'Of course I don't. You're in your own unique world of shit right now. But that doesn't mean the rest of us can't see what's going on.'

'Tell me then,' I say. 'Please, tell me.' I'm not being at all sarcastic. I'm deadly, deadly sincere. 'Tell me how to get this right.'

'It's time. Just tell Sylve the truth.'

'Or what? Or you will?'

'Just tell her the truth. Stop lying to her.'

'And if she kills herself? If her heart gives out? I can't make my daughter a martyr to your holier-than-thou ideas of honesty.' I stand up, the chair making an ugly scraping sound. 'Don't come round here any more,' I say. 'And don't go to the hospital. I'll take you off the visitor list.'

'Don't be stupid.'

I'm crying and yelling at once. 'If you're not willing to help me, just get out.'

She picks up her bag. 'Just ask yourself: who are you doing this for?'

Sylvie

Mum and Teddy come in on Saturday, straight after Teddy's soccer game. Mum takes the chair, and Teddy sits on the end of the bed. He's still in his long socks and muddy shorts. His knees look too big for his little legs. Mum's wearing an old scarf of Dad's, looped twice around her neck. She keeps fiddling with the tassels at the end.

For three years I've been watching only myself. I've been fixated on this body. Each rib. My hip bones. The negative space between my thighs. I've watched myself, and the others watched me too.

Then Dougie had his accident. When they told me about the cave and the flood, fear lodged in me like a fishhook. It made me look back at my family. I see them now.

I see Teddy, trying to fix me.

I see Dad, or his absence. I see him hiding from me.

I see Dougie, his letters coming more often than ever, relentlessly upbeat, trying to stop me from worrying about him.

I see Mum, and her new brittleness, since Dad left. She's too quick to answer questions; too cheerful. She spends more and more time in here with me. I watch now as her hand moves from her scarf to the chair, traces the piping along the edge of the vinyl seat-cushion; goes back to her scarf.

I think she's afraid, but I don't know what she's afraid of. It might be me.

It's a new feeling, this: curiosity. A turning back to the world. For a long time, I've looked only inwards. I have been my own object, my own subject. Now, I see everything.

Mum's bottom lip, flaky where she bites it. Teddy, stopping himself from talking. What have I done to them?

At the Neck, the stingrays will be waiting in the shallow water, lying right on the sand so they touch their own shadows. The tide goes out, holds its breath, and comes back. The house will sit empty, an abandoned shell. The penguins that nest under the jetty will have laid their eggs.

I want to go back there, squat quietly at the edge of the jetty and see the hatchlings. Not breaking out of their eggs, but breaking into the world. There are so many things I want to find out, things I want to try. For such a long time I was impatient for my life to end. Now I'm impatient for it to start.

Gabe

'I haven't told you everything about what happened in the cave.'

For an instant I'm afraid I might shake her. I imagine grabbing Rosa and shaking her until all the truth about Dougie's final moments comes rattling out.

'You said you'd told me everything. You said you didn't remember anything else.'

'I lied.'

I try to calm my breathing. Two minutes ago we were kissing. Now I'm imagining the cave. The blackness.

'Why did you come here every day, and watch me trying to work out what happened, when you hadn't told me the truth?'

'Maybe that's why I came. I don't know. I wanted to be close to you, because you knew Dougie.'

'You should've told me.'

'I'm telling you now.' She takes a deep breath. The red wine has stained black the creases in her top lip. 'I told you we were holding hands, when the flood came. You know how it is.'

I don't know. I can never know how it was, to be there in that cavern, with the water coming up in the blackness. I can imagine, though, how skin would seek skin.

'So when Murphy came for you?'

The question sits between us. I wait.

'I let go of Dougie's hand.' She sniffs, her breath jerky. There's a tear on her cheekbone, magnifying one of her freckles. 'Murphy was pulling me towards the entrance.

Dougie didn't let go. So I kind of—' She wiggles her empty hand in the air. 'I pulled away from him. I let him go.'

'You should have told me,' I say eventually. My voice is quiet. 'That's all. I wish you'd told me.'

'It doesn't change anything. It won't matter to the inquest. It doesn't make any difference.'

'It does to me.'

'Why?' she shouts. 'It happened to me, not you. It's mine, not yours. It belongs to me.'

'He was my son.'

'He was my boyfriend.' She's standing up, glaring at me.

It's true that what she's told me tonight doesn't change anything. I still don't know whether he died then and there, in Cavern 3, or whether he struggled for minutes or hours. I don't know whether he was already dead when the floodwater dragged him through to Cavern 4, or whether he swam there himself, looking for a way out. I don't know what was in his mind.

'I won't come here again,' Rosa says.

I nod. 'I think that's best.'

She shuts the door behind her.

Gill warned me, when she said she couldn't bear to see Dougie's body: once something's in your head, it's there forever. I can't stop picturing Dougie's outstretched hand, as Rosa's slips from his grasp.

I go to the kitchen and I get the knife.

All the way there, on the train, I'm aware of the unyielding pressure of the metal against my thigh. The cold of the handle, when I slip my hand into my pocket to grasp it.

It's nearly midnight when I get to the house. The lights are all off, rain dripping noisily from a broken gutter on the roof.

I ring the bell. No time to hesitate. There's no answer, and I ring again. A light comes on inside, and I hear voices.

Murphy opens the door. He's wearing a navy dressing gown. He looks worried, or angry. His partner, in striped boxer shorts, is a few steps behind him, holding a phone.

'I'm Gabe Jordan,' I say.

And at exactly the same time he says, 'You're Douglas Jordan's dad.'

It hasn't occurred to me that, all those nights when I was Googling him, he was Googling us. What has he found? It would only take two minutes online to find all kinds of stuff: pictures; newspaper articles; my profile and photo on my work website.

The man in the background says, 'Phil? Should I call the police?'

Murphy doesn't say anything. He's waiting for me to speak. I'm waiting for the same thing. My tongue has become an inert thing in my mouth, too big, too heavy. My hand's still in my pocket, gripping the knife.

In the end, I slip back into the juvenile mathematics that has troubled me all this time:

'If you go into a cave with two adults and ten children—'

'Eight children,' Murphy says quickly. 'Eight children, and four adults.'

'You know what I mean. Dougie and Rosa were barely adults. They were in your care too.' The knife isn't cold any more – it's warmed to my hand. It feels like a part of me.

'And so were eight twelve-year-olds,' he says. 'I got them all out. I got the Campbell woman out too.'

'If you go in with ten, and you come out with nine,' I repeat. I feel dizzy.

His face looks formless – so stricken that it changes shape, the bones all gone, everything hanging.

'I don't think you should be here.' His voice is shaking.

'If you don't leave now, I'll call the police,' his partner says. He lifts his phone to his ear.

'Did Dougie say anything to you?' I ask Murphy. 'At the end?'

'I'm not supposed to be speaking to you,' he says.

Then he starts talking, and he doesn't stop. The words fall out of him, sand from a slit sandbag. 'I'm sorry I'm sorry I'm so sorry I'm so sorry, he seemed like a good kid, such a good kid, I'm so sorry, so sorry—'

I can't even make out most of his words. My hand on the knife. My hand on his arm.

And I'm squeezing him, and I don't know if I'm trying to crush him or to comfort him, and he's squeezing me back, his strong arms, and we're both crying, and all my maps have led me not to the cave and its secrets but here, this moment, standing in the dark with a stranger's arms around me.

'I have to go,' I say, and I leave them standing there, backlit in the hallway.

Bouillabaisse for when you're afraid that your daughter won't come home from hospital, and afraid that she will

When softening the fennel and onion, use both olive oil and butter – this is not a time for holding things back. Later you can watch the oil marbling and pooling on top of the stock.

The fennel flavour takes on a new dimension if you throw in a tablespoon of fennel seeds at the same time as the chopped fennel and onion. Wait until the seeds snap and explode. Savour those small, contained detonations.

Toss in some star anise with the prawns. If you're squeamish, you can take off the prawn heads before you condemn them to the pan – but if you were squeamish, you wouldn't have got this far, through these three years. And the flavour's better if you leave the heads on. The prawns surface like commas in the broth. Like pauses in a sentence you haven't yet said out loud.

Gill

I fell in love first with the word: *bouillabaisse*. Those three languorous syllables: *bwee-ya-bess*. I learned in culinary college that the *Baisse* comes from *Abaisser* ('to lower the heat and simmer'). But in my imperfect French, the *Baisse* is close enough to *Baise*, that emphatic, glorious *Fuck*. Every bouillabaisse I ever cooked was just an attempt to live up to the name. Mostly I failed.

This one, though, comes close. I dropped in some long, curled strips of lemon rind to lean against the sweetness of the saffron. Prawns, heads and all, and chunks of Tasmanian salmon, slipped in right at the end for barely enough time to cook, the flesh still glassy in the middle, glossy as the inside of a shell.

I serve it with homemade bread. I never used to have the patience to bake bread – but since Sylvie went into hospital, patience is no longer a choice. And I like the kneading. I like holding the dough up against the light and stretching it until it's nearly translucent, thin as the webbed skin between base of thumb and forefinger. I like leaving the ball of dough to rise and coming back to find it fat with air. I like the optimism of that process – leaving the dough to rise in a bowl on the windowsill and hoping, each time, that the yeast will perform its small miracle.

I call out to Teddy and Papabee that dinner's ready, and take one final taste of the soup, a slurp straight from the wooden spoon, scalding my tongue.

I think: *Dougie will like this one.*

Sylvie

On my bedside table is Mum's latest Tupperware. I made myself eat three spoons of the seafood soup. That's the rule (I'm good with rules): I force myself to have three spoons every day of whatever she brings. Full spoons – so full that if my hand shakes at all, the food spills on the sheets and I have to start again. These spoonfuls are the hardest part of my day – much harder than drinking Sustagen or eating my safe foods, because I don't know exactly what's in Mum's meals. In this soup, the oil's congealed in little specks on top, and I close my eyes when I eat it so I don't feel sick. It's important, though. I'm learning that I have to pay attention. I need to understand why Mum's so brittle; why Dad sounds so vague and tired when he phones; why Teddy's so tense; why Dougie's writing to me so often, but why he's never there when Dad rings me. If I want to understand these things, then I have to start with these little plastic containers Mum brings in every day. I can't understand Mum without tasting her food.

I think I'm starting to understand now. I think I know what I have to do. And when Teddy comes in, all by himself, I say: 'I need you to do something for me.'

Teddy

When she asks for my help, I'm afraid. I've always been a bit afraid of Sylvie, even before she put her bones on the outside. She's always been way, way cleverer than me. If she asks me for the truth, I don't know what I'll say. But I promised Mum not to tell Sylvie. So whatever I do I'll be letting somebody down.

And what about Dougie? How do I do the right thing for him, when he's in a box at Dad's flat in London, and can't tell me what he wants?

But Sylvie doesn't ask me anything – she just tells me exactly what she wants me to do. Then she gives me her bank card.

'You'll need this,' she says. 'It's going to be expensive. Use my Papa J money.'

'You sure?'

'I'm sure.'

She writes down her pin and her online security code. I don't realise straight away what it is. 1103Sau5ag3, she's written – just a lot of numbers and letters. Then I get it: Eleventh of March – my birthday. And Sau5ag3, for SausageDog. And even though Mr Brindle in Computer Tech at school always says you should never use pets' names or birthdays in passwords, when Sylvie tells me hers it makes me think that maybe all this time we've been missing her, she's been missing us too.

That night, after dinner, I tell Mum I need to use her laptop for homework. She's busy in the kitchen anyway, and she hardly seems to hear me.

In my room I double-check and triple-check the details.
I can remember Dad's birthday (ninth of February) but not
which year, so I have to go back out to the kitchen.

'Mum,' I say. 'I'm doing a family tree project for history.
What year was Dad born?'

I'm worried that she'll ask more about the project, but she
doesn't even look up.

'67,' she says.

'1967?'

Mum laughs. 'Come on, Teddy. It's hardly gonna be 1867.
Does Dad look 149 years old to you?'

Sometimes, I think. *Since Dougie died, sometimes he does*.

Back in the study, I triple-check Dad's details, and press
Purchase. Then I send an email and a text.

The email is to Dad. I attach the plane ticket, and the
booking number, and type the message that Sylvie wrote
down for me on the edge of one of my geography worksheets.
There, next to Mrs Conway's diagram of the water cycle, is
Sylvie's handwriting:

Dad.
Come home. We need you here. Don't tell Mum.
Sylvie.

At the hospital today, when Sylve told me what to write, I
said: 'But doesn't Dougie need him?' I made it into a question,
so it was less of a lie.

She looked at me for a few seconds, and I'm nearly sure
she was going to ask me something, but in the end she just
said, 'We need Dad too.'

The text I send is to Sue. Sylvie said I could just tell Sue the
message, if I could get her on her own, but Sue hasn't come
round for a while, so I text her instead.

Dad's arriving back on Sunday. His plane lands at 11am. Mum doesn't know. It's important. Please can you pick him up?

Mum can't pick him up, because she doesn't know he's coming back. And it's a school day so I can't guide Papabee to the airport. 'Dad can just catch a taxi,' I'd said to Sylvie, but she told me to ask Sue. I get it. If Dad was in a taxi, he could change his mind, or go back. But nobody gets away from Sue.

Sue rings my phone straight away.

'Are you going to tell Mum?' I ask.

'What do you think?'

'I think, if you did, she might tell him not to come home.'

'Probably.'

'It's not that she's mad at him,' I say. 'But if he comes back, things will have to change. And she wants things to stay the same.'

'How about you, Teddy? What do you want?'

In the whole time since Dougie died, I don't think anybody's asked me that. I close my eyes and squeeze my hand tight around the phone.

'I want my dad back. And I want my mum back too.'

Sue takes a deep breath.

'Email me the flight number so I can check if it's on time. I don't want to be hanging around at the airport for hours if it's delayed.'

'Thank you,' I say, and even though she just says, 'You got it, Tedster,' and hangs up, I think she knows my *thank you* is as big as my fear.

Gabe

When I get back from Murphy's I'm still shaking, and the knife that was in my pocket is gone. Did I drop it at his house, or somewhere on the way back? I hardly remember catching the train home. I'm drunk, exhausted. I run a bath.

For the last two months, I've wanted to know everything. I wanted to know the angle of Dougie's body when they found him, and the contents of his stomach, and what happened to the carabiner that was on his harness when they started but wasn't on his body when they found it. I wanted to know why the force of the water punctured his left eardrum but not his right, and whether he felt it, or heard new sounds. I wanted to know if his eyes were open or closed, and the expression on his face, and whether his final thought was of Rosa or of us.

I bend my knees and let myself slide down until the bathwater creeps over my face. I hold my breath and force myself to open my eyes. The lights in the ceiling are blurs of white. Was this how Dougie felt, as the last air escaped him? Did he hope, or did he forgo hope? Which of these do I need to learn from him?

I lie on my back in bed and listen to the sirens in the distance, and the night buses carrying their emptiness from stop to stop. I call Gill. She doesn't answer – she often doesn't, these days. I don't blame her.

I've spent two months here, amassing all those facts now stacked on the dining table – those reams and reams of paper. But the only true answer to all my questions has been silence. And the person who can teach me the most about silence is sitting in a bed in Paediatrics 3, on the other side of the world.

And Teddy – little Teddy. I abandoned him to all the things I cannot face. Gill too. I've failed all of them.

When I sleep, I dream that I'm hanging on to Dougie's hand.

Let go, he says. *Dad, you dork. Let go.*

It's four in the morning when the email from Teddy comes in.

I pack my bags. Clothes, wash bag, wallet, laptop. The things that Rosa brought me from Dougie's room: his old t-shirt, which still smells of him. The photo of Sylvie that was stuck above his desk. Not the Sylvie that I remember from when she was a child, or the Sylvie that I've wanted her to be. This is the actual Sylvie, the one who's waiting for me now, at home, all bones and glare.

This has all gone on too long – my obsession, and Gill's, neither of us daring to call out the other in case they respond in kind.

There were only two things I needed to learn here in London:

Dougie is dead.

My other children are not.

In conversations since Dougie died, I've sometimes balked at saying, *I have two children.* Now, I'm learning to remember it: *I have two children.* I cannot save Dougie. But I might be able to save them.

I leave the rope on the coffee table, on top of the book about cats.

The last thing I pack, rolled carefully in a jumper and tucked into my hand-luggage, is Dougie's ashes. Gill's been writing to Sylvie for months about my travelling with Dougie. Now it's time to do it for real.

I should call Rosa before I leave, I think. I want to say goodbye. I want to tell her that she should go on and do all the things she's talked about. Visit her sister in Mexico. Go to Iceland. Fall in love with someone. I want to say that she was right, to let go of Dougie's hand, and to survive.

I want to say to her that it's not her that I'm angry with. It's Dougie, for going where I can't follow.

I want to give her my blessing, but I don't. She doesn't need my blessing, or my absolution. She doesn't need anything from me.

Teddy

'Did you do it?' Sylvie asks me as soon as I get there. I've skipped soccer practice and caught the bus straight to the hospital. On Tuesdays Mum usually meets me here at five, so I've got almost an hour before she's due.

'Yup,' I say. 'Sue's picking him up tomorrow, if he comes.'

But that's not why I've come in to the hospital early today, without Mum or Papabee.

'I've got something for you.' I take the plastic bag from my backpack.

'Here we go again.'

She doesn't take the bag, so I open it myself. I take out the bundle of pine needles and let them fall onto the bed. One of the needles sticks to my palm; I peel it off and put it on the covers with the others.

Here in the ward, where everything's clean and white, the little pile of needles looks like something from another world. Sticky pine-sap smell, and bits of dirt.

'Where are these from?'

I don't answer, because she already knows.

'When did you go?' she asks. 'Mum didn't say anything about going to the Neck.'

'She didn't go. I went.'

'How the hell did you get there?'

'Papabee. Don't tell Mum.'

'It's not safe for him to drive all that way any more.'

I hope that if I don't say anything, she'll have to stop changing the subject.

She scrapes the needles into a pile and starts putting them back in the bag. 'I'd forgotten about the Secret Tree,' she says, with a laugh that doesn't quite work.

'Then how did you know where these were from?'

'You aren't even meant to know about it,' she says. 'It was just for me and Ella. It was meant to be our secret.'

The big kids never understood how much I know. Mum and Dad don't either. You can hear and see a lot when people forget to notice you.

'We were the ones who found the hole in the tree,' Sylvie says. 'Me and Ella, years ago, when we were ten or eleven. It was our own private game.'

The big girls. Their laughing voices when I knocked on the door of the girls' bedroom in the attic. *Go away, Teddy. Girls only.* Sylvie's a year younger than Ella, but their birthdays are both in August, so most years they had a joint party, until Sylvie went into the Boneyard.

'That hole in the Secret Tree was our letterbox,' Sylvie says. 'We'd leave little notes for each other. Just silly stuff. You know: *I hate Nathan – he's such a pain in the arse! Meet me by the beach after dinner for a swim – DON'T TELL THE BOYS! Let's paint our nails tomorrow!* Stuff like that.'

Her voice is a bit croaky. It might be from all those years of having the tube down her throat. Or it might be that she's not used to talking this much.

'And then?'

'Then nothing. I don't know. We got older. It just stopped. You know what it was like: she came back from Spain and she was different.'

That was the summer before Sylvie got sick. Ella had gone on exchange to Spain. That summer she wasn't at the Neck,

357

and Papa J was there instead, taking Ella's place as Sylvie's partner for Pictionary.

'She was still nice to me, when she came back the next year,' Sylvie says. 'She was never mean – but you could tell that she just wasn't interested any more. Not like before. It was like all our old games, our old secrets, they'd become boring to her. Or like she'd just forgotten about them, which was kind of worse. And even though we were still sharing a room, she didn't talk to me like she used to. She was always hanging around with the boys, laughing at Dougie's stupid jokes. It made me feel like I was suddenly so much younger than she was.'

I know that feeling. I know the exact shape and taste of it, like my tongue knows my teeth.

'Then I saw her going to the Secret Tree,' Sylvie says. 'One morning, near the end of that summer. And I couldn't believe it – because we hadn't used it for the whole summer, and she hadn't even mentioned it. But I saw her going there, sneaking off after breakfast. It was the first time all summer that I felt happy. So I went, straight after, and I found the note: *Meet me at the island, midnight tonight.*'

We all call it *the island*, but it's actually not an island most of the time. It's the headland at the far end of the beach, a big mound of rocks that pokes out into the water. It only turns into an island at high tide, when it gets cut off.

Sylvie's still talking. 'It was like she was giving me back all my memories: making it all OK again. That I didn't have to feel embarrassed about all our old games, or for missing her. That we were still a team. So I wrote on the back: *OK!* And I put it in there for her. All through the rest of the day I was so happy. I didn't say anything to her about it, because it was more special that way, using the Secret Tree like we used to.

'Then, that night, I went down to the beach. Ella'd already left, earlier – I thought she was just going to the loo, but she didn't come back. And I lay there, too excited to sleep, waiting for midnight.

'Then I sneaked out too – out the window, because I was scared of waking up the boys if I went down the stairs.' Again, her laugh doesn't come out right.

'I sneaked right down to the beach. I didn't have a torch or anything, but it was pretty light – a really big moon. And there was Ella. The tide was out, and she was lying on the sand, right by the island. I could see her all the way from the tessellated pavement.'

Another one of those laughs. It frightens me a bit.

'Then?' I ask.

'You don't want to know all this, Teddy.'

That's stupid. I still have the scrapes on my arms from where I climbed the Secret Tree. I wouldn't have done that – I wouldn't have done all that sweating and scrambling – if I didn't want to know.

'Stop treating me like a baby.' My voice sounds angry. It sounds exactly as angry as I feel.

She looks at me for a long time before she speaks.

'It wasn't just Ella. It was her and Dougie, lying there together. She must've told him about the Secret Tree. The note was for him. He probably didn't even notice my *OK!* on the back.

'At first I thought they were just lying there, the way Ella and I used to when we were younger, looking at the sand-worm trails, and waiting for the crabs to come out.'

I wait, too. Her words come out slowly, slowly, like a hermit crab coming out of its shell.

'They weren't just lying there,' she says.

'What were they doing?'

I know the answer already. I'd forgotten that I knew: I'd seen it, that summer, after Ella came back from Spain. I didn't know what it meant – only that it was something I hadn't seen before. All the clues that I didn't realise were clues. Once, when I was lying under the table playing with cards, I saw Dougie's leg reach out to Ella's. *Pat pat pat*, his foot on her leg. I thought he was kicking her – I remember wondering why she didn't kick him back or tell him to get stuffed. Another time, when we were walking down to the beach, Dougie and Ella were way behind the rest of us and when I looked back they were holding hands. They didn't normally do that.

'What are you doing?' I'd asked.

They let go right away and Ella laughed at me. 'What do you mean?' she said. 'Just holding hands, you goose. Like I do with you.' And she grabbed my hand, and swung it, forwards and backwards, a bit too high, and held it all the way down the gravel road to the beach. And we were both pretending: pretending that was normal. Pretending that what I'd seen with her and Dougie wasn't something new.

'Were they doing kissing and stuff?'

She nods, and I'm relieved she doesn't want to tell me any details. I know about sex – enough to know that it definitely isn't something that I want to talk about with my sister.

I try to picture Dougie and Ella, there on the sand, under a big moon all full of its own roundness. I picture them as much as I can, and then when it gets too clear I try to picture Sylvie instead, standing on the beach, watching. Her bare footsteps in the wet sand, and how they stopped.

'It shouldn't have mattered,' she says. 'I walked away, quietly as I could, and it shouldn't have mattered as much as it did. It wasn't even that they were sleeping together.' She's picked up one of the pine needles and she's breaking it, very neatly, into pieces. 'I just felt so stupid. I thought the note was for me. It was always our special thing, the Secret Tree, and our special place. She'd told him about it – that was the worst bit. And all of a sudden I was the idiot, and they'd gone off somewhere without me. I was being left behind. And I didn't want any part of it.'

The sex? Or the growing up?

It's like she's heard the question in my head.

'Any of it.' She tosses the little pieces of pine-needle back onto the bed. 'Everything was changing. I didn't want it all to change. I wasn't ready.'

'You knew they were growing up. You were too.'

'I didn't want to.'

'Why not?'

Even I know that everyone has to grow up. A lot of it doesn't seem like much fun – more homework; exams; being sensible. Even the stuff that's supposed to be fun – like sex, or the taste of wine – seems a bit gross. But even I know that you can't stop growing up – it happens whether you want it to or not.

It takes her a while to answer. 'I just felt like they'd outgrown me.' She gives a big shrug. 'Like I was being left behind.'

'Is that the story? Is that why you stopped eating?'

She shakes her head. 'No. But it's part of the story.'

Sylvie

When Ella came back from Spain at fifteen, she suddenly had boobs. Not pathetic little beginner boobs like I was just starting to grow, but proper boobs. She didn't have them when she went away, and when she came back, there they were. She was tanned, and she said *choritho* instead of *chorizo*, and she had amazing clothes from vintage shops in Barcelona, while everything I owned had been bought for me by Mum at Sportsgirl or Target. Ella showed me photos of a boyfriend she'd had in Spain. In one of them, he was sitting up in bed, laughing, with no shirt on and the sheets rumpled all around him. I tried not to look embarrassed.

I could feel it again – that sense that everyone else was in a hurry. Dougie and Nathan were always jockeying for a seat at the grown-ups' table; sneaking to the far side of the headland to smoke cigarettes. I hated the smell of smoke on them; hated the feeling that everything was going too fast.

That summer at the Neck, everything was changing. I saw how Dougie looked at Ella. We all looked at her – her long red hair turning blonde in the sun. Before, I used to feel like her beauty was a secret that only I knew. Now the secret was out. Her legs hanging over the edge of her beach towel, her toes digging into the sand. Upstairs in our little room at night, I wanted to talk to her about everything that happened the summer that she wasn't here. But I didn't know how to tell her about the footsteps on the stairs. I wanted to pretend that nothing had happened after all.

All summer I waited to find the words. The days kept passing, as if they weren't full of secrets. Dan caught a bucketload of flathead and Mum cooked them, full of tiny bones. Teddy smashed the kitchen window with a cricket ball. I saw Ella and Dougie on the beach, and stood there feeling like I might throw up right there on the sand.

I wasn't angry – not at Ella, or even at Dougie. I just knew that something was starting, for them, but for me it was something coming to an end. I didn't want anything to change – not ever. I wanted summers at the Neck to always be the same: me, Dougie, Nathan and Ella sunbaking on top of the water tanks. Running barefoot to the beach, Teddy trailing behind with SausageDog. Squatting at the edge of the headland, poking at our reflections in the rockpools.

Everything was changing. Everything. The tide was coming in, and I couldn't stop it.

PART SIX

Sylvie

I've been watching them. I've been tasting Mum's food, listening to her silences, the spaces between the things she says. I've seen how Mum avoids the subject of Dougie, or talks too much about him, her words coming out too fast, too full of details.

And Teddy's drawing nearer to my secrets too. He's creeping closer, sideways, crabwise, following the stories he's been able to collect. What will it cost him to find me? And what will it cost me to keep him away?

I want to grab his narrow shoulders and say, *What you're doing is dangerous. Don't get any closer. Don't get any closer to me.*

Soon enough, we're both going to work it out. The tide's coming in. We're both going to arrive at our answers.

Look: here is a picture of a family on a beach. A happy family. The gum trees are white and straight, and the rocks are the red-brown of an old blood stain. Look: the children are playing in the water, the parents are talking. Two grandfathers sit on beach towels. A dog is digging in the heavy sand.

Look closer.

Teddy

Something's about to happen. Dad's coming home, if he uses the ticket we bought him. Sylvie's supposed to be coming out of hospital this afternoon, if she stays stable. And Mum – Mum's spending all her time writing those letters, and cooking her weird recipes.

This is my last chance – the very last go. But I know what to do now, and where I have to be.

Mum wants to get the house ready before she goes to pick up Sylvie, so she's happy for me to be with Papabee all day.

'Just be back by five,' she says, 'when Sylvie and I get home from the hospital, OK?'

Papabee misses the ramp towards the bridge again, but he gets it right the second time, and then we're on the bridge and pointing away from town. In my head, that rhyme comes back: *Sister in the Boneyard, brother in the water.* I'm going to the water, and the Boneyard – both at once. I'm going right deep back to where it all started.

Just past Copping, where the road gets really winding and twisty, Papabee overtakes a tractor and stays on the wrong side of the road. I remind him to get back into the left lane, trying to keep my voice polite, and he says 'Indeed,' and wanders back over. But it isn't Papabee's driving that's making me feel like I might throw up. It's not even the twisty road. I'm afraid. Proper afraid, with hand-sweat and everything – like when I nearly fell out of the Secret Tree. I wind down the window (Papabee's car is so old it has actual winding handles) and take small breaths so I don't vomit.

We stop at the service station at Dunalley, just like we used to with the whole family on the way to the Neck. I buy a custard tart with my pocket money, and a lamington for Papabee.

'How very kind,' he says. 'What would you call this delicious confection?' Bits of coconut are stuck in his moustache.

Back in the car we drive through the first thin stretch of land, water on both sides like a gate made of sea. I know it has to be the Neck, for Sylvie's price, and I know it's going to be the beginning or the end of something. I just don't know what.

Instead of going to the house, I get Papabee to park above the tessellated pavement. Down on the beach it's pretty cold, but we take off our shoes anyway. I like the way the wet sand squishes up between my toes.

'That's where I'm going.' I point at the rocky headland, way at the far end of the beach. 'Want to come?'

Papabee looks at the steep rocks. 'I think that would require me to be rather more intrepid than I am,' he says. 'But I shall have a walk along this charming stretch of beach, and meet you back here.'

'OK,' I say, relieved that he isn't coming with me. I can't explain to him that I'm looking for the final clue, to unlock Sylvie's secrets. That I'm like a detective, but this isn't a game or a story any more. I'm trying to find the magic that's as strong as the magic of nails and crosses – a magic that belongs just to us. Something that I can take to Sylvie and say: *There. That's the price. Now tell me the whole story.*

Gill

I carry Sylvie's bag from the car to the house. It's not too heavy, despite all the books, but she still looks too frail to bear any weight at all.

I call out when I unlock the front door, but Teddy and Papabee aren't back yet. Sausage comes to the door, smells Sylvie's hand and licks her ankle, then waddles back to his basket to resume his sleep.

'They'll be back soon,' I tell Sylvie. It's quiet here – quieter than the hospital, with its food pumps and monitors and the low chatter of nurses. I wish Teddy and Papabee would arrive. I don't know how to be in silence with Sylvie yet.

I put her bag down by her bedroom door. She's behind me, moving in the way that anorexics do – her posture stiff, as if she might break in half.

In the kitchen doorway, she reaches out her hand. It hovers just above my arm, not quite touching me. I notice that her hand looks different – the knuckles less spur-like, the veins less prominent.

'Mum,' she says. 'There's something I have to tell you.'

Sylvie

Before I speak, I take three breaths.

If I say it out loud, it will become real. From living so close to silence for so many years, I've learned that every word is an incantation.

Teddy

It was always going to be the Neck. It seems obvious now –
like Papabee searching for his glasses when they're on top of
his head the whole time. Of course it's the Neck. I could have
saved a lot of time – all these weeks and weeks of looking
in the wrong places.

There's no one else on the winter beach – just us and
all that heavy sky. I walk right down the far end, until
Papabee's just a wiggly line wearing a hat, and then
I scramble onto the rocks of the headland. Squatting
over one of the rockpools, I poke my finger into a sea
anemone, making it squeeze shut, then I feel bad, because
Sylvie always used to say it was mean to trick them into
thinking they've caught food.

I know the *where* but not the *what*. I know I'm in the
right place, but I still don't know exactly what I'm looking
for. I pick up rocks and squeeze them, checking which ones
feel like the right size for Sylvie's story. Some are too rough
or the wrong shape for my hands, so I chuck them into the
water. It's so windy I don't hear them go *splosh*. Other rocks
are smooth but too big to carry, or too small – way too light
for all Sylvie's secrets. I find one stone with a white spiral on
it – a fossil, Dad would know what kind – and I think of the
ancient snail shell in *The Lorax*. I left my bag in Papabee's
car, so I put the fossil-stone into my pocket.

A fossil's just a stone that remembers. I jump from rock to
rock and think about the memories of stones. I wonder if the
stones here can remember us, and all those summers before
it went wrong and people's names stopped working. Can the

stones remember the feel of Dougie's bare feet? Sylvie's too?

I walk right around the headland to the far side, checking stones as I go, and filling my pockets with rocks until each step goes *clink clink*. The tide's changing more and more of the headland into rock pools. On a flat rock higher up I find a dead crab claw, turned completely white from the sun. I open and shut the pincer like a mouth. I sniff it. It smells of salt and secrets, so I put it into my pocket with the stones.

Gill

Sylvie says, 'Dougie's dead.'

She looks right at me. 'Those letters weren't from him, were they.' She's telling me, not asking me.

I nod.

'He didn't just break his leg.'

I nod again.

I say to her, my voice tight, 'I'm so afraid.'

'I know.' Sylvie breathes in, her nostrils pinched tight. 'Tell me.'

'He drowned.' I hear myself say it. We're telling each other. 'He died in the cave.'

She gives a small gulp, half swallowing a sob.

I wait, ready to tell her more. If she asks, I'll tell her everything. But she doesn't.

'How did you know?' I ask.

Sylvie

There are lots of things that I could say to her. The letters. All of Mum's silences, and all of her words. Dad being gone for so long. Teddy, and the urgency of all his little bribes and offerings.

What I most want to tell her: *I tasted it.* I tasted the grief in the mourning notes of cumin, and in the sharpness of the ginger in her lentil soup. I listen to food the way other people might listen to music – the same attentiveness. I've learned that a meal can be a love letter or a eulogy or a prayer, or all of those at once. So I ate my mother's grief.

Gill

She talks about how my food tasted different. She tasted my mourning. She ate it.

'What about the letters?' I ask.

'You sounded a lot like him. But there were just too many of them. He never wrote that often, before.'

Of course. I'd been too conscientious – I got carried away with trying to make it real. He was a good brother, but he was still a nineteen-year-old boy – of course he hadn't written that regularly.

'I didn't want to hurt you,' I say. 'I was trying to protect you.'

'And there was all that stuff about museums.' She rolls her eyes a bit. 'That was you, not Dougie.'

I laugh through my sobs. I understand, now, Louise's measured stare, and why she didn't push me about telling Sylvie. Louise had given Sylvie more credit than I had.

'Remember how he complained when you made us go to MONA?' Sylvie says.

I nod. I'd herded the kids into the car to visit the new art museum. 'Just this once,' I said, 'we're doing something for me. God knows I've spent enough hours of my life watching you kids play sports.'

Dougie had imitated my voice, calling out to Teddy and Sylvie, 'Pack your bags, kids! We're going on a guilt trip!'

His voice, our laughter. Dougie. The actual Dougie – funnier and more annoying and more real than anything I managed to conjure in those letters. Dougie. And there's a noise now that takes me a minute to recognise: it's me and Sylvie laughing and crying together.

Sylvie

Mum says, 'I'm so sorry. So, so sorry.'

I shake my head. I know what it is to hide from things. I haven't told her my secrets. I haven't even told Teddy, for all his trying.

'I get it.' I get that it wasn't me she was protecting. Or not only me, at least.

'I was so terrified that you couldn't handle the news. But I shouldn't have done it.' She wipes her face with the back of her hand. She looks old, for a moment. Properly old – older than Papabee. 'Dad wanted to tell you. I didn't let him.' She swallows and stares at me. 'We've got to get better at telling each other the truth.'

She waits, like it's my turn. Like I'm going to open my mouth and let it all out: all the reasons, all the secrets.

Her phone rings.

Gill

It's Papabee, calling from his mobile.

'Gillian? It's your father.'

'I know it's you, Dad. It comes up on my phone.'

'Not now.'

'Yes now,' I say. 'I'm looking at it right now. It shows on the screen: *Dad, mobile*. I've told you this a thousand—'

'No, I meant, let's not discuss that now. I think I may have made a mistake. I rather think something's gone wrong.'

'What do you mean? Is it the car again? Have you lost the car?'

'No – I'm at the car now, in fact. It's Teddy. I've waited, but it's been a long time now, and I'm wondering where he's got to. It's getting very cold, you see. And it'll be getting dark soon.'

'Where are you? Dad, where exactly are you?'

'That's the thing. I'm not entirely sure.'

Sylvie

'It's Teddy,' Mum says, when she hangs up. 'He's missing, and Papabee doesn't know where they are.'

'What did he say?'

'He's at a car park. And he said something about a beach. He can still see the car. A car park, a beach.' She's repeating herself, as though she's afraid she'll forget a detail. 'He says he can't see Teddy. Hasn't seen him for a long time.'

Certainty settles in my gut. 'He's at the Neck.'

'How the hell would they get to the Neck? Papabee can't drive that far.'

'He'd do anything that Teddy told him to. And he took Teddy there just a couple of weeks ago.'

'What are you talking about? We haven't been to the Neck.'

'They have. Teddy just didn't tell you.' Oh Christ, all these secrets.

'Why would he go there? And why again now? Sue and Dan aren't even at the house this weekend.'

'They haven't gone to the house. He's at the beach.'

'He's probably fine,' Mum says. 'It's probably just Papabee being Papabee. They'll just be at Nutgrove, and Teddy'll have wandered into the ice cream shop, or gone off with some friends, or something.' Nutgrove's the small, suburban beach just ten minutes away, in Sandy Bay, where there's only the sluggish estuary, and not the real sea. 'They'll be fine.'

'Of course they will,' I say. We both know it's nonsense: people in other families are fine. That isn't what happens in our family.

We run to the car. As soon as we're out of the driveway, Mum tosses her phone onto my lap. 'Call the police.'

I ring 000, and I try to explain to the operator.

'You have to send a police car. He's only eleven, and we don't know where he's gone.'

'And this was reported by who, your grandfather?' the operator says. She asks me for Papabee's name.

'Edward Barwell?' she repeats. 'We have a note on file – is this about his car?'

'No, not this time. I mean, it's sort of about his car, but it's not lost. He drove my brother to Eaglehawk Neck.'

'Can we speak to Mr Barwell directly?'

'You can – I can give you his number – but it won't do any good. He hardly ever answers. And he doesn't know what's going on most of the time—'

'But he says your brother's gone missing at Eaglehawk Neck?'

'He didn't say at the Neck. But we think that's where he's gone.'

Even as I'm saying it, I can hear how unconvincing it all sounds.

'You have to do something,' I say. 'My brother's already dead.'

'He's already dead?'

'My other brother. Look, it doesn't matter. You have to send someone to look for Teddy.'

'We can let the local station know. But I'm sure you understand that we're going to need a bit more information before we send anyone out.'

I give them Papabee's number, and beg them again to send somebody, but she's saying something about it not sounding like a cause for concern, and telling me to stay calm, and in the end I just hang up, so I can call Papabee again. But he doesn't answer, and it goes through to voicemail, and I don't know whether he's on the phone to the police, or whether he just hasn't heard his phone ringing.

Usually it takes just over an hour to get to the Neck. Mum does it in fifty minutes, driving our beaten-up old station wagon like a race car. She comes skidding into the car park, bits of gravel flicking against my window.

I don't know what to feel when I see Papabee's car there. Relief, because we've come to the right place. Or fear, because there's a reason there are no other cars here, and no tourists to be seen: it's cold, and already almost dark. Beyond the car park the unforgiving sea is churning the dark with its waves. The tide's in, turning the tessellated pavement into segmented pools, and the headland is cut off altogether.

Teddy

I climb right to the top of the headland. A few years ago we saw whales from here – two of them, surfacing again and again, making their own islands in the sea. We watched for hours, and the grown-ups let us bring our dinner down to the beach so that we could watch the whales until they'd gone.

Today there's nothing to see. Nothing to the sea but waves, high and messy. It's getting dark – like somebody's colouring in the edge of the sky grey. Getting so dark I can't tell any more which bits are sea, and which bits are sky.

I look back down. The headland has got a lot smaller, and a lot more island-y. I've been here for longer than I'd realised. I scramble down, scraping my knee, and rush to reach the path back to the beach. But the path isn't there. The tide's sneaked up on me and snatched it away, and the headland is an island now.

Dougie would have remembered to check the tide. He was always sensible that way – always watching out for the rest of us, in a bossy, big-brother kind of way. That was one of the reasons it's so stupid that he drowned. He knew all about tides, and water, and not swimming near the rip. I forget to be sensible about things like that. I can imagine what Mum and Sylvie will say, when they hear what I've done: *Teddeeeeeeee!* they'll say in that impatient way that I've heard a million times.

But I don't have time to worry about getting into trouble. I'm worried for Papabee. I've already left him alone on the beach for way too long. If I'm really stuck – truly, actually stuck – the worst that will happen to me is that I'll get cold and probably a bit scared, when it gets pitch black. But Papabee won't know where he is, or what to do. He can't drive home without me. He might not even find the car without me. And when I think about him being frightened and confused in the dark, I start to cry, and I'm crying a little bit for him, and a bit for me, and then the crying gets bigger, and now for Dougie, and Sylvie, and Mum and Dad too. I cry for all of us.

Gill

I leave the car door open and run straight down to the beach, straight past my dad, who's standing not far from the water. I run towards the island. I'm looking for Teddy's footprints but the tide's high and it's taken most of the beach. Two seagulls are above me, screaming. It sounds like perfect outrage, perfect hunger.

I spot him, a tiny figure on the island. He's squatting on a rock at the edge, not far above the rough water. He sees me, and stands up, and I shout *Teddy for God's sake stay where you are, stay out of the water,* and wave madly with my arms, *Go back up up up I'll get help.* But he doesn't get it, he thinks I'm just waving, because he waves back, and I think *I should never have come here* because that's when he does it: steps closer, down onto the small plateau just above the water, and the next wave comes and hides the plateau altogether. At first he's OK, he braces his little legs wide and manages to stay on his feet, and the wave starts to withdraw and I think *Maybe he'll be OK, he'll climb back out,* but the wave going out takes him with it, sweeps his feet away so he's dragged on his back over the rocks and I see his arm go up, and then a leg, and then I can't see him at all.

Teddy

It's dark and my pockets are full of stones. It's not just that. The water's so heavy when it's on top of me. The cold's heavy too.

Is it because I tricked the anemone? I should have listened to Sylvie. I should have listened.

Too heavy, too much water pulling down my clothes, my skin, my hair.

And I'm the brother in the water. It's me.

It's dark. I'm slipping out of my name.

Too heavy. Stone for bones.

Gill

I see the dark water take him and I shout, *Dougie. Dougie.*

And I turn back to see Papabee and I think *Fuck fuck if I go in and get into trouble, he'll follow, and Sylvie too.* Caught between my father and my children and where are the fucking police.

I shout: *Dad Papabee Dad don't follow me whatever you do don't come into the water* and he waves cheerfully and I turn to yell the same thing to Sylvie but it's too late she's already in.

Sylvie

My brother's name follows me into the water. *Dougie, Dougie,* Mum yells, and then *Teddy* and then my name, too, *Sylvie.*

The water so cold it wrings the air from my lungs. A wave hits me in the face, knocks me down and under the water.

I am not strong. My heart's not strong. I'm too thin, too wasted, to fight all that water above and around me.

But I have this stubborn body. This faithful body, that has refused to let go, refuses still. I have lost enough, and I will not lose him.

I swim through the dark water. I reach for him. I grab his hand.

Gill

They're both in the waves. Papabee too, down the beach but in the water now, knee-deep and edging deeper, watching the children.

This is where it ends. Who am I waiting for, to end it? Not Gabe, who isn't here, or Sue, who has her own children to care for. Not Papabee, of whom I've already asked too much. I'm the only one who can end it. The only one who can save them, or myself.

I'm in the water, the outrageous cold making my body a stranger, clumsy and slow. The dark sky squats over me as I search for my children in the waves.

Sylvie's found Teddy but she can't hold him up, and she's being dragged down. When she comes up to gasp for air, her hair is a net thrown over her face. I grope for Teddy in that tangle of water and limbs.

I'm rough with him – no time for tenderness. My elbow hooks around his neck, his jaw sharp against my arm. Sylvie, too, surfacing again now that I have Teddy's weight.

We drag our bones towards the shore, through the black water. When did water get so heavy? Gabe tried to tell me about this – tried to tell me something about the weight of water – in one of his phone calls. I get it now. I carry the weight until the sand steadies under my feet and all I have to bear is the weight of our own sodden bodies, and I stand.

Teddy

Ever since Sylvie went into the Boneyard, I've wanted to know if it's better to be alive or dead, and how to choose. The water teaches me that it's not a choice. My body chooses: *live live* it sends me kicking and squirming but the stones in my pockets can only say *down down down*. Even when Sylvie grabs me I still can't stop fighting up towards the air but I only drag Sylvie under with me. My body wants that air it wants to live and Mum's pulling us up and dragging us to the beach but my body already made the decision for me it was done.

I'm on the sand at Sylvie's feet. Maybe this is the price I have to pay, the very last one: my body, on the sand.

Sylvie bends to whisper in my ear.

Gill

I slump over, hands on my knees, and take a breath. Another. I'm shaking, in great ungainly jerks of cold. Sylvie is beside me; Teddy lies on the sand between us, breathing in noisy gasps.

Further up the beach, Papabee's still standing knee-deep, watching the horizon with an expression of vague interest.

I cough up seawater and phlegm. I can still hear my own screams: *Dougie. Teddy. Sylvie.* I say the words again and again, giving my children's names to the sea.

Sylvie squats down to where Teddy lies.

She bends to whisper in his ear.

Sylvie

I am not here to drown him in my secrets. There are no easy answers and no simple stories.

I want to tell him: *There is never just one answer. I am not just my wounds and my secrets. Yes, there were footsteps on the stairs. But they're only one part of the story, which is also a story about Cordelia, and the Fool, and Dougie and Ella on the beach, and the way that girls find themselves carrying the weight of being women.*

He thinks I'm going to tell him my secrets. They are my own. Instead, I want to tell him about himself. I want to say: *Teddy, don't be like me.* I want to tell him: *You can live in books, but you can't only live in books. The price doesn't have to be everything, or nothing. You don't have to erase yourself to be seen. You don't have to seek the answers in the sea, or write the answers with your bones. Your body doesn't have to be the price.*

There are other currencies, other voices, other languages to learn.

We can learn them together.

I bend to whisper in his ear.

Papabee

I watch an egret, and admire the question mark of its elegant neck. At least I think it's an egret – the line between egret and heron and cormorant has become rather blurred lately. I used to know a lot of names of birds – my wife was very keen on all of that. Now, egrets and herons and cormorants tend to coalesce into a vague mass of long-necked water birds.

Nonetheless, I very much enjoy watching them. I've always thought they look discerning, the way they peer down their beaks at the world. This one sits on a rock among the waves, and the curve of its neck is like the arch of a raised eyebrow – imperious.

It seems to me to be far too cold for swimming, and too dark, and the waves look distinctly hostile. But Sylvie has gone in. It looks as though she's swimming with her clothes on, which strikes me as eccentric. Still, I ought to at least try. I like to join in when I can.

I walk a little way into the water. Much too cold, unpleasantly so, and so I go no further. Gillian is in too now, but I stay here, in the shallows, and try not to wonder why they're all behaving in this manner. I try to concentrate on pleasant things: the egret (if indeed it is an egret). The last bit of light touching the clouds at the horizon. I wait. I do a lot of waiting. Often I don't remember precisely what I'm waiting for.

They're coming out now: Gillian with an arm hooked under Teddy's armpit and wrapped around his chest. Dear Teddy – I wondered where he'd got to. And Sylvie on the other side of him. I still think she has been allowed to get far too thin – I'll talk about it with Gillian, after they've all dried off.

Teddy's lying on the ground now, in all his wet clothes. What a lot of sand we shall have in the car on the way home.

Perhaps they told me they were going to swim. Perhaps they told me why. I do forget a great deal. I suspect I'm a burden to them, though they're far too kind to say it. But I'm not the only one who forgets. I see them doing it too: forgetting who I was, before I became this old man who can't tell an egret from a cormorant; who can't always remember my family's names. I'm mainly Papabee now, not Edward or Dad. *Dear old Papabee*, and there are worse things to be, but it is difficult, sometimes, all this forgetting.

Gillian's bending over with her hands on her knees, all her clothes soaking. Sylvie's close to Teddy. She bends over too now, saying something in his ear.

Teddy

Sylvie whispers to me. She tells me lots of things. Some of them make sense, and some of them don't. She doesn't tell me how to save her. She tells me that I don't need to save her. That it's not my job.

Some of what she tells me, I realise I've known all along. I can see now: all the clues that I didn't realise were clues. I remember how she'd pushed his money away, when I'd tried to give it to her. How she'd held the envelope by the corner, the same way Mum holds the little black bag after she's picked up one of SausageDog's poos, carrying it carefully between the tips of her finger and thumb. 'I don't want his money,' Sylve said. I remember her after *King Lear,* how her body turned sideways when he hugged her. The tissue that she ripped up at his funeral – those angry little white shreds.

She doesn't tell me because of nails, or magic, or any price that I could find, or because I nearly drowned. She tells me because she's ready, and I listen.

But she doesn't tell me everything. I know that what she tells me are only some of many answers, and I know that it isn't over. There'll be more hospital visits; more doctors; more of those awful afternoons in the family therapist's office.

'And I know about Dougie,' she says. Water's dripping off her hair and her nose. 'I know he's dead.'

I swallow. My mouth still tastes like the sea. 'I didn't like keeping it secret from you.'

'Someone once told me I had to keep something secret, too,' she says. 'You don't have to do that any more.'

Mum steps closer to us, now she's finished coughing. She puts her arm around Sylvie's shoulders. Then Mum looks at me, and says, 'Oh, Teddy. Teddy. There you are.' She sounds surprised, as if it's the first time she's seen me in ages.

Gill

Over the crest of the sand, from the direction of the car park, a policeman is walking.

Papabee reaches us first. He looks down at his legs, his suit wet up to the knees.

'I appear to be wet,' he says. 'Has it been raining?'

Behind him, a cormorant stands on a rock among the waves. It spreads its wings wide and holds them like that, crucified against the sky.

PART SEVEN

....

Gill

The next day I'm on the front verandah with Sylvie, and Sue's car pulls up. Gabe gets out, squinting against the sharpness of the light.

Sue holds the gate for him while he drags his suitcase through, but she doesn't follow him up the path. She stands at the gate and sees me watching from the verandah.

I raise my hand, a kind of salute, and she raises hers back.

I let the children have Gabe first. Teddy runs to him and jumps up like a monkey, Gabe staggering under his weight. Even Sylvie gives him a hug, and I try not to wince when her spine protrudes as she raises her arms to him.

Then it's just the two of us.

I tell him what happened yesterday. He keeps saying, 'Christ. Christ. I should've been here.'

I nod. 'Yeah. Or I should have been there with you. I don't know. We both got it wrong, didn't we?'

After the kids and I had come out of the water, the policeman insisted on getting us checked out at the local medical clinic. They kept us for a few hours, monitoring Sylvie's heart carefully. They gave us hospital gowns to wear, to replace our soaking clothes. Papabee only needed to change his trousers, so he wore a gown over his shirt and tie, and kept wandering around the clinic with the back of his undies showing, making Teddy giggle.

We left Papabee's car there and I drove us all home, Teddy and Sylvie falling asleep in the back seat.

'I should have been there,' Gabe says again.

'You're here now.'

I've been denying my grief; he's been running from his. We face each other now, in the shadow of the mountain, in the space that Teddy and Sylvie have created for us.

'I should've tried harder,' says Gabe.

'Yes,' I say. 'But you were trying. I know how hard you were working over there, for the inquest.'

He shakes his head. 'I was working hard at the wrong thing.'

'Me too.'

It's not a happy ending. It's not an ending at all, but a kind of beginning. I have work to do – the job of grieving for Dougie, which I've dodged for more than two months. There are days I long to slip back into the comfortable old lie. But when a lie breaks, it breaks the way an egg breaks: incontrovertibly.

Gabe and I talk. At night, the kids in bed, we talk so much that sometimes our words pile up, a mound of words, things we haven't said to each other during these last months. He tells me some of what he found out in England, and I tell him about Sylvie, and Teddy, and all that they've done.

'It was them who brought me back, you know,' he tells me. 'I don't mean metaphorically. I mean, they actually booked the flight. They sent me the ticket.' In his voice I hear the mixture of shame at himself, and pride in them.

There are things he's learned about Dougie's death that I'm not yet ready to know, and moments of Sylvie and Teddy's lives that Gabe has missed and can never make up for. That's OK, or, if it isn't OK, at least we've accepted that it can't be changed.

I go to see the therapist that Sue recommended, and he listens to me and passes me a box of tissues when I cry. I have tissues in my bag, nice ones, not the thin, single-ply ones that he proffers, but it seems rude to refuse him, so I cry into his scratchy tissues.

'It's more exfoliation than therapy, really,' I say to Sue, and she laughs.

I called her the day after Gabe came back. Before I could even begin to apologise for everything, she just said, 'See you in five? Don't forget the lemon.'

At her house, I told her what had happened at the Neck.

'Teddy went straight under. Went down like an anchor.'

'Shit,' she said. 'Why? He's a decent swimmer.'

'It was freezing cold. And he had stones in his pockets. Full of them.'

'Oh Jesus.' She was hysterical. 'Your bloody family. How on earth does an eleven-year-old go full-Virginia Woolf?'

'No, no,' I said, laughing too. 'He was collecting the stones, apparently. I'm still not sure exactly why. Something to do with him and Sylvie. He said he couldn't explain, but that's why he went there in the first place—'

'OK, so not suicidal, but still batty.'

'Probably, yes,' I said, but I felt proud of Teddy – of his determination. His total commitment to his schemes, even when I don't understand them.

I think a lot about what happened on the beach that evening. I know that it wasn't a miracle, and it wasn't a baptism. It wasn't any kind of metaphor. It was real, and it was nearly deadly. But something changed. I don't know who saved who, but we all went into the water, and we all came out.

After dinner one night I walk with Papabee up to his flat, Sausage leading the way.

'I should've been there,' I say. 'That day at the Neck. I should never have left Teddy with you for all this time. It wasn't fair. Gabe and I were neglecting him – and you.'

It takes Papabee a few goes to get his key into the lock. 'Teddy? We've always been fine, Teddy and me. We make an excellent team.'

'And you've done a great job, taking care of him when I couldn't.'

'He takes care of me,' he says, as the door finally swings open.

'I know. But you've still been wonderful. I don't think I'll ever be able to repay you.'

'Far the best thing to do,' he says, already busying himself with his hat and scarf, 'is to write me a cheque for a hundred dollars.'

A packing crate arrives from the school in England, with a note from the headmaster, in old-fashioned handwriting. There's a photo, too: a rowing boat with *Douglas Jordan* painted down the side, the headmaster and his wife standing in front of it, looking suitably solemn. Another photo, this one of the boat in action, being rowed by eight glowingly white boys. Gabe and I laugh over it, and I remember Dougie's letters – the real ones – where he'd laughed about those posh kids. Gabe tells us about Dougie pissing in the shampoo bottle, and Teddy can't stop laughing, and Sylvie says, 'That's gross. Completely gross.'

Inside the crate are all Dougie's possessions from England – the ones that Gabe hadn't brought back already. Together, we pack them up. We keep his photos, and some of his t-shirts, which will fit Teddy one day, if he wants them. The rest goes to the charity shop.

'Do you still have those letters?' I ask Sylvie.

She nods. 'Why? D'you want them back?'

I'm not sure. I don't know how I'd feel about getting rid of them. They're lies, but they're part of our story, and so I leave them with Sylvie for now. Who do they belong to, anyway? Her? Me? Dougie?

A postcard comes, one day, for Gabe. It's from Mexico – a picture of palm trees, aqua water. On the back, it says: *I still miss him. Rosa.*

Gabe

I'll tell Gill, one day, about what happened between me and Rosa, and about what I nearly did to Murphy. I won't tell her right now – she has enough demands on her, and I don't want to place my mistakes at her feet, demand forgiveness of her when she's already given so much. Sometimes the kiss with Rosa seems a small thing – at other times it takes on a huge weight. And sometimes I'm using a knife in the kitchen and I can't believe it ever went that far – that I really carried a knife with me to Murphy's house that night. The knife and the kiss are the same: nothing happened, but it was still too much.

It's not for me to decide how much forgiveness any of this warrants. And Gill might not be interested in forgiveness. But we've done enough keeping of secrets, and soon it will be time to tell her. She may ask me to leave – I'll understand if she does, and it will be no more than I deserve. But Dougie's death has taught me that few people get what they deserve, so I find myself hoping that Gill and I will find a way through.

I'll tell her, too, that I understand what she did. That there was a kind of courage in her refusal to let either Dougie or Sylvie go. I'll tell her that it might not have been the right thing for us to do, but that it was right in the way that love is always right: because it has no choice.

What remains of love, after decades? Maybe it's no more than a kind of selfishness: I want to be around her. When Gill drags a chair into the patch of sun on the front verandah and sits there reading the papers, I want to drag my chair next to hers. That doesn't feel like a small thing.

We talk about the children. For hours, we pass our memories backwards and forwards to each other. Gill and I are handing each other back our children, dead and alive.

I don't begrudge either of us the consolations that we sought. But it's time to stop seeking.

The inquest comes and goes. I am not there. The coroner records a narrative verdict – some recommendations about due diligence for caving instructors in adverse weather. The findings seem restrained, sensible. I don't read the whole report.

Sylvie is still at home. She doesn't join us at the table yet, for meals. Instead, she eats secretly, in her room. It takes her two hours, sometimes more, to get through a bowl of cereal. There are days when it feels like all she does is eat – so many hours, for such tiny amounts of food.

But she does it. The bowls that she brings out of her bedroom are empty. I check, and check again, more carefully, but there's no more sneaking food to SausageDog; no more of those hidden parcels of food, scrunched in balls of paper or silver foil and shoved in her wastepaper basket.

'The wanting doesn't go away,' she says to me, when I ask her one night. 'I just get better at managing it. The voice that says: *You're fat, don't eat that,* is still there.' She shrugs. 'But I know it's a bullshit voice.'

The plan is for her to go back to school next year, and she's studying already. She's started using Dougie's room to work in. Her books on his shelves; her Ugg boots under his desk. Some evenings Teddy joins her in there, lying on Dougie's bed to read while Sylvie works at the desk. They still call it *Dougie's room*, but it's not dusty any more. I like to hear them talking together in there, their voices stopping and starting, while Gill and I sit together on the front verandah and watch the mountain propping up the clouds.

Teddy

After dinner Mum puts on the SBS news and Papabee says what he always says about Lee Lin Chin being *handsome for a Chinawoman*, and I shout, 'You can't say that, Papabee!' and Sylvie says, 'Actually, she's not even from China – she was born in Indonesia,' because Sylvie knows everything. And I remember the game Dougie used to play: one point for every time Papabee says something embarrassing, 'and two points for casual racism'.

Mum's started taking me to my soccer games, now Papabee doesn't drive. Mum and Dad talked to Papabee and his doctor, and agreed that it was time to take away Papabee's licence, and sell the car. He doesn't really seem to realise. I still go to his place after school most days, but I catch the bus. Every now and again Papabee calls the police and tells them his car's been stolen.

On Friday afternoons, when Sylvie goes to her therapist, Mum takes me to the bookshop café and we have cake and sometimes she buys me a book. 'Because that's what we need in our house,' she says, rolling her eyes. 'More books.' She lets me eat the froth off the top of her cappuccino, and she listens to me tell her about school, and about how I'm teaching SausageDog to shake hands, and about how Alasdair-Down-The-Road stole a cigarette from his gran, smoked it, and coughed so much that he vomited.

I give Mum all my stories. I don't think there are going to be any more prices paid for stories in our family. I think we've all paid enough.

Some of the names in our house have changed again. Mum's calling Dad 'Gabe' now, and not 'your father', unless I'm asking her too many questions about the International Space Station and then she says, 'Go ask your father.' And Dougie seems to be Dougie again, and not Douglas, now that the lying's done with.

We don't talk about Papa J now – he's come out of his name altogether. Maybe Sylvie talks about him to her therapist, or to Mum and Dad. I don't know for sure – that's her business. The dark water taught me that in the end you mainly save yourself, and that's enough.

Mum and Dad are going to family therapy with Sylvie again. After the second session, I heard the three of them staying up late talking, and the next day the photo of Papa J and Dad was gone from the kitchen, and all that was left was the nail it used to hang on. I thought about the weird magic of nails, and I thought about how somebody can be like the Onceler in *The Lorax*: you only ever see a bit of them at a time, or see them in glimpses, and never really get the full picture. When I get angry at Papa J now, I don't have anywhere to put all my anger, because he's underneath that whole digger-load of dirt. But at least I know my anger doesn't belong with Sylvie any more.

With all these names changing, I decide my name should change too. I've tried imagining being Bird-Teddy, Silverfish-Teddy, Crab-Teddy. It's time to imagine what it's like to just be Edward.

I tell Mum, when we're at the bookshop one Friday.

'I think I'll be Edward, from now on.'

She opens her mouth to say something, then closes it again.

'For high school, next year – you know.'

'Okay,' she says. 'Okay. Right.'

Since then, she and Dad and Sylvie are trying really hard, and they're getting better at it, even though right now it feels like my name is *Teddy-I-Mean-Edward*. Papabee forgets, of course, but he forgets everyone's names anyway, so I don't mind.

I know being Edward will be pretty much the same as being Teddy. But it's the rhyming that made me decide. I remember when Mum or Dad used to call for us, on the beach at the Neck: *Dougie! Sylvie! Teddy!* And Mum shouting our names that day we almost drowned. All of our names rhyming.

I'm Edward now. Edward doesn't rhyme with anything except itself.

Sylvie

Sue comes into Dougie's room. I'm sitting on his bed, reading.

'Oh Christ,' she says, seeing my copy of *Ulysses*. 'They've got you reading that?'

'It's for school. It's not on the syllabus, but Mrs Lewin said I should read it. She reckons I need to be pushed, academically.'

'Pushed? *Ulysses* is enough to push anyone right over the edge. Here,' she gestures impatiently. 'Pass it over.'

I give it to her, and she flicks through to the end, brows drawn close together as she concentrates. When she finds what she's looking for, she presses her hand down on those final pages. Then, with quick, decisive movements, she begins to tear out the rest.

'What are you doing?' I yell.

She doesn't stop. 'Saving you a lot of time. Most of this,' she says, nodding down at the pages massing on the bed and slipping onto the floor, 'you don't need. A man wandering around, being a tosser, and thinking he's being profound. Don't punish yourself with reading this just to impress your teachers. Or your parents.

'But this bit,' she taps the final pages, which she's still shielding with her right hand while her left hand rips methodically, 'that's the only bit you need. Molly's soliloquy. You could spend weeks reading the whole bloody thing, and I guarantee that this would still be the only bit you'd remember afterwards. It's the bit that matters.'

She holds out the hollowed book, just two hard covers, folded loosely around the few pages that remain at the back. 'Done.'

I start laughing, and more of the ripped-out pages fall from the bed. Sue's grinning too, as she tosses the book on the bed.

'There you go,' she says.

The covers flop open like two hands fallen from prayer.

I read Molly's soliloquy three times in a row, right away.

I want to read all the books, and love them, and rip them up. I want all of it. I'm greedy for all the words that I've denied myself for so long.

Nothing has its own power, but the price is too high. Cordelia, dead as any of them in the end, for all her virtue, and for all the purity of her silence. The Fool, too, just disappears.

I read Molly's soliloquy and I want *Yes*. Not the dutiful *Yes* of the good girl, the good daughter, the good student. The desiring *Yes* of wanting, for myself.

And if I'm to be the girl that books built, then I'll take Molly's *Yes* over Cordelia's *Nothing*. But I won't take Molly Bloom's ending for the ending of my own story. I want to find new books – ones that weren't given to me by adults; ones that weren't written by men. I want to find more words, and make new ones – new forms of *Yes* and *More* and *Everything*.

Gill

Sylvie told us about Gabe's father. For weeks, I couldn't say his name at all. Gabe smashed the glass in the frame that held his photo.

Because Papa J will never be here to answer for what he's done, we turned our anger at ourselves, and how we'd failed her.

'Why didn't you tell us?' I begged her. 'We would have believed you.'

She says she couldn't. And if I'm to show her that I will always believe her, I have to start by believing what she's telling me now. I have to trust that she was telling the truth all along, when she said, 'It's not about you.'

There are habits that take a long time to break. Putting mail for Sylvie on the hallway dresser, to take in next time I go to the hospital. Automatically scanning Campbell St for parking spaces whenever I drive down it, even though there's no reason for me to go to the hospital any more. Setting the table for three, because for so long it's been just me, Teddy, and Papabee. But now Gabe and Sylvie are here too and, on good days, Sylvie's even starting to eat at the table with the rest of us.

You never know which discharge from hospital is going to be the final one. You only realise later – when it's been two and a half months, and Sylvie's weight's been stable, and at our weekly appointment Louise says, 'I think we might just play it by ear from now on – cancel the standing appointment and just get in touch as and when, no? You know what to watch out for.'

Sylvie's spending less time weighing her food and more time debating politics over the SBS news with Gabe every night. Her friend Esra has been coming over, as well as Ella. I find an open tab on the laptop, a student forum about the best universities for Journalism and Politics courses. And at last, at last, I let myself believe that this isn't finite. That perhaps this isn't just a respite between hospital admissions, but that it might actually be real.

Sue calls. 'Work talk, not gossip,' she says. 'We've had an offer.'

'Uh huh,' I say, waiting. It's late October; all the broadsheets and long-lead magazines will already be planning their Christmas food supplements. I haven't been writing so much, since Sylvie and Gabe came home, but it's time to get back into it, the daily work of proper writing.

'Is it *The Australian*?' I ask. 'I was thinking something about vegan Christmas meals. You know: *Turning the Tables on Turkey*, that sort of thing.'

'Not for the newspapers. For the book.'

'The book?' I sound stupid, even to myself.

'*The Cookbook of Common Prayer*.'

'That's not a real book.'

'I didn't want to tell you when I sent it out on sub. Didn't want to get your hopes up. But they've gone for it. Peregrine are really keen – they've put a good offer on the table. They're talking about making it a lead title for next spring.'

'Are you serious?'

'They are,' she says. 'And they're offering six figures, Gill. More money than your Seasons books put together.'

She's waiting for me to say something, but I don't have any words, so she continues.

'They say they want to market it as part-memoir, part-recipe book.'

'It wasn't even really meant to be a book at all.'

'I know. And if the recipes were crap, I'd say it's just a gimmick, and you should've kept it in the drawer. But they're not – they're really good. Sylvie was the one who told me to give them a proper go. She asked me, *Have you actually cooked them? Even the ones that seem crazy – they taste perfect.*'

'I don't know. I wrote it for myself, really. Is it going to be any use to anyone else?'

I can picture her rolling her eyes. 'Peregrine obviously think so. I say: who cares? Take the money.' She pauses. 'It won't bring Dougie back. And it won't even fix bloody Sylvie, though it'll pay for more therapy – and I'm not just talking about her.'

'We're still going twice a week to family therapy with her,' I say. 'And I'm seeing that guy, too. The therapist.'

'The scratchy-tissue guy? Good. So see him more, then. Plus, the money'll buy you time to write the next two books. Or to not write them, and sit in your study and cry, if that's what you need.'

I don't think that's what I need, any more. I want to get back to writing. I'm already thinking about figs, and Christmas recipes. Something about mulled wine pudding.

Gabe

On weekends, Sylvie and I go for long walks along the Cornelian Bay foreshore with the dog. Sometimes we stop on a bench and talk, or don't talk, for a while. SausageDog brings us sticks, and we throw them, and he looks at us mournfully and ignores them.

Sylvie doesn't want to talk much to me about Papa J. I understand, although I'm relieved that she's talking about it with her doctors. I do my best to hide my anger and my guilt; I don't always succeed.

'I hate him,' I say to her, wrestling a stick from the dog.

'I didn't,' she says. 'And I do. That's why it's complicated.'

She doesn't want to talk about it beyond that, and we won't push her. As for my own anger at my father, it's no good to Sylvie, who deserves her own anger, and her own answers.

Sylvie and Teddy – Edward, I mean, though I get it wrong more often than I get it right – are helping us plan something for Dougie. Not a funeral – too late for that – but some kind of memorial service. Sylvie wants to write a speech, though she's not sure if she'll be up to reading it herself, so Sue's going to read it for her. Gill and I will give a brief speech, too. Ella wants to read a Jane Kenyon poem. Nathan and some of Dougie's other friends are choosing the music. I've emailed Rosa to tell her that she's welcome. If she comes, she might even want to give a speech. It's up to her. I haven't heard back yet.

Teddy's organising a slide-show on the computer: photos from through the years. Dougie as a scrunch-faced baby, fresh into the world. Dougie, Sylve and baby Teddy on the balcony; Dougie at six, in just his undies, laughing. Dougie as a boy, knees scabby, leaning over a Tintin book. Dougie with his huge rucksack at the airport, walking away from us.

Gill

November brings an early heatwave. There's a fire on the road to the airport; smoke in every breath. It's been thirty-five degrees all day, and even in the evening the heat hasn't dropped. A storm's coming in, heavy grey cloud massing over the mountain.

I hear the crack when the first pod explodes, pinging into the French doors. I've seen the wisteria pods burst before, but never like this – all at once. The heat and the moisture from the storm must have set them off, and they crack in a frenzy. The seed pods are big – six inches, the largest of them, and hard, despite their velveted surface. They twist open with a percussive crack, firing their seeds wide, and landing, broken, with a clatter.

'Come out here,' I shout to Gabe. Teddy (sorry – Edward) and Sylvie come too, to see what's going on.

The pods are going off like popcorn. Some of the seeds hit the glass doors; others land on the table or scud along the paving stones. It drives SausageDog berserk, leaping in the air to snatch at the falling pods, and chasing the seeds that skitter along the ground. We're laughing, mouths open, hands up to shield our eyes.

I hold one of the seeds in my hand. Perfectly round, light as a communion wafer.

Another snap. 'Jesus,' Sylvie says, 'it could take an eye out,' and although we flinch each time a crack comes, there's no question of leaving. We keep waiting for it to end, and it keeps coming: every twenty seconds, another crack. The magic of broken things.

We go to the Neck to scatter the ashes. We haven't been back there since that day the kids almost drowned.

'Are you sure you want to?' Gabe asks. 'It doesn't have to be the Neck. There are other places Dougie loved.'

'No,' Sylvie and Teddy say together. It has to be there, for the same reason that Teddy went there that day, and for the same reason that Sylvie knew where to find him. It's always been the Neck.

We drive down in convoy with Sue and her family. For dinner I cook mussels, and send Ella and Sylvie to the fish and chip shop for chips, now Ella has her licence. Nathan's here too, but seems to spend most of the time inside, on the phone to his boyfriend. Ella and Sylvie are sharing the upstairs room just like old days, though there's less giggling now. After dinner, they climb to the top of the water tank and lie there talking.

Sue sits beside me on the sun-bleached wooden bench. We're so quiet I can hear the tonic fizzing in my glass, and Sylvie and Ella's distant voices. Gabe, Nathan and Dan are playing cricket on the driveway, an upturned cardboard box as the stumps. In the hammock, Papabee and Teddy – Edward, I mean – are reading, top to toe.

A gull is flying from the west, dragging the sunset across the sky. I look around at all of us – my family, smaller than I wanted, but bigger than I realised. And I don't know what it is to pray, but it must be something like this: a kind of noticing. Seeing the line of ants, a row of stitches on the dirt near my bare feet. Hearing the silence of the water from beyond the gum trees. Letting the world be enough.

Mussels for the day before you scatter your son's ashes

Use as many mussels as your children have gathered from the beach. Rinse the mussels of sand, and de-beard them, yanking off any gritty chunks of seaweed.

Roughly chop two onions. (Better: ask somebody else to do it for you. There's no greater act of love than willingly chopping onions for someone.) Toss a lump of butter and a big glug of olive oil in a deep-sided pan, and soften the onion over a low temperature, with four cloves of garlic, thinly sliced so that they look like slivered almonds. When the onion is translucent and barely beginning to turn golden, pour in a glass of white wine (nothing fancy – use whatever's left over).

When the wine has finished its initial heady sizzle, add the mussels, and put a lid on the pan. Leave for a few minutes, stirring occasionally.

(Meanwhile, if you found any wild samphire on the rocks, blanch a greedy handful quickly. No need to salt the water – samphire brings its own salt.)

If there are any mussels that haven't opened, don't force them. Just put them aside.

Take the mussels off the heat and stir through a whole tub of pouring cream. Season with black pepper (lots) and salt (only if you must). Top with a handful of roughly chopped parsley and (if you fancy it) de-seeded red chillies.

Eat barefoot, at an outside table, with toasted ciabatta to dunk in the boozy, creamy sauce. Or (best of all), eat with a bag of chips from the chippy down the road, bundled in paper already turning see-through with grease.

Lick your fingers.

Gill

In the morning, we go down to the beach with the ashes: me, Gabe, Sylvie, Teddy, and Papabee. No cormorant today – just seagulls, threaded on the string of the horizon. The November sun makes the sea sharp with light. A gusty wind is scudding clouds across the sky.

Gabe passes me the box. We open it together.

Edward

We each get a turn with the box. When it's my go, I tip some of the ashes out and the wind chucks them back at me, white dust all over my jeans. Mum and Dad laugh and Sylvie screams and I brush it frantically, slapping at my jeans, my hands all chalky.

I shake my hands. Even though it's kind of gross, I don't actually mind. Part of me quite likes the idea that there might be a bit of Dougie rubbed into the seams of my jeans, or stuck under my nails.

Sylvie goes next, turning her back to the wind so that when she shakes the box, the ashes fly away and it looks like smoke. Dad helps Papabee sprinkle a bit too. Then Mum and Dad take the box and shake it together, the very last bits.

Today's Dougie's birthday – he would have been twenty.

'What do you think he'd make of this?' Dad says.

Sylvie tugs at a bit of hair that's blown across her mouth. 'He'd say: this is the shittest birthday present ever.'

'Language,' says Dad, but he's smiling, and his hand's on Mum's shoulder.

'Will Dougie be joining us?' Papabee asks.

'No,' Mum says, putting her hand in Papabee's. 'He won't be, Dad. Dougie died.'

Gabe

Afterwards, Sylvie and Edward swim. I take three steps in, and then four, feeling the sand shifting underfoot, the persuasive tug of the tide. My children are in the waves beyond me.

And if I cannot forgive the water, I can at least step into it. I follow them.

Sylvie

Everything changes. Nothing changes. There will always be secrets. There are words that I've whispered to Teddy that I might not say again, to anybody. There's still a place for silence.

I let the water reach my waist. My body's stronger now – a body for doing things. For reading books, for pulling myself up to the top of the water tank. For dragging my brother from the waves.

I lean back, letting the water take my weight. Far above me, a gull makes its hoarse prophecy. I close my eyes, and I am not afraid. This water has its appetites. But I have my own.

Acknowledgements

My agent and friend, the inimitable Juliet Mushens, has had faith in my writing even when I didn't. This novel has benefitted greatly from her patience and wisdom.

The wonderful team at Allen & Unwin UK has given me the best possible home for this story. Particular thanks to my brilliant editor Kate Ballard, for her insight, generosity, and enthusiasm.

I'm grateful for the diligence and care of my copyeditor, Nicky Lovick, and my proofreader, Sarah Chatwin. Any remaining errors are, of course, my own.

For her understanding and support, thanks to Clara Haig-White.

For perceptive feedback and encouragement, thanks to Peter, Alan and Sally Haig, Tony Johnson, and Andrew North. Particular thanks to Alan Haig for attention to detail to a degree that was extraordinary, and only occasionally annoying.

For fruitful discussions about Lear, Cordelia and nothing-ness, thanks to Margaret Ellis.

For his friendship and his steadfast belief in me, I will always be grateful to the late Derek Alsop.

This is a book about family, so I also want to thank my second family. Thank you to the Norths, for the gift of Andrew; thank you to Andrew, for the gift of the Norths.

And for everything else: my beautiful son.